Two Way Mirrors

Just Jewel

ISBN-10: 0615864309
ISBN-13: 978-0-615-86430-3

Book cover design by Innovative Insight

Printed in the United States of America

Dedicated to Ryan, whose simple words, "It's not too late, you know," inspired me to start writing again.

ACKNOWLEDGMENTS

I would like to extend a special thank you to Poetiic and Jasmine for your help with this project. I'd also like to thank my mother, Patricia, and the rest of my family and friends who encouraged me along this journey.

Two Way Mirrors

CHAPTER 1

Mrs. Shay,

How's life treating my Queen? Good I hope! As for ya husband, I'm well! Damn Baby I miss the shit out ya sexy ass! ☺ For real, no bullshit! I know what Usher meant when he said he got it bad! ☺

You should get this by your b-day! I want you to be happy on ya day. I wish I could be there and make sure you are happy on ya day. But I got you on the next one. I owe you that! ☺ Just know that you mean the world to me, and I only want the best for you. And that's all I'm striving to do for you and my princess.

Baby, I want you in my arms so bad it's scary at times, but it feels good, so damn good. I know it will be soon, but soon can't come fast enough! And I know you know what I mean! But I don't want to get you back on that subject because I know how it stays on ya mind. I'm just letting you know it's on mine as well. Not being able to see you this weekend is going to be hard. I want you to spend your b-day with your husband, even if it's the day after or two days after. I want my wife on her b-day! And I know I don't always get what I want! But I have to let you know how I feel!

Baby girl, I love you and that won't change! Have a happy birthday!

Love You,
Ya husband

-Cal

E/H

I had already told you that I thought they were going to move me to the compound, and they did! So I'm on B-Unit, not 2 wing. That don't have nothing to do with our sessions! <u>Hopefully</u> same time, same place this weekend! Morning or afternoon! Whenever you feel like kissing me! ☺

I love you Baby!
I'm out for now!

With a painted smile on my face, I breathed in deep and exhaled slowly. As soon as I saw the handwritten envelopes in the mailbox, my heart skipped a beat. My stomach fluttered every time I received a letter from Cal. Getting Cal's letters always left me feeling warm inside. It's amazing how I could yearn for someone so much that I never even knew on the street. It had only been seven months, and already I felt in love.

Calvin Shay was my future husband. One of my more embarrassing secrets, I met Cal through my ex-boyfriend Durell. Rell and I were together, on and off, for three crappy years. I might have felt a little bad had it been anyone else, but Rell was the worst boyfriend I ever had. He cheated on me the entire time we were together. He was spoiled and a user in addition to being outright mean at times. It's a wonder I stayed with him as long as I did. I guess I was the walking definition of young and dumb. That's the only way I can explain it.

Rell was facing armed robbery charges when we met, and his indictment landed him a three-year sentence. During that time he would send me pictures and letters of his fellow inmates, begging me to hook them up with other females. Hooking them up was how he got favors on the inside. However, I had a shortage of close friends, and the ones I did have had no interest in linking up with a jailhouse boyfriend. Who could blame them? So I held on to Cal's picture since no one wanted it.

Standing in his crisp khaki prison uniform with a white T-shirt peeking from underneath, in his 'G' stance, right hand cupped over left wrist resting at the waist, hair neatly twisted and falling at his shoulders with such a serious look on his face, his whole presence in the photo intrigued me. Rell had also given Cal my phone number to pass along messages to me. Cal was one of the few that had a cell phone in prison that someone boofed for him. I knew he was the big man on campus, and that shit turned me on.

Eventually, Rell dug his own grave. I got some sense, and we broke up. I was pleasantly surprised to get Cal's phone call months later. He called trying to see if I knew any connects for some things he was trying to get sent in from the outside.

I still remember our first conversation like it was yesterday. We were both high, which would explain why I was more forward than I usually am. After I gave him the number for the contact he was looking for, there was a brief awkward silence on the phone.

"So you still with that girl? What's her name?" I blurted out. I knew Rell had eventually found a female to link Cal up with on the outside.

He chuckled first, "Nah … so you and ol' boy done, huh?"

He opened the door for me to go right in, telling him how I was through with Rell's sorry ass and how he had done me wrong.

Cal was blunt and told me straight up, "I ain't try'na hear all that. I wanna talk about me and you!"

I remember feeling embarrassed and getting shy when he said that. I was happy at the same time because I was about to get exactly what I wanted that night—him. We got to talking regularly, then writing, next visitations, and the rest was history.

I smiled to myself as I licked the nasty-tasting Dutch paper, daydreaming about how I would spend my birthday with Cal the next year. I couldn't wait. It was Friday night, January fourteenth, my twenty-fifth birthday. I was ready to smoke a blunt, get tipsy, and hit the club. I had a stressful week at work, and I was ready to let loose. I was happy that I requested to be off for my birthday night.

I looked at the alarm clock on my nightstand, ten o' seven. *Damn, neither one of these chicks ain't call me yet,* I thought to myself. I was already dressed in a low-cut navy blue blouse, some dark stretch boot-cut denim jeans, and some fly navy blue leather boots with the gator detail on the heel and toe. I had rushed out right after work to take a special trip to the Village in New York just to get the boots. I was proud of my two hundred dollar Italian boots. I worked hard for them, and I wanted something new and sexy to wear on my special night. These were it. Even though I was in my apartment, I was walking around in them to break them in.

My girls, May and Cherlise, were supposed to meet up with me at ten so we could head back out to the city. Finally, my phone sounded and lit up with a text message from May: *"Sorry, I have a really bad headache. I'm not going to make it out tonight."* Wow we had been talking about this for like two weeks, my big two-five. I was looking forward to this night! Disappointed and a little hurt, I hit her back: *"Okay, feel better."* I knew she just didn't want to go because she didn't know Cherlise like that and would feel uncomfortable. *Lying-ass bitch,* I thought to myself.

After I finished rolling, I sparked my blunt and took two deep pulls. I could feel myself start to get lightheaded. It felt great. My body sank into the bed paralyzed as I thought about how messed up it was that May cancelled on me. Headache or no headache, this was my twenty-fifth birthday! Shit, pop some Advil or something, and let's go! Oh well, I knew for sure I could count on Cherlise.

She was my club partner and we had been friends for eight years now. She was more on the spontaneous side and pretty much down for whatever, whenever. We would decide at two o'clock in the morning to go get tattoos or go on a road trip to somewhere we've never been before. We would go to the club, meet random guys, and let them take us to breakfast after the club let out in the AM. We knew some of each other's deepest secrets. Although we were totally different, we never judged each other on our flaws or mistakes. That's just how we were.

I flipped on the television and turned to Court TV. I loved to watch Forensic Fridays where Court TV would show episodes of *Forensic Files* for three hours straight. I slid off my boots to get comfortable, lay back on the bed, and took five more pulls before putting the blunt out in my self-made ashtray. Because I didn't like to have ashtrays lying around, I used the lids to my Yankee Candle jars instead. I didn't want people to know I smoked. It was a dirty little secret of mine. Only Cherlise knew, and it was a while before she did. As I could feel myself zoning out, and my eyes getting low, I reached over and put the blunt out again. I always checked, checked, and re-checked to make sure it was out because I was afraid of starting a fire. I felt my body unwind as I blinked slowly and heavily.

I was watching an interesting case about a woman whose body

had been stuffed inside a barrel and hidden in a crawl space under a house for three decades. The autopsy revealed that she was three months pregnant at the time of her death. That was the last thing I remember seeing before I drifted off to sleep.

CHAPTER 2

Island Calypso music started to play in the background of my dream. Awakened by my phone, I knew that ring tone. I reached over and slammed my finger on the "END" button. I never understood why my mom insisted on calling me so early in the morning on Saturdays when she knew I would be sleep.

I blinked a couple times and turned over to look at the clock, nine twelve. My phone beeped twice, and I knew she had left a message. I looked at the phone and saw that her call was the only missed call. What the hell happened to Cherlise? Some birthday, both of my so-called friends had stood me up and cancelled on me.

It was winter, and it felt and showed outside. The baseboard heat in my place wasn't doing the best job. I didn't want to get up as I snuggled into my blankets in the fetal position. Eventually, I decided that since I was up and it was still early, I would head to the gym. I knew it might be crowded because a lot of people liked to work out on Saturday mornings. I hoped the cold weather would keep them home though.

It was a slow drive there even though it wasn't that far from my apartment. Black ice and snow banks lined the streets of Newark from the snowfall days before. I could hear the slush against my tires as I tread carefully along my way. I felt bad for the few people that I saw waiting for the bus on days like these, bundled up, cold with their snow boots on, trying not to slip and fall on sidewalks.

Once at the gym, I tied on my paisley grey bandana, got my bottle of water, plugged in my headphones, wiped down the elliptical machine, and went to work. I always loved to work out to the beat of the music. After about fifteen minutes, I closed my eyes as I felt my heart start to speed up. Sweat dripped down my forehead, and I started to breathe out loud through my mouth. As I switched my step to work the elliptical in reverse, I reached down to my waist, where I had my mp3 player clipped, and turned up the music. Eyes still closed, I felt my thighs tightening up as I continued working the machine with my arms and legs.

Have you ever had that feeling someone was watching you? I grabbed my towel from the holder, still working the elliptical with just my legs. I dabbed around my eyes before opening them, and there she was again! I looked in the full-length wall mirrors in front of me. In the reflection, a short, pudgy, dark skinned woman dressed in an all black sweat suit was standing near the door, staring at me. She wore her hoodie tightly secured around her head and face with the drawstrings pulled. Her long bangs were all that peeked through the hood. They fell just to her eyes. Still, I could tell it was her.

This was my third time seeing this woman recently. She didn't seem threatening, but it did make me uneasy to think she was possibly following me. She seemed curious more than anything, curious about me. Now that I saw her again and she was staring at me, I knew it couldn't be coincidence. First the grocery store, then the bowling alley, and now she was at the gym. Newark, New Jersey isn't a huge city but it's not small either. So what were the odds of me continuously running into this woman? She looked young, like she could be in her early or mid thirties, not a bad-looking woman.

Just then, her eyes met mine in the mirror. I hopped off the machine ready to confront her. As I spun around to walk across the floor, she disappeared around the corner of the doorway. I quickened my pace through the rows of stationary bicycles to a slight jog until I reached the doorway. I peeked my head out and looked left, then right. She was gone just like that. I shrugged it off and turned back around.

"BOO!"

Startled, I jumped. "Rock, you scared the shit outta me!" I exclaimed through a nervous chuckle.

"Now, what's a pretty lil' lady like yourself doing using that type of ugly language?" Rock replied with a wide grin on his face.

Rock was sexy as hell, but a little too pretty for my taste; a little conceited too. Standing at about six feet, with pecan skin, he had deep dark, wavy hair in a Cesar cut, hazel eyes with dark long lashes, a perfectly trimmed mustache and connecting goatee. He had thick dark eyebrows too, but the fact that he looked like he got them waxed turned me off. He had a strong jaw line and juicy, moist lips. Of course his six pack, huge muscular tatted arms, and defined back didn't hurt either.

Even though I made it clear to Rock that I had a boyfriend and that I wasn't interested, he still wouldn't quit. He worked out every day, so whenever I'd come, I already knew he would be there ready to flirt. He was Dominican, but he looked black, and I think he was used to black girls flocking to him because of his looks and "good hair." Although I wasn't interested, it still felt good to be pursued. Plus, I enjoyed working out and talking with Rock sometimes. He was good company.

"Oh please!" I replied, rolling my eyes, being sure to flash my dimples at the same time.

"Aww, did you miss me? Is that why you were looking for me? Well I'm right here, Sweetness." Rock said, licking his lips with his arms extended as if expecting a hug.

"You swear it's all about you!" I walked past him, headed back to the machines. Rock followed behind, and I knew he was looking at my butt.

"One of these days you'll stop playing hard to get, girl."

"Oh, I'm not playing, sweetheart." I shot back.

An older white lady had gotten on the machine already. Damn, didn't she see my stuff there? I stood in front of the machine, reached over, and grabbed my towel and water bottle from the holder.

"You could've wiped the machine down!" the old lady snarled at me.

I just rolled my eyes, mumbled under my breath, and walked away, "I wasn't finished yet, you old bat!"

"Aaah haaa!" Rock taunted. "C'mon let's go do our squats," he said as he snapped his towel popping me on the thigh. I followed his lead over to the mats to start our sets. I stayed at the gym for another hour then headed to my mom's house.

I used my set of keys to let myself into mom's apartment. "Hellllloooo?" I called as I walked up the stairs.

"Hi! Happy birthday!" she said popping her head over the top of the stairwell. "I called you this morning. Did you get my message?"

I replied in a singsong annoyed tone, "Thank you, yessss I got your mess-aaage. I was still sleep! Did you cook anything?"

"No, you should've stopped and bought something. How was your night out with the girls last night?" she asked.

"There was no night. They both stood me up—well May said she had a headache, and Cherlise was just a no show."

"Oh well, forget them! I hope Cherlise is okay though." She said, genuinely concerned.

Every three weeks, I would go to mom's place for her to do my hair. She did hair professionally out of a shop in South Orange where she lived. I still wasn't used to visiting her at her apartment. After my father passed years earlier, she had to downsize from the home I grew up in. I preferred to go to her place instead of the shop, so we could talk without ears around. We were very close. I was her only child, and since my father died, we grew even closer. I told my mother almost everything. Our standing appointments were our bonding time. We would use this time to catch up and gossip. So naturally, once we got started, I told her about the strange woman I kept seeing.

After washing my hair, I grabbed a peanut butter Tandy cake from the fridge and took my place on the floor between my mother's legs. She sat on the futon. This was the way she had been doing my hair since I was a child. "The strangest thing happened at the gym today," I started to tell her about the woman. "This woman was staring at me while I was working out on the machines. It was weird, though, because she was dressed in all black and staring as if she were on some kind of secret undercover mission." I chuckled at the idea.

"Well, maybe she wanted you," she replied, laughing back.

"No, it wasn't like that. And this was my third time seeing her."

"Maybe she just goes to the gym at the same time you do. Maybe she was looking at your hair or something." My mom always thought people were looking at me because they liked my hair or they were jealous of how slim I was. Mothers always think their children are the best looking children in the universe.

"No, she wasn't looking at my hair because I had a scarf on, and this was not my third time seeing her at the gym. First, I saw her at Shop Rite. Then, I saw her at the bowling alley in Linden, and now the gym. I'm almost convinced she is following me!"

"Why would she be following you? It's probably just coincidence, or maybe it wasn't really the same person you saw all three times," my mom tried to rationalize.

"Well, I don't know why she would be following me, but it is definitely the same lady! I'm positive!"

"What does she look like? Maybe you look like somebody she knows." She replied.

I described her to mom, and she grew a little quiet as if in deep thought. Eventually she just said, "Well, just be careful of your surroundings. It's probably nothing, but people are crazy these days. No telling what kind of nut case she might be." Then she changed the subject. "Guess what happened at the shop yesterday ..." I zoned out as she began to tell one of her many shop stories.

"Angela!" mom snapped me out of my daydream. "Are you listening to me?"

I answered back reassuringly even though I wasn't listening anymore "Yes!"

"Oh, okay, 'cause you just kept on saying 'mm hmmm.'" My mom knew me so well. Whenever I wasn't listening, I would be sure to throw in a couple of "mm hmm's," "wow's," and "really's?" I was always right on cue too. Those three acknowledgements seemed to fit in well to any breaks I heard in the conversation when my mom would pause for my reply or reaction.

"So what do you think?" she asked. I burst out in laughter because I was caught!

"I'm sorry, think about what?"

"See, I knew you weren't listening." She laughed back. "I said I was thinking about going to church at Fountain in the morning. Do you want to go? No pressure." I felt bad, but I had to tell her no. Sunday was my visitation day. I was going to see Cal, and I couldn't wait nor would I miss our visit for the world.

"Oh no, I'm not gonna go. I have something to do in the morning," I explained. I knew the probing would start here.

"What'chu doing tomorrow?" she asked inquisitively.

I smiled, "I just have something to do."

She left it alone and just replied "Oh, okay. You don't want to tell me."

She was right. I didn't want to tell her. I had managed to keep Cal a secret this long. I didn't want her to know about him. I felt silly carrying on a relationship through the mail with a man I had never met outside of the prison walls before. I was embarrassed that my love life had come to this. Still, I was enjoying the feelings while they lasted.

At that moment my phone started ringing. I didn't recognize the number, but I answered anyway in fear that it could be Cal. I never wanted to miss a call from him. To hear his voice was rare, so I cherished every moment I heard it. "Hello?"

"Hello, cuh' speak to Angela?" a woman's voice came through. I knew it was probably somebody else calling on Cal's behalf. Whenever his cell phone was on the move throughout the jail, he would still find a way to get a message to me.

"This is Angela. Who is this?"

"Dis is Dae Dae." She sounded a little rough around the edges. Then again, all of his people usually did. She continued, "Dis is Stink's wife! Cal wanna know if you gonna come up tomorrow." I had spoken to Dae Dae a few times by now, and I still cringed every time her or Cal referred to her boyfriend as "Stink." Who would answer to a name like that? I got up from the floor and walked into my mom's bedroom as I held my finger up to her signaling that I'd be right back. I closed the door behind me, so she wouldn't hear my conversation.

"Oh hey, yeah I'll be there." I replied.

"What time? He wanna know if you coming in the morning or the afternoon."

"Tell him I'm coming to the afternoon visit, twelve o'clock."

"Alright I'ma tell 'em. He said to tell you to hit up Wally to get that. He said you would know what he was talking about."

I responded, "He want me to bring it tomorrow if I get it?"

"I guess so. He didn't say. He just said hit up Wally."

I just said "okay." She repeated the same back and we hung up.

I knew what Cal was talking about, but he hadn't said anything about bringing anything this weekend in his letter. I had been smuggling weed into the prison to Cal for a couple of months now. He would have me cop a lot of the cheapest stuff I could find and a little bit of the best haze. Then he would sell it for much more than it was worth on the inside. I never thought about how much trouble I could get into if I got caught. I had to admit, it was a bit of a thrill.

Plus, I was obedient and loyal to Cal. I would do anything he asked. That's just how I felt about him, a man I barely knew. I didn't mind anyway because all the profit he made was being sent to me. I saved most of it for him, but I kept some for myself too.

By this time, I was sitting on mom's bed. I thought about calling Wally then, but decided I would call when I left. As I got up from the bed, a piece of paper fell from between the edge of the mattress and footboard. I reached my hand down in the crevice to grab it, but instead my hand fell upon a cold box. I looked down to see if I could see where the paper went. I saw it lay up against the grey box. I wondered what was in it, but it was none of my business. Besides, it appeared to be locked.

Just then the door burst open startling me. "What are you doing? I would like to finish your hair today!" mom said, eyeing me as I brought up the paper from behind the bed.

"Nothing, I dropped this paper behind the bed." After placing it on top of the blanket, I led the way back out of the bedroom, but I saw her do a quick look at the box, as if checking to make sure it wasn't touched. This made me even more curious, but I didn't think too much more about it after that. She finished my hair, and I was off to my weekend job.

CHAPTER 3

I looked cute, as usual, on the weekend. My locs freshly twisted, I pinned one side up to give myself a sexier look. I wore my black, tight skinny jeans and black flats with my Gel-ins inside. The long-sleeved lace top I had on was sexy, tight, and fell right at my waist making my butt look bigger. I had round hips, but since I wasn't naturally blessed in the butt area, I had learned different fashion tricks to give an appearance of a fatty, which was always a plus and ensured more tips at work. But I always kept it sexy and not sleazy, just like mom taught me. The top was a low-cut V-neck and plain in the front, but the sleeves and entire back was lacey see-through. All the bartenders had to wear all black. I guess Ronnie, the owner, thought it made us look a little classier. I finished off the outfit with silver and black bangles, a silver and black half moon costume necklace that fell right at my exposed bosom, and I swapped out my gold lip ring with the silver one. For some reason, unbeknownst to me, customers always found my lip ring a good conversation piece, that and my dimples of course.

I didn't mind bartending too much. It was way better than selling insurance, which is what I did for my regular nine to five. Bartending tips were good. The music kept me moving and made the time go by quick, and I liked *most* of the people I worked with. That always makes a difference. *Ronnie's Girls*, even though the strip club closed at two in the morning, we would still go hang out together after we got off. When I say "we," I mean the other bartenders.

The bartenders chilled with the other bartenders, the dancers with the dancers, security with security, and so on. Occasionally there was a mix, but usually there wasn't. Most of the dancers liked me. This was good because when they were ready to drink, they would tip me. When a customer was ready to buy them a drink, they would send the business my way, so I could get the tips. Sometimes we would even double-team the guys that came in there. One of the dancers would entertain a man, either by lap-dance or just giggling at their jokes, and I would converse with them both at the same time and/or do bartending tricks for them. That way, we both got tipped well before it was all over with. I even picked up a few stripper tricks to do at home with Cal when he got out.

Of course there were a few of the girls that didn't like me. I know it was just because I was cuter than them. Not to toot my own horn, but a lot of those girls and women had serious bodies and could do serious things with those bodies, but they looked like dogs in the face. Don't get me wrong, I have a nice body that I am proud of, but where I may be lacking in the butt and titty areas, my face definitely makes up for it. I didn't pay those ignorant bitches any mind, though. I was there to do what I did best; get money!

I had my radio on blast, bumping some club music as always to get amped: "GET ON THE DON-KEY! GET ON THE DON-KEY!" I circled the block around the club a few times before finding a spot around the corner and down the street. I never liked parking right in front of the club because I didn't want customers knowing my car or trying to follow me when it was closing time. There were a lot of nut cases that came in there.

Just like clock work, I performed my ritual. Even though I had been working here for six months now, I still got nervous each and every night. I was nervous that I might mess up someone's order, give the wrong change, break a bottle, or who knows what else. So I popped the cap on my water bottle and took the rest of my Grey Goose and cranberry concoction straight to the head, then sat the bottle back in the cup holder. I turned the radio down, got some gum out of my purse and popped it in my mouth. I flipped down my visor mirror and glossed up my lips extra heavy, but not too heavy, and threw on some mascara. I tossed everything in the glove box and locked it except for my lip-gloss, gum, phone, and car key. We couldn't keep our purses behind the bar, so I only brought my necessities in. I double checked my left shoe to make sure the forty dollars was stashed under my Gel-in just in case of an emergency. You never knew what might jump off.

I shut the engine off, and just as I started to step out of the car, my phone started vibrating and ringing. I looked at the screen. It was Cherlise. *Oh boy, here we go with the excuses,* I thought to myself while debating if I should answer. I got out, activated the car alarm, and answered, "hello?"

"Heyyy Angie! What'chu doing?"

"Hey Cherlise, what's up? I'm about to walk into work," I said in a dry, bored tone.

"Oh, you working tonight? I should come through then!" she replied excitedly.

"Alright, I'll be here."

"Oh, my bad last night! I'm sooo sorry. Matt had an asthma attack, and I had to take him to the ER!" *Lies, lies, lies. Why was this woman always lying when she knew damn well I always knew when she was lying?*

I was getting so sick of hearing about Matt. Every time I turned around, it was Matt, Matt, Matt. Cherlise had been my girl since high school, and I'd seen her date many different guys. It was different with Matt, though. She was changing. Her world now revolved around him and whatever he wanted. One of the smartest people I knew, she had quit college in her senior year. Matt even convinced her to start stealing from her job at Applebee's. Every time we wanted to go out when it was her turn to drive, it became a big issue because Matt always wanted her car. Whatever Matt wanted, he got from Cherlise. Whenever we did go out, she was always in a rush just to get back to be with Matt. She knew he had a lot of women and she didn't even care. She just made excuses for him and accepted it. Now she had started lying to me about silly shit just to accommodate Matt.

I didn't know what the real story was why she stood me up, but I knew it wasn't because Matt had no damn asthma attack! I bet he didn't even have asthma. She could've at least come up with a *good* lie. I just simply replied "Oh, no problem. Is he okay?"

"Yeah, I was so scared! The doctors got it under control, though. But, um, what you doing next weekend?"

Here we go again. She was going to try to make it up to me the next weekend. I wasn't beat. "I don't know yet. I might be going out of town."

"Oh, okay, well maybe the weekend after that we can do something then" she replied.

"Okay. Well just text me if you decide to come through tonight." She said she would, and with that, we hung up. I think she could tell by the tone of my voice that I wasn't in the mood to see her. She probably wouldn't come anyway, and that was fine by me at the moment.

I reached the door of the club and said hello to the bouncers. They knew me now, so Freddie opened the door for me, and Chucky teased me like he always did, "Hey wifey! Y'all know this is my future wife, right?"

I always flirted back, "Hey baby, when you gonna have my ring ready?"

I could still hear him as I walked into the loud music "Soon baby! Soon! Watch!" I turned and flashed him a quick grin before letting the door close behind me.

Ying Yang Twins' "Salt Shaker" blasted throughout the club. The speakers vibrated through the floor up through my whole body. As my eyes adjusted to the dim lighting, I passed by big booties shaking and bouncing all over the place. Hips gyrated to the music and thick silhouettes slid up and down poles on the stage. I made my way to the bathroom passing a couple lap dances along the way.

I always took a leak before I got behind the bar because I knew once it picked up there wouldn't be a chance to go. The bathroom was always disgusting. I hovered over the toilet praying my ass wouldn't touch the toilet seat. I wiped myself, then used my foot to flush the toilet and stepped out of the stall to the sink. Ugh, once again out of soap! Ronnie was the cheapest club owner I knew! Fifty percent of the time, we were out of soap. The other fifty percent of time that we had soap, there wasn't any toilet paper. Whenever we let him know he just said, "okay," and did nothing about it.

"What's up Ang?" Princess, another bartender, said as she flew past me into the stall.

"What's good?"

"*Shit!* These niggas ain't tipping tonight," she said in a disappointed voice.

"Oh boy here we go."

"We all going to IHOP tonight. You in?" she asked.

"Yeah, I'll probably roll wit'cha" I said as I ran cold water over my hands. I dried them and fixed my hair in the mirror as Princess came out.

Princess was pretty cool. A little unpolished, but it probably wasn't her fault. She was on unemployment and raising her little boy alone. So those under the table tips were her livelihood. She always asked Ronnie for more hours, but for whatever reason, he never gave them to her.

Back out in the thick of it, I made my way through the club to the bar. I said "hi" to Tee Tee, Keisha, and Britt as I joined them behind the bar. I looked around to see what needed to be done. I got right into the groove of it by cutting up some fresh lemons and topping off the well bottles.

Fast-forward two hours later, and the bar was packed and the club was jumping. My tip jar was full, and I was still adding to it, so it was a good night. I don't know what Princess was talking about with the slow tips. I crouched down under the bar to grab some napkins for re-stocking. As I popped back up, there he was.

That night would be the first night I laid my eyes on Gordon Hopkins. "Uh, can I get a whiskey sour with Johnnie Green?" he said.

"Sure," I replied with a courteous smile. He was cute, but so what. Cute men came into the club all the time. "Fourteen," I said as I tossed a straw in the glass and placed the drink in front of him on a napkin.

He took two sips and pushed the drink back towards me saying, "Can you add some more whiskey to this, please?" I had already turned my attention to another customer that was standing next to him.

Damn, I hate when muthafuckas ask for more liquor! I thought to myself. I hated it because Ronnie was so cheap that he made us measure each ounce we poured, and we had strict rules to charge for an additional shot when people wanted more than the measured amount. It was so annoying because people always said they couldn't taste the liquor. Obviously that little jigger full of liquor was never enough. Then the people never wanted to pay for the extra shot, so it always ended up being like some type of stand off battle between the customer and me. The customer is supposed to always be right, so usually if I didn't think Ronnie or any of his spies were around, I would just give in and sneak some extra liquor into the person's cup.

As I turned to engage in battle with him, he said "Oh, go ahead and finish with him first."

I said "okay," and served the other guy. When I was done, I took a quick look around and snuck some more whiskey in his glass.

As I returned his glass, the bigger guy next to him started laughing and said "Damn, she acting like she don't wanna put no liquor in this!" So I let out a huff and grabbed his glass, ready to put some more in his as well, but he held his hands up in protest and said, "nah, nah, it's okay," as he continued to laugh like it was the funniest thing in the world.

Cutie started laughing too, nudging big guy in the arm, saying, "I know! I asked for more whiskey, and it still taste like it's just ice in here!" That's when I noticed it. The warmest, friendliest, most genuine, beautiful laugh I had ever seen. His semi-full lips gave way to some gorgeous, perfectly aligned pearly whites.

I explained to them laughing back, "Sorry, my manager is real strict about the liquor. We gotta measure it and charge extra if you want more." That's when cutie reached in his back pocket for his wallet and quickly pulled out some bills. They hiked on my bartending skills a little more, but not in a mean or obnoxious way, more in a playful way. I didn't mind because they both tipped well.

Big boy asked me, "What you working for? To pay that tuition?"

I replied, "something like that." The truth was I had finally graduated the year before, but I was paying off the student loans I had taken out. However, patrons were likely to tip more when they thought I was still a struggling college student. That's when cutie asked what I was going to school for.

It turned out he had majored in business when he was in college too. We talked about that for a while in between me helping other customers. I could tell he was more than a little older than me, but he looked damn good. I had never been attracted to a man that much older than me, but this was different. He had a boyish charm about him. He was on the lighter side, but not yellow; more of a caramel, I guess. He was clean-shaven, which was a first for me. I wasn't usually attracted to men with no facial hair. He had sincere looking eyes. He wore a blue pea coat over a crisp, white button-up with a navy blue and yellow striped tie. He wore slacks and hard bottoms. I wasn't usually attracted to the "office look" either, but he made it sexy somehow. He wore a navy blue wool hat, and I wondered if he had a bald spot under that hat.

"Do you have any kids?" he asked.

"No," I replied with a puzzled look.

"So can I call you some time?"

"How old are you?" I shot back, ignoring his question.

"Thirty-eight" he answered.

Older than what I estimated, but what the hell. I ran the receipt ream near the register for paper and jotted down my number for him. Just as I was about to hand it over, I glanced down at his hand and asked, "Are you married?"

"No—Yes! Yeah, but we're separated." I could tell he really wanted to lie and say no.

As soon as he said that, I crumpled up my number, smiled politely, threw it in the trash next to me and said, "aahhh never mind. I don't think so."

He tilted his head back in laughter and tried to protest. There it was again, that beautiful smile. The light hit him just right this time too, so I could make out dimples. I turned and walked away shaking my head as he yelled out "Wait! Let me explain!" I went to pretend like I had something to tend to at the other end of the bar. I saw him grab his boy laughing and telling him what had just happened.

Really I went to tell Princess what had just happened. As we laughed with my back turned to him, Princess looked up behind me and pointed, "He wants you, girl." I rolled my eyes and told her to go help him. She did, and was back in two seconds. "He asked me to tell you to come here."

I rolled my eyes again and walked back over with a slight smile. "Look, my manager doesn't like seeing me stand around, so if you're not ordering more drinks—"

"Okay, gimme another whiskey sour!" he replied before I could finish. I did as told. When I returned with the drink, he held a twenty in his hand close to his chest. I held my hand out for the money, but instead, he went on to explain. "Yes, I'm still legally married, but I'm getting a divorce." I rolled my eyes as if to say I wasn't falling for that one. He wouldn't hand me the money until I listened, though. "For real, we've been separated for almost a year. She moved out the house already, and my roommate moved in."

Still hesitant, I said, "Mmmm hmmm. Nah, I don't talk to married men."

He grabbed my arm gently, "For real, that's the truth. Let me get your email address at least or something." Reluctantly I agreed and wrote my email down for him. "Oh, and I don't have any kids either!" he said proudly. Mesmerized by his charm, I totally forgot to ask him that.

I slammed the paper on the bar in a playful way as he handed over the twenty. Just then, I heard somebody in my other ear, "BOSS LADY!!!" *Oh shoot! I totally forgot to call Wally!* It was him. It's a good thing he knew where I worked. Then again, maybe it wasn't if he had just seen me give my email address to cutie. I didn't need that kind of information traveling back to Cal.

"Hey, what's up Wally? My bad, I completely forgot to call you so I could come get that!" I exclaimed.

"Yeah, damn girl! I was like *did something happen to her?* What the fuck?"

"My bad. I'm sooooo sorry." I said, really meaning it.

I knew Cal was depending on me to bring the weed up the next day, and I had totally forgotten. "So you still going up there tomorrow?" Wally asked. I glanced over at cutie who was still standing there, but talking to one of his boys.

"Yeah, I'm still going. I was just so busy today. I started to call you earlier, but got side tracked doing something else—hold up," I said as I ran over to the register to get cutie's change. When I turned around, he was walking away.

I held up the change, and he waved his hand towards me saying, "Keep it."

He held up the piece of paper, motioning that he would email me, and I mouthed, "okay" to him as he made his way to the door.

I tossed the bills in my tip jar, and I turned my attention back to Wally. Wally was about an average build, brown-skin, short afro, and black lips from smoking too much. His hair looked like it hadn't been washed or picked in a while, and he wore a black skully cap tilted to the side. He had a lazy eye and thick bushy eyebrows.

Working a toothpick around in his mouth, he continued, "yeah, so you definitely going up there tomorrow?"

"Yes! Yes! Yeeeesssss!!" I replied impatiently. I couldn't stand when people asked me the same thing over and over after I had already answered the question the first time.

"Alright 'cause I just wanna make sure he gets that. Don't oversleep, okay?" he said through a chuckle.

I didn't really get the joke, but I smiled back, "I won't. You got it on you right now?"

"Of course," he replied, reaching in his inside flight jacket pocket.

"Hold up! Hold up!" I said pulling his arm away from his pocket.

I walked over to Britt and told her I would be right back. I walked around to the other side of the bar and tapped Wally on the back, signaling him to follow me outside. Once outside, I pulled him over to the doorway entrance, two doors down from the club. The gate was down because the store was closed, and it was dark enough where no one could see what we were up to. It was freezing, especially since I had no jacket on. I breathed into my cupped hands. I could see my breath.

Wally reached again into his inside jacket pocket and pulled out a small zip-loc baggie filled with some good purple haze. I could smell it before he even whipped it out. It was the eighth that I was expecting. I rolled up the baggie, slipped off my right shoe and laid it under my other gel-in. I was afraid the baggie might be too long for my shoe, but it fit perfectly.

Once I had my shoe back on, I said, "good lookin' out" and started to walk back.

"Hold up, Boss Lady" Wally said. He reached back in his pocket and pulled out something else. It was a small, rectangular-shaped package. It was about the size of a fun-sized Snicker bar and wrapped in white paper; it was almost like a tiny present.

"What is this?" I asked as he handed the package to me.

"That's the bundle of dog food!" he replied as if I should know.

"Bundle of *what*? What am I supposed to do with this?" I asked puzzled.

"Ohhhh Boss Lady, you don't know what that is? Cal didn't tell you?"

"Nah, I just know I always get an eighth from you and that's all I usually bring up!" I explained.

"Well he told me to give you the eighth and a bundle. When is the last time you spoke to him? He told me he wrote you to tell you what's up!"

"I spoke to him about two weeks ago. I probably just didn't get his letter yet."

"Oh yeah, I spoke to him on Sunday and that's what he said." He replied.

"Damn, I don't even know what to do with this. All I ever bring up is the weed and he always tells me what to do with it."

"So do the same thing with that that you usually do with the sticky then!" he said.

"Yeah, but how is that thing supposed to fit in the balloon?" I asked still puzzled and still unsure if I even wanted to be handling dope. Weed was one thing, but now Cal wanted me to bring in dope? We hadn't discussed that.

Wally started cackling. Through his cackle, he managed to get out, "Nah, Boss Lady, you gotta unwrap the bundle first! Then just empty out all the envelopes into the loon. You shouldn't need more than two loons."

I chuckled back at my own ignorance and innocence. "Oh, okay." Needless to say the bundle wouldn't fit in my shoe so I shoved it deep down in my front pocket, hoping it wouldn't work its way up during the night and slip out.

"Alright you all set, Boss Lady!" Wally said as he stuck his hand out for some dap. I gave him some while still chuckling from embarrassment.

"Alright Wally, thanks" I replied.

As I turned to walk away I heard his voice say, "Tell my dude what's up for me and be careful, Boss Lady!"

"Okay!" I responded and walked back to the club. My walk was almost a limp now due to my uneven footing with the baggie in my shoe.

The rest of the night went by fast, and I made two hundred dollars in tips, which was a good night for me. Two hundred dollars just for four hours was what I called an easy night. An easy night at the club for me meant no drama, no fights, all tabs paid, and good tips. I overheard Britt complaining about her tips saying how she thought she had done better than that. It seemed like all the bartenders were busy the whole night so it should've been an easy night for all of us. Princess turned up the lights behind the bar a little to signal it was close to closing time.

"Last call for alcoholllllll!!" the DJ sang into the mic over the music. I never understood why people never came to the bar when they heard last call. Instead, they would wait until they were passing the bar on their way out to leave. Fifteen minutes later, he played my favorite club song of the night "Get-get-get, get the fuck out! Get-get-get, get the fuck out!" That meant the party was over, and everyone had to leave. Security started clearing the place out. All the half naked strippers limped and staggered back to the dressing room. You could tell they were tired and their feet hurt.

This is when we wiped down the bar, put away everything, and topped up all the bottles. This was also the time when all the last minute alcoholics would come up to the bar with "Is it too late to get a drink?" or "I'm sorry, I know y'all closing and y'all ready to go home, but can I just get a glass of water?" or simply "lemme get a Henny n' coke!"

The last minute "Henny n' coke" line always pissed me off. *It's like, what the fuck! Y'all didn't hear last call fifteen minutes ago? You can't see the bar lights are on, the bartenders are counting their tips, and the bar is completely cleared off? Helloooooooo!!! We're closed now; time to get the fuck out like the song said!*

Of course I couldn't say this to the customers, and Ronnie would have a heart attack if we turned one dollar away. So I would try to ignore them and keep my back turned in hopes they would go away or one of the other bartenders would serve them. Most of the time, all the bartenders would do this at the same time until one of us gave in. If I didn't do so well in tips, then I would just go ahead and make the drink to get every single last tip I could. However, usually the last minute alcoholics weren't tippers. Thankfully, on this night, I didn't get any last minute alcoholics.

We all finished counting our tips, grabbed our coats from the coatroom, and headed for the door. As we stood congregated outside the club, I said my goodbyes and started to walk away. "Ang! You still meeting us at IHOP, right?" Princess yelled out to me.

"Oh shoot!" I said out loud to myself as I spun around. That quick I had forgotten about IHOP. My mind was already into tomorrow. I couldn't wait to see Cal, and I was thinking about the work I had to do when I got home bagging everything up in the loons. "Nah, my bad, I'm not going tonight. I completely forgot that I gotta be up in a couple hours." I replied to her. I just wanted to go straight home. I didn't want to be driving or walking around with all that stuff on me.

"Aaaahhhh, you can't hang! You supposed to be young and

vibrant," she replied, teasing me.

I laughed back, "Shit, you right! I *can't* hang the way I used to girl! Next weekend!" I turned my back and waved goodbye all in one motion, then continued walking to my car.

The drive home was short. After I got settled in, I pulled up a chair to my little wooden table. I grabbed a handful of little black water balloons from the table drawer. I started with the haze, breaking off a little at a time into the open hole of the balloon. I squeezed the base of the balloon with my fingertips, clumping it in a ball. Once the balloon-ball reached the size of a grape, I tied it in a tight knot, cut the tip off, and placed it down into another balloon. I did this three times to triple it. By the time I finished, I had four balloon-grapes.

Then I started on the bundle. I did the same thing using green balloons. It was harder to do the dope because it didn't stick together like the weed did. I only ended up with two of the green balloon-grapes.

Next, I tried on several outfits to see which one looked the sexiest, but would still be able to camouflage the loons, and wouldn't be *too* sexy at the same time. You see, if you wore outfits even a little revealing, too fitted, or too sexy, the hating-ass female C.O.'s wouldn't let you in, so almost all of the visitors wore a big, white T-shirt because it covered all the curves, mainly the ass. You had to wear a shirt long enough to cover your butt. Cal always wanted me to try to be sexy, though, and I really didn't want to wear what everybody else had on either. I always kept an extra shirt in the car, just in case, but I wanted to make Cal happy, so I always tried to go for sexy.

I decided on some dark denim jeans. They were boot-cut and hugged my curves in a subtle way. I picked a Chinese-styled mini dress to wear as my shirt. It was tight, but long enough to cover my butt and had slits on each side, accenting my hips. It was black, but the Chinese mock collar and trim on the hem was red with gold.

I tried out the loons along the inside of the waistline in the front of my jeans. I placed them neatly in a line going across my lower abdomen, just above my panties, right behind my belt. I checked myself out in the mirror from all angles to make sure my abdomen area looked and felt flat. That was one of the areas where the C.O.'s patted you down.

I finished the outfit off with some basic black leather boots. I lined them up by the front door and hung my outfit up on the hook on the back of my bedroom door. I was set to go, and I was really excited to see Cal. Each moment we spent together was precious because we only got about two and a half hours per week to visit. I set my alarm clock, snuggled up in my bed, and drifted off to sleep.

Two hours later I was startled by the faint sound of rattling. I couldn't quite make out what the noise was. Sleepily, I opened my eyes and blinked a few times, but I lay still trying to listen where the noise came from. I wanted to make sure it wasn't the heat kicking on and off through the baseboards again. I listened closely. It sounded like it was coming from the kitchen.

I slowly sat up on the edge of my bed, and slipped my feet into my slippers. I grabbed the small steak knife I kept on the nightstand next to my bed. I crept slowly into the kitchen with my heart racing. *Damn I watch too much Forensic Files and Cold Case Files!* I thought to myself. I watched those types of shows religiously. Then I would start being paranoid afterwards, thinking someone was going to sneak in my apartment and try to attack me or assault me.

When I got to the kitchen, I could still hear the noise, but now it sounded like it was in the living room. I continued walking until I was able to pinpoint what it was. It was the doorknob to my front door! Someone was jiggling it back and forth, trying to get in from the outside. My heart raced faster as I flipped on the light. I stood at the door and I could feel someone standing on the other side; just standing there. Then it sounded like they walked away toward the stairwell to the right.

I heard voices in the hall at the apartment next door to my left. I cracked the door open and stuck my head out. I looked to the right and saw no one. I looked to the left and could see the girl next door letting her boyfriend in. As he walked in, before he closed the door behind them, he looked down the hall at me. I could hear him laughing and saying something to the effect: "I thought that was your door down there!"

I breathed a sigh of relief. Obviously it was him trying to turn the doorknob. He must've been drunk or something. Now that I officially had the shit scared out of me, I had to do one of my paranoia checks of the apartment. That was when I turned on all lights, checked all corners and closets, and checked under the bed and behind the shower curtain for intruders. You would think my place was huge the way I carried on. If someone was in my apartment, they had very few places to hide. Either way it just made me feel safer to do it. I drifted back to sleep with no problem and the next sound I heard was my alarm clock going off.

CHAPTER 4

I smiled as soon as I awoke. I was always excited to see Cal. I was like a little kid on Christmas morning. I could feel the butterflies in my stomach. Even though I was excited, I was always extra nervous when I knew I was bringing something in. Anything could go wrong. The dogs could be there. One of the loons could slip out or the C.O. might feel them during the pat down. I could get caught passing the loons off to Cal, anything. He always tried to reassure me that nothing would go wrong, but I knew he couldn't know that for sure.

I sat on the toilet for a while. I always got diarrhea from the nerves. Nothing came out though, so I got showered and dressed. I pinned one side of my hair up like I had the night before and sprayed some oil sheen in it. I looked good. I hooked up some grits, a beef sausage, and a scrambled egg. I washed that down with some orange juice. After eating breakfast, I carefully lined the loons up inside my pants again, checked my purse to make sure I had my I.D., and tossed in the bag of leftover tokens I had from the last visit. The tokens were to buy Cal some snacks from the vending machines during the visit. He usually never wanted anything, but I always brought them just in case either of us got hungry.

Just as I was about to head to the door to put on my boots, I felt my stomach bubble. Just like clockwork, the nervous diarrhea kicked in. It never failed. I would always try to go before I got in the shower, but it always waited until I was good and ready to walk out the door to come out. *Dammit!* I didn't want to be running late, but there was no way I was about to hold in diarrhea for the next three hours.

I sat back on the toilet and did my duty. It came pouring and plopping out my ass like juice. It smelled something awful too, like somebody crawled up inside me and died. I pushed out loud, long farts. Some sounded like machine guns and some like shotguns. I hoped all the gas was out, so I wouldn't have to sneak any silent assassins out in front of Cal. It felt like I was wiping for days. I looked at each wad of toilet paper with no end in sight and my suspicions were confirmed. I had mud butt. I used a couple of baby wipes to freshen up since there definitely was no time to jump back in the shower.

I had to get a move-on. Time was ticking and I definitely didn't want to be late because those bitch C.O.'s would definitely turn me away. I farted in the car the whole way there. I let it rip so much and so hard, I thought I was sure to burn a hole right through the seat of my pants. I cracked the windows even though it was freezing outside. I lifted my butt from the seat and wiggled around a little to air out my jeans. I didn't want the fart smells to settle in my clothes.

I arrived at Western State Prison just in time to see the buses roll up. They didn't look like regular city buses. They looked more like tour buses. All the girlfriends, mothers, kids, and baby mamas stepped off the bus in their white-T uniforms. Most of these women were project chicks and hood rats. They didn't work or do anything really except make babies and visit their men in jail. There was a sprinkle of men here and there. They were usually brothers or cousins of the inmates.

I reached the sidewalk, and as I went to reach for the door, I felt some little hands on the side of my thigh. I looked down and there was a little girl no more than two. She looked up at me with her mouth open as if she had startled herself. She was a cute little dark-skin child, but it was hard to see that cuteness through the dried snot under her nose and crumbs around her mouth. One side of her head had some five-week old plats, and the other side wasn't braided. It was pulled up into a nappy afro puff. She was a pudgy little thing with a big round face. Her dingy T-shirt had Elmo on the front and gave way to a little potbelly.

As I wondered where her coat was, I heard her mother yell at her, "Zahkwanzaa watch where you going! Look at you running into people n' shit!" I looked up to see Zahkwanzaa's mother who wore her hair slicked back with a long weave ponytail. Her hair was dark brown and the weave ponytail was black and blonde, probably some kind of Yaky something or other. She wore a big white-T like the rest, but I guess she was jazzing it up with an arm filled with gold bangles. She had on three sets of big gold hoop earrings. One set had her name on them, and a gold nameplate necklace hung from her neck. With fingers decorated with different gold rings on each one, she wore long acrylic tips. They were painted red with a black and silver marble design on the tips.

No wonder her little girl's face was so dirty. She probably couldn't do anything with those long ass nails on. She wore these long ridiculous fake eyelashes and foundation that didn't match her complexion. Her neck was brown and her face was damn near white! Her look was finished off with some bright red lipstick.

She herself was a tiny little thing and she struggled, leaning over towards one side as she held an infant on her hip with one arm. I didn't get a good look at the baby. In her other hand, she held the hand of a little boy. He looked a little older, maybe around six or seven. He didn't look as dirty as the little girl but he needed a haircut bad. He was light skin and needed some chap stick on those dry, cracked lips.

"Zaheim, get ya sista!" she ordered the little boy.

He did as told, calling out to his sister, "Zah Zah, com'ere! Mommy said to take my hand!" I could see fresh snot starting to roll down little Zah Zah's nose on top of the old dried up snot. She grabbed her brother's hand reluctantly as she coughed a phlegmy cough without covering her mouth.

I proceeded through the door as my mind was in a little panic. I didn't want to be so obvious and look at that moment, but I was hoping in my head that none of little Zah Zah's dirt or snot was transferred to my clothes when she bumped into me. *Ugh!* Dirty ass little kids made me cringe. I didn't want them anywhere near me if they weren't clean.

The lines were long as usual, all the usual faces. After being in line for about forty-five minutes, I finally made it to the window. I handed the lady C.O. behind the glass my license and Cal's inmate number rolled off my tongue from memory. "Okay, step back please?" she said as she eyed my outfit.

Here we go with the bullshit, I thought to myself as I stepped back. It took everything in me not to roll my eyes from annoyance.

"Turn around" she ordered. I did as told as I felt her eyeing my behind to give my outfit the once over. This is when not having a fat butt came in handy. "Okay, go ahead" she said giving me the green light to move on to the next room.

I went to the bathroom to touch up my lip-gloss and make sure I looked good. I decided that was a good time to check the loons too to make sure they were secure and wouldn't be felt through the pat down. I found a locker and stuffed my coat, keys, and purse inside. Then I got into another long line. This line was to go through the metal detector and get patted down. Here is also where they would have the K-9 dogs if they were out that day. I said a silent prayer in my head that they wouldn't be. My heart sped up as the line moved and I got closer to the metal detector room.

The pat down went smoothly and there were no dogs. I entered into the main room, which was the size of a gymnasium. Tan plastic chairs were lined up all across the floor. Women and children scattered all over the room, rushing to their loved ones, embracing them with hugs and kisses. Cal and I never did that. I guess both of us just thought we were too cool for that.

I walked towards some plastic chairs nearby the picture table. This was where the picture man sat, waiting for the inmates to come and sign up to take pictures with their visitors. This is where Cal had instructed me to sit because that's where he usually was if he got out there before I did. I scanned the area, but didn't see him, so I took a seat and waited. I preferred to get out there before him anyway because I loved to sit back and watch him walk through the door.

You would think we were at an NBA game waiting for the starting lineup to run out. An inmate would come walking out in their khaki suit with their head held high and chest poked out. Then their kid would run up yelling, "Daddy! Daddy!" and they would scoop them up into their arms, hugging and kissing them. If there were no kids involved, the inmate would stroll over to their woman in their best cool gangster walk. That was the cue for the woman to stand up at attention with all smiles. She'd hug and kiss her man like it would be the last time.

Not Cal and me, we never went through those charades, but my heart would flutter every time I saw him walk through the door. I think it was because he was the tallest of all the inmates standing at six foot three. He had a presence about him, a cool swagger, but he didn't even have to try. Plus, everybody knew Cal. When he walked out, there was always a series of given acknowledgements from other inmates, some visitors, and even some guards. He was quiet, but everyone showed him respect.

After waiting a minute or two, he came through the door. He looked crisp and handsome as usual; his hair was freshly twisted. I was glad to see he had taken my advice and stopped doing that thing all the guys were doing back then, shaving their front edges down for that "O'marion look." His hair was on the peezy side, so it just made his edges look knotty.

He scanned the room looking for me. It was a little game that I liked to play, like *Where's Waldo*. He knew what section I'd be sitting in, but he still hadn't spotted me yet. It took him a full circle around the section of chairs I was sitting in for him to find me. I wanted to give him a big smile like the other women there did, but I never wanted him to think I was that open. I was smiling on the inside with excitement, but kept a cool face.

I leaned back in the chair as if not excited to see him. "What's up?"

"*You* what's up! I couldn't find you for a minute" he replied.

"I know. I watched you walk around in a circle looking lost." I said with a smirk.

"Why you didn't say something? Why you let me walk around like that?" he said as he gazed at me with loving eyes.

I loved those eyes, milk chocolate brown. I loved the way he looked at me. I could always tell his undivided attention was on me, and he was taking me all in. He sat down and his hair fell over his shoulders and back. I loved the color of his hair too; light sandy golden-brown as if kissed by the sun. He was beautiful, fucked up teeth and all.

Yeah, that was the only thing wrong. His teeth were crazy, out of this world! They were all kinds of crooked. I remember the first time I laid eyes on them. I couldn't help but stare. It must have been apparent because immediately following our first meeting he felt a need to send me a letter explaining the situation. He said he busted up his whole face in a motorcycle accident, and before he could get his teeth fixed, he got locked up. I made a mental note that the dentist would be first priority when he came home.

"So what's up?" he asked. I don't know why, but we always asked each other that question about five times before we actually started having a real conversation. I think it must have been the excitement for both of us. We didn't know where to start and it felt awkward, but that was always only in the beginning. Once we got to talking, time would go by so fast.

"Yo, you got that on you?"

"Oh, yeah! That reminds me! Yeah, I got it. I had completely forgot to hit Wally up, but he showed up at my job. He gave me the weed but he gave me something else too." I replied to him inquisitively.

"A bundle right?" he asked, and I nodded in confirmation. "Good. You didn't get my letter yet?"

"No, I didn't get any letter. I was confused when he gave it to me and he said you was supposed to be telling me." I explained.

"Yeah, I tried to send you a kite so you would know what was up, but I guess the mail is slow again …you forgot to call Wally? You slippin' baby," he said as he shook his head. Even though I did slip up a little, I knew he was only joking.

He always liked to go sit outside, so he could smoke a Black n' Mild and take pictures. So that's where we went. I never had to bring him any blacks either, like the other chicks had to for their men. There was always a minimum of two inmates that had one ready for him. I loved that. My nigga was like Mr. Big or something.

We chilled, and like I said, the time flew by. We talked about my jobs, his daughter, sex, my mom, and our plans together for the future. Before we knew it, the C.O.'s were making us go back inside because the visit was almost over. I didn't want our visit to come to an end, but I was freezing out there. I knew what was coming next and the butterflies started to flutter around in my stomach like crazy. I hated this part because I was always so nervous. It was time to make the transfer.

We sat back down in the plastic chairs across from each other. "Where you got the loons?" he asked. I pointed to my waist where I always had them. "How many is it?"

"Six altogether" I responded.

"You used a different color for the bundle I hope?"

I rolled my eyes and answered, "Yeeessss, duuuhhh. There's four black. That's the weed. Then the bundle is split between the two green ones."

He smirked and rolled his eyes then patronized me, "Pardon my soul. I don't know what I was thinking to question your intelligence." I just rolled my eyes again in response and sucked my teeth while shaking my head. "Alright, take 'em out and just put them between your legs for now."

"Now?" I asked as my heart started racing. He hesitated, taking a quick scan around to make sure no C.O.'s were walking by and nobody was looking.

"Yeah, you good. Take 'em out now!" he said in a hurried whisper.

I sucked in my skinny woman's gut, reached under my shirt, and tried to scoop them all out at once. I dropped them between my thighs and held them there. *Damn!* I didn't get them all. "I'm still good?" I asked worried.

"Yeah, hurry up!" So I did a quick scoop again and got the last two dropping them between my thighs with the rest. I squeezed my thighs tight together so that no one walking by would see the loons peeking out, especially the green ones.

I could hear my heart pounding through my chest in surround sound now. "Slide up. I'm 'bout to slide in there and get 'em." Cal instructed. I did as told while still trying to keep my thighs squeezed together. He rested his hands on my thighs and leaned forward to kiss me. Our tongues wrestled but my mind was not on the kiss. I felt his hand slide in and scoop up the loons. Then he quickly stuck his hands down his pants and secured them wherever he put them.

I asked him once before where he always put them. It played with my mind that he might be boofing them up his anus. He tried to explain to me that he kept a rubber band tied around his dick, and he secured them somehow that way. I still didn't get it, but that part wasn't my job. Right now, all I was worried about was finishing my part of the deal.

"Damn, I only got three. You gotta move up some more," he demanded. I scooted up in the chair. When I did, I felt the loons drop into the chair.

Shit I thought to myself. "Damn, now they fell into the chair!" I alerted him.

"Don't worry about it. I'm gettin' all them shits. Com'ere." He said as he leaned in for another kiss with his hands back on my thighs again. I sat stiffly as I kissed him hoping he would get all the loons this time. He slid his hand in again way deeper this time sliding past my coochie, grabbing more loons to put in his pants.

"I hope you got them all that time?" I asked wanting this to be over.

"Nah, there's one more! Where the fuck is it?" he said getting a little agitated.

"Shit, when I slid up I think it fell in the chair. It's all the way under my ass." I replied.

Just then the C.O.'s started yelling out "THAT'S IT!! VISIT IS OVER!!"

I panicked. When visiting time was over, normally, we would all stand up and give our last kisses goodbye. The inmate had to switch over and sit in the chair on the side where their visitor had been sitting. "What are you gonna do? How are you gonna get it?" I asked with wide eyes.

"Get up! Come on!" he replied not breaking a sweat. Right as I was about to get up a C.O. started walking towards us. I froze and my armpits began to burn and sweat. If I got up now, the C.O. would see the loon in the chair and that would be it.

"Come on! Get up!" he repeated with urgency.

I responded in a scared voice "No, here she comes! The loon is still in the seat!"

Now she was just a few feet away and she spoke to us directly this time, "That's it guys! Visit's over!" Cal told me to get up one more time and this time I had to listen since the C.O. had spoken to us directly. Right as I stood up, she walked past the chair. I didn't even hug Cal. I just scurried off with my heart racing.

Oh my God, I know she probably sees the loon! Shit, we're gonna get caught! I thought.

As I hurried away, out the corner of my eye, I saw Cal plop himself in my chair not missing a beat. "Excuse me Miss!" I heard the C.O. call out to me, "Is this yours?"

Oh shit this is it! I thought to myself as I slowed my pace and turned around nervously.

"Is this yours?" she repeated holding up a baby's blanket. I guess someone had left it in a chair.

"No," I responded and hurried to get in the line to leave.

Once I got my stuff out of the locker and was secure in my car, I was able to breathe a sigh of relief. That was a close call. My heart rate slowed as I drove back home. As I reached my driveway, I heard my phone chime signaling I had an email. I stepped through the door to my apartment, and checked my phone. It was from a Gordon Hopkins.

I didn't recognize the name, but opened it since it didn't appear to be junk email. The subject line read "hi." Once I had it open, I read:

Hi, how are you? I met you at Ronnie's last night. My name is Gordon, by the way. I don't remember if I told you that last night. What are your plans for tonight? I would like to take you to dinner if you're not too busy.

I had completely forgotten all about cutie from the night before. Aww, he seemed sweet. Guilt started to set in as I thought about my feelings for Cal. What was I even thinking giving my contact info out? I wasn't thinking at all. He would be home in less than a month! Not to mention, I loved him dearly and didn't want anything or anyone to come between us. I had to be honest and let cutie know. I knew that I would be mad if I found out Cal was talking to any other women. I replied:

Hi, no you didn't tell me your name. Sorry I forgot to ask. I'm also sorry that I've wasted your time. You never asked me if I have a boyfriend. I have to be honest with you. I have a boyfriend, and I should've told you that last night. So sorry, but I won't be able to go out with you.

I felt really horrible. I didn't know why though. I didn't know this man. What the hell did I care about his feelings? For some reason, I did care. He seemed like a genuine, nice guy. Oh well, he did say he was married anyway, separated or not. Besides, I did meet him at work. Not only was this a conflict of interest, but he probably just wanted to fuck. I did work at a strip club after all.

Confident I made the right decision, I tossed my phone on the table. I was feeling a little sleepy, so I prepared for a nap. Unzipping my boots, I kicked them off by the front door. That was the beauty of living alone. I could drop things wherever I wanted without having anyone to answer to or anyone seeing the mess. I walked in my bedroom and peeled off all my clothes, then slipped on some plaid boxers and a white tank top.

I grabbed a granola bar from the kitchen cabinet and a Capri sun from the refrigerator. I sprawled out on the couch, grabbed the remote, and flipped on the TV. My body sunk into the comfortable, soft suede. Lifetime was always good on Sundays, so I left it on that channel. After munching down the granola bar, I drifted off to sleep.

CHAPTER 5

Boom! BOOM! BOOM! The front door came flying inward, kicked in by a man dressed in all black. Startled, I jumped up off the couch. Before I could even get to my feet good, I felt a hard thud come across my face as he bunted me with his gun. The vision now blurry in my right eye, I was only able to make out a brown skin man, average height, dressed in all black from head to toe. I could only see his eyes because he had a black bandana tied across the bottom half of his face. I had no idea what kind of gun he hit me with but I could see that it was pretty big and silver.

As I fell back onto the couch, I could see another man had followed in behind him. Also wearing all black, this man was black too, but a little shorter and stockier. He wore panty hose over his face. "Where is it bitch?" the first man demanded with his big gun pointed right in my face. Now crouched up in the far corner of the couch with my legs folded up against my chest, my heart pounded through my tank top hard and loud.

"Wha-what? Where's what?" I stammered.

"Oh, *where's what?* She wanna play dumb. Just shoot that bitch!" the short one spat.

The first man replied, "Nah she gon' tell us where it's at!" Then he came across my face again with the gun. This time he clocked me right in the forehead leaving a knot as blood started to trickle out. My head throbbed in pain and confusion. I had no idea who they were or what the hell they thought I had.

"Please," I started to sob "Where is *what*? I swear I don't know what'chu talkin' bout!"

The short man grew impatient, "Gimme this!" he said to the first guy as he grabbed the gun out of his hand. He came at me full force, grabbed me by my hair in the back, and came down hard with the gun in his other hand. Once, twice, three times! I was feeling woozy, nose broken, lip busted, the blood gushed down my face. "You still wanna keep playing dumb, bitch? I'm only gonna ask you one more time where the fuck is it!" he hissed at me through clenched teeth. I could tell the short one meant business, but I was so confused, scared, and dizzy.

I felt myself fading in and out of consciousness. The room grew darker, dimmer. "She 'bout to black out man. Wake her ass up!" the first guy ordered. The short guy gave me a nice back slap across the face. Sure enough, the sudden sting lit the room right back up.

"Look! I really don't know what you want! Is it money? My wallet is in my room. Take whatever you want. Please!" I pleaded with them.

"Maybe she really don't know man," the first guy said as if thinking out loud.

"Here, keep an eye on this silly hoe" stocky guy said as he handed the gun back to his partner. He disappeared through the kitchen. I could hear the thumping and thuds of him going through my room, ransacking the place. It seemed like forever as the other assailant and I sat there in silence (with the exception of my sniffles) with his gun pointed at my face. He never even flinched for a second.

Stocky guy reappeared even angrier than before. Stopping in the kitchen, he emptied out all the cabinets tossing everything in every direction. Once done there, he joined us back in the living room and stopped for a second, looking around as if out of options. Then he got behind my entertainment center and proceeded to push the entire thing over. Everything came crashing down making a loud thud. He kicked and picked through my scattered CDs and DVDs. He found nothing. There was nothing to be found.

"Shit! It ain't here man!" stocky guy sounded exhausted and irritated.

"Damn, now what? What the fuck we gon' do with her?" the first guy replied. The stocky guy didn't have to say anything. He just looked at me, then back to his partner with cold eyes, and gave a quick tilt of his head, as if to say "off her." The first guy turned back to me, and pressed the barrel right to my forehead. Before I could get any words out, my eyes grew big with fear as I watched his finger pull back on the trigger.

CHAPTER 6

My eyes shot open as I lay on the couch staring up at the ceiling. Blinking a few times, I got my breathing under control. Once again, I had that dream. I had been having nightmares of being executed for some years now. Although it didn't always happen the same way, it always ended with someone shooting me in the head. This dream was more violent than the others though.

For some reason, I was still hearing the thumps and thuds. I turned over on my side and lifted my head to see if I could make out what the sound was and where it was coming from. I felt and heard a big thud against the wall. *Oh, they just over there fighting again,* I thought to myself. My next-door neighbor, Mr. Burkwell, and his grandson were always fighting. Sometimes it would get physical.

I put the TV on mute as I listened in. I was always worried that his grandson would seriously hurt him one day. "Get off me, Granddad!" I could hear the muffled sound of the boy's voice. He had to be about fourteen by now.

"What'chu gon' do? You wanna be bad don'tcha?" I could hear the older man reply. I could hear them wrestling around. "This is what happens when you wanna be big n' bad! Think you gon' raise your hands at me in *my* house!" the older man continued to taunt.

"Get off me, Granddad! Get the fuck off me! I swear to God!" the boy's voice was even more muffled now as the thumping and tussling continued.

"Or what? You swear to God what? You gon' stop disrespecting me in my house boy!" The older man continued chastising.

This went on for another ten minutes before I heard and felt a real loud THUD. Silence. Now I could only hear what sounded like the boy's footsteps leave and walk down the hall to the front door. That's the way it always ended. They would fight until they got tired, and the boy would storm out. One time one of the new neighbors called the cops on them. I always minded my business.

The sun was going down now. I grabbed my phone from the table as I thought about what to do with the rest of my evening. I had a reply from cutie, now known as Gordon:

Wow, I guess I should've asked you if you were in a relationship. My bad, I should've known someone as attractive as you would have someone. Thank you for being honest. Take care, beautiful...

Part of me still felt bad, but the other part was super excited that Cal would finally be home in a few more weeks. I couldn't wait! I had to start doing some shopping, so he could be fly when he came out. I had close to ten thousand dollars saved between the money he had sent to me from his weed customers and my tax return. I was giving him the whole savings, so he could get on when he came home. Neither of us liked to ask people for anything. He wanted to be able to come home and buy right back into the game. I didn't think it was the smartest idea, but he was a grown man from the streets. Talking sense into him wasn't really an option. So long as he didn't bring any of that shit into my home, his life was his own to ruin. All I could do was hope for the best.

It was going on eight o'clock. My stomach growled loudly as I continued sitting on the couch. Besides that granola bar, I hadn't eaten anything since breakfast. I decided to cook and call it an evening. I had to be up early for work the next morning. I let out a big yawn and stretch then made my way to the kitchen.

Chicken stir-fry sounded good I thought as I rinsed out my skillet. While slicing the chicken up, I cringed at the thought of having to go to work the next morning. The weekends always flew by whether I was doing anything or not. *Ronnie's Girls* was just my weekend, part-time job. I hated my full time job at B.I.G. Insurance.

I hated working in corporate America period. I tried to be grateful because the money was decent, and it kept food on my table and clothes on my back. Working there was a sacrifice that I made to stay in a position where I didn't have to ask anyone for anything. Wearing uncomfortable business suits, fake-laughing at corny dry humor, people actually getting excited about insurance, and trying to teach "know-it-alls" fresh out of college that they actually knew nothing; ugh my stomach tied in knots every Sunday night. I had been working there for six long years. Every Sunday night, the depression would start to set in at the thought of that place.

I was an account manager. I know, it sounds way more important than what it really is. I hated that job so much sometimes I actually would sit and cry in the car in the job parking lot when I arrived in the mornings. Prayer before walking in had become a daily ritual, but on the crying days I would find myself praying extra hard. Praying I would be able to keep my composure, praying things went smoothly that day, and thanking God that I even had a job.

After taking a seat at the small table in the living room, I wasted no time digging in. For once, it actually tasted as good as it looked. I wasn't the best cook, but I was learning. Cooking was not something that I enjoyed, rather a necessity.

Just as I approached the middle of my tasty meal, my phone began to ring. In mid-chew, I jumped up and grabbed it from the coffee table. I studied the number as I returned to my seat. I didn't recognize it, so I just hit the "end" button to send it to voicemail. I always screened my calls, and I knew it wouldn't be Cal since I had just seen him. The phone rang again right away. I sent it to voicemail again. Whoever it was did not like leaving messages. Two minutes passed as I went back to eating my dinner. Then the phone rang a third time. It was the same number. The area code was "609." This was a South Jersey number. I couldn't think of anyone that would be calling me from South Jersey or why; I just let it ring again. Whoever it was should just leave a message.

I finished up my dinner, then lay back on the couch and watched a little more TV. Every Sunday night I stayed up late trying to prevent Monday from coming, but it was inevitable. I came to terms with it and got up, cleaned the kitchen, and got my clothes out for work. After brushing my teeth and washing my face, I changed and hopped into bed.

My rest was peaceful, but was interrupted before my alarm clock could go off. My phone seemed to be blaring as it jolted me awake. I grabbed the phone and saw it was Cherlise. I glanced at the time. It was five o' three in the morning. *What the hell is her problem?* I thought to myself as I reluctantly answered.

"Cherlise, why are you calling me at five o'clock in the morning?" I answered in my deep, raspy-sleepy voice.

"Ang! I know. I'm so sorry. I need a really big favor if you can do it. Please, please," she was begging.

"What? What's up?"

"I'm in jail. Can you bail me out?"

It took me a second to register what she said. "What? No you're not!" I said through a soft chuckle.

"Angie, Angie listen to me. I'm for real. I'm in jail. Can you please bail me out?"

"No you're not! I don't believe you!"

"Oh my God, Angie I'm serious for real. I really need you to bail me out! I been in here since yesterday! I been trying to call you, but you wasn't answering!" she explained.

I still wasn't buying it. It was a shame. Cherlise was one of my closest friends, but at this point I barely believed anything that came out of her mouth anymore. She had become such a liar since meeting Matt. Part of me wanted to believe her, but part of me felt like she was lying and had some kind of hidden agenda.

"What? You're not in jail. They don't let you use your cell phone in jail. They confiscate everything when you get locked up. Stop playing. It's too early in the morning," I said to her, still not convinced.

"I know! I was trying to call you collect yesterday but you weren't answering. I couldn't remember anybody else's number, and I knew you probably weren't answering because you didn't recognize the number. So the guard gave me back my cell phone, but I only have a few minutes. He's gonna take it back in a second. Please! For real, Ang!" she said.

Okay, now I was more convinced. That must have been her trying to call me the night before from that "609" number. "Oh shit! Why they lock you up? How much is your bail?" I responded now in concern.

"I don't have a lot of time. The guard is telling me I have to hang up now. I'll tell you later. Look, my bail is five hundred."

I had five hundred dollars to spare, but I didn't want to let her know that. Her credit was all messed up, so I already knew she didn't pay her debts. I would have liked to think that she wouldn't jerk me for the money, but you never knew with Cherlise these days. She wasn't the most trustworthy person. I decided to play it safe.

"Oh damn! I don't have the full five hundred. I can probably do like two hundred— But I'll need it right back!" I said quickly.

"Okay! Okay! That's fine. I can pay you back in two weeks when I get paid!" She sounded desperate and grateful at the same time.

"So where are you? Are you in South Jersey somewhere? I won't be able to get there until this evening. I gotta go to work." Cherlise was my girl, but I did have to go to work. Besides, she had been in there since yesterday. A few more hours wouldn't hurt.

"Yeah, I'm in Burlington, but you can just put the money into my account. My friend Travis is gonna help bail me out too. He's gonna take the money out my account after everyone puts it in, and he's gonna come down to get me out. I been trying to call my mother to help too." She explained.

I felt uneasy about putting the money directly into her account. I would have felt much more comfortable going directly to the jail to put the money towards her bail. For all I knew, I could put it in there and she and Matt would skip off to another country the next day. I wouldn't put it past her. Now I was wondering where the hell *was* Matt? Why wasn't he bailing out his woman? There was no time to ask that question.

"Okay, the guard is telling me I have to get off now. Look I'm gonna text you my account number and bank info right now. Do you think you can go there before you go to work?" She asked. I glanced at the clock again. I had plenty of time, so I agreed. With that, we hung up.

I drifted right back to sleep, but the time went fast. Before I knew it the alarm clock was going off already. After showering and getting dressed, I scarfed down a pop tart and some orange juice. The Chase bank was not on the way to work, and it wasn't near my bank either. I went off-route to stop there. I glanced at the clock on the dashboard of my car. Great, the street in front of the bank was a no parking zone. I circled around the block once to find there was no parking lot either. So I pulled up to the curb right in front of the ATM. Traffic was building now as rush hour began to settle in. I waited for a man to finish at the ATM, and then I jumped out taking my chances. I threw my hazards on while glancing at the time once more. I was going to be late anyway despite my efforts to leave early.

I was appalled to find that there would be a three dollar and fifty cent transaction fee for me to take money out of my account since Chase was not my bank. I sighed in annoyance and thought to myself, *I should remember to tell Cherlise that she needs to pay me back for those transaction fees too.*

I got the cash and deposited it right back into her account. Just as I was waiting for my receipt to be dispensed, I heard a car behind me. I turned to see flashing lights behind my car. *Dammit,* I was about to get a ticket. I snatched my receipt as soon as it came out. I sprinted to the car just as the officer had arrived towards the front of my vehicle with his pad out. "Wait! Wait! I'm right here! Please don't write me a ticket!" I yelled out of breath as I made my way to the driver door.

"Sorry ma'am, but you know you're parked in a no parking zo—," the officer stopped short as we came to realization that we knew each other. It was Rock from the gym.

"Hey! I didn't know you were a cop!" I said smiling at him. I was sure he wouldn't write me the ticket now that he recognized me, but I threw on the charm anyway.

"Yes, ma'am, I am! Now why would you park here, beautiful? You're causing more traffic."

"I know; I'm sorry. I just needed to run to the ATM real quick to help a friend and there's nowhere to park here!" I responded in a pleading voice.

He shook his head and crossed his arms while eyeing me up and down "Tsk tsk tsk. This is my first time seeing you outside the gym. You on your way to work?"

"Yes, and I'm already running late. You're not gonna give me a ticket are you Officer … Johnson?" I said while scanning the nameplate on his uniform.

I smiled to flash my dimples and batted my lashes. I was glad that I had picked a halfway decent outfit to wear to work. At least I looked cute, so that helped. "Hmmmmm," he said while still eyeing me up and down. "I'll tell you what. I won't write you a ticket under one condition."

Oh boy, here we go— strings, I thought to myself. "What's that?" I asked with eyebrows raised and wide eyes.

"You have to let me take you out."

Dammit I knew it! "Mmmmm sorry, I can't do that. I already told you I have a boyfriend, Rock." I said with puppy eyes trying to let him down gently.

"I don't care about that nigga! Fuck him!" Before I could say anything, he caught on quickly that I didn't find his last comment funny, and I wasn't laughing. "Syke. Nah, you know I'm just messing wit'chu, sexy." I looked at him with one raised eyebrow. "Okay, I won't give you a ticket ... *this* time."

"Thaaaaaanks, Rooooock!" The smile reappeared on my face.

"You going to the gym tonight?" he asked.

"Yeah, you already know! Gotta keep it tight!"

"That you do," he said with his eyes focused on my breasts. "See you later then, baby."

"Thank you, later," I replied, closing the driver door.

I saw that I was losing time as I sped away. I racked my brain trying to remember if my manager would be in the office or traveling today. I hated talking to her. I decided to hold off on calling her until I was sure I would be more than ten minutes late. That was the rule I had set for myself.

My manager for the last two years was Danika Roe. She was a black woman, and she was very institutionalized, a real square. She did everything by the book and kept an umbrella stashed up her ass. Insurance was serious business to her and it showed. I knew if I called to say I was running late, she'd make sure to lend her disapproval over the phone. I didn't feel like dealing with that today.

I finally made it to the highway and burned it up. I pulled into the parking lot at exactly eight o' five. There was no time to sit and procrastinate this morning. So I hurried and grabbed my purse. That's when I realized I had forgotten my lunch in the refrigerator at home. *Oh boy, is this the kind of day this was going to be?* I braced myself and said a silent prayer as I power-walked to the side entrance of the building.

I walked quickly to my side of the floor and was glad I didn't pass anyone along the way. I didn't want to have to stop and make small talk. I also didn't want anyone to see me walking in late, not that anyone other than Danika would dare say anything to me about it. Still, I didn't want to fit into the stereotype of black people always operating on "C.P.T." Unfortunately I would have to speak to the people who sat in my row only because it would be rude for me to walk past and not speak. "Good morning, good morning" I said in a dry tone as I rushed down my row and slid into the seat inside my tiny cubicle.

I could hear my co-worker, Renee, on one of her daily, loud personal phone calls, "WHAT? For what? Look I'm broke. It's just gonna have to wait 'til next payday ..."

I started up my computer and took a walk to the kitchen to get my morning water. I didn't drink coffee. I didn't like drinking hot stuff, and I didn't like having coffee breath. Bad enough I had to smell everyone else's stale ass coffee breath when they came to talk to me.

"Good Morning." It was the pantry guy. His name was Donny, but unfortunately everyone referred to him as the pantry guy because that was his job. He came and stocked all the cups, coffee, water, etc. in the kitchen pantry. He was a sexy lil' thing too; brown-skin complexion, nice neat cornrows, and a nice slim toned frame. His features resembled that of Trey Songz the singer. He was very friendly and helpful too, always spoke in passing. I remember one time when I couldn't get my window to go up in my car, and he came out to help me with it.

For some reason, I always got nervous around him. I would stutter or trip or do something else embarrassing, which was so unlike me. I didn't know why. I just thought he was cute. I didn't even like him, and of course, I had a boyfriend. From what I heard, he had a girlfriend too. Still, I said another silent prayer in my head. *Be cool. Be cool.*

I could feel my armpits start to perspire as I responded, "Mornin'."

"How was your weekend?" he asked.

"It was okay; I didn't do much. How was yours?" I turned my back to him to get water from the cooler. I prayed he wasn't looking at my butt.

"It was cool. One of my boys had a party at his crib, so I went to that. Then my niece's christening was yesterday, so I went to that too."

I pretended to be interested, "awwww, that's nice. How old is your niece?"

"She's like six months old. She's so cute. You wanna see a picture?" he asked, reaching in his back pocket.

I really didn't, but I couldn't be rude and say no. I said, "sure," still pretending to care. By now, my pits were burning with perspiration. I just wanted to get out of there before I did anything embarrassing. He dug in his wallet and pulled out a small photo of his niece. Thank goodness she was actually cute. Nothing I hated more than when people showed me pictures of kids that weren't too good looking. I felt obligated to lie or just change the subject to avoid lying.

Thankfully, I was able to give an honest response this time, even if I did play it up a little for theatrics. "Awwwwww oh my God! She's a cutie! Just gorgeous!"

"Yeah I can't wait to have my own." he responded.

I gave another "awww" because I didn't know what else to say to that. I was ready to get back to my desk now, so I said, "well back to the grind, see ya later!"

"Okay, see ya."

Yes! I exclaimed internally. I had made it out without embarrassing myself. Now I just needed my pits to adjust back to a normal temperature. Thankfully the sweat hadn't come through my shirt, so I was good. I sat back down to my desk. Before I could start anything, one of the underwriters popped up in my cubicle.

"Hey Angela, how was your weekend?" Bob asked. I never understood why the underwriters always felt a need to make small talk.

We both know you don't give a shit about my weekend or me. So just tell me what the fuck you want. "Mornin', it was okay. What's up?" I asked, cutting right to the chase.

"Can you do me a favor? I need these two accounts issued as a rush." Everything was always a rush with these people. It was so frustrating and annoying but what could I say? No?

"When do they need to be done?" I asked.

"By the end of today."

"Okay, just set them over there in the rush pile," I directed him while pointing to a huge stack of files that were about to topple off of the desk. I had made that pile to be sarcastic and give a hint to the underwriters that everything they brought over was in the rush pile. It's too bad they still didn't catch on.

I opened my email and braced myself for the day ahead of me. Thirty-six new messages; gosh, I was only gone for two days. I skimmed through the emails to see what was urgent and what wasn't. I saw one from May. I always opened my personal emails first because nine times out of ten it would be something funny. This one wasn't funny though. It was just an email apologizing again for canceling on me over the weekend. I just replied:

No problem. I hope you're feeling better.

I tried to change the subject, but she replied asking how was the club and if I had fun.

I never understood this about people. You didn't care enough to come, so why do you care what happened there? You should've showed up. Then you would have all the details you need. I let her know that I didn't go anywhere because Cherlise had also stood me up. She had the nerve to reply:

Aw man. I feel so bad now. You should've called me! If I had known she backed out too, I would've gone. I'm sorry, I'm gonna make it up to you. What are you doing this weekend?

What the heck? Who says that? I thought she was in so much pain? Now all of a sudden she would've come just because the other person backed out? Don't do me any favors. What do I look like, some kind of pity birthday case? I replied completely ignoring her whole email:

I have so much work to do. I don't understand why everything has to be a rush!

I decided to change the subject entirely. Then I continued skimming, and saw an email titled *"Shhhh it's a surprise!"* I wondered what this was about, probably somebody's baby shower or something. The email was from another lady on my team, Renee. Renee was the stereotypical black woman at work: loud, ghetto, and always late or calling out. She was really nice, though, got along with everyone. She was the type of person that made everyone feel welcomed. When my car was broke down, she even gave me a ride home a couple of times. Renee was the type to help however she could. So it was no surprise that this email was coming from her. It read:

Hey All,

Tomorrow is Vanessa's birthday. I thought it would be nice if we did a little something for her. I'm asking everyone to donate $5. I'm going to get some balloons and a card for everyone to sign. Please bring the money to me before the end of this week. Also, please remember that this is a surprise so please try to be discreet in giving me the money. Thanks everybody!

Regards,

Renee

I couldn't stand office birthdays. Somebody was always collecting money, or everybody had to chip in to take the person to lunch, or they would go through all these crazy actions to try to surprise the person when the person was never surprised. I never told anyone at work when my birthday was because I was smart enough to know that no one really cares about your birthday, especially at work. It might sound mean, but in reality, no once cares about your birthday except you and your mama. I wished people at work would realize this.

In addition, I wouldn't say I hated the people that I worked with, but we definitely weren't friends. I barely even talked to them. Why in the hell would I want to give money towards their birthdays? It didn't make any sense to me. I thought May would get a kick out of this. She felt the same way about office birthdays as I did. So I forwarded her the email and just typed at the top:

"Look at this sh*t!"

I spent the rest of the morning replying to all of my emails and working on my huge rush pile. The hours dragged by as they always did. It was getting close to one o'clock, and I was getting hungry. I always liked to take a later lunch to make my afternoon seem shorter. Sometimes it worked and sometimes it didn't. As I gathered my purse and saved the accounts I was working on in our system, an email popped up from May in response to the birthday email I had forwarded earlier.

She was asking what I was going to do, if I was going to give the five dollars or not. I was in a hurry and replied real quick:

Yeah I'm just gonna give the $5. It's only $5. There's like ten of us on this team. This chick is ghetto as hell. I know she's just going to go to the dollar store and get the card and balloons. That's only like $5 at the most. What is she gonna do with the rest of the money? Plus she was just crying broke on the phone, so how is she gonna ask everyone else for money when she don't even have none herself.

I clicked send and hurried off to lunch. My stomach was growling by then. I decided to go out for lunch instead of going down to the cafeteria. Popeye's chicken was on my mind and stomach, so that's where I went. It was finger-licking good too just as I anticipated. I took it to go and ate at the park.

I decided to call Cherlise after I finished scarfing down my two-piece and licking the grease from my fingertips. I sat and watched two squirrels chase each other through the grass as the phone rang on the other end in my ear. "Heyyyy, Ang! I was just about to call you!" she answered. These continuous lies really weren't necessary.

"Are you out? What the hell happened?" I asked inquisitively.

"Oh my God, Angie! I was so scared. I don't wanna ever go to jail again!"

"Well I should hope not! I don't think anyone ever *wants* to go to jail." I replied with a sarcastic chuckle.

"I know. I know. Lemme see, where to start. Okay, I got pulled over on the parkway on my way back from my friend's house in South Jersey for speeding. I thought the state trooper was just gonna write me the ticket. You know me, I'm always speeding!"

"Yeah, I know." I replied shaking my head on the other end.

"So after he ran all my information and he started walking back to the car, I could tell something was wrong. He was like, 'Miss Hickins you're gonna have to come with me.' Oh my God, Angie there was a warrant out for my arrest! I didn't even know it!" she said in disbelief.

I didn't really understand why she was so surprised. Cherlise stayed getting speeding tickets, and she never paid them. What the hell did she think would happen? "Wow, so they took you right then and there? They handcuffed you? What happened to your car?" Now I had questions a mile a minute.

"Oh my God, Angie yes! They handcuffed me and put me in the back of the police car. They let me call my friend, Travis, to come get the car. Thank goodness it didn't get impounded."

"Wow, that's crazy. Wait, where was Matt?" I had to ask.

"Oh, he had his son, so he couldn't come get me." She was starting with the bullshit excuses.

I pressed on, "*He had his son?* So he couldn't come bail you out either? That was an emergency!"

Her voice dropped as she responded hesitantly, "I know. I know. He had some other stuff going on. He really couldn't do it." Was I really hearing this? This is the type of stuff that annoyed me with her relationship with Matt. Her whole world revolved around him, but whenever she was the one in need he was never anywhere to be found. I could tell there was more to it that she wasn't telling me, but I didn't press the issue.

"So what happened after you got there? Was it really like on TV? Did Big Bertha try to make you her bitch?" I laughed.

She laughed back, "No, no Big Bertha. They brought me in and fingerprinted me. Angie, they made me get completely naked. I was so embarrassed. Then after they gave me my uniform, I just sat in the cell. I didn't use the bathroom the whole time I was there. I didn't take a shower either because I was scared."

"Oh my God, that's crazy. Damn, so who gave you the rest of the bail money?"

"Travis gave me one-fifty, I had one hundred in the bank already, and my cousin gave me the other fifty. I called my mother, and she didn't even help me. She was like, 'I don't know. I'll have to see what I can do.' Can you believe that? I cursed her out today. I'm like I had to ask all my friends for money and my own mother wouldn't even help bail me out. Like *wait?* Wait for what? I'M IN JAIL! THIS IS YOUR DAUGHTER! She really let me sit there all weekend. That's some bullshit!" I could hear the hurt in her voice as she told me about her mother.

All I could say was, "Damn. That *is* fucked up. Well at least you're out now!"

"Yeah, oh, and I will have your money week after next when I get paid. So don't worry."

"Okay, just let me know when you have it." I said trying to sound like I wasn't worried. "Well, I'm on my lunch break and gotta get back, so I'll talk to you later."

"Okay, what are you doing later tonight? I might stop by." She asked.

"I don't know. I might go to the gym. Then I'll just be home after that."

"Okay, I'ma call you!" she said. With that, I said goodbye and ended the call.

Reluctantly, I drove back to the office. It wasn't a far drive. Every time I went out for lunch, I always dreamed about just going to lunch and never coming back. It was just a fantasy, though. I took my time getting out of the car and walking back into the building.

As soon as I sat back in my seat, I heard Renee's loud voice booming, "UM, MS. DELIMAR!" There was a small pause. She sounded angry, "UM I *GOT* MONEY *THANK YOU!*" As soon as she said that a rush of emotions ran through my body.

Oh my God, did I do what I think? I thought to myself. I hurried and opened my email up. Yup, sure enough. Instead of replying to May's email about the birthday situation, I had replied directly to Renee's original email. I felt the blood rushing to my face with embarrassment. *That's exactly what I get!* I thought to myself.

I panicked inside thinking what I should or could do to redeem myself. There was no way to play it off or make it seem like a joke, so I thought of the next best thing I could do. I sent her an email that read:

I'm sorry, I didn't mean anything by this. Can we talk outside for a minute?

After a few minutes I got a reply saying:

Yeah we can talk, but not right now.

My mouth was dry, but I gulped in embarrassment. I stayed glued to my seat for the rest of the day. I knew Renee had a big mouth, so I was wondering just how bad it was. Had she told Vanessa? I didn't want Vanessa to think I had a problem with her because I truly didn't. Had she forwarded my email to the entire group? Did everyone know? When we talked, was she going to curse me out? I felt like crap. For the rest of the afternoon, I scolded myself in embarrassment. Eventually, I realized I heard no sound or movement coming from Renee's cubicle. I was too embarrassed to get up to see if she was in her seat, so I tried to stay focused on my work until the end of the day came. When I got up to leave for the day, I realized she had left early. Oh well, maybe we'd have the talk on the following day. This would give me time to prepare exactly what I was going to say.

CHAPTER 7

I couldn't wait to get out of the office! I thought about the situation with Renee the whole way to the gym. Once I was on the elliptical machine, I was fine, though. As much as I disliked working out, it always cleared my mind. It was never physically easy, but some of my best ideas came to me during my time on the elliptical. I had my headphones plugged in my ears. I closed my eyes and worked my arms and legs faster while I got lost in the workout to Eminem's song *"Lose Yourself"*.

Once I got into the groove of the music, the hour flew by. It was time to go. I headed to the ladies' locker room to get my gym bag. I glanced at the front entrance and saw Rock coming in. I quickened my pace before he saw me. I just wanted to get out of there. Although I was grateful for the favor he did for me earlier, I wasn't in the mood for his flirting this evening.

I got to my locker, entered my combination, and popped the lock open. Sitting on my gym bag was a folded piece of small white notebook paper. I opened it and written on it in pretty purple cursive was just one sentence: *"The truth shall set you free."* This was strange. Of course I didn't recognize the handwriting. I looked around. There were two women walking by and another lady walked over from the showers to the bench next to me. She stripped from her towel exposing her whole, pale, flabby body, and plopped down on the bench. Seeing that, I spun back around to my locker. I folded the note back up and put it in my bag.

I walked out of the locker room in a hurry, eyeing every person I saw with suspicion. Just as I stepped out into the hallway, Rock appeared. "Hey!" he said startling me.

"Hey Rock, why do you insist on scaring me?" I exhaled while grabbing my chest.

"Sorry love, you know I would never want to intentionally scare you." He answered leaning with his hand on the doorframe. He had me cornered. I tried to step around him, but he blocked me and leaned in a little. I didn't like people in my personal space—not random people anyway.

"Ah ah ahhhh, not so fast, lovely. You still owe me, so we need to work something out." He explained in a whisper.

"Rock, I already told you, I'm not going out with you because I have a boyfriend—"

"So if you didn't have a boyfriend, we'd be going out?" He cut me off.

"I didn't say that either! Look, I know I owe you but we'll have to figure something else out."

"Well what you got in mind?" he asked licking his lips like a pervert.

"I don't know yet, but I'll definitely let you know something. For real."

He stood up straight, and let his hand drop down to his side allowing me to pass by. "Okay, but don't keep me waiting too long, baby. You know I won't forget!"

"I know you won't!" I said with a fake smile as I walked away.

I was excited to find a letter from Cal waiting in my mailbox. This must have been the letter he was asking me if I got during our visit. Even though I had just seen him over the weekend, I was still always excited to see what he had to say. I couldn't make it up the stairs to my apartment fast enough. I couldn't wait to rip open the letter. My smile beamed at the sight of his handwriting. The letter was short but sweet as always. One page covered how much he missed me and how he couldn't wait to see me at our visitation. The second page pertained to the business with Wally.

The rest of the night flew by quickly. Cherlise actually did stop by. I should have known. She only stopped by because she needed someone to vent to about Matt. Matt cheated on Cherlise for the majority of their relationship, and she knew this. He was the type of dude to borrow Cherlise's car to go floss and pick up other women in it. He would pick fights with Cherlise almost every Friday just so he could get away and go be with other chicks. Either she never caught on to the pattern or she was in plain ol' denial. Either way, I was getting sick of the Cherlise and Matt Show.

This particular night she discovered he was still messing around with his son's mother. I didn't think it took a rocket scientist to figure that one out, but I guess it was brand new news to Cherlise. For some reason, she never got mad. She always seemed hurt more than anything. I don't know if it was love or what, but she needed Matt the way she needed air to breath. The thought of losing him to another woman drove her crazy, literally.

Whenever we would go out, she would start calling his cell phone as soon as we got out of his sight. She would continue calling him several times until he was back in her sight. If he didn't answer, she would continue calling him back to back. Cherlise was the type of girl to call a dude one hundred times back to back and not think twice about it.

I didn't understand. She was pretty, smart, and I knew she could do much better than Matt. She was half white and half black, light brown skin, long straight black hair, and pretty long black eyelashes that outlined bright eyes that always seemed to be gleaming. She was taller than me, maybe around five eight, and filled out solid. She was thick in all the right places. Cherlise was always smiling, except for when she was venting about Matt, and always kept a pleasant disposition. A lot of men would have jumped at the chance to have her on their arm.

Although I thought it was pretty sad and pathetic, I tried to understand and put myself in her shoes. All previous advice and/or opinions had fallen on deaf ears when it came to Cherlise. So I learned it was better for me to just be there to listen and be her sounding board.

After Cherlise finished venting and filling me in on her brief brush with the law, we ate dinner. I made fried chicken and spinach. She made the mashed potatoes. That's what we did sometimes, got together and cooked dinner. She was better at it than I was, though.

It was going on two o'clock in the morning by the time Cherlise left. I said my prayers before hopping in the bed for the night. I had forgotten about the incident with Renee for those few hours. Now lying in the bed, waiting to drift off to sleep, I suddenly remembered. I wasn't sure exactly what I was going to say the next day to her. I sincerely felt bad and wanted to make things right, but I was so embarrassed.

I rolled back out of bed and knelt on my knees again. I was desperate and prayed to God to help me work out the situation and to give me the words to say to apologize to Renee. When I finished begging God for his help, I climbed back in bed and slowly drifted off to sleep.

CHAPTER 8

The rest of the workweek went okay. Renee actually called out for the rest of the week, so I didn't have to worry about confronting her for the moment. Maybe this was God's way of buying me some more time to figure out what I would say to her. I genuinely felt bad, but Friday was here already again.

I lived for the weekends. As soon as five o'clock popped up on my computer screen at work, I high-tailed it out of that place. I was scheduled to work both Friday and Saturday at the club this weekend, but I still had a few hours to kill before I went in. I decided to get some ox tails and peas n' rice from a Guyanese spot I knew of in East Orange. It was the next town over, but not too far from my house.

It was packed as usual on Fridays. It was always hot in there, all year round too. I squeezed into the crowded storefront to wait in line. A tall metal fan stood in the corner blowing more hot air. The aroma teased my palate as I looked through the cloudy windows where the food was laid out. Macaroni pie, cabbage, ox tails, stewed beef, jerk chicken, peas n' rice, curry chicken; all the good eats were lined up on the other side of the window.

There were about four people before me in line, so I people watched as I waited patiently. There was a couple sitting down at one of the tables lined against the wall and a lady with her two kids sitting at another table behind them. The man sitting with his girlfriend or wife was yelling back and forth through the glass to the lady working behind the counter. It was always the same woman. She was a very dark-skinned woman with smooth skin. She had a short haircut, but she always wore something to cover her head. That day she wore a shower cap as she yelled back through the glass to the man. I couldn't really understand what they were saying, but I could tell that they knew each other by the way they teased and laughed with each other.

There was a middle-aged man in front of me. I assumed he had just gotten off of work as well because the jacket he wore had a nametag on it. He looked like one of those guys that worked for Verizon or PSE&G or something. He wore a denim cap on his head, but I didn't see the point because it wasn't all the way on. It was more just sitting on top of his little peanut head. He kept turning around and looking at me. The third time he did it, I decided to engage in battle with him.

"Engaging in battle" was a term May and I had come up with. Whenever some one stared at us for too long, we would engage in battle or simply just "engage." That is, we would catch them staring, lock eyes, and stare back as though playing the staring game. Whatever it took, we would stare back with a blank stare until the other person became so uncomfortable or came to the realization that they were staring and looked away. Usually it worked. Sometimes it didn't.

I locked eyes with Mr. Peanut Head, and it didn't take long to take him down. I guess he realized that he was staring, and he gave a polite smile and nod. I was a little irked by his staring, but you can't *not* smile back when a person smiles at you, so I gave a fake, warm smile. To ease the tension, I turned and glanced out the big window behind me. There were a few young guys standing at the bus stop. I turned back around as I secretly hoped that they would be gone by the time I exited the store.

Even though I was grown, I hated walking past a group of guys. It made me nervous for some reason. I didn't want any of them to try to kick game to me. I knew they would probably look me up and down and size me up as I walked past. I was good for tripping or doing something else embarrassing when I was in those kinds of situations. So for all those reasons, I hoped the bus would come by the time I got my food.

The line was moving, and it was finally my turn to order. I didn't have to think about it because I always ordered the same thing when I came here. I never understood why, but the lady behind the counter would always stop smiling when I came up to order. I would say "hi," and she would never say it back. It could have just been my imagination, but I think it was because she knew I was American. Oh well, one of them or not, I still liked their food. So on I went with my order.

"Hi, do you have any roti skin today?" I asked. Depending how late I went, sometimes they didn't have anymore.

"Roti skin? Yes, but it's puree." She responded.

"Okay, yes can I have one roti skin, a small ox tail dinner with peas n' rice and cabbage, two pine tarts, and two beef patties?" I ordered. She walked to the back to get the roti. She returned and grabbed a tin pan to start fixing my dinner order. I turned back around while she proceeded and glanced out the window.

There she was again! It was that lady who had been following me! She was across the street leaned against the corner of the Easy Pickins store. She was just standing there looking directly across the street at me. "Sixteen fifty!" I spun around at shower cap lady's request. I shuffled quickly through my purse for my wallet. I didn't want to loose sight of the lady. I pulled out a twenty, handed it to the shower cap lady behind the counter, grabbed the plastic bag with my food in it, and hurried towards the door. "Excuse me, gal! Your change!" the lady behind the counter yelled out to me. I thought about leaving my change but thought better of it and doubled back to the counter. I grabbed the money quickly trying not to snatch it and shoved it down in my purse.

I managed to squeak out a quick "thank you" as I hurried back to the door.

I forgot all about the guys at the bus stop. I didn't care at this point. I was ready to confront this woman and find out why she was following me. I practically ran pass the guys. I heard one of them say, "How you doing Ma?" I didn't look. I didn't even wait for the light to change. I looked for my chance, and dashed right into the street. I ran fast enough not to get hit by the two cars coming from my left. I made it to the double yellow lines in the middle of the street and waited there for the cars from the right to cease so I could continue my dash across the street. One car blew their horn at me, but I didn't care. Just as they did, the lady saw me. She looked right at me and began power walking down a side street.

She was getting away. "HEY!" I called out to her. She peeped over her shoulder and doubled her speed down the street. The light turned yellow and my heart raced as I waited for it to turn red. "Wait! Please stop! I just want to talk to you, PLEASE!" I begged. The number thirty-four public bus slowly rolled up on the other side of the street blocking my view. The light finally changed and I ran across the street around the back of the bus. I looked down the side street, left and right. She got a way again! As I spun around looking lost, a crowd of people stepped off the bus one right after another. I got caught up in the small crowd, and I knew I had lost her again. *Dammit*, I thought to myself as I turned to walk back across the street.

CHAPTER 9

I was happy and surprised to see another letter from Cal waiting in my mailbox. He must have written me right after our last visit. I immediately forgot all about the strange woman following me. As usual, the butterflies started. I was excited, not only for his letter, but we only had two and a half more weeks before we would be together forever. I was counting down the days, sixteen and a wake-up. I couldn't wait for him to get home. We were gonna take the whole world over together.

As I walked down the hall approaching my door, I came upon an odor. As I stood outside of my apartment, fingering through my key ring to find the right key, the smell grew. It was faint, but it smelled like hot garbage. I couldn't get the door open fast enough. As soon as I walked in, I kicked off my shoes, placed the food on the kitchen table, and tore open Cal's letter. He didn't have to say much to brighten up my day. Reading his letters was like a short escape from reality. It allowed me to be in this fantasy world where I had the perfect boyfriend and relationship.

It may sound pathetic, but being in a jail relationship was one of the best relationships. I had all of my man's attention. I got to decide if and when I wanted to see him, and each time I did see him, it was a precious moment. If he should ever upset me, all I had to do was stop writing or going to visit and that would have him right back on track. I also knew exactly where he was all the time, no guessing.

I sat back for a minute and imagined what it was going to be like to make love to him. I was nervous. Although I copped a feel at visit and even managed to get a peek once or twice at the goods, there was never a guarantee that he knew how to work it. What if we weren't compatible in bed? I giggled a little to myself as I thought about how tall he was and how short I was. I wondered if it would be awkward for us to get into positions.

I only had about two more hours before it was time for me to head off to work. I took my time eating my dinner and put the leftovers in the microwave. I was usually hungry when I came in from the club. I really didn't feel like going into work, but I didn't like calling out either. I knew it would be worth it once I was back at home counting my tips though.

After I ate, I squeezed in a quick one-hour nap. I headed off to the club where I parked and did my usual ritual. Once inside, I got right into the swing of things. The music always had a way of putting me in a festive mood and giving me the energy I needed.

Work flew by even though it wasn't that busy. I was glad to see that Ronnie wasn't hanging around tonight. I was always more relaxed when he wasn't there. I glanced up to see Jillian, one of the dancers, walking over towards the bar. She was holding a man by the hand leading him over, and they grabbed a stool near me. She sat on the man's lap.

Jillian was one of the dancers that I was cool with. We worked well together. Whenever I saw her walking over to me leading somebody by the hand, I knew that was my signal to get ready to work my charisma. It meant they had money and were ready to spend it. Jillian had an average face and brown skin with full lips. Her makeup was always done to perfection, not too much and not too little. She had a long, straight, black wig with flat bangs across. It looked cute on her. Her body made up for her average face. You could tell she probably hit the gym on the regular. She was very fit and toned with a nice flat stomach. She had a classic coke bottle shape. Her hips gave way to a big, round butt. Tonight she was wearing a one-piece teddy-like body suit. It looked more like a monokini swimsuit, gray with bright pink piping.

The man she led over looked to be in his mid to late forties. He had a receding hairline and a salt and pepper mustache and beard. He wasn't bad looking, but he did have a bit of a stomach on him. Before they sat down, I was able to get a quick peek at his shoes, nice, shiny, clean hard bottoms. I thought they might be Stacy Adams. He was dressed professionally and wore a Rolex watch. Even in the dim lights of the club, the diamonds on the watch and on the big pinky ring he wore dazzled and gleamed. He was a good pick. We could tell he was there to spend money.

Once perched with her legs crossed, Jillian said with a smile, "Annngie! This is our new friend Michael. I told Michael that you're my favorite bartender, and you're gonna take good care of us. So he would like a …."

Her voice paused as she looked at Michael to finish her sentence, "a double shot of Jose Cuervo with salt and a lime." I was glad to see that he wanted an easy drink as opposed to something fancy I didn't know how to make.

"Coming right up, Michael" I said, flashing a big smile before turning around to make the drink.

"And whatever the lady would like," he added.

"Oh, you're gonna buy me a drink? What a gentleman," Jillian responded while batting her fake eyelashes. "I'll have a shot of Patron." I knew that was code for water in a shot glass.

I was surprised to learn when I started working at Ronnie's that most of the ladies that danced there didn't drink. Customers would get offended if you turned down a drink, and Ronnie would get mad, so the ladies would say Patron, and we'd give them water while charging the customer for the real thing. They looked the same and the customer couldn't tell it was water. This made everybody happy.

I returned with drinks in hand and sat them down. "Would you like to start a tab, Michael?"

"Sure, and please have a drink with us, Angie," he responded, reaching inside his interior suit jacket pocket. He handed over a black credit card. Jillian and I both saw it and glanced at each other in silent confirmation that we were about to make some good tips from this guy.

"Thank you, that's so kind of you." I said while taking his card and stashing it securely in a wine glass behind the bar. "I think I'm going to have a shot of Patron too," I said, pouring myself some water out of the same Patron bottle I used for Jillian.

"Cheers to you beautiful ladies!" Michael said, smiling as he raised his glass. We tapped glasses exchanging cheers and threw back the water.

The three of us chatted for a while. I didn't worry about the other customers because I knew the other bartenders could take care of them. I was content to stay right there with the big fish. Michael continued buying us rounds, and we continued stroking his ego by flirting with him. I made sure to laugh at all his jokes and tapped his hand lightly as if dying in laughter. Meanwhile, Jillian stayed perched right on his lap with one arm swung around his neck and the other inside the top of his crisp button-up stroking his chest. Every now and then, she would lean in and whisper something in his ear. We knew we had him, and he was probably feeling like a king. That was the point.

It was close to closing time and Michael was good and drunk. I closed out his tab and handed him his credit card in preparation for his departure. "It's been a delight ladies." He said as he patted Jillian's thigh signaling her to get off of his lap.

"Our pleasure, Mr. Michael! Make sure you come back and see us!" I said as I grabbed his hand and squeezed.

"That's right, Daddy!" Jillian chimed in.

He left me an eighty-dollar tip; well worth it. Jillian walked him out, and I'm sure he tipped her way more for her services. I joined in and helped Britt and Tee Tee wipe down the bar and bottles. "You coming with us to IHOP tonight, Miss?" Britt asked.

Since I backed out the weekend before, I agreed to go. "Yeah I can go for some French toast and bacon."

"Cool, we out soon as Ronnie comes to lock up the doors." She responded.

"Heeeeeyyy ladiiiiies!" droned a drunk Ozzy as he leaned over the bar to keep himself up. Ozzy was a regular. He came to the club almost every night. He was married, but he hated going home. He would come in and make us listen to stories about the fights he was having with his wife while he drank shot after shot of F&J. Sometimes he would break Ronnie's rules and get extra fresh with the dancers. He had been thrown out on several occasions but never banned.

"Hey Ozzy," we all said in unison.

"Angie, let me get another shot of F&J!" I don't know why, but Ozzy always wanted me to serve him. He never asked the other girls to serve him, and I know they were happy because he was a true pain in the ass.

"Ozzy, we're about to close, and I don't think you need another shot." I responded.

"C'mon Angie. Don't start tonight. You know you too fine to have all that attitude, girl! Just give me the fuckin' shot please!" He demanded.

"Ozzy, you can barely stand up. I can't serve you another drink. We gotta make sure you make it home in one piece to the Mrs."

"The Mrs.? Shit! I need more to drink, so I can go home and deal with that bitch." He said as he put his forehead down on the bar and shook his head in exaggerated despair.

"I don't know Ozzy …"

He lifted his head and grabbed my arm tightly, "Stop playing Angela, and just give me the fuckin' drink! Wait 'til I tell Ronnie you not treating his customers right!" He said, licking his lips. I could smell the five shots of E&J he had drank already on his breath.

"Let go of my arm, Ozzy. See, you're already too drunk!"

He pulled harder on my arm "Why the fuck you playing? AYE ONE OF Y'ALL BITCHES GON' GIMME A SHOT OF E&J DAMMIT!" he demanded as he grew more agitated.

I was glad to see Britt leave from behind the bar and return with Freddy, the bouncer. He finally got Ozzy to let go of my arm and escorted him out. I shook my head as I watched them leave. Ozzy didn't scare me. He was more annoying more than anything, and I was used to his behavior by now.

I went to go close out my register, and Jillian popped up leaning over the bar. "Good teamwork tonight, Ang!" she said as she raised her hand for a hi-five.

"Hell to da yeah!" I said laughing while slapping her hand.

"We always know how to tag team 'em, huh?" Jillian said as she winked.

"Yup! We sure do!"

"Michael liked us! He was feeling' Jillangie, the Jillian-Angie combo!" she sang as she did a little cabbage patch dance. I laughed as I continued counting out my register.

"But that's 'cause we know how to work it together, know what I mean?" she continued.

"Yup, we got this thing down pact, girl!"

"You got a boyfriend, Ang?" she asked out of nowhere.

I wondered why she was asking, and responded "Yeah but he's

locked up at the moment. He'll be home in a couple weeks, though."

"Oh word? Damn! ... Well, we need to hang out some time outside of work before he comes home. 'Cause I know he gon' have that ass on lock when he touch down!" she added.

"Yeah, that's what's up! Do you like to club?"

"You know it, and I bet you and me would probably have fun." She said.

"Okay, just let me know when you wanna do something, and I'm game."

"Where's your phone? Lock my number in," she instructed. I grabbed my phone from behind the counter and put her number in as she dictated her digits to me. "And call my phone now, so I have your number." She said as she stood up straight to walk away.

"Alright, later Jilli!"

Just as I finished and closed the drawer, I could hear my name being yelled. "ANGIE! What's good? We ready!" Britt was holding the door calling out to me as Tee Tee and Kiesha walked out. Princess wasn't working that night, so it was just the four of us.

"I'm right behind you!" I yelled towards the door as I grabbed my phone and dashed to the coatroom to get my coat.

Tee Tee and Keisha usually rode to work together. So they rode together and Britt and I drove separate cars to the IHOP on Bergen Street. I wasn't even that hungry anymore, but I went just to hang with the girls. We settled into a booth near the back window. It never mattered what time you went to IHOP. It was always packed. We chatted and giggled about Ronnie and some of the dancers we didn't like. I ordered some French toast with some beef bacon on the side and an orange juice.

"Girl, I saw your favorite customer, Ozzy, giving you a hard time tonight." Tee Tee teased.

I rolled my eyes, "Oh my God, don't get me started. Can't stand his ass ..."

"Me neither! You know he followed Keisha to her car last week right?" she went on.

"What? Get outta here!"

"Yup, he sure did. He grabbed my arm just like he did yours tonight and tried to kiss me!" Keisha chimed in.

"Oh my God, what did you do? I would've been scared shitless!"

"I just started screaming for my life at the top of my lungs.

Luckily, Ronnie was just closing the gate and heard me. Him and Freddy came running around the corner and got him off of me." She recounted.

"That shit is crazy. I don't know why they don't ban his ass for good from the club. That should've been it right there." Said Britt.

"Girl, you know Ronnie is not about to turn away a dollar, especially from a drunk like Ozzy. Shoot, he keeping the place in business!" Tee Tee said, and we all started laughing.

As I wiped the bacon grease from my fingers, Britt mentioned Jillian. "So Angie, I noticed you and Jillian are becoming best friends 'n shit lately. Sup with that?" Tee Tee and Keisha were quiet as they looked at one another as though they knew a secret I wasn't in on.

I replied, "I don't know 'bout all that, but she's cool … She always brings me the big tippers, so I can't complain. Why you ask me that anyway?"

"Hmmm, she must like you! She don't bring the rest of us the big tippers." She replied as she winked at the girls who snickered in response.

"We just got a little system of how we work together. That's all." I said.

"Yeah, I bet y'all do!" Tee Tee interjected as she busted out laughing.

"What? Why y'all laughing? Y'all know something and y'all not telling me?" I begged in reply.

Britt answered, "nothing, really it's nothing. Just be careful that's all."

The girls wouldn't tell me no matter how much I begged. So I got up to go to the bathroom. On my way back from the bathroom, I glanced towards the front door and who did I see? It was the mysterious lady again. *What the fuck? How the hell is she everywhere I go?* I thought to myself. This time she wasn't alone. She was there with a man and a young girl. The girl looked just like the lady and looked as though she could have been around fifteen or sixteen. The way the man stood close to the mystery woman told me it must've been her husband or boyfriend.

She hadn't spotted me yet, meaning it must've actually been coincidence this time. For once, she wasn't following me on purpose it seemed. I wasn't letting her get away this time, though. I walked right past our booth as I heard Keisha say, "Angie where you goin'?"

I was just about ten feet away before the lady spotted me. Her eyes grew wide as she whispered something to the man and nodded in my direction. Now, seeing her up close, I could get a good look. She looked a little older without the hood tied around her face, but I knew it was the same woman.

I walked right up to her and said, "Hey! Who the hell are you and why do you keep following me?" The man stood between us as she hurried to usher the young girl out of the IHOP. I could hear the girl asking who I was. The man restrained me as though he was her bodyguard. "And who the hell are *you*? Take your hands off me! You tell that bitch to stop fucking stalking me!"

The man spoke in a hushed voice "Look miss, we don't know you. Please just leave us alone."

"Leave *you* alone? I'm not the weirdo lurking around every corner. Tell that weirdo to leave *me* alone! How 'bout that!"

POP! POP! POP! POP! Just as the man let go, shots rang out, startling us both. They sounded close by, but I couldn't tell where they were coming from. I just knew they were coming fast. The man grabbed me and pulled me to the floor. I covered my ears and buried my head down into my chest. Panic shot through my heart as I listened to the gunfire. It was coming from two different directions now. I heard the glass shatter right above where I was laying. I peeked up for a second to see people running and screaming in different directions, but I was too scared to get up.

I looked down one of the aisles. I saw two men with guns running towards me. The one in the front seemed to look directly at me, so I ducked my head back down. They ran right past as I listened to the glass crunch under their feet. I stayed on the floor a few more minutes until I knew for sure the gunshots had finished. I opened my eyes to see the man acting as the bodyguard was nowhere to be found. He must've run out at some point. At that point, I wasn't thinking about the strange lady anymore. I had to get to the girls and see if they were okay. All I could hear was screaming as I stood up slowly and cautiously. I walked timidly back towards our booth as I came upon the screaming. It was a woman sitting on the floor, cradling a man in her lap. His body lay lifeless in her arms. Blood steadily seeped from his shirt.

I froze. "Please, help me! Help me! Call 911! PLEASE!" she cried out to me. I couldn't move. It felt as though time had stopped and gravity had me stuck in that one spot. "Oh my God! Oh my God! Marquis, please baby! Marquis, please get up!" I heard the woman crying and pleading, but my body wouldn't budge. Just then, I felt someone grab me by my arm.

"Oh my God, Angie! What the fuck? We didn't know where you were! Come on, let's get the hell outta here!" I heard Britt, but I still couldn't move.

"Come on girl!" Keisha said as she pushed my purse and coat into my chest and nudged me towards the direction of the door. I took one last look at the woman and the man in her lap as I felt Keisha's push nudge me back to earth. I grabbed my stuff from her and took off right behind Britt. By this time, the IHOP was practically empty.

Once we were out in the parking lot, Britt gave us strict instructions. "Aye, y'all get right in your car and go straight home. Don't stop, and hurry up before the cops get here. We don't need to be caught up answering no questions about nothing!" As her words set in, I agreed. I gave a quick "bye" and hurried off to my car. A quick glance around the parking lot gave no sight of the strange lady and her family. Once I was locked in my car, tears streamed down my face as I began to cry. I didn't know why I was crying. I didn't know that woman in the IHOP or her Marquis. I don't know if I cried out of fright, out of shock, or what. I could hear the police sirens getting close, so I quickly started the car, wiped my face, and peeled out of the parking lot. I couldn't wait to be safe in my own home.

I don't even remember the drive home. All kinds of thoughts were running through my mind. Why did those guys kill that man? Did they see my face as they were running out? What if they knew I saw them and had followed me? I reasoned with myself and tried to convince myself that I was being totally paranoid. Still, I looked around cautiously as I walked from the parking lot in the back of my building inside.

I breathed a sigh of relief once I had entered the building. As soon as I did, that horrible smell hit me right in the face again. It had gotten way stronger just in those few hours I was gone for work. As I made my way up the stairs, the smell grew worse. I passed my neighbor's door, and it seemed as though the odor was coming from there. *Why don't they take out their goddamn garbage?* I thought to myself as I covered my nose and mouth and hurried inside my apartment. I lit an incense as soon as I got in, and I put it on the table near the front door. I didn't want that awful smell seeping into my apartment.

I heated up my leftover food in the microwave while I changed into my pajamas. I tried to focus on the excitement of seeing Cal the following afternoon. No matter how hard I tried, the images of that woman and the dead man she cradled kept creeping back into my mind. I knew I would probably have nightmares, if I was able to sleep at all. I fell asleep on the couch watching TV.

CHAPTER 10

To my surprise, I had no nightmares at all. I slept like a baby considering the night's events. The warmth of the sunlight peering through the window shade is what woke me up. I slowly peeked my eyes open as I looked up at the ceiling. I felt well rested, but a little hungry. I squinted at the time on the cable box and tried to focus.

"Oh shit!" I exclaimed to myself. It was already eleven o' eight AM. I had to be at the jail by noon or they wouldn't let me in. I sprung from the couch and made a dash for the bathroom. I didn't even get my outfit together the night before and had no clue what to wear. That was the fastest shower I think I had ever taken.

I knew I would be pushing it for time, but I had to at least try. The thought of not seeing Cal felt like it would kill me, and I knew he would be disappointed too. I threw on some jeans and a white-T just like everyone else would be wearing. I didn't care. I didn't have time to take any chances with any risky outfits today. I grabbed a granola bar out of the cabinet and a bottle of water. This would have to do until I got home from the visit.

I threw on my white air forces, grabbed a coat and my keys, and swung my front door open in a hurry. I was surprised to see one of my other neighbors jump back from Mr. Burkwell's apartment door. I had startled her. She was still dressed in her pajamas with a head wrap on and fuzzy slippers. We had only spoke in passing before now.

"Mornin'," I said to her dryly.

"Hey, do you smell that?" she asked with her face scrunched up.

"Yeah, it smells horrible and it's been smelling like that for a few days now. I don't know what that is!"

"I think it's coming from him," she whispered as she pointed to the old man's door.

"Yeah, I know. I wish he'd do something about it, but I haven't seen him in a few days. Maybe he's away or something. Were you just knocking on the door?"

"No, I was trying to track down the smell to see where it was coming from." She said in an almost embarrassed chuckle. "If he doesn't do something about it soon, I'm gonna call management." She added.

I was thinking maybe we should knock on his door and just ask him to do something about the smell, but I was in too much of a hurry to deal with it then. So I replied, "Yeah because it's just getting worse and worse."

I walked past her towards the stairs as I heard her mumble under her breath, "don't make no sense." She turned and walked into her apartment as I made my way down the stairs.

I wasted no time letting the car warm up. I only had fifteen minutes to get there. I broke all speed limits, weaving in and out of traffic as I burned down McCarter Highway. I pulled into the parking lot at eleven fifty-five. I jumped out the car and jogged into the building. I didn't want to make a scene running like a wild woman, but I didn't have any time to spare either. I made it just in time. The check-in window was still open with two people in line in front of me.

I breathed a sigh of relief as I got to the window. I recited Cal's inmate number to the C.O. as I handed her my license for identification. "Ummm, inmate's last name Shay?" she asked.

I answered quickly, "yes."

"He's already got a visitor, ma'am. I'm not going to be able to let you in." she said uninterested.

"Excuse me?" I didn't think I had heard her correctly.

"Someone has already signed in to see this inmate today."

I stood there confused thinking to myself, *I know she didn't just say what I thought she said!* I didn't know what to say or do next. I was dumbfounded. "Are you sure? Who is it?" I asked.

"Sorry, I can't give you that information." That was all she said.

I felt my heart sink as I wondered who in the hell was there. He knew I was coming. I had been coming every weekend. He always told me beforehand if his grandmother or brothers were coming up. Even though I didn't like the idea of his ex visiting him, he always told me beforehand when she was going to bring his daughter too. So who could this be? My mind immediately went into paranoia. I was ready to flip out if he had another chick up there to visit him.

I thought about waiting around until visit was over, but I didn't see the point in waiting around for three hours if I didn't even know who exactly I was looking for. If it was a chick, I didn't know what she looked like, so it would be of no help. Even if I did know, I wasn't going to confront her. For what? Cal was the one who owed me an explanation, and his ass better have had a good answer.

I walked slowly back to the car feeling almost broken-hearted. There was nothing I could do except to go home and wait for him to call me later or have someone else call me. I started up the car and gave a deep sigh. As I made my way to the highway, I decided I didn't want to go straight home. I called Cherlise to see what she was up to instead. Matt was out with her car as usual and she was home doing nothing, so I went by to pick her up. We decided to go to the mall. Shopping always made us both feel better.

"Well, you have his grandmother's number, right? Just call her now before visit is over, so you can see if she was there. At least that'll narrow down the possibilities." Cherlise had a good point. Though I felt kind of out of place to call her up and ask her that. It seemed kind of intrusive of me.

"Yeah, I guess I could do that, but I don't know. You don't think that's a little nosey of me?" I asked.

"Hell no! She knows who you are and you wanna know who the hell was up there visiting him don't you?" She asked.

I forgot who I was talking to. Cherlise would go through any means necessary to get information about her man Matt. She didn't care if she had to hire a private detective or call the producers of *Cheaters* to find out what was what. I did want to find out, but I felt really weird about calling his grandmother giving her the third degree, especially since I hadn't even met her in person yet. Sure I had spoken to her a couple times on the phone to pass on messages from Cal, but that was it.

"What am I gonna say?" I wondered out loud.

"Shit, just ask for her and if she's not there just ask whoever answers the phone if she went to see Cal." Cherlise instructed slowly as though I was slow.

"I'm not going to ask whoever answers the phone that and they don't even know me!"

"Fine, you want me to just call and say I'm a friend of Cal's?" she asked. It was sneaky and immature, but I knew not knowing would bother me until I knew something.

I chuckled and grinned with wide eyes "Okay yeah, and call from your phone so my number doesn't come up. They might not answer if we block the number."

"Alright, if I get her on the phone, do you want me to ask her if his brothers went up to see him?" she asked.

"Mmmmm, I highly doubt it was his brothers seeing as they haven't been up to see him in months, but no, don't ask her. When she says she didn't go to visit, just say you're Cal's friend and were supposed to go see him, but somebody else went to visit and you weren't sure if maybe she or his brothers had went up. That way you're not outright asking her, but casually mentioning them to see if she volunteers the information." I told her.

"Okay, what if she's not home and someone else answers?" she asked.

"Tell them the same thing." That still seemed a little nosey, but I didn't care at this point since I wasn't the one doing the talking or calling.

We sat down near the food court as Cherlise took out her phone. My stomach growled lightly as I took in the aromas of all the fast food. I inhaled pizza, Chinese food, and McDonalds. The smell of Auntie Anne's Pretzels teased me the most. I gave in and stood in line to get Cherlise and me a pretzel while she made the call.

All that conversation preparation was wasted as the call to Cal's grandmother went unanswered. Since I wasn't getting any closer to an answer right at that moment, I decided I would just have to wait to see what Cal had to say. Now we only had one more visit left before he came home for good. I would have to wait until the following weekend to see him. I wondered for a second if he felt as disappointed at the moment as I did.

Next we stopped at a small jewelry kiosk. There was really nothing I wanted on display. Cherlise asked to see a chain. "What'chu think about this, Ang?" she asked. It was a plain, thick white gold chain.

In between licking the sour cream and onion pretzel powder from my fingers, I answered, "Mmm, I don't know. It looks a little man-ish honestly. You like that?"

She chuckled and replied "Not for me! I think I might get it for Matt and maybe get this "M" to go wit it." She pointed to a white gold charm that had diamond cuts in it. The charm was nice and it probably would go with the chain.

Just at that moment I realized she was in the mall shopping with me and hadn't paid me back yet. Although we agreed that she could pay me back the following week when she got paid, a feeling of annoyance rose over me. If she had money to be buying this dude chains n' stuff, she could pay me back now! Where the heck was he when she needed help getting out of jail? I decided to just leave the topic alone. We agreed on the following week, so I would just wait until then.

"Yeah, I like that charm. That'll look nice against a nice black sweater or something." I replied less enthused.

"Ooooh yeah! He can wear it with this black Coogi sweater I bought him last month!" She sounded excited at the thought. I could see her picturing it on him in her mind. I never saw a woman get so excited over buying her boyfriend stuff that he would more than likely be wearing out with another chick. I didn't get it, but maybe it wasn't for me to get.

"Okay I'll take it! Can you clean it first?" she asked the saleslady.

As the saleslady complied, I remembered the night before. "Oh shoot! I completely forgot to tell you what happened to me yesterday!"

"What?" She asked as the saleswoman handed her the chain and charm in a little bag.

"Oh my God, Cherlise. Girl I was in the middle of a shootout last night—well early this morning!" I started to tell her. We continued walking around the mall after she paid for the chain as I told her how everything had went down the night before. With my mind so preoccupied on Cal and the mystery visitor, I had completely forgotten about it all.

After being in the mall for hours, I had only gotten a belt. I drove back to Cherlise's house, and we just chilled there for a while talking and watching TV. She did most of the talking, as usual, about things going on with her and Matt. There was always some type of baby mama drama or other woman drama going on with them. Since it seemed like Cherlise was content in staying in such a relationship, there wasn't much for me to say. I just extended a listening ear.

Cherlise turned to me and lowered her voice to a whisper. "Angie, I have something to tell you."

I faced her, intrigued by whatever was about to come out her mouth. "Awww shit! What?" I asked her with a worried smile. Whenever Cherlise spoke like this, I knew it was something juicy and something mischievous coming.

"Um, I been doing something kind of bad with Matt." She gave a partial confession.

"Something like *what*?" I asked perplexed.

"Well ... him and his friends robbed a couple bars and stores in Patterson ..."

I jumped out of disbelief before she could continue. "Whaaaat? Are you serious? Oh my God you stuck somebody up, Cherlise?"

She threw her head back in a silent cackle as she continued, "Noooo, he and his friends did the stickups. I just drove the car."

I didn't know what to say "Oh my God. Damn, y'all crazy! You weren't scared you would crash or get caught?"

"No, well you know how I drive anyway. But nah, I park down the street from the bars or whatever and they always pick somewhere that's close to the highway, so I can just jump right on and off the highway."

Cherlise was the fastest and craziest driver I knew. She had gotten so many speeding tickets and had been involved in so many accidents; more than I could keep track of. I still couldn't believe what I was hearing. She had really let this guy Matt brainwash her into doing some crazy shit! Then again, who was I to judge? Cal had successfully brainwashed me into sneaking drugs into a prison for him. I got sidetracked as I started getting mad all over again thinking about that and him having another visitor.

"Damn, so did y'all use guns? Like give me the whole rundown." I said, wanting to know all the dirt. She went on to explain that they had robbed about four stores and bars. She would park down the street and Matt and his two friends would go in and rob these places with guns. Then they returned to the car, and Cherlise would hop on the highway and take them to a motel room they had checked in beforehand. There they counted and split the money. It was really like something out of a movie. She even went on to tell me how one time they boxed in a car full of gay guys at a red light and robbed them at gunpoint as well. She laughed when she told this story. I didn't find it too funny.

"Damn, y'all swear y'all on some real Bonnie and Clyde type shit!" I said making fun of her.

She laughed, "I know right. I know you not talking!" There was nothing I could say. I had already told her about what I was doing for Cal, so she was right. I had no room to talk.

"Damn, just be careful." I told her.

Cherlise always had some type of hustle going, but this was the first of its caliber. Every job she worked at she found some way to steal money, services, or both. She had no conscience about it. I hadn't really thought about the consequences of what I was doing either, so I understood. I tried to make myself feel better about it by reminding myself it was a temporary hustle. Once Cal was home, I wouldn't have any parts of it.

We both fell asleep on the couch, and were wakened by Matt banging on the door, yelling and cursing from the hall. "CHERLISE! WHAT THE FUCK ARE YOU DOING? OPEN THE DAMN DOOR!" I heard him first. I looked over at Cherlise who was still knocked out with slob streaming out her mouth onto the couch pillow.

"Cherlise!" I said, nudging her. She wasn't budging, so I shook her harder. Her eyes popped open as she wiped the slob from her mouth. "Matt is knocking on the door." I informed her. Before the words could barely escape from my mouth, she hopped up off the couch like a mad woman.

"Oh shit!" she said as she ran to the door.

Matt walked in visibly upset. "What the fuck you in here doing? You got a nigga in here? What the fuck took you so long to answer the door? I been calling you!"

She laughed nervously as she answered, "No, Angie's here. We just fell asleep."

"Damn, I was waiting outside mad long. What's up Annnnngie?" his mood had instantly softened once he saw me sitting there.

"What's up, Matt!" I greeted him from the couch.

Despite my disapproval of his treatment of my good friend, I had no personal beef with Matt. He was always pleasant to me and since he was my friend's boyfriend, I showed respect and hid my disapproval. I glanced at the time on Cherlise's cable box. It was almost midnight. I checked my phone, and still no calls from Cal or his people. I got up and used the bathroom in preparation to leave.

As I came out, I could hear Matt telling Cherlise he was hungry and demanding she cook something. I found her in the kitchen following orders, bent over pulling out pots and pans from the lower cabinet. "Okay, Chef Cherlise! You 'bout to get it poppin' in the kitchen?" I asked jokingly. She grinned back and nodded. "Alright, well I'm 'bout to be out myself." I notified her.

"Okay, I'll call you tomorrow!" I let myself out, and headed home.

I could see flashing lights before I made the turn onto my street. As I made my way down the street, I could see police cars and an ambulance. Neighbors stood outside on both sides of the street in their nightclothes speculating to one another. It wasn't until I came right up on my driveway that I realized all the commotion was taking place at my building. I tried to turn into the driveway leading to the parking lot, but a police car had it blocked.

I let down my window, and called out to an officer standing near the police cruiser. "Excuse me! I live here. Can I get into my driveway?"

It was a white, militant looking officer who appeared to be taking his job very seriously. He responded in a stern voice, "We're not letting anyone in or out right now, ma'am. You'll have to park down the street."

I sucked my teeth and sighed. "Well, will I be able to get in?" I asked.

"You said that you live here, right?" he replied.

"Yes."

"We should be able to let you in in a few minutes, but you'll have to park down the street for now. And please have ID ready." He instructed.

"Okay," I said as I pulled off in search of parking on the street. I had to park far at the corner, and I wondered what was going on as I walked back towards my building.

I walked up to the cop who I had just spoken to and pulled out my ID. "Here's my license. Can I just go on in?" There were policemen blocking the front door and spread all over the walkway and grass. The officer looked at my license, then at me and answered, "Yeah, just show this to the gentlemen at the door and they'll let you into your apartment." He called out to the officers by the door, "Joey! She lives here! Please escort her to her apartment!" I flashed my ID to Joey who escorted me upstairs as instructed. As soon as we were inside the building, I almost gagged from the strong odor.

"Oh my God!" I gasped as I cupped my hand over my mouth and nose.

As we arrived at the top landing, I found even more police standing near my front door and I could see Mr. Burkwell's front door open with police walking in and out. "Okay, which apartment is yours?" the escorting policeman asked.

"Right there, number twenty-four" I pointed as I answered.

"Oh!" he said as though surprised. "Hey Rogers! She lives next door to the victim. Is she good to go in?" he called down the hall to one of the officers as we approached.

"She can go in her apartment, but Clark might want to talk to her first!" he responded as he looked me up and down.

Victim? I said to myself in my head. I wondered why they wanted to talk to me. I wasn't even home. I had no idea what was going on.

As I stopped in front of my door, a familiar face walked out of the old man's apartment. "*Angie?*" Rock said in surprise to see me. I was just as surprised to see him.

"What are you doing here? What's going on?" I asked.

"You live here?" He retorted, not answering my questions.

"Yeah, what are you the only cop working in this city?" I asked joking, but in a serious voice.

He gave a little chuckle and said, "How well did you know this guy?" I still didn't know what guy he was talking about, and I was still unsure what was going on.

The longer I stood there, the worse the smell got. It was overwhelming, and I guess Rock read my mind by the face I was making. "Yeah, death has a distinct smell. Why don't you go on into your apartment? My boss is probably going to want to ask you some questions, so I'll be right back." He explained. I opened my door in a hurry and exhaled forcefully. I could still smell a faint odor from inside my own apartment, but it wasn't nearly as bad as in the hall.

I waited in anticipation, but more so to have my own questions answered. Who was dead and is that what we had been smelling all this time? Was the body still over there right now? How did they die? So many questions flew through my mind as I waited. Finally I heard a knock at the door.

I cracked the door and saw Rock's pretty face. I opened it more as he spoke, "Angie, this is Detective Clark. He just has a few questions for you and then you can go get your beauty rest."

I gave a slight bashful smile and nodded, "okay." The detective extended his hand, and I introduced myself.

"Is it okay if we come in? We know that smell is horrible." The detective asked.

"Sure," I replied as I opened the door more and waved out my hand to usher them in. I sat down on the couch as they both stood nearby.

"How well do you know your neighbor, uh … Mr. Burkwell?" he asked, searching his pad for the name.

"Um, not *that* well. We just say 'hi' and 'bye' in passing. He let me use his phone once when I was locked out of my apartment. That's about it, though." I explained.

"And what about his grandson, Mikell?" he asked.

"Same there; we just say 'hi' and 'bye.'"

"And how did they seem to get along?" he asked in a Dr. Phil type of voice.

"I really couldn't tell you. I mean I've heard them argue and fight before, but that's only sometimes." I answered honestly. I didn't want to be a snitch, but I wanted to find out what had happened. Why did he use the past tense "how *did* they get along?"

"Why? Did something happen to Mr. Burkwell?"

"Well, what would make you think something happened to Mr. Burkwell?" the detective asked. Rock just stood by silently, eyeing my apartment. I was a little embarrassed that it wasn't as clean as I would've liked it to be for company.

"Well, because he's kind of old you know? Getting into fights with his teenage grandson, I was always a little worried for him that things might escalate." I explained.

"Uh huh, I see." He paused for a second to write something down. I regretted saying that. I didn't want to be involved in whatever was going on. "So, Miss Delimar, did you ever call the police to report the fighting?" the detective continued with his questioning.

"No." *Hell no I ain't call the cops! I mind my own damn business!* I thought to myself. "Can you at least tell me is Mr. Burkwell okay?" I asked partially out of nosiness but partially out of genuine concern.

"We're not really sure. That's what we're trying to figure out. We can't confirm anything, but we believe the deceased body we've found next door is that of Mikell's. So we're just trying to find out what happened." He explained.

"Oh my God! How did he die?" I exclaimed.

"We can't release that information right now." He continued with his questioning, "So I know you've noticed that smell. One of your neighbors called us to report it."

"Yeah, it's been smelling for a while now and every day it's gotten worse. Me and the lady over in twenty-seven were just talking about it this morning and trying to figure out where it was coming from." I told him.

"Miss Delimar, how long would you say you've noticed the smell?"

"Mmm, it's hard to say. I can't say exactly how long, but I know it's been at least five days or more." I said while looking up at the ceiling trying hard to remember.

He scribbled something else in his pad and continued with his questions. "Do you remember the last time you saw either Mikell or Mr. Burkwell?"

I looked back up at the ceiling. "Mmmm, it's been a while since I've seen either of them, probably weeks." I answered. I started to tell the detective that I hadn't seen them, but I knew exactly the last time I heard them fighting. Then I decided not to. I didn't want to get involved. Whatever had happened had nothing to do with me.

"Okay, well I think that's all the questions we have for you right now. I'm going to leave my number with you in case you remember anything else that might help. We're trying to locate Mr. Burkwell for some questioning. If you should happen to see him, please give me a call." He said while handing me his business card.

"Okay, sure" I said while getting up from the couch to let them out. I had no intentions of contacting Detective Clark about anything.

"Thanks for your help, Miss Delimar," he said while leaving.

"No problem,"

"Johnson, I want you to go down and check on Micki's team. See if they've gotten anything yet." He instructed Rock.

"Okay, boss" Rock responded, but not moving right away. Instead he waited for the detective to walk back into Mr. Burkwell's apartment. "Soooo …." He said, grinning at me.

"So what?" I said, wanting him to leave.

"This is your spot, huh?" he said, still eyeing the place.

"Yep, this is my humble abode."

"Su casa es mi casa?" he asked still smiling.

I rolled my eyes and responded, "I don't know about all *that*!"

"You know you still owe me for letting you slide, right?" he reminded me as if I'd forgotten.

Before I could answer, my phone rang. It was Cal. I didn't even bother to excuse myself. I just answered. I couldn't even get a "hello" out before Cal started in on the phone, "Yo! What the fuck happened today? Where the hell were you?"

"What do you mean where was I? I was there and they said you already had a visitor. What the fuck is *that* about?" I shot back.

"That's bullshit! I ain't have no visitors. I was waiting for you. You lying, yo!" he accused.

"What? I'm not lying! I came up there and that's what the C.O. told me. Now *you* stop lying. Who the fuck was up there?" I was getting heated.

Cal continued cursing me out on the other end of the phone as Rock talked shit in the background. "Trouble in paradise?" he laughed.

"Cal, hold on for a second!" I demanded. I covered the phone and turned my attention to Rock. "Is there anything else you need? I gotta take this!"

"You know what I need!" he said loudly and I knew it was on purpose. "You owe me! You keep acting like you forgot!"

"I know. I know. I told you I got you, but you gotta go. We'll talk at the gym." I said while practically closing the door on his face.

He said, "okay" as I closed it.

"Hello?" I said, now back on the phone with Cal.

"*Hello?* What the fuck you mean *hello?* Who the fuck was that?"

"Calm down, babe! That was a cop. The dude next door got killed or something." I said trying to reassure him.

"Nah, fuck that! That wasn't no cop! What the hell he talkin' 'bout you *owe* him? Owe him what? Lemme find out that's where ya ass was today!" he was getting more furious by the minute.

"Oh my God! I told you already I was *there* today! Like I'm always there! That really was a cop, but I know him from the gym too. That's it!" I explained.

"Yeah, alright, whatever Angie! You must think I'm stupid! I'ma let you go, so you can go talk to your cop!" he said.

"Wait—" Before I could finish he had hung up the phone on me.

I tried to call him right back, but it went straight to voicemail. "Fuck!" I said out loud. I was even more pissed because now Cal thought I was messing around when I could give two shits about Rock. On top of that, I still didn't get any answers about what happened with our visit. Was he really trying to pretend like he didn't have some other bitch up there? Did *he* really think *I* was that stupid? Then I thought what if he was telling the truth. I just don't see why or what the C.O. would have to gain by telling me he had a visitor if he really didn't.

I was confused, annoyed, and upset. I wanted to smoke a blunt so bad, but couldn't with all those police officers roaming around the building. I was still getting a faint whiff of death. I lit an incense and put a towel down to the bottom of the door where there was a little space. I was too upset to sleep, so I decided to just pop some popcorn and watch a little late night TV. The TV was on, but I was thinking about Mr. Burkwell. All this time I was worried that his grandson would hurt *him*. Would he really have killed his own grandson? I wondered where he was.

CHAPTER 11

All day Sunday I waited for Cal to call me back, but he didn't. I grew antsy and uncomfortable sitting around the house dwelling in my thoughts about the shooting from Friday night, but more so about Mr. Burkwell's grandson. I decided that I would hit the gym and then head to my mom's to see what she was up to. She always complained that I never came to see her any other time than when I needed my hair done.

As I entered the gym, I hoped Rock wouldn't be there, but something told me that he would. Sure enough as soon as I found a mat in the corner to start my crunches, he appeared. I lay back with my back flat on the mat after finishing my second set, and he was standing over me. Any closer, and I would've been able to see straight up his shorts. Knowing Rock, that was probably intentional.

"Good afternoon, Miss," he said with his usual smile.

I gave a sigh as I came up to start my next set of crunches. "What's up, Rock?" I replied in a voice to let him know I wasn't too thrilled to see him.

"Crazy night last night, huh?"

"Yeah, I still can't believe it. What happened anyway? Did Mr. Burkwell really kill his grandson?" I probed.

"Now you know I can't tell you that. That's official police business."

"Aw, man, what good are you!" I joked with him hoping he'd spill a little of what he knew.

That's when he bent down close to my face and dropped his voice to a sensual whisper. "I could be a lot of good if you would just let me show you how."

I rolled my eyes and sat straight up on the floor trying to create some distance between us. "Ugh, anyway ... well can you at least tell me how he died?"

"How who died?" It was like his mind was totally somewhere else. He had forgotten that quick what we were even talking about.

"*Mikell!* Mr. Burkwell's grandson!" I exclaimed.

"Oh, blunt force trauma." He said quickly reuniting with the conversation.

"Blunt force trauma? Like he got beat in the head to death?" I asked, wanting the details.

"Well yeah, we found a hammer. It looks like he was beat with that, but we're not entirely sure yet."

"God that's crazy! What did the body look like?"

"Damn, girl! Let me find out you have some kind of sick obsession with murder! Who asks that?" he said now looking at me with a screwed up face.

"*I* ask that! And no, I'm not obsessed with murder. I just wanted to know. His body was stinking really bad!"

"Yeah, I know! Well how much is that info worth to you?" he asked slyly with a smirk on his face as he raised his eyebrows up and down.

"It ain't worth shit!" I said getting up off the floor without finishing my sets.

As I turned to walk away, he grabbed my arm by the bicep. I gave a look first at my arm, then up at him, as though to say, *"If you don't get your hands off me ..."* He dropped my arm quickly.

Then he tried to joke, "Don't look at me like that! I'll do it again!" I didn't smile or reply. I just looked at him with a straight face. "Calm down, girl, you know it's all love. I was just messing with you. Daaaaang, why you getting all serious?" he tried to soften me.

"Yeah, okay," was all I said as I continued walking off.

"Where you going, though?" he asked while following me like a puppy.

"I'm 'bout to be out."

"You didn't even finish all your sets!"

"How would you know that?" I wondered in my head and said it out loud.

"'Cause I just know. You know I know your routine." He said with a smile and a wink. I didn't like him saying that, and I definitely didn't like him knowing any of my routines.

I just shrugged him off and said, "bye, Rock" as I walked away.

Yeah Rock was cute, but he was becoming way too pushy. I didn't like him in that way, and I didn't want him thinking that I did. Every time I saw him, I tried to let him know more and more the best way I could that I wasn't interested, but he just wasn't getting it. I relaxed in the comfort of knowing that Cal would be home soon and hopefully could put an end to this. All I would have to do is bring him to the gym with me a few times to let Rock know what the deal was. Then he'd have to leave me alone.

I had so much on my mind that I sped up the highway without even realizing it. Before I knew it, I was at my mother's house. I knocked on the door first even though I had a key. I didn't tell her I was coming, so I didn't want to just walk in. I waited a few minutes then let myself in. "Ma!" I called out. I didn't get an answer. I jogged up the steps and called out again out of breath "Mother! Are you home?" Still, I got no response. I checked her bedroom, as the living room was empty. She wasn't home.

I noticed the same gray metal box sitting out on her bed with some papers sprawled out. I didn't feel comfortable snooping through her things, but I did wonder what was in the box. It was unlocked this time, so I lifted the lid. A bunch of handwritten letters sprung out. There were no envelopes, just a bunch of letters written on notebook paper. I opened one and read quickly not knowing when my mom would return.

Angela,

I hope this letter finds you well and happy. Today I saw a young girl around your age that looked how I picture you to look. She was beautiful. She had a beautiful smile. She was with a group of her friends at the mall. She looked like she was having a great time with them.

That is my hope for you. I hope and pray every day that you are having an amazing time in life and that you are smiling every day. You are sixteen by now, and still I haven't heard back from you or your mom. Still, I pray for the day that you will respond. Furthermore, I pray for the day that we will meet.

I want you to know that I have always loved you and will never stop loving you. I don't blame you if you are angry with me and don't wish to speak to me or get to know me. I don't know if you have gotten any of my letters, but I will never stop writing you either. My door is always open whenever you are ready to come in.

Love Always,

Rainy

Great, more confusion to add to my life, I thought to myself as I placed the letter down. Who the heck was Rainy and what kind of name was that anyway? Why did she want to meet me and why was she writing me? I sifted through the box to find about forty more letters. Some were written to me, and some to my mom. None of the letters were dated, and I found no envelopes for postmarks. I wondered how old these letters dated back since she had referenced me being only sixteen. Why hadn't my mom given me the letters or at least told me about them? I had a lot of questions for my mom at that point, but how could I address her? I had no business going through her things.

I heard the key in the door and I quickly closed the lid to the box. I took a quick check to make sure I left things exactly how they were as I hurried off to the living room. I flicked on the TV quickly and sat down. She looked surprised as she came up the steps. "What'chu doing here?" she asked.

"I just thought I'd come by to see you. I have soooo much to fill you in on." It was true. I did.

"Oh, you been waiting here long?" she asked.

"Nope, just got here like five minutes ago."

"Oh ...why you ain't call me?" she asked.

"I don't know. It was kind of a last minute decision. I just came from the gym and didn't feel like going home."

"Oh," she said as she walked in her room to put her purse down.

She swung the door behind her, but it didn't close all the way. I could hear her shuffling the papers on her bed. It sounded like she was locking the box back. I couldn't tell if she had slid it back under her bed or not. The questions about this Rainy person continued to come to my head, but I decided that I wouldn't mention the letters. I trusted my mom and knew if she had kept those letters from me or didn't want me to know who Rainy was, it had to be for a good reason.

She reappeared and started to walk into the kitchen then paused. "Were you in my room?" she asked with a suspicious look.

"No, I just peeked in to see if you were in there then came out here." My mom always knew when I was lying, so I tried to keep my voice low so it wouldn't crack.

"Oh …" she said, looking off to the side as if in another world of thought. She continued into the kitchen.

I filled her in on all the happenings except for my visitor dilemma with Cal. I still wasn't ready to tell her about him. I would tell her when he came home. I told her everything else about Mr. Burkwell and his grandson and the shooting at IHOP.

"Oh my God! You better be careful hanging out with those girls after work." She said, showing genuine concern.

"Well, it wasn't *them* that was shooting!" I told her with a light chuckle.

"No, I know that. I didn't mean to sound like I meant hanging with them was a problem. I just mean just be careful where y'all decide to go." She said, trying to redeem herself from her previous comment.

She had a point, though. I didn't know the next time I'd be hanging out after work at the club. If it wasn't even safe to go to IHOP anymore, then maybe I just needed to go home after work.

"That's really sad about the man and his grandson, though." She said shaking her head. "What do you think they were fighting about?"

"I don't know."

"Well you just be careful coming in and out, especially when you come in from work at the club. You hear?"

"I know. I know." I assured her.

"And if you see that man Mr. Burkwell, you just stay clear of him." She continued to instruct me.

"I highly doubt he's gonna come back to the crime scene, mom. Shoot, for all I know, he could be dead somewhere too!" I said.

I looked my mom up and down. Something was different. She looked older for some reason. She looked older just from the last time I had seen her. She looked thin too, and her eyes were dark. "You look like you lost some weight." I said, not hiding my stare.

"You think so?" she said through a cough.

"Yeah, you look really thin. Have you lost weight?"

"I don't know. I did have a little cold last week and not much of an appetite, so it's possible." She explained.

"Well how are you feeling now?"

"I feel fine! Really!" she said, trying to convince me. I wasn't convinced, but I left the topic alone.

I stayed and talked for a few more hours. I finally decided to head home knowing that I had to get ready for the workweek. I couldn't put it off any longer. When I got into my building, it was refreshing to see that the odor had died down tremendously; although there were a few horse flies flying around the building. *I hope they bring the exterminator in,* I thought to myself as I walked down the hall towards my door. Once inside, I showered and changed into my pajamas. I didn't feel much like cooking, so I just had a bowl of cereal.

I was feeling a little hurt that Cal had not called me back. Did he really think I was out here cheating on him? I convinced myself there was no way he could possibly believe that. He just needed some time to cool down. That was all. Since he was still mad and not calling me, I decided to write him.

I told him everything that was going on with me; everything from the situation at work with Renee to how Rock had helped me out of a parking ticket. I let him know over and over in the letter how much I loved him and couldn't wait to be with him. I also made sure he knew that I came up to visit and that I was not happy to hear that someone else was there. I sprayed the envelope lightly with some of my cucumber melon perfume. I knew he liked when I did that, and hopefully it would help soften him. I would mail the letter in the morning. Then all I could do was wait; hopefully he'd come around.

CHAPTER 12

Renee finally returned to work the next day. The conversation wasn't as bad as I expected. I didn't waste too much time because I wanted to get it over with. After about an hour into work, I emailed her asking if we could step outside to talk. She agreed. "First of all, I just want to apologize for the email. There's no excuse for it, and that's exactly what I get for talking shit." That was the best apology I could come up with considering the awkward situation. I didn't want to be phony and say that I didn't mean the stuff I said. I was more so just sorry for talking behind her back.

"I mean, I just don't know what to think. I was shocked when I got that email like '*no she didn't!*'" she said as she let out a chuckle. I was glad that she was able to find humor in it.

"I know. I know. Like I said, there's no excuse for it. I just have a thing about the birthday collections. I honestly just feel like why would I contribute for someone's birthday that I'm not friends with or anything? Either way, I should've just told you that I didn't want to contribute and left it at that." I explained.

"I see. Well just to let you know, I do have money, and I was going to put the extra money in the card, so Vanessa could have some cash. But I understand." She said, sounding as though she really understood. Then she continued, "I was just surprised to hear that coming from you because I felt like we were kind of like family, you know?" My heart sank when she said that. I genuinely felt where she was coming from, and it made me feel two inches tall.

"I know. I know, and that's why I had to talk to you and apologize. I couldn't just leave it like that because I am genuinely sorry for talking about you like that. You don't deserve it." I meant what I said too.

"Well, it's fine. We're still cool. It's water under the bridge." I thought she was finished. Then she asked, "Who did you mean to send that email to anyway?"

"Oh, a friend of mine. She doesn't even work here. You don't know her." I quickly replied.

She looked at me with squinted eyes and said "Uh huh …"

I tried to reassure her. "No, really. It's not anyone you know!"

"What's her name?"

I didn't really understand why she wanted to know, but I told her, "May, you really don't know her. For real." I said, laughing lightly.

"Oh, okay." she said.

Then I had a question, "You didn't tell or show anyone the email did you?"

"No, I didn't tell anyone on the team except Vanessa, so don't worry." She said.

I laughed nervously "Great, the one person I didn't want to know. I just don't want her to think that I have any personal bad feelings towards her or anything because it's really not like that at all."

"Oh no, she was cool about it. She doesn't think that." She said, like it was no big deal. Great, now I would feel weird every time I saw Vanessa too. Oh well, I had dug my own grave. I was just glad they were both mature enough to just let the whole thing go.

Though I still didn't feel too good about myself for what I had done, I did feel like a weight was lifted by hashing it out with Renee. Mondays always dragged by, and this day was no different. So when my cell phone started to vibrate, it was something to break up the monotony. It was Jillian. I looked at the phone wondering what she could want. I didn't like to talk on my cell phone too much at my desk, because I didn't want to be unprofessional. So I waited for her to leave a voicemail. I checked the message she left from my desk phone. "Hey, Annnngie! It's Jilli! I wanted to see what you were doing tonight. Hit me back when you get this!"

I called her back to see what she had in mind. I didn't really like hanging out on work nights, but I thought it might be good to get out and get my mind off of Cal. "Hello, can I speak to Jillian?" I asked, even though I was pretty sure it was her who had answered the phone.

"Hey, Angie! What's up, girl?" she sounded excited, but I had never really seen her not be excited.

"Not much, I'm at work. I was just calling you back." This was my way of telling her to talk fast.

"Oh Ronnie got you working *today?*"

"No, I'm at my other job today. I work at B.I.G. Insurance. Ronnie's is just my part time job." I explained.

"Ooooh okay, look at you! Gettin' that paper! I ain't even mad at you! So what time you get off?"

"I get off at five. Why? What's up?"

"We should hang out! My friend is hosting Martini Mondays at this club tonight. We can get in for free."

"I don't know. I gotta be up early tomorrow to be back at work." I said, sounding like a real square.

"Are you serious? That's so wack! Stop being an old hag and come!"

I thought about it for a quick second and decided what the hell. "Okay, I guess I'll go. What's the name of the club and where is it?" I said, still chuckling at the old hag comment.

"I forget the name of it, but you can just drive to my house, and we can ride together."

"Okay, well what kind of club is it? Can I wear jeans?" I hated when I was over or under dressed.

"Yeah, you can probably wear jeans but just be grown n' sexy! We should leave at like ten."

I laughed again, "Okay, well I'll hit you later when I'm ready to leave. You can just give me your address then." She agreed and we said our goodbyes.

I was kind of excited to hang out even if it was on a weeknight. It gave me something to look forward to and something to keep my mind off of everything that was going on. Cherlise and May weren't the only people in the world to hang out with after all!

During the drive home, I wondered if I had time to squeeze in a quick workout before going out. Then I thought better of it because I definitely didn't want to run into Rock. I decided to just go home, cook and eat, and see what I was going to wear. I opted not to wear jeans. Instead I decided on a cute cream-colored sweater dress with some black leggings and black pumps. I didn't expect the place to be jumping on a Monday night, so I wasn't trying to do too much.

I was pleasantly surprised when I pulled up to Jillian's house on a quiet cul de sac in Maplewood. I was pretty sure she lived alone, and her house looked nice from the outside. A two-story townhome, it looked new. She met me outside as she started up her black beamer. I was impressed. I knew dancers did well for themselves, but I didn't realize just how well.

"Heyyyyy, Ang!" she said excitedly as she popped the lock for me to get in the passenger side. She looked me up and down. "Okay, okay, I see you got your grown n sexy on!"

I laughed, "Girl please, I just threw this on, but thanks." She wore a black mini dress that fit like a glove. Although a little spicy for my taste, her thigh-high black leather boots fit her well.

I wasn't sure how it was going to be hanging out with her outside of work, but I actually enjoyed our conversation as we rode to the club. Jillian was cool, real down to earth. She had nice things, but she wasn't showy about it. She was generous too. Once we got to the club, she insisted on buying the drinks. The spot was nice. The lights were low and the décor very laid back. It gave a very sexy, sultry type of ambiance.

She introduced me to her friend that was hosting. She seemed nice enough, and she looked a little butch. Actually, she looked a lot butch. Her hair was cut like a man's, and she was dressed like a man in hard bottoms, jeans, and a crisp black button-up. She looked like she was probably an attractive lady at one point.

That didn't matter to me. The music was good, so I was ready to hit the dance floor. As we danced, I noticed no guys had tried to dance with us yet. That's when I took a good look around. There actually weren't too many guys there period. There were maybe ten or fifteen throughout the whole club of about a hundred people. I would say at least five of those guys were employees.

"Jilli, where the hell are all the dudes?" I asked looking confused.

"You got me!" she said then spun around and continued to dance. She was enjoying herself. She didn't seem to care that there wasn't too much eye candy. I didn't really care either. As long as the music was good, I was good.

I danced until the muscles in my legs began to hurt, and Jillian kept the drinks coming. All of a sudden, I felt someone squeeze my butt firmly. I spun around with the quickness, ready to smack whatever dude thought he could just grab my ass like that. To my surprise, it was a woman! It caught me off guard. "What the hell is your problem? You try'na get fucked up?" I said, feeling violated. Before she could respond, Jillian got between us and started arguing with the chick.

"My bad, I didn't know she was with you." The woman said and backed away with her hands up in the air in the stick up position.

"Are you okay?" Jillian asked.

"Yeah, I'm fine. I don't know what the hell that was all about!" I said, still confused.

"Don't worry about it. She's obviously drunk out her mind." She said, trying to calm me down.

I didn't drink anymore after that, and as my buzz wore off, I started to look around the club. That's when I noticed. The few men that were there were there with a chick. Other than that, it was a club full of females. Women were grinding on each other on the dance floor. I even saw a female couple huddled in the corner with one woman sitting on the other's lap. It was like the needle scratched the record in my head. *This broad done brought me to a lesbian club! What the hell?*

"Why you ain't tell me this was a lesbo club?" I asked her with my face tore up.

She looked around and laughed, "It is not!"

"Umm, yeah it is! Take a look around, Jilli!" I said getting annoyed.

She took a slow survey around the club. "Oh my God, I think you're right!"

"Uh ya! You think?" I said, sarcastically.

"My bad, you wanna leave?"

I was real confused. I thought to myself, *Uh, don't you?*, but I didn't want to say that out loud. "I mean I really wasn't feeling that chick grabbing my ass just now, Jilli. That's not what's up!" I said, trying to answer her question indirectly.

"Okay, it's all good. We can leave. I'm sorry, ma ma." She said, not phased at all.

The ride back to her house was an awkward one. The girls had tried to warn me. I guess this is what they were talking about. Jillian was a lesbian. Did she think I was a lesbian too? Is that why she asked for my number? No, I told her I had a boyfriend though.

I guess she was reading my mind through the awkward silence. "Look, I'm really sorry about tonight. You seem like a real cool down to earth chick, so I thought you wouldn't care what kind of club we went to. I didn't know you was a homophobe."

I couldn't believe she had just said that. "I'm *not* a homophobe! I just don't like bitches grabbing on my ass!" I said offended.

"No, I know. Okay, maybe I shouldn't call you a homophobe. I just thought you would be cool with it." She said.

"Look, I don't know if you're a lesbian or not, but I'm not! I don't know if you thought I was one but —"

"Nooooo, I don't think you're a lesbian. I just thought you was a cool chick." she cut me off.

"I *am* a cool chick thank you very much! But you don't just take somebody to a lesbian club and not tell them. That's the type of shit you should tell a person before you go. Gimme the chance to decide if I wanna be felt up by some bitches!" I said getting angry.

"Okay, okay relax; I'm sorry. It's not like I planned for her to grab your ass!" she said laughing.

I was annoyed that she was so calm about this and that she had the nerve to laugh about it too. I couldn't wait to get out of her car. "Look, I don't want you to be mad at me or anything. I said I was sorry. Next time I'll know..." she said, trying to sound sincere.

Next time? I thought to myself. There wasn't going to be a next time if I had anything to do with it. "Yeah, okay." I said dryly.

"Come on! I don't want it to be weird between us at work now and stuff. Next time I'll make sure we go to a regular club, okay?" she assured me.

"Yeah okay ... so *are* you a lesbian?" I blurted out. I didn't care at that point. She had put it out there.

She smiled coyly and replied, "Nah, I'm not a lesbian, love."

I didn't even wait for her to turn the engine off when we finally pulled up to her house. "You wanna come in and chill for a little?" she asked. Was she serious?

"No thanks, I gotta go get some sleep, so I can get up for work tomorrow."

"Oh yeah, I forgot. Okay, well, you sure we good?" she asked with a smile.

"Yeah, we good!" I called out right before closing the door to my car. I couldn't get away from there fast enough.

As soon as I walked through my door, I kicked off my shoes. I wasted no time changing and going straight to bed. I only had a few hours to sleep before it would be time to get back up again. It took me no time to fall asleep. Not too far along into my sleep, a faint rattling sound awakened me. I was so sleepy it took me a minute to focus. It was that same rattling noise at the front door again. "Great that guy down the hall thinks this is his apartment, must be drunk again," I mumbled to myself.

Reluctantly, I swung my feet to the edge of the bed and slid on my slippers. I walked into the living room and turned on the light. "You have the wrong apartment again, man!" I called out through the door. The rattling stopped, so I walked to the door and looked through the peephole. There was no one there. I figured he had already made his way on down the hallway. Not giving it a second thought, I turned out the light and headed back to bed. I went right back to sleep.

CHAPTER 13

The next few days drifted by, and everything was seemingly back to normal. Things were cool at B.I.G. Insurance, no more odors when I came home, and I hadn't seen that weird stalker lady since the shootout at IHOP. I avoided the gym when I thought Rock would be there, and it seemed to be working. Even Cal had come around.

He had gotten my letter, and it served its purpose. He called me one evening after I had gotten off of work. "I still don't like you talking to that guy at the gym." He said in a stern voice.

"Baby, I don't like talking to him either. He just always seems to be there! No matter how much I tell him about you, he doesn't seem to care."

"Well, stop going to the gym!" he demanded.

"Come on, you know I gotta keep it tight for Daddy" I said, trying to sound sexy.

"I know that's right! Well, don't worry. I'll be home next week, and that pig is gonna know exactly what it is!"

"Exactly, so stop wasting our phone time to talk about his wack ass! Are you nervous about coming home?" I asked, changing the subject.

"Nervous? Hell no! I'm excited. Excited to see my grandma, excited to see my princess, and excited to see my wife and skeet skeet all up in that!" He did sound excited.

We never got to talk long, but before we hung up, we confirmed our visit for the weekend. I still wasn't satisfied with the explanation I got for what happened with our previously scheduled visit. He insisted that there was a mistake made on the prison's part. He swore that he had no visitors and was up and ready waiting for me, but they never called him down. There was nothing I could do but take his word for it, so I decided to drop the issue.

Soon after we hung up, the phone rang again. I didn't recognize the number. I knew it wasn't anyone calling on Cal's behalf since I had just gotten off the phone with him. I answered anyway, "hello?"

"Yes, may I speak with Miss Angela Delimar please?" the voice on the other end said.

"This is Angela. Who's calling?"

"Hi, my name is Deborah Collins. I'm a nurse at First Trinity Hospital. We're trying to get in contact with the immediate family of Ms. Candice Delimar." She explained. My heart sped up when she said my mother's name.

"Yes, I'm her daughter. What's wrong?" I asked in a panic.

"Okay, we need you to come to the hospital immediately. Your mother is here in our intensive care unit." She said calmly.

"Oh my God! What's wrong with her? What happened?"

"We're still trying to find out, but right now we really need to have someone from Ms. Delimar's immediate family up to the hospital as soon as possible. Can you or someone from your immediate family get here?" she asked, still not saying what was wrong.

"Yes! I'm on my way. It will probably take me about thirty minutes, but can you please tell me what's wrong?" I pleaded.

"Well, why don't you just come up to the hospital, and then the doctor can explain everything to you. Right now, we really just need you to get here as soon as you can." She said, still remaining calm.

"Oh my God, okay. Well if she's in ICU it must be serious. Can you tell me if she's conscious at least?"

"She's been in and out of consciousness since she arrived. That's really all I can tell you over the phone, ma'am." She said, sounding sympathetic.

"Okay, I'll be there as soon as I can." I said, sounding defeated from not getting all the details.

I started breathing heavily as I rushed around the apartment to prepare for my departure. So many thoughts flew through my mind as I wondered what was going on with my mom. Tears started streaming down my face as I thought the worst of thoughts. I ran down the stairwell so fast that I tripped and slid down three of the steps. I didn't have time, nor did I care if anyone had seen me trip. I just needed to get there, ASAP!

The tears flowed the whole drive there. I seemed to catch every single red light and rode behind every Sunday driver on the highway. I parked crooked in the parking structure. I didn't care. I ran all the way from the structure to the main entrance.

Heaving in and out of breath, I asked the receptionist at the main desk where the intensive care unit was. Once she told me, I took off running. I forgot to even say thank you. Hopefully, she was able to understand it wasn't intentional.

Once I made it to the floor of ICU, I burst through the double doors. I didn't even give the nurse at that desk a chance to ask how she could help. "Candice Delimar! Where is she? I'm her daughter. I got a call saying she's here." I blurted out.

"Oh yes, okay. She's right this way. The doctor is still in with her right now." The nurse replied in a gentle voice as she walked me over to the room.

I walked in to find my mom lying stiffly on a bed that sat about three feet high from the ground. Her eyes were closed, and she looked even thinner than the last time I had seen her. Tubes ran into her nostrils and up and down both of her arms. I could see she was hooked up to several beeping machines, and I noticed a catheter running from under the sheet.

I grabbed the only chair that sat in the corner near her head and slid it close to the bed. I sat down and collapsed with my head buried into her shoulder. "Oh, mom," was all I could manage to get out in the midst of the tears. I was afraid to touch her because I didn't want to accidentally yank out any of the many tubes or wires. "Oh, mom." I repeated while looking at her face. She looked peaceful, but still I couldn't stand seeing her like this.

"Miss Delimar, I'm Dr. Smith. I'd like to talk to you about your mother's condition." The doctor said sternly.

I lifted my head, wiped my face with my sleeve, and tried to sniff back the fresh tears that wanted to continue coming out. "Okay," I said, already knowing everything I needed to know. My mom was lying here on this bed not able to talk back to me. That was a clear enough message.

"The cancer has started to spread at a more rapid pace throughout functional parts of your mother's brain. She's had a—"

"*Cancer?*" I cut him off before he could finish.

He replied impatiently, "Yes, you didn't know your mom has Meningioma?"

"Meningioma? What is that exactly?"

He took a deep breath as if annoyed that I was asking any questions, "Meningioma is a type of brain cancer. Dr. Fonneli has been treating your mom for it for the past three months." I couldn't believe what I was hearing. My mom had brain cancer and hadn't bothered to tell me. Why wouldn't she tell me about something so serious?

"Oh my God," I said, starting to weep softly. I bit down hard on my thumbnail trying to control my emotions.

"The cancer is spreading rapidly. In addition, she has a small aneurism at the base of the cerebral cortex." He explained in a monotone voice. He looked like Jim Carey and sounded like Ben Stein, from all the *Clear Eyes* commercials. All I could do was gasp as he continued on. "We've been able to stop the bleeding from the aneurism, but the damage is already done. She's stabilized right now, but that can change at any moment. You need to understand that her condition can worsen and turn fatal quickly."

"So can she hear us? Is there still brain activity?" I asked.

"She's breathing on her own, and she can most likely hear you, but she can't respond." He explained.

"So what happens next? What are you guys going to do to help her condition?"

"Well, I'm sorry, but there's not much more we can do at this point. We'll continue monitoring her aneurism and brain activity, but at the rate the cancer is spreading, it's not likely that she has a lot of time." He explained.

"Oh my God! Like how much time?" I asked as I cupped my hand over my mouth.

"I can't say exactly, but anywhere between twenty-four hours to two weeks." He said it so casually. "Miss Delimar, you need to prepare yourself for the worst. If you're religious, you may want to call in your priest soon. I'm sorry."

He turned and left the room. I guess there was nothing else to be said. He had just told me that my mom was basically about to die at any minute. I didn't know what to do. I was her only child, and my father had died years before. Mom's only sister lived in Florida, and they hadn't spoken in eighteen years. My grandparents had all died before I was even born. There really was no immediate family to call that was close by.

I unzipped my coat and hung it on the back of the chair. I got comfortable and laid my head on her shoulder again. I felt funny talking to her without her talking back. So I just listened to her breath as I felt her chest go up and down. That was the least bit of comfort I had at that point. After a few hours, I fell asleep. A nurse came in to check on her at one point.

"Just press the button if you guys need anything. We'll be right out here at the desk." She instructed.

"Okay, thank you," I said as she closed the door. I used my jacket as a blanket, and I huddled up in the chair. I looked at my mom one more time before I closed my eyes to go back to sleep.

"Angie," I heard a faint voice calling my name for the second time. I sleepily cracked my eyes open just a tad. "Angie, love" I heard the voice again as my mom struggled to clear her throat.

"Mom!" I said as I came to my senses. My eyes popped open in excitement and hope now that she had awakened and was talking. "Oh my God, mom! I was so scared! How are you feeling?"

She struggled to get her words out, "I-I ..." She cleared her throat again "I'm sorry, Angie."

What was she sorry about? She must've been disoriented. "That's okay. Don't try to talk. Just stay here. I'm gonna call the doctor and let him know you're awake!" I said to her. She was still struggling to say my name as I hurried off to get the doctor. I returned with Dr. Smith who was accompanied by another nurse.

"Miss Delimar, we're gonna need you to just step outside and give us a minute while we run some tests on your mother." The nurse instructed. I did as told, but only after I reassured my mom that I would be right outside and would return once they were done. She was still repeating my name and apologizing as I left the room.

"Excuse me, what time is it?" I asked one of the nurses at the nurse's station.

"Uh, three o' four," she responded. I decided to take a walk down the hall, so I could turn my cell phone on and make some calls. I needed to let both of my jobs know that I wouldn't be in the following day, which was Friday. I knew at this hour I would just get voicemails, but it would be one less thing I would have to do later. Besides, I needed something to keep me busy while I waited in anticipation to find out about mom's progress.

I had two messages myself when I turned on my phone. I decided to check them after I made my calls. The first one was from Jillian apologizing again about the club scene. I erased that without a second thought. I couldn't think about her or her lesbianism right now. The second message was from May, "Hey, it's me. I was just calling to see what you have planned for this weekend. We still gotta do something for your birthday. I was thinking we could do lunch somewhere on Saturday, my treat. Call me back when you get this!" She was still stuck on making up my birthday to me. While I appreciated the gesture, I knew it wasn't because she really cared about my birthday. It was more so just to even the score so to speak. She just wanted to feel like she did her part. Whatever. I couldn't deal with that right at the moment either.

The doctor and nurse were still in with mom by the time I had made it back down the hallway. I decided to just sit in the empty visitors' waiting room. I was bored, but I fought to stay awake. Finally, after an hour of waiting, the doctor came into the waiting room. "Okay Miss Delimar, although your mom is conscious now, we still need to keep a close eye on her. Her condition remains the same as we discussed before; so she can go in and out of consciousness at any time." He explained.

"Can I see her?" I asked.

"Yes, go right in. She's heavily sedated, though. She may be a little incoherent." He warned.

When I went back in the room, her eyes were closed, but I wanted her to know that I was there. I touched her shoulder gently. "Mom?" I said softly as I studied her little frail body.

Her eyelids lifted slowly. "Annngggie," she was slurring. "Annggie I have to tell you …" her voice trailed as she fell back into sedation.

"It's okay, mom. Just rest. I'll be right here."

My voice prompted her to try again: "I have to tell you … I'm ssssorry Ang …" her eyes closed.

I could tell the morphine had her really out of it. She looked so tiny lying there. I wondered why she kept apologizing, probably for not telling me about the cancer in the first place. I didn't get why she wouldn't tell me something as important as that. We talked about everything. Why would she keep something so serious a secret? I guess she didn't want to worry me. I made myself comfortable as I prepared to go back to sleep for the night.

I spent the rest of the night waking up periodically to check on her. The next morning we were both awakened by the nurse checking my mom's progress or lack thereof. She was heavily sedated for most of the day. I didn't want to leave her side, but I wanted to get her some things that I thought she might need or want. I decided to make a quick run to her apartment.

I picked out a fresh outfit for her to wear once she was released in the spirit of remaining optimistic about her condition. I put together a toiletries case for her with two washcloths, toothpaste and toothbrush, mouthwash, deodorant, and a few pairs of underwear. At some point, I hoped the nurses would give her a bath.

I noticed the letters and metal box were no longer on her bed, but didn't have time to give it much thought. I wanted to get back to the hospital after I made phone calls to my only aunt, mom's co-workers at the salon, and the couple of close friends that would be concerned about her. I couldn't decide if I should call a pastor at this point. I didn't want to offend or scare my mother by assuming she was about to die. Besides, I wasn't ready to accept that possibility either.

I went back to the hospital, dropped off the items, and got an update from the doctor on mom's condition. Still in and out of her heavy sedation, she slept most of the time. I still needed a shower bad. Though I didn't want to leave her side again, one of mom's close friends, Sandy, offered to stay while I did that when she came to visit. She was the only one of mom's friends that came up to visit after I had made all the calls.

My stomach started to grumble as I rode home. I realized that I hadn't eaten in almost twenty-four hours. When I got home, I went straight in the bathroom and peeled off my clothes. The warm water felt soothing against my body. I closed my eyes and breathed in the steam. Tears started to stream down my face as the thought of losing mom crept into my brain. I tried to get control over my emotions and be strong. I let the water hit me in the face washing away the tears.

Feeling refreshed, I stepped out of the shower, grabbed a clean towel from the shelf, and dried off. My body felt relaxed wrapped in the softness. I walked into my room, and that's when I noticed it.

Something was wrong, out of place. I stood frozen, looking around the room trying to figure out what was different. I wasn't the neatest person, but I always remembered exactly where and how I left things.

My top dresser drawer was slightly open and the strap of my rose petal pink baby doll was hanging out a little. I knew for sure I hadn't touched that thing in at least a year. Or did I? I was so tired and a little delirious at this point. My mind went back and forth, but it came to the conclusion that I had definitely not left that drawer open or touched that baby doll. There was no reasonable explanation for why or how it would be disturbed. My heart sped up as I thought about who had been in my apartment and why. To my knowledge, the super was the only one with keys. However, sometimes his son would come fix things in his absence. His wife also had access to the keys, but I couldn't see her going through my lingerie.

I had noticed things in the past out of place when I came home. It happened on two other occasions, but it was something simple like once someone had helped themselves to a piece of candy from my candy jar I kept on the coffee table. Another time, I could tell someone had used my toilet. I complained to management that particular time, and the super didn't deny it, but assured me it wouldn't happen again.

This time I called the super directly to confront him. The phone rang a few times then went to his voicemail greeting: "Hello, this is Juan. I am on vacation for two weeks, so please call the management with any problems at five five five zero four nine two. Thank you." Juan didn't speak English that well, so he spoke slowly on the greeting. I hung up and called management with the intent of complaining. I was surprised to find out that Juan and his entire family was on vacation, had been that entire week, and would be the following week. They were all in Puerto Rico.

I asked if someone else was filling in for him who would have access to the keys. The woman from management assured me that no one else had access. They had a super on call for emergencies from one of their other properties, but he would have to go to the management office first to get the keys for each apartment. My heart sank when I heard that. It almost made me feel crazy because I knew I had not left my drawer open like that. That's when I thought back to my neighbor rattling my door the other night. I hadn't actually seen his face on the last incident, but who else could it be?

Feeling uneasy, I dressed quickly without even putting any lotion on. I scarfed down a bowl of cereal as my eyes darted all around the apartment looking for any other signs that anything was out of order. I saw nothing. Still, I felt uneasy as if I was being watched. I took one deep breath and spoke to myself out loud, "Angela, you're paranoid. You have *got* to stop watching so much TV!"

I grabbed a few things for myself and tossed them into an overnight bag. I didn't know how long I would be at the hospital and didn't want to have to come back home for anything. Feeling extra paranoid, I opened the junk drawer in the kitchen and sifted around with my hand until I found a roll of clear scotch tape. I tore off a little piece, and after making sure both locks were locked on the front door, I stretched my arm high above my head and placed it on the outside of the door. This way when I returned, if the tape was out of place, I'd know someone had been in my apartment.

Halfway to the hospital my phone rang. It was May. I answered and switched the phone to speakerphone. "Hey girl, sorry I haven't had a chance to call you back" was how I answered.

"That's okay. You got my message, though?"

"Yeah, thanks but I'm gonna have to take a rain check. My mom is real sick. I'm on my way back to the hospital now. She's in ICU." I explained.

"Oh my God, I'm so sorry. What happened?" she asked, sounding genuinely concerned.

I filled her in on mom's condition. There wasn't much she could say except to call her if I needed anything and to keep her posted. I thanked her and told her I would. Before we could even say our goodbyes, the phone beeped. It was Sandy on the other line. I told May that I'd call her later on.

I clicked over to Sandy, "Hi, Aunt Sandy, I'm on my way back to the hospital right now." She wasn't a blood relative, but she was close enough to it, so I always referred to her as aunt.

"Yeah, you need to get back up here right away. Candy isn't doing so well this evening Angie." She said, warning me cautiously.

"What's wrong? What happened?" I asked in a panic.

"Why don't you just get up here? I don't want to have this conversation while you're driving. Besides, I think it's best if you talk to Dr. Smith when you get here. Drive carefully, and try not to worry. I'll be here and I'm not going anywhere." She said compassionately.

I felt the tears starting to well up again as I got off the phone. I blew air from my mouth upwards to my eyes to try to dry them. My vision was getting blurry, and I couldn't see. I turned on the radio and tried to find something upbeat to take my mind off of what was going on. I wasn't big on gospel, but one station was playing "Stomp" by Kirk Franklin. I happened to like that song, so I let it play.

When I finally made it back to the hospital, Sandy met me at the doorway of mom's room blocking me from entering. "Angie," she said with tears in her eyes as she hugged me.

I hugged her back, and my voice cracked as I asked, "what's going on?"

"Well the doctor will have to tell you the specifics, but she's stopped breathing on her own, Angie. It seemed like she was doing a little better for a moment. She was awake and talked to me for a couple minutes, but then she had a seizure and fell into a coma." She explained.

I couldn't believe what I was hearing. I looked in the room and rushed to my mother's side. I could see even more tubes hooked up to her now. As the respirator pumped air into her, I could see her chest rise and fall. Her eyes were closed but not all the way. They were more so rolled in the back of her head. I broke down sobbing seeing her like this.

My head was buried into her thigh when the doctor startled me. "Miss Delimar?" he said, back in his stern tone. I sniffed and lifted my head with red watery eyes. "I need to talk to you about your mom's condition. Can we step outside?" he continued. I took another look at mom, and reluctantly headed out to the hallway. "As you can see, your mom has taken a turn for the worse. Remember we talked about this being a large possibility?" he asked.

All I could manage to get out was, "yeah."

He went on throwing out a bunch of medical terminology and conditions explaining my mom's state of being. I heard what he was saying, but I wasn't really listening. All I remember him ending with was, "I know this is a difficult time for you, but you're the only one who can make this decision. If you decide to take her off of the respirator, you may want to start making some arrangements. I don't know if you and your mom are spiritual, but if you'd like to arrange for the hospital priest to come in I'll have a nurse set that up for you." He said looking at me waiting for a decision right then and there.

"Okay, can you just give me a few minutes with her?" I asked.

"Sure, sure, but I have to tell you that we need to make the decision relatively soon like within the next hour or so." He explained. I nodded and went back into the room where Aunt Sandy was sitting next to her.

"I don't know what to do!" I said to Aunt Sandy while I looked at mom. I knew she was gone, but I wasn't ready to let her go.

"I know this is hard on you. I'm here for whatever you need." She replied as she got up to let me sit in the chair.

She rubbed my back and asked, "do you want me to give you guys a minute alone?"

"Oh, that's okay. I wouldn't know what to say to her anyway. I don't even know if she can hear us." I replied as I sniffled.

"You don't have to say anything if you don't want. She knows you're here, and she knows you love her." She said trying to console me.

"Yeah ..."

"Do you want me to call my pastor?" she asked.

"Yes, I guess so."

"Okay," she said in a whisper as she patted my back and walked out to go use the phone.

I held my mother's hand and cried some more. I didn't know what to do. I didn't want to keep her hooked up to the respirator if she was in pain, but I didn't want to just pull the plug either if there was a chance for recovery. The doctor made it seem as if there was no chance for recovery, but doctors don't know everything. The more I thought about what to do, the harder I cried. I didn't know how to make the decision.

I walked out to the nurses' station and asked them to have Dr. Smith come to my mother's room. I wanted to ask him more questions. "Doctor, I don't know what to do. Is there any chance for her to recover?" I asked, already knowing his answer.

"Miss Delimar, it's highly unlikely in her condition. Even if she did recover, the amount of fluid that is in her brain at this point, she would not be able to function the way she once could. She is close to brain dead at this point." He said as though not wanting to share that with me.

"Do you think she's in a lot of pain right now?" I asked, hoping for what, I don't know.

"Yes, she is most likely in constant pain, Miss Delimar."

I paused for a minute. "Well, my aunt went to contact her pastor to come here. Can we hold off removing her from the respirator until he comes?"

"Sure, we can do that. Are you expecting him shortly?" he replied.

"I think so, but I have to wait to see what my aunt says. She's on the phone with him right now."

The doctor disappeared again. I turned my focus back to my mother. Her body was lifeless, just a shell. Although not at peace with it, I knew I was making the right choice by removing her from the respirator. I held her hand in mine as I stroked the back of it with my other hand. I laid my head next to hers, closed my eyes, and let the tears stream down. Sandy returned a little while later to let me know the pastor was on his way. Then she went to the hospital cafeteria to get us something to eat.

A part of me wanted to laugh once I saw Sandy's pastor. He was an odd-looking man that seemed to have never left the seventies. He was an older man, short, and wore an oily jeri curl. He had an off-white button up shirt tucked into some tight, brown corduroy, high water pants that flared at the bottom. The pants were pulled up over his belly. The bottom of the flared pants gave way to penny loafers with actual pennies placed in the slits near the toe of each shoe. His feet were clearly bulging out the sides of the loafers as they leaned. The top few buttons of his shirt were open, exposing some curly chest hair. I wondered if he put activator on the chest hair too. A gold chain with a little gold cross hung around his neck resting on the patch of hair. He wore a pair of huge bifocals. The lenses looked pretty cloudy.

I knew my mom would be laughing too if she could see this. That thought was the only thing that temporarily stopped the crying as he read the twenty-third Psalm. We all held hands as he said a prayer and anointed my mom's forehead. Before he left, he offered his church's services if I needed a church to have the funeral. I thanked him and took his information. I hadn't thought that far yet.

Sandy and me both said our goodbyes and were asked to leave the room as the doctor removed her from the respirator. Moments later, Dr. Smith found us sitting in the visitor's room. We stood up to greet him, and Sandy grabbed my hand as he gave us the news. "I'm sorry, Miss Delimar, we did everything we could." I squeezed Sandy's hand extra hard as a retched sound escaped from my mouth. I didn't even realize it was coming from me. It came from my soul and through my gut as I hollered out in despair. I sobbed heavily and doubled over as if someone had punched me in the stomach. Sandy did her best to try to console me, but she was trying to get her own bellowing under control. It was the hardest I had ever cried.

I guess it wasn't Dr. Smith's job to console us. He just simply said, "You can go in when you're ready to see her if you'd like."

Then he walked away and a nurse came in. She ushered Sandy and me over to the chairs to sit us down. "Can I get you something to drink? Some water?" she asked compassionately. I shook my head as no words formed to come out. We stayed in there crying for a good forty-five minutes before going in to see mom one last time before they removed her body from the room.

I took one look from the doorway and couldn't bring myself to move my feet any further. I just cried, shook my head, and walked down the hall. Sandy went in for a minute. I spent the rest of the night talking to the nurses about the next steps and filling out paperwork. I felt like a zombie going through the motions. I can't even tell you what half of the paperwork was. None of that mattered. My mother was gone; just like that.

CHAPTER 14

I decided not to go see Cal the next day. I wasn't feeling up to it, and there was so much to do with preparing for the funeral and burial service. He would be home in a few days anyway. Since I had no way to immediately contact him before the visit, all I could do was wait for him to call me or have someone call me on his behalf. I knew he would be disappointed, but he'd have to understand.

The scotch tape didn't appear to be disturbed on my apartment door, but I still felt uneasy being there. I sat on the living room couch staring into space. My brain was in such a fog that I didn't know where to start with everything I needed to do. My phone rang snapping me out of it. It was Ronnie. I hadn't spoken to him, but left a message, so he was probably calling to see if I would be in to work.

I answered, and let him know everything that was going on. Surprisingly, he was very compassionate and told me to take the following week off as well. This was a Ronnie I didn't know, but could definitely get use to. In the past, any time I requested time off, he would fuss and have a fit. I guess there was no case to be made against an employee whose mother just passed.

After Ronnie, I started making all the necessary phone calls. I had an appointment to meet with the funeral home later that day. The rest of the calls were to notify more extended family and friends. Jillian beeped in while I was on a call, but I didn't answer. She left another message asking me to call her back. I decided to call her back to get it over with, so she'd stop calling.

She picked up on the first ring, "Angie! What's up girl? I been calling you!"

"Hey, Jillian. Yeah I know. My mother passed away so I haven't had a chance to return phone calls." I replied dryly.

"Oh my God, I'm so sorry, Angie. I had no idea. I thought you were still upset about the other night. Then when I didn't see you at work last night, I thought it was because of me." She was rambling.

"No, I been at the hospital for the past two days."

"Oh God, well I know you probably have a lot to do, so I won't keep you. I just wanted to make sure you were okay. Call me if you need anything, okay?" she said, waiting for a reply.

"Thanks" I replied uninterested.

"No, Angie I'm serious. I know you might still be mad at me about the other night, but forget all that. I'm serious. I'm here if you wanna talk or anything. You hear me?" she said again, waiting for a response.

"Okay, I hear you. Thanks." With that we hung up.

I decided to call Cherlise and May last. May was already waiting to hear the update, so it was no surprise when she offered to go with me to the funeral home later that day. I was surprised when I called Cherlise, but I guess I shouldn't have been. "Heyyyy, Angie! I know you're calling about your money. I didn't forget about you!" she said as soon as she answered the phone. I had actually forgotten that she was supposed to pay me back this weekend.

"Oh, actually that's not even why I was calling." I said.

"Oh what's wrong?"

"My mother passed away last night." I said flatly.

"Oh my God, for real?"

No, for fake, I thought to myself sarcastically. I guess she didn't know what else to say. "Yeah, apparently she had brain cancer and an aneurism too. That's what did it." I said while trying not to break down and cry again.

"Wow, how are you doing? Are you okay?"

"I'm okay. I just don't know why she didn't tell me." I said.

"Yeah, it seems like she would've told you something like that … so when is the service and everything gonna be?"

"I'm not sure yet, most likely Tuesday or Wednesday of next week. I'm going to the funeral home later today, so I'll know more after that." I explained.

"Oh okay—hold on!" she said and then clicked over on her phone. It took her a while to click back over. I was just about to hang up when she came back on the line. "Angie! That's Matt on the other line. I'm gonna call you back, but let me know if you need anything and let me know when the funeral is." She said, trying to rush off the phone.

"Okay, bye" I said and hung up before she could even say bye back. Fuck the fact that my mom had just died, and Cherlise was supposed to be my best friend. Everything was all about Matt, even at a time like this. I didn't even have the energy to get angry. I was hurting too much.

I had no idea there were so many choices involved in a funeral. I had to choose from about forty caskets, choose flower arrangements, choose how I wanted mom's makeup done, choose how her hair should look, choose a headstone and what to put on it, choose pictures for the program and the program layout. It hadn't even dawned on me that I needed to bring an outfit for her to be buried in. After I made the rest of the decisions, I let the funeral director know that I would be back with the outfit later. May went with me, and Sandy met us there for moral support.

On our way out, Sandy pulled me to the side and asked me to walk with her to the car. "I have something to give you." She informed me. Once at her car, she lifted out a metal box from her backseat. It looked exactly like the one in mom's room. What was *she* doing with the metal box? "Your mom wanted me to make sure you got this. You can look through it and call me with whatever questions you have when you feel up to it." She explained as she looked me deep in my eyes with a sympathetic look.

With a puzzled look on my face, I just replied, "Okay...thanks ..." I didn't know what else to say. I didn't want to reveal that I had already read one of the letters in the box. I decided I would wait a few days, see what else was in the box, and then reach out to Sandy. I didn't know what questions she was expecting me to have, but I guess I'd know better once I cracked the box back open.

May and I ended up going out to eat after all, even though the occasion was no longer for my birthday. It felt good to get a heavy meal in my stomach since I hadn't really been eating the way I should have for the past few days. Now I was ready for a nap. It was dark now, and I felt uneasy about going back to my apartment. I decided to drop May off and stay at my mom's. I would need to start packing up her things at some point anyway.

It felt weird being in her room without her there, so I stretched out on her couch. I placed the metal box across my lap and stared at it, unsure if I wanted to find out what it was all about. I didn't think I could handle anything else. My phone rang startling me out of my daze. My stomach fluttered when I realized it was Cal. I was happy he was able to sneak a call to me from his cell phone.

"Hey, love," I answered.

"Hey love my ass! Where the fuck was you at today?" he blasted into the phone.

"Calm down! A lot has been going on." I said, too drained to bark back.

"Here we go again with the bullshit excuses. What was it this time? I bet you was somewhere fucking that cop wasn't you?" he accused.

"What? No!"

He cut me off before I could say anything else. "Uh huh then what? You better get to explaining!" he demanded.

"I will if you gimme a chance to talk DAMN!" I said, getting a little irritated.

"Well talk then, shit! And don't fuckin' yell at me!" He was steaming.

"Cal, my mom passed away last night." He got quiet on the other end of the phone. "Helllooo? Did you hear what I just said?" I asked like I was talking to an idiot.

"Yeah … are you for real?" he said, softening his voice.

"Yeah, I'm serious" I said as my voice began to tremble. I was trying hard to hold the tears back.

"Aw, baby, I'm so sorry. Damn!" He said. I could tell he was sincere.

"She …she" I couldn't hold the tears back or finish my sentence as I began to weep into the phone. Before I knew it, the weep turned into heavy sobbing. I could barely catch my breath.

"Damn, baby. I'm so sorry … go 'head n' let that shit out. I'm right here for you." He said, trying to comfort me. It felt good to hear his voice. I didn't like crying in front of people. Even though he couldn't see me, I still felt embarrassed.

It took me a little while to regain my composure. "Sorry, I just can't stop crying."

"Don't be sorry, baby. Go 'head and get it out. I'm sorry I can't be there right now to hold you like I want to." His response just made me cry more.

I ran down the events leading up to my mother's departure to him. "What day you gonna have the funeral?" he asked.

"It's gonna be on Tuesday at Rupert's Funeral Home."

"Damn! I wish I was gonna be home in time to be there for you. You know I'll be home Thursday, though, right?" he asked, still trying to comfort me.

"I know. I wish I could've came to visit today, but I was at the funeral home making arrangements and stuff." I explained.

"I know. I know. Sorry I spazzed on you like that, baby. You know how I get when I don't see you." He said, lightly chuckling.

I laughed back, "I know, crazy ass. What time am I picking you up on Thursday?"

"Be up here like nine o'clock and bring me an outfit to change into. I don't wanna have to walk out in that little paper suit they give us." He instructed.

"Okay."

"I gotta get off this phone now, baby. I'll try to call you tomorrow or Monday to check on you, though. Okay?" he whispered.

"Alright," I said in a child-like voice.

"If you need anything, call Wally. I'll let him know what's up. Okay, I love you."

"Okay, love you too, babe." I replied, and we hung up.

I wished he could've stayed on the phone longer, but I knew he couldn't take any chances getting caught having the cell phone. Still, talking to him made me feel a lot better. I couldn't wait for him to get home. I thought about the fact that I never got to tell my mom about him and how she would never get to meet him now. It saddened me, but I turned my attention back to the metal box that was sitting across my lap.

I cracked it open and the same papers sprung out of it. I pulled all the letters out to see what else was in the bottom of the box. There was a yellow document. I unfolded it and saw that it was a birth certificate. I don't know why or how, but until now I had never seen my birth certificate. Whenever I needed it, my mom made excuses and always told me to just use my passport for I.D. Something was

117

wrong with this birth certificate. It had my first name on it, but a different last name. *Reynolds? Who is that?* I thought to myself. That wasn't the only thing that was wrong. The line for my father's name was left blank and in the mother's field, "Rainy Reynolds" was filled in.

My mouth dropped open as I stared at the birth certificate. Now I was really confused. I didn't want to accept what I think I had discovered. This couldn't be! There had to be some explanation for this. I looked at the clock, ready to call Sandy to get answers. It was close to midnight. I really didn't want to call her that late; especially since she had been by my side practically for the past twenty-four hours. I knew she had her own life to tend to.

I decided I'd wait to call and read more of the letters instead. At the very bottom of the metal box in a corner was a necklace. It was thin, brown leather with my red garnet birthstone hanging from it wrapped in a silver wire metal. There was also a picture. It was an old Polaroid. My mom was in the picture standing next to a woman holding me as a newborn. I studied the picture trying to figure out who the woman was. She looked like someone I had seen before, but I couldn't put my finger on whom.

Most of the letters were along the same line as the first one I had read. There was one letter that was different, though. It was a letter to my mom.

Dear Candice,

I hope you and Ricky are doing well. Once again, I'd like to thank you for everything you're doing. I've written close to twenty letters by now to Angela, but I haven't received a response, so I'm sending this letter to you. Can you please let me know how she is doing? I know that I have no right, but I would love to see pictures of her. I'm in a program now and have been clean for one year today. I would never dream of trying to interfere in Angela's life or trying to take her away from you. I would just like the chance to get to know her. Even if she's not ready to see me, can I at least talk to her on the phone? If she doesn't want to talk to me either, can you call me then? I just want to know that she's okay. My number is still the same, but just in case you don't have it anymore, it's 555-0198.

Thanks,

Rainy

I had read enough. I felt sick to my stomach. I don't know if it was from the confusion of trying to figure out who this Rainy person could be or from the fact that my mother was hiding this from me, whatever *this* was. Between her holding back about the cancer, the letters, and the birth certificate, I was starting to feel like I didn't know my mother at all. I always felt that we had the closest relationship, but maybe we weren't as close as I thought. I continued reading through the other letters until I fell asleep.

CHAPTER 15

Tuesday couldn't come fast enough. I was ready to get the funeral over with. I spent the remainder of the weekend moping around mom's empty apartment. I must've read and reread Rainy's letters a dozen times. She gave an account for everything that was going on in her life throughout the years as well as asking for an account of what was going on in mine. The content of the letters led me to believe that my mother had not answered any of them.

I can't tell you much about the funeral because I slept-walked through the whole thing. I was in such a daze. It was a small service with only about thirty or so people in attendance, including my Aunt Tina who flew up from Florida. She flew right back afterwards, and I was surprised she even came up at all. May and Cherlise came. To my surprise, even Tee Tee and Britt came from the club. Ronnie sent flowers. B.I.G. Insurance sent flowers as well.

I think I must have been all cried out at the cemetery. Although I was hurting deeply inside, no tears came out as they lowered mom's casket into the ground. Sandy stayed there with me after everyone else gave their condolences and left. I thought this was the perfect time to ask her about the letters in the metal box.

"That was a nice service. I'm proud of you for pulling this together, Angie. I know it wasn't easy."

"Thanks, Aunt Sandy. I can't believe she's gone." I replied, looking at the pile of dirt where they had just buried my mother. "Aunt Sandy?"

"Hmm?" she replied, also staring at the pile of dirt.

"Who is Rainy, and why is her name on my birth certificate?"

Sandy blinked back tears as she turned her attention to me. "I see you've looked through the box."

"Yes, I read all the letters … a few times!" I said.

"Why don't we take a little walk?" She suggested as she put her arm around me, guiding me through the grass to the paved road. "I wish your mom would've told you this herself. I've been after her for years to tell you the truth, but …" she trailed off.

"But what? Tell me the truth about what?" I pressed.

"Candy was not your biological mother. Angie, you're adopted." She said quietly. I didn't respond. I didn't know what to say. My heart sank for a moment. "A woman named Rainy Reynolds is your birth mother." She continued hesitantly. I stayed quiet some more. "Rainy was just a teen when she gave birth to you, Angie, and she was involved in a lot of things. I guess she thought the best thing was to put you up for adoption, but I do know that she loved you very much. That's why it was supposed to be an open adoption where she could maintain contact with your mother and father."

"I can't believe this. And my father?" I asked.

"I don't know who your biological father is. I'm not sure that Rainy knew either." She replied.

"That's why no one's listed on my birth certificate." I said to myself out loud.

I stopped walking and put my face in my hands. I couldn't believe what I was hearing. What kind of person was Rainy? What kind of things was she involved in that were so bad that she didn't want me? My mind raced with questions as anger rose in my spirit.

"And my mom and dad didn't tell me! Why? And you knew all these years too?" I said angrily.

"Angie, it wasn't my place to tell you. I guess Candy and Ricky just wanted you to always feel like you belonged with them. Who knows why they did what they did. I think they wanted to tell you the truth, but they were scared you would want to go find your real mother or something."

"And the letters? There's so many of them, and they never let me have them! Why would they do that?" I said, almost shouting as tears began to roll down my face.

Sandy hugged me, trying to comfort me. "Angie, you have to understand Rainy was into some heavy drugs, and she hung around a pretty tough crowd. Candy and Ricky just wanted to keep you safe."

"But I have a right to know who I am and where I came from! I can't believe this! Who else was in on this little secret?" I asked.

"Only a few people know, just the people closest to your mom and dad. But who you come from doesn't make you who you are, Angie." She said sympathetically.

"All these years … all these years" I said shaking my head.

"I'm sorry you had to find out this way. Candy wanted to tell you herself, but I guess time got away."

"I just don't even know what to do with this. You mean to tell me that I have a living, breathing mother somewhere out there who has been trying to contact me for practically my entire life?" I was in disbelief.

"Yes, to my knowledge she's still living."

"Do you know how I can get in contact with her?"

"I'm sorry, Ang. I don't." She said.

We walked the rest of the way back to the cars in silence. This was a doozy. So much had been going on the past couple of weeks. My head was spinning. I thought about the number that Rainy had put on the letter for my mother to call. I would try to call her when I got back to mom's apartment.

After I changed my clothes, I paced the floor back and forth looking at Rainy's number. I had butterflies in my stomach thinking about what I would say. I had already found enough excuses to waste time. I had eaten, watched TV, reread more of the letters, and taken a nap. What would she say? Would she be happy to hear from me? I wanted to call before it got too late; it was already going on ten o' clock. I built up the courage and dialed the number.

A man answered the phone, "hello?" My heart sped up. I wasn't prepared for this. I was expecting Rainy herself to answer. No words reached my lips. "Hello?" he repeated.

Hurry and say something, Angie! I thought to myself in my head. "Uh, I'm sorry. I have the wrong number." I said quickly and hung up.

I couldn't do this. I was feeling too anxious. I really wished that I had a blunt at the moment to calm me down and mellow me out. I decided it was still early enough for me to make the trip to see my weed man. I turned off all the lights and locked up mom's apartment.

During the drive to Newark, I hoped the man wouldn't try to call me back. I shouldn't have hung up on him like that. Why didn't I just ask for Rainy? My thoughts were racing. I called Mike, the weed man, to tell him I was on my way. He was a young video game nerd that never left the house. He didn't fit the description of someone you would think would sell weed, but I guess that's why he had gotten away with it for so long. He was cool. Sometimes I would chill with him for a few hours and smoke. This evening wouldn't be one of those occasions, though.

I usually only bought a dime bag from him, but when I told him that I had just buried my mother that day he tossed in an extra one for free. He even reached in the car and gave me a big hug, which was out of character for him. I was grateful for the extra bag, though because that meant I wouldn't have to come back for a while. I stuck the bags down in my pants pocket and pulled off in route to my apartment.

I pulled slowly into my parking space. It was a ghost town out that night. No one was on the street, and the parking lot light was blown out. I got out of the driver seat, and closed and locked the door. I walked a few feet then realized I had forgotten the metal box on the floor of the passenger side seat. I walked back and bent down into the car to get it. When I got up about to close the door, I felt something hard hit me in the back of my head. I fell to the ground, dropping the box, and the next thing I remember is waking up to a man's voice.

My pants and panties had both been pulled down. I groaned from the throbbing pain in the back of my head. "Make one sound, and I'll blow your brains out," the voice said as he pumped in and out of me from behind. I lay on my stomach, disoriented and in panic. My heart was pounding so hard and loud that I was sure I would have a heart attack. I thought to myself, *This is it! This is how I'm going to die. Who knows where they'll find my body!* So many times I had the dream in so many ways, but I always ended up being shot in the head. I closed my eyes and opened them again to make sure I was indeed awake. It wasn't a dream this time.

"See, I try to be the nice guy, but none of y'all bitches appreciate that. This is how y'all want it, huh? You like it rough, don't you?" he asked as if really waiting for a response. He stuck a gun to the side of my face and said, "I can't hear you. I *said* you like it rough, don't you bitch?"

I winced at the sight of the gun and whimpered out a plea "Please,

please don't do this."

"Oh, you want me to stop? You mean you don't like it rough? Okay, turn over. You want me to stop; you gotta beg for it." He said as he held the gun to my face and flipped me over. He wore a black ski mask. I looked into his eyes. They were cold, psychotic eyes. "Don't look at me! Look over there!" he instructed. I turned my head to the side and tried not to anger him.

Lying in between the cars, I prayed for someone to come out and see us. My back ached from rubbing up against the hard gravel. I shivered from the cold as I saw my breath in the air. "Yeah, that's right quiver for me baby. See, y'all bitches always wanna play hard to get, but I know your type. I know y'all just want a man to take control, huh?" he said. All I could do was cry in response. The next thing I knew, a figure appeared standing over us dressed in all black. Like a black ninja, the figure came down across the back of his head with a brick. His body fell on top of me, and the ninja smashed the brick in the back of his head again.

I struggled to push his body off of me but he was too heavy, and I was too weak. The ninja rolled him off and helped me up. Holding on for support, I stumbled to the front of my building. I sat down on the steps and peered up into the ninja's face under the light. He was kind of short and wore black jeans and a black hoodie tied tightly. Still feeling woozy I saw the face again. The ninja wasn't a *him*! It was *her*, the lady that had been stalking me! I jumped up and took a few steps back out of fear. The street started to spin, and I fell flat on the sidewalk.

CHAPTER 16

When I came to, I was lying in a hospital bed. I looked around the room and tried to sit up. My head had a massive throbbing. I reached to feel where the pain was coming from to find a bandage had been wrapped around my head. That wasn't the only place I felt throbbing. I ached between my legs too. I started to whimper as it all started coming back to me in bits and pieces.

A nurse walked in, took one look at me, and backtracked calling out into the hall, "Dr. Irvin! Patient Delimar is up!" She walked over and fluffed the pillows behind me. Rubbing my shoulder she asked, "How are you feeling?"

"My head hurts really *really* bad and ... and ..." I couldn't bring myself to tell her about the pain between my legs. I clutched my hospital gown instead and continued to whimper.

"It's okay. The doctor is going to need to ask you a few questions. You just answer the best you can okay?" she informed me. I nodded in response. "And she's a female doctor too, so don't worry" she said, trying to comfort me. "Can I get you any water or maybe some chips or something?" she asked softly.

"No, thank you." I replied, trying to regain my composure.

"Okay, the doctor will be right in," she said and walked out.

"Hi! We're glad to see you're awake." Dr. Irvin walked in with a big warm smile. "I'm Dr. Michelle Irvin." She extended her hand, and I let go of myself only long enough to shake it. "You're at University Hospital, Angela." She reached in her front pocket and pulled out a light. "Please look up ... good ... down ... good. Now follow the light with your eyes." I did as she instructed. Next she listened to my heart and asked me to breathe in and out.

Dr. Irvin was a petite woman who looked to be in her early thirties. She had blonde hair with strawberry highlights and bright blue eyes. She was swimming in her oversized, white doctor's cloak. She looked very comfortable in her little white orthopedic shoes.

Sitting down on a low stool on wheels, she wrote some things down on my chart. "Do you remember how you got here, Angela?" I wondered how she knew my name. Then I glanced over at a chair in a corner and saw my purse sitting on it. I thought hard, but I couldn't remember how my purse or I had gotten there.

I burrowed my eyebrows thinking hard finally answering, "no."

"Okay, that's fine. Can you tell me the last thing you do remember?" she probed on.

"I remember feeling something hit me hard in the back of the head ... when I woke up, a man was on top of me. He had a gun ..." My voice trailed as fragments of the night's events came back to me. "There was a woman there too."

"A woman? Was she with the man?" Dr. Irvin asked.

"No—no, she hit him with something and got him off of me. I don't know where she came from, but I know her."

"You know her?" she asked.

"Well, I don't *know* her, *know* her. I recognized her face. She's a woman that's been following me for weeks now. I don't know her name or anything, though. She just seems to keep popping up everywhere I go. I know it sounds crazy."

"I see. Well you suffered a pretty bad concussion. You have a really deep gash in the back of your head. It took seven stiches to close it." The doctor continued on as I put my hand up to my head to feel the bandage again. "You were also raped, Angela. There's a little vaginal tearing as well as some trauma. The good news, depending on how you look at it, is that there were traces of spermicide. So whoever did this used a condom. We're still running tests for the full range of STDs as a precaution." All I could do was let the tears stream down my face and nod in understanding. I started to rock back and forth to comfort myself.

"Now, although he used a condom, we still offer the morning after pill to all our victims as another precaution. It's totally voluntary and up to you if you want to take it. The sooner you take it, the better chance you have of not getting pregnant. But like I said, we think he did use a condom, so you're probably not pregnant." Dr. Irvin explained to me.

I shook my head enthusiastically, "yes, I want it please!"

"Okay, I just need you to read over and sign this form. It basically lets you know your rights not to take the pill if you don't want to, and that we went over this information with you." I just glanced at it, not really reading, and signed at the bottom.

As she pulled open a drawer to take out the pill, she continued talking, "The police were here to take your statement earlier, but since you weren't coherent, they said they'll return a little later. They did confiscate the clothes you were wearing for evidence."

"Okay, well can you just give them my address to come talk to me? I'm ready to get out of here." I said.

"I understand, Angela. However, we're not going to release you for at least another few hours. Like I said, you suffered a pretty serious concussion, so we need to monitor you for the next few hours to make sure you're okay to be released. During this time, we'll need you to stay wide awake too." She said matter-of-factly.

I sighed out of annoyance and tiredness. I just wanted to be home in my bed. "Okay," I responded.

"Angela, I understand this is a hard time for you, an emotional time. Here is the name of a psychologist. She specializes in post traumatic stress from rape." She said, handing me a business card.

"Thank you," was all I said as I eyed the card. I had no idea if I would need to talk to someone or not. I hadn't really thought about it yet.

"Is there anyone we can call for you? A friend or family member?" she asked.

"Um ... yes, can you call my friend, Cherlise? Can you hand me my purse, so I can get the number from my cell phone?" After dictating the number to her the doctor left the room to have one of the nurses make the call.

I tried to get comfortable in the stiff sheets of the hospital bed. My head was throbbing as I tried to piece the events together. I replayed the parts of the attack that I could remember. I closed my eyes and tried to lay my head back gently. I winced from the pain. All I could see were the eyes of my rapist. They were almost familiar.

The things I could remember him saying made me wonder how many other victims he had raped. I tried with everything in me to recall if I might've known him from somewhere. Nothing came to me.

Then my thoughts wandered to my stalker. Her round face was clear as day in my mind. She had been my stalker up until this night. This night, she had become my guardian angel, but where was she? My eyes, still closed, moved back and forth beneath my eyelids for about an hour until I was interrupted in my thought process.

"Angela Delimar?" a deep, serious voice said. I opened my eyes to two police officers dressed in suits.

"Yes?" I answered.

"I'm Detective Ramsey, and this is Detective Green. We're here to interview you about your attack. Are you up to talking with us?" he asked, as if he was really going to give me a choice.

I grimaced a little when answering, "uh, I guess. The doctor said I have a concussion, so I don't know how much help I'll be."

"That's okay. We know you're probably still in a lot of pain, so we'll try not to take up too much of your time." He said. "Now why don't you start from what you remember? Where were you when you were attacked?"

"Okay... I was at home. I just remember walking back to my car to get something out of it. Then I felt a hard blow to the back of my head." I started.

"Now which side of the car were you on?"

"The passenger side."

"Okay so after you were hit in the head, did you fall down right away or ... what happened next?" he asked.

"Um, I don't remember exactly. I think I must've fell out because I just remember waking up to him on top of me. He had me laid on my stomach on the ground ... oh and he had a gun! I do remember that! He held a gun to my face." I said, remembering the important piece of information.

"A gun? Okay, good. Do you remember what the gun looked like?"

"I don't really know what kind it was. I'm not that familiar with guns. I just know it was black." I answered.

"That's okay, you're doing great. About how big was the gun?"

I held my fingers up to show him the length "about that long."

He and his partner were both scribbling notes in their pads. "Uh huh, and was it a revolver, you know the kind that spins in the middle? Like a handgun?"

"No, I don't think it was a revolver." I said, glancing down at the gun hoisted on his hip. It was peeking from beneath his suit jacket. "Actually, it looked a lot like your gun." Both cops glanced at each other when I said that.

"So while he was on top of you, did he say anything?" he asked.

"Yes, I vaguely remember him talking to me, but I can't remember exactly everything he said."

"Okay, just tell me what you do remember." He instructed.

"Well, I just remember him saying something about trying to be a nice guy, but women—no, bitches not liking that and something about women playing hard to get." I paused for a minute trying to remember, but that was all that came to me. "That's all I really remember him saying. I think he said more stuff, but I just can't recall."

"Okay, that's fine. So did his voice sound familiar to you?" he asked.

"I really can't remember the voice so much, but I think he must've turned me over at some point because I remember looking into his eyes." I said, getting chills.

"You saw his face?" Detective Green interjected excitedly.

"No, no he had on a black ski mask. You know like a robber? But the mouth and eyes were cut out so I saw his eyes." I explained.

"What color were they?" Detective Ramsey asked.

"It was kind of hard to tell in the dark," I answered, disappointed that I wasn't able to answer anything with sureness.

"Okay, so he's on top of you, and you're facing him, what happens next?" he asked.

"This lady came out of no where and hit him in the back of the head." I answered.

"A lady? What did she hit him with?"

"I don't remember" I replied.

"Okay, and you're sure it was a woman who hit him?"

"Yes, because I thought she was a man at first until I saw her face close up. Her face, I recognized." I told him.

"Where did you recognize her from?"

"From everywhere, she's been following me for weeks now. I

don't know who she is or why she's been following me, but I'm sure it's the same woman." I answered.

"Have you ever spoken to her or do you know where we might find her?" he asked.

"I have no idea. I've never spoken to her. She just pops up in random places."

"Did you ever report her for stalking or try to take out an order of protection or anything against her?" he asked.

"No, I didn't think it was that serious. She didn't seem dangerous … more weird than anything."

"Uh huh, so after she hit your attacker, what do you remember after that?" he asked.

"I just remember he fell on me, and she rolled him off. I can't remember much after that." I said regrettably.

"Okay, that's fine. Now Angela is there anyone that you've had a fight with recently or anyone that you can think of that would want to harm you?" he asked.

"No, no one that I can think of."

"Anyone paying any extra attention to you at work or have you noticed anyone else following you besides the woman you mentioned?"

I thought for a brief moment and only one person came to mind. "Well there is just one aggressive customer at the club where I bartend."

"Okay, what about him? Did you have words? Did he ever threaten you?" he probed.

"No, he's never threatened me, and he's probably harmless. But one of the other girls said he did follow her to her car and tried to kiss her, and he grabbed my arm and wouldn't let go the other night at work. He was pretty drunk, though. He's a regular, and he's always drunk." I explained.

"Okay, what's his name? We want to check out every possibility."

"I only know him by Ozzy. I don't know his whole name."

"Okay, that's good enough. Do you think you would be able to sit down with a sketch artist to have a picture of the woman drawn? She's probably our only hope in finding your attacker." He explained.

"Sure, but do I have to do that tonight? My head is killing me." I said, wanting them to leave.

"No, you've been a great help tonight. Maybe you can come down to the station within the next day or two to do it. We want to get it while it's still fresh in your mind."

"Okay," I agreed.

"Please give us a call if you remember *anything* at all. Okay?" he said while handing me his card.

I told him that I would call, and after taking down all of my contact information, they left. One of the nurses came in with a glass of water and some painkillers for me to take. "Thank you," I said to her as I swallowed them.

"You're welcome. We called your friend, Cherlise, for you and let her know you were here. She said she's on her way." I was relieved to hear that.

"Thank you." I repeated to the nurse.

"Sure, can I get you a magazine or something? Sorry, we don't have cable in these rooms." She said apologetically.

"Sure, thank you." I said not knowing what else there was for me to do since I couldn't sleep. Plus, I needed something to take my mind off of the evening's events.

I looked at my phone. It was three thirteen in the morning. I was getting sleepy and wanted so badly to close my eyes and drift off. I was afraid of slipping back into unconsciousness, so I fought the urge. Wondering how I got to the hospital, I called for the nurse. She came in out of breath "Yes? What can I get'cha?"

"Oh, nothing, I was just wondering if anyone here knows how I got to the hospital." I asked.

"All we know is someone left you lying in the doorway of the emergency entrance. They didn't even come in to tell us you were out there, and nobody saw who put you there unfortunately. Sorry ..." she said sounding genuine.

"Oh ... okay."

I spent the next couple of hours looking through magazines until the doctor came in to check on me one last time. Dr. Irvin released me, but I couldn't leave until I had a ride to pick me up. They needed to make sure that I wasn't driving. I looked at the time on my phone again wondering where Cherlise was. It was after five o'clock at this point. One of the nurses wheeled me in a wheelchair to the exit where we waited patiently.

"Let me give her a call and see where she's at." I said, feeling bad for having the nurse waiting.

The phone rang for a while before she answered, "Angie! Oh my gosh, I'm sooooo sorry! Are you okay?"

"Well, I was attacked and raped but other than that, yeah I'm fine. Didn't the nurse call you hours ago?" I asked feeling annoyed.

"Oh my God, yeah she did. I'm coming, but I let Matt borrow the car. I'm still waiting for him to come back. I been calling him, but he's not answering." She rambled on.

I rolled my eyes and said, "It's okay. I wanted you to take me home, but never mind. I'll just call a cab."

"Are you sure? I can try to call him again!"

"No, it's okay. The cab will probably get here faster anyway." I said.

"Okay, well call me when you get home," she said as if she really cared if I made it home safely or not. I agreed and hung up.

I was too through with Cherlise now. Not only did she still owe me money, but she couldn't even be there for me when I needed her the most. I was so done with her. "Um, my friend can't make it. Do you have the number to any cabs?" I asked, embarrassed that I had no one else to call. I knew May didn't drive, and I didn't feel like talking about what happened to anyone else.

"Sure, let me go get it from the front desk." She said, wheeling me to the side of the doors. I shivered from the gusts of cold air that were coming in and out as people entered and exited. I was cold, wearing the thin scrubs the hospital provided me with since the police confiscated my clothes.

I was happy to finally see the cab pull up. I couldn't wait to be safe and sound in my own bed. Although it did worry me that my rapist was still out there running rampant. Then I remembered the day my dresser drawer had been disturbed. My heart started to speed up in panic. I thought about telling the cab driver to take me to my mom's instead, but I knew I would have to go home some time. Besides, the sky was starting to lighten as it prepared for daybreak. Someone would have to be pretty bold to approach me or break into my apartment in broad daylight.

It wasn't until the cab dropped me off that I realized I didn't have my keys. I figured I must've dropped them at some point during the attack, so I walked around the building to the parking lot in the back. I was surprised to find them still laying there in the snow next to my car. Thankfully neither my rapist nor anybody else had gotten away with the keys.

After I had my keys in hand, I noticed the interior car light was on due to the door not being completely closed. I opened the door and slammed it shut. I was happy to see my metal box was still there too. I looked down at the ground and saw what looked like blood. I wondered if it was my attackers or mine. I got in the driver side and turned the keys in the ignition to make sure the battery hadn't died. Luckily, the car started right up. So I removed the keys, grabbed the box, and took special care to make sure all doors were securely closed and locked.

I did the same once I made it into my apartment. I did my paranoid check of all closets, shower, nooks, and crannies to make sure no one was in there or had been in there. All was clear. I took a shower. Instead of relaxing the way it usually was, it was a painful experience. Not so much physically, but emotionally. I started having all kinds of paranoid thoughts. Would someone be waiting for me when I got out of the shower? All of a sudden I started feeling dirty as I remembered looking into the rapist's eyes while he was on top of me. Without noticing, I started scrubbing my body harder and harder. I huddled in the corner of the shower and began to cry as the soap rinsed from my body. I missed my mother now more than ever.

I wished she were there to hold me and comfort me. I needed her to make me feel safe again. But she wasn't even my real mom anyway. Anger started to set in as I thought about what a faker she had been. My entire life she had been a fraud, a phony. I exited the shower and bathroom cautiously doing another paranoid scan of the apartment. I dressed quickly and sat on my bed. It did feel soft and inviting. I wanted to crawl under the blankets and let myself sink in and nod off to sleep. Something kept me up, though. I opened the metal box, which I had sat on the foot of my bed. I took out the picture and studied it closely. My heart began to race as the connection began to develop in my brain.

The woman holding me in the Polaroid was the ninja! This was the same woman that had been following me for weeks now! My breathing sped up as I thought about all the times I had seen her. Her face played over and over in my head like a slide show. Yes, this was definitely the same woman, only a lot younger in the picture. I couldn't believe it! This had to be my biological mother. It was all making sense now. I still didn't quite understand why she had been following me, though.

I couldn't be still after that. My body wanted to sleep, but my mind wouldn't let me rest. I took out the letter with her number on it again. I wanted to call, but I felt it was too early in the morning. I tried to force myself to sleep. I closed my eyes and eventually drifted off. I dreamt of the attack, of course. I couldn't get the attacker's eyes out of my head. They haunted me.

CHAPTER 17

Although it startled me out of my nightmare, I was happy when the phone woke me. It was Cal. I was happy, but that soon turned to panic as I watched the phone ring. I didn't know if I should tell him about the attack. I wasn't sure how he would react. I answered the phone quickly before I missed the call. "Hello?" I said, trying to sound normal.

"Heyyyyy! What are you doing? Sleeping?" He sounded cheerful.

"Yeah, but that's okay. How are you babe?"

"I'm great. I'm 'bout to see my baby tomorrow! What more could I ask for?" he said, sounding giddy.

I forced out a fake chuckle, "I know, just one more wake up!"

"Yeah, how you feeling though? How'd everything go with the funeral?" He asked.

"Everything went fine, and I'm okay. I'm glad it's over."

"Just okay, huh?" he said, dropping his tone.

"Yeah ... it's just been a lot going on lately, babe. More than one should have to bare, you know?" I was still contemplating if I should tell him or not.

"Like what? What else happened? Talk to me baby. That's what I'm here for." He said, sounding concerned.

"Well, check this out. Turns out the woman that died wasn't even really my mom. I mean she was my mom, legally I guess, but not biologically."

"What? Say word!" he said in disbelief.

"Yeah, apparently I'm adopted, and no one ever told me."

"Daaaaamn, that's crazy! How'd you find *that* out?" he asked.

"My mom's friend, Aunt Sandy, gave me this box my mom was hiding. It had my real birth certificate and letters from my real mom in it. She's been writing me all these years, and my mom never told me or gave me the letters." I explained.

"Wow! I can't believe that. I guess she was just trying to protect you. You know our parents always have the best intentions, but sometimes they fuck up too, you know?" What he said had a point.

Leave it to him to make excuses for my mom and dad. "Yeah I guess, but Cal I'm twenty-five fucking years old! When were they planning to tell me?" I said, getting angry all over again.

"I know. I know. I'm not excusing what they did, but at least you know the truth now."

"Yeah, I guess. Oh and how 'bout she's been following me around. I've been seeing this woman in all these random places."

"Who been following you?" he asked.

"The woman that's supposedly my birth mom! I saw her at the gym, the store, everywhere! I told my mom about it, and she acted like I was being paranoid."

"How you even know what she look like? And why you didn't tell me somebody was following you?" He asked defensively.

"I don't know. She seemed harmless. There's a picture of her—well, I *think* it's her—with the letters." I explained while still debating on whether or not to tell him about the attack. I decided not to. He would see the damage soon enough. I would just tell him in person.

We talked for a few more minutes about the plan for the following day before hanging up. I was excited. At least with all that was going wrong in my world, I had finally seeing him in person for good to look forward to. I had my outfit picked out for weeks for what I would wear when I saw him. I was bummed that I had to have this head bandage on though. It kind of took away from the outfit. Nevertheless, nothing would keep me from seeing my baby. I lay there playing out the fairytale in my head of how I would greet him outside those prison walls. I would walk up to him calmly with a smile on my face. Then I would reach up and wrap my hands around his neck as he wrapped his arms around my waist. We'd lock lips, and he'd pick me up off the ground then put me down and feel on my booty a little. I giggled to myself at my own imagination.

I was wide-awake now even though I had only slept a few hours. I lay still for a while, looking at the ceiling while replaying my fantasy in my head. I rolled over on my side as my eyes landed on the letter with Rainy's number sitting on my nightstand. I thought about calling again. It was afternoon now, but I kept making excuses. What if she was at work? What if that man answered again? What would I say? I thought back to the night I saw her at IHOP. I wondered if the young girl I saw her with was her daughter. I got excited at the thought of having a little sister. If this mysterious ninja was in fact my mother, why would she just dump me at the hospital like that? More importantly, how did she seem to always know where I was?

I decided I would call later that evening in case she was working during the day. I called the apartment management instead. They would definitely have to change the locks on my doors. I had no way of knowing for sure if someone had been inside my apartment, but considering the rape, I wasn't taking anymore chances. I explained everything to a lady named Melissa.

"I'm going to need to have the locks on my door changed." I informed her.

"Oh my God, really? What happened?"

"Well … I was knocked out and raped when I was getting out of my car last night." I said calmly.

"RAPED?" she said loudly into the phone.

"Yes, and I think someone has been in my apartment, so I need to have those locks changed immediately please." I insisted.

"Sure, of course we can do that. I'll try to get someone out there tomorrow."

"Okay, thanks" I said ready to hang up.

"And I'm going to let my boss know about this when he gets in today. We've been trying to get you guys some cameras over there for the longest. Maybe this will help." She explained.

"Yeah, that reminds me! The outside light in the back parking lot is blown out."

"Okay, thanks for letting us know. We'll get someone to fix that too. I'm so sorry that this happened to you. Did they get the guy?" she asked, wanting details.

I didn't want to go into detail. "No, they didn't. That's why I'm so insistent about the locks, so thanks for your help. I'll keep an eye out for the locksmith tomorrow. Bye bye now."

"Okay, you be careful. Bye." She ended the call.

I spent the rest of the day trying to relax, mostly snacking and watching TV. Cherlise hadn't even called to check on me. I didn't know what kind of friend she was becoming, but I didn't like it. I thought about calling her to tell her I was coming to get the money she owed me. I wasn't going to ask for it, and I wasn't going to keep watching her shop and not pay me. Besides, since she was a career robber now, she could afford to pay me. Then I looked out the window and saw the sun was about to set. A fear set in of being out alone at night. So I changed my mind. I decided to just text her instead. I let her know that I would be by first thing in the morning to get the money.

I tried on my outfit to make sure everything still fit in all the right places. I stood in front of the mirror trying to decide what I could do about the bandage that was tied around my head. It really wasn't a good look, but the doctor said I shouldn't remove it until I went for my follow-up appointment. I decided to be obedient and tried on a few hats. None of them really worked with the outfit. I sighed in defeat knowing that there wasn't much I could do about it.

Next I turned my attention to his outfit. I had bought him a few things, but not too much because he wanted to go shopping for himself. I laid out some jeans, a black, long sleeve, casual button up, and the black Timberlands I bought for him. I pulled the shopping bags out of my closet and broke open the packs of boxers, tank tops, and socks that I bought. I wanted to make sure he had everything he needed. I took out the black two-holed belt as well. I stood back and looked at both of our outfits. Yup, we were going to look good together.

I took a look around the room and realized the room was in a bit of disarray. I started cleaning. I must've been working off nervous energy because the next thing I knew, I had cleaned the entire apartment from top to bottom. Mopping, vacuuming, dusting, and tidying up, the hours had flown by. I checked the time to see if it was a good time to call Rainy. It was.

I paced back and forth a few times in the living room before picking up my phone. My hands were shaking as I dialed the number and waited on the line. All I heard was dead air, then three beeps, and "We're sorry, the number you have dialed is temporarily out of service. Please try your call again later." My heart sank in disappointment. I hung up and dialed the number again, receiving the same recording. I double-checked the number to make sure I had dialed correctly. How could the number be out of service and why?

I don't know why it affected me so greatly, but I sat down and began to cry. I had no idea how I would get in contact with Rainy now. I grabbed the phone book from the bottom of my coffee table and searched for Rainy Reynolds. There wasn't one listed. That's when I realized I didn't even know what city she lived in. I didn't know what to do next, so I just set my alarm to get up in the morning. Then I fell asleep on the couch watching TV.

CHAPTER 18

The next morning I was nervous. I was so excited that Cal was finally going to be released. I had more butterflies than I had ever had before any of our visits. Thankfully, I didn't have diarrhea this time though. I kept turning around in the mirror in circles making sure every angle of me was perfect. I wanted to look my best for my baby. I did the best that I could with my hair with that bandage being in the way. I hated that I still had to wear it. I didn't wear perfume too often because it made me sneeze profusely. However, today was an occasion that called for it. I picked up my Marc Jacobs fragrance from the dresser and sprayed one puff on my wrist then rubbed both writs together. Then I sprayed three little puffs into the air and stepped into the mist twirling around.

I checked and rechecked to make sure I had all of the pieces to his outfit neatly folded in a big duffel bag. I was ready. I thought about calling Cherlise first to make sure she had gotten my text since she hadn't responded, but then I thought it would be better to just show up at her door. That way she had no chance for excuses.

I double parked on the crowded street in front of her house, put my blinkers on with the car running, jumped out and jogged up the steps to her front door. I had to ring her bell three times before she answered half awake. "Angie! What'chu doing here?" she asked surprised.

My words rolled out slowly as I zoomed in on a puffy, black eye. "I texted you last night to tell you I was gonna stop by this morning to pick up the money."

"Oh, my battery died last night, so I didn't even get the text. I'm sorry." She said as if I was going to say never mind about the money.

"Oh …" was all I said followed by an awkward silence.

"I don't even have any cash on me, Ang—"

"Oh, well I can take you to the ATM right quick. Just go throw something on real fast." Before she could finish with that excuse I cut her off, not backing down.

"Uh—hold on let me see if Matt has any cash on him." She said as she disappeared back into the building. Miraculously she reappeared with the money. "Thanks again" she said as she handed it over.

"No problem. You getting ready for work?"

"Nah, I'm not going today," she said with a sullen smile on her face.

I didn't want to know why and didn't ask. However, I couldn't ignore her injured eye. "What happened to your eye?"

"Oh, Matt's dumb ass wasn't paying attention and swung the kitchen cabinet door open too fast." She said shaking her head after sucking her teeth.

"Oh, damn. When did that happen?"

"Last night. I hope it goes down by the end of today, so I can go back to work tomorrow. I don't feel like hearing my manager's mouth." She went on, "What'chu you doing out so early?"

"Today's the big day! I'm bout to go pick up my baby!" I said with a big grin spread across my face.

"Aw shit! Wait—what is that bandage on your head like that for?" she said as I turned my head to the street checking on my car.

"Stiches … seven of them."

"Oh snap! I totally forgot about your attack! Oh my God, how are you?" she asked, stepping out of her self-absorbance for a minute.

The time had passed when I needed her though. I didn't feel like talking about it. I didn't feel like giving her the juicy story that she thought she was about to get. "I'm doing okay, thank God. I'll be better once I get my hubby in my arms." I said, smiling.

She smiled back and then straightened her face a little, "So what happened? The guy actually raped you?" she asked, intrigued.

"Yeah, but I don't really wanna talk about it." I said, brushing her off. "I gotta go." I took a few steps back towards the stairs.

"Okay, I understand ... well, call me later."

I told her "okay" knowing good and well I had no intentions of calling her.

Happy at least one thing had went as planned, I got back in the car and headed to the prison. It was a different scene at the prison than the usual visits. No long lines or big tour-like buses. There weren't too many people at all. As I walked to the building, I saw some inmates dressed in white aprons and shower caps out behind the kitchen. Although there was a tall metal fence and barbwire between us, it still made me uncomfortable when they started howling and calling out to me. I guess they couldn't help it. I ignored them and hurried inside the building only to find more desertion. I walked up to the glass. No one was there, but I could hear talking from the back, so I called out, "Hello?" No answer.

I called out again, this time sticking my neck through the window opening trying to see to the back, "Helllooo?"

The talking stopped abruptly and a woman's voice snapped back "One minute!" The over-sized prison official took her time waddling to the window, "Yes?"

"Hi, I'm here to pick up an inmate that's supposed to be released today." I said as pleasantly as I possibly could. This would be the last time I had to deal with these bitches. I tried to keep that in the front of my mind.

"Okay, well just have a seat. If and when he gets released today, he'll come out of that door over there." She said as she pointed to a door off to the side.

"Okay, am I allowed to give you these clothes to send to him now?" I sounded silly to myself asking that.

I guess I sounded silly to her too because she started laughing, "No, what'chu think this is? He has to wear the release outfit we give him. They're not allowed to change on the property." She informed me.

"Okay, do you know about what time he'll be released?"

After giving an annoyed sigh she said, "If he's cleared and has no warrants, then he should be out around ten."

I was annoyed I had to wait another hour. I told Cal they wouldn't let me give him the clothes. I felt like a dummy. I walked back to the car to put the duffle bag in the trunk and returned to sit and wait. I must've asked Cal about five times if he had any other warrants or any holds in any other counties, anything that would hold up his release. He assured me he didn't. I began to get nervous as one hour turned into two. I perked up every time someone came through that door, but it was usually just a guard.

By eleven thirty I was back at the window calling for the guard again. I knew it would be lunchtime soon, and I didn't want to wait until no one was available to give me an update. No one answered when I called out to them this time, and I heard no talking in the back. A different male guard happened to be walking by out in the lobby where I was, and noticed I was still waiting.

"You're still waiting for a visit?" he asked.

"No, I'm actually waiting for an inmate that's supposed to be released today. I've been waiting for two and a half hours." I informed him wearily.

"Oh, I think all the inmates that were scheduled for release today have already been let go. What's the name? I'll check for you."

"Calvin Shay, do you need his number?" I asked, prepared to recite Cal's inmate number to him.

"No, just the name is fine. I'll be right back." He said as he disappeared through a side door to the office. This time he reappeared from behind the glass window. "Miss?" he called out to me. I walked to the glass prepared for bad news. "Okay, Calvin Shay was released this morning, but he had a warrant in Essex County, so he's already been taken to the Irvington Police Department." He informed me.

My shoulders drooped as I let out a disappointed sigh. "Really? He told me that he had no warrants. Do you know if he'll still be released today or what happens next?"

"I don't know. You'll have to go to the Irvington Police Station to see. They may allow him to post bail and be released or they may hold him. It depends."

"Okay, the Irvington Police Station is next to the library, right?"

"Yeah, you know where the courthouse is?" he asked.

I shook my head "nope."

"*You don't know where the Irvington police station or courthouse is?*" he asked in almost an outrage.

"No, I've never been incarcerated and never had a reason to know where the police station or courthouses were." I answered dry and sarcastically. "But thanks for the information. I'll find it." I walked away as he stood there dumbfounded. I found it offensive that he apparently assumed all black people knew where all the jails were.

I was sure I had passed the police station before, so I drove to the general vicinity to see if I could find it, and I did with no problem. As soon as I pulled up, my phone began to ring. I answered hoping it was Cal "Hello."

"Uh hi, Miss Delimar?" the voice said.

"Yessss, this is she. Who is this?" I asked hesitantly.

"This is Detective Ramsey with the Newark Police Department."

"Yes?" I answered, still not sure who he was.

"I took your statement the other night at University Hospital. I'm following up regarding your attack. I wanted to see when we can schedule a time for you to come down to the station to do that sketch we talked about."

"Ooooh, okay. Ummm I can probably come in some time tomorrow." I said.

"Okay, tomorrow is fine, but is there anyway you can come in today? The sooner you sit down with our sketch artist the better. It's better to do it while everything is still fresh in your mind."

"Well I'm just not sure if I'll be able to get there today. If I can, I'll give you a call back but it will most likely have to be tomorrow." I didn't want to make any commitments until I knew what was going on with Cal. Right now that was more important to me.

"Okay, well tomorrow is fine. You can come any time. Just give me a call before you come to make sure the artist will be here. You can call my direct line. Do you still have my contact info?" He asked.

"Yes, I still have your card. So I'll give you a call tomorrow." I replied and then we said our goodbyes.

With my attention turned back to the matter at hand, Cal, I put two quarters in the parking meter outside the station and went in. It was a lot smaller than I expected. I was surprised to see a little white female officer working at the front desk. She seemed out of place there to me for some reason.

"Hi, I'm trying to see if you have my boyfriend here. He was released from Western State Prison today, but they said he was sent here because he has a warrant." I explained.

"Okay, what's his name?" she asked pleasantly. I said it for her and then spelled it. "Yep, he does have a warrant here, but he's not here yet. I don't show him as checked in to our station yet. He's probably still in transit."

"Okay, so what does that mean? Is he still going to be released today? When is he going to get here?" I fired off the questions.

"Well, there's probably a few inmates in transit so they have to go to each station and drop off each inmate where they have warrants. Unfortunately, I don't know what order they drop them off, so I can't tell you exactly when he'll be here. You're best bet is to just go home and wait for him to call you." She explained.

Feeling defeated, I said "okay" and turned to leave.

I couldn't stand the fact that I would have to play the waiting game now. I was ready for him to be home, in my arms. We had waited long enough. For some reason, I had already had the feeling it wouldn't go as smoothly as we hoped. The lady was right. All I could do now was go home and wait for his call. I started to drive, but I felt too anxious to go home and wait. I did go home, but only for a second. I decided to go get some work out clothes. I would go try to burn off the anxious energy by exercising.

I secretly hoped to run into Rainy there since that was one of the places she had stalked me. Of course, when you *want* your stalker to show up, she doesn't. I got on the elliptical machine as usual. I worked the machine hard trying to clear my mind while keeping my cell phone by my side in case Cal called. It felt good to be back in the gym. I hadn't been in a while in fear of running into Rock. I thought I saw him for a second too. When I glanced up into the mirror, I saw a man that looked just like him. He glanced at me too, but instead of coming over to bother me, he hurried off to leave the gym. That wasn't like Rock at all. Plus, this guy was wearing a bandana tied around his head. Rock wouldn't be caught dead looking like that.

I was surprised to see that Cal still hadn't called me by the time I finished my workout. I went home reluctantly, showered, and put the same outfit on from earlier. I was still holding on to the hope that I would see my Cal before the day was over. I ate and called May to fill her in on my life's events. She started to cry for me when I told her about the rape and attack. She was insistent about coming over to check on me, but I was able to talk her out of it. She said she just needed to see me and know for her own peace of mind that I was okay. I told her I was waiting on Cal to call me to come pick him up and didn't want her to take the bus all the way over and I have to leave. We stayed on the phone for a good two hours, which helped kill time.

Still, by seven o'clock in the evening, I hadn't heard from Cal. I decided since it might be too late at this point for us to go out to eat, I would cook us a nice dinner. I made a steak, two baked potatoes, and a nice mixed vegetable medley. I went around the apartment making sure everything was in its place, neat, and clean. It was. There was nothing else to do. I tried to hold off and wait, but I was growing hungrier and hungrier. I ate my plate and wrapped up the other plate in some foil for Cal.

I went in the living room and watched some TV hoping to relax and kill more time while I waited. Eventually I drifted off to sleep. It wasn't until about eleven o' clock that night that Cal called me. I answered the phone sleepily, "Hello?"

"Baby, you up? Wake up!" Cal said on the other end. It felt good to finally hear his voice.

"I'm up! Where are you?" I said, lying.

"I'm at the Irvington police station. They took forever to bring me here." He said, sounding a little tired himself.

"I know! I went there after Western State said you had warrants there. I asked you if you had warrants, Cal."

"I know. I know, but I didn't know I had this one. I still don't even really know what it's about, but yeah, the lady at the front desk told me you was here looking for me." He said.

"Yeah, that was way this morning! So what's the deal?"

"You gotta come post bail for me for this warrant. It's five hundred dollars, so just take it out the stash. We gon' get it right back when I go to court in the morning." He instructed.

"Ugh! Okay, I'm on my way."

"Baby, hurry up because they'll send me to lock up if you not here by midnight. I already told them you was coming, so just hurry up, okay?" he instructed further.

"Uggghhhr okay, well I'll get there as soon as I can. Let me go!" I said so I could hurry up and get ready.

"Alright, I love you."

"Love you too, bye." I replied hanging up.

I jumped up in excitement that I would finally see him. Lord knows it had been a long wait. I washed up in the bathroom quickly making sure my breath was fresh and face clean, no eye boogers. Although, I couldn't imagine that he would look any better than me, having been just released from prison and all.

My heart raced the entire ride to the jail. I was beyond excited and could barely contain myself. He must've been worried he'd have to go to lockup because he called three times to see how far away I was while I was still in route. After assuring him during the third call that I'd make it, I arrived there just in time. Ten minutes to twelve I posted bail for him and sat down to do more waiting. This time it was only about another half hour before he came out.

There he was, bigger than life itself. He had on some stiff, dark denim jeans that looked too small and a matching denim jacket. Even in this ridiculous outfit, he still looked handsome and he still owned the room. He had a small brown paper bag in his hand holding all his worldly possessions. As usual, we both played it cool. We just said, "what's up" to each other and gave a hug, the kind with space still in between our bodies. Maybe it was because the lady at the front desk was sitting right there or maybe because we were both so tired after having waited all day long. I don't know, but it was nothing like the fairytale I had replayed in my mind so many times.

The ride home was quiet except for when Cal asked me to pull over so he could pee. When we finally made it back home, I heated up Cal's plate only to find that he wasn't really hungry. I guess we had made enough small talk because he was mostly interested in just going to bed—or I should say getting me into the bed. I expected this. I mean it had been two years for him.

I was nervous, but tried to go along with it. "Come here," he whispered to me in his raspy voice. I obeyed and moved in closer. He kissed me passionately, but to my surprise I tensed up instead of getting aroused. I took a deep breath and tried to relax running my hands over his back and through his locks of hair. He totally skipped over all the foreplay we had discussed so many times through our letters. Instead, he went straight for the gold, pulling down my panties and trying to penetrate me. I tensed up even more as images of those haunting eyes popped in my head. Now all I could think about was the rape. It felt like it was happening all over again. I didn't even realize it until Cal said something.

"Baby, relax. Why are you pushing my hand away like that?" he asked, confused. I looked down, breathing short, heavy breaths to see my hand tightly grasped around his wrist while he was holding his dick trying to put it in me. The thought of him inside of me terrified me.

"I'm sorry, stop … please." I said in a soft voice. He did as told, but only for a moment. He went back to kissing me, but then tried to penetrate me again, this time more forcefully. I tried to relax and let him, but couldn't. "STOP! STOP! PLEASE!" my voice was louder this time accompanied by me pushing him away forcefully.

"What? What the fuck?" he asked, losing his patience as he thrust himself to the side of me lying on his back. He was hard as a rock, and I wanted to give him what he wanted, but I wasn't even wet. Nor was I horny. I was scared, scared, and more scared.

"I'm sorry Cal. I'm sorry." I said as tears started to stream down my face.

Hearing the fear in my voice, his voice softened as he took a deep breath, "It's okay, baby. I know you're not comfortable with me yet. It might take some time, I guess. Come here." He said, pulling me closer to his chest. My breathing eased up as I felt comforted by his embrace.

"No, it's not that babe." I said sniffling and wiping away tears. I continued, "I didn't tell you …"

"Tell me what?" he asked, now looking into my face for an answer in the dark.

"A few nights ago I was attacked outside in the back." I held my breath as I waited for his response.

"*Attacked?* What'chu mean *attacked?*" he exclaimed.

"When I got home the other night, a man raped me outside in the parking lot."

"What!" He now broke the embrace and sat up in the bed. "What the fuck you mean? Why wouldn't you tell me this Angie?" he said, sounding upset and betrayed at the same time.

"I didn't know how to tell you. I just wanted everything to be perfect when you came home."

"That's some bullshit, Angela! I can't believe you wouldn't tell me something like that. I'm your man! What the fuck?" he repeated.

"I know. I should've told you, but I didn't know how. I didn't know how you would respond or if you would still want to be with me." I started to ramble.

"Oh, and this was the best way to tell me?" he said sarcastically.

"I know, and I'm sorry. Please try to see this from my point of view! I still have stitches in my head for God's sake! I'm probably not even thinking clearly."

"Where?" he asked. I guess he hadn't noticed the bandage on my head after all.

I turned on the lamp sitting on the nightstand closest to me. "See," I said, turning around so he could see the bandage.

"Damn ... I still don't understand why you wouldn't tell me that shit! ...Well what happened? Who did it?" he asked. I spent the next hour retelling the story and answering all of his questions. By that time, we were both tired and it was clear we weren't having sex that night. We both turned over with our backs to each other and went to sleep.

It took me a while to fall asleep, but it took him no time. He was snoring right away. I clung to myself as I kept seeing those eyes staring back at me. I thought about that night. I thought about Rainy's face, and how I could find her. I thought about Cal and if he would leave me now. I invested so much time into him and our relationship. I waited months for him to come home to me. So far things were not going how I had envisioned for us, but it was only the first night. I swore to myself that night that I would turn things around starting the next day. We would make it. We had to.

CHAPTER 19

Things were a little awkward between us the next day. We spent all morning in court waiting for the judge to call Cal's name for that warrant. It turned out someone, I don't know who, had put a restraining order on him and called in a violation of that order. He claimed he didn't know the person. We spent about three hours there before we got the bail money back. It had already been decided that the stash would be used for Cal to get back to hustling. So without hesitation, I handed over the entire stash we saved up.

We barely spoke as we strolled through downtown shopping for clothes for Cal. We always had so much to talk about before, but not so much now. He seemed more focused on buying a cell phone, so he could start making calls to all his boys. He sold his illegal cell phone he had in prison to another inmate since he wouldn't be able to bring it out with him without getting caught.

"So what we gettin' into tonight?" I asked.

"I don't know. What do you wanna do?" he asked, sounding disinterested.

"I don't know. I have to go to the police station, but after that it's whatever."

"Police station? For what?" he said, looking at me like I was crazy. I guess he wanted to stay as far away as possible from any police stations, and I couldn't blame him.

"I have to go sit down with a sketch artist." I explained.

"Oh, you know what he looks like?"

"No, not my attacker. I only saw his eyes. I have to do a sketch of Rainy—or at least the lady that I'm pretty sure is Rainy. I told you she's the one who saved me. They want to put a sketch out to see if they can get her in to get more information." I replied.

"Oh … well she did you a big favor. Why you wanna rat her out?" He asked. I knew that he lived by the code of the street never to snitch on anyone, but this was different. I wasn't snitching in my eyes because she had done nothing wrong. Plus, I had my own motives of course.

"I'm not snitching!" I answered defensively. "I want to find her too. This may be the only way I can get in contact with her."

He raised his eyebrows as if he was considering the validity of my argument, "True, true …"

I continued, "So what will you be doing while I go to the police station?"

"I guess you can just drop me off at my daughter's house." He replied.

I got quiet for a minute. I hated when he referred to his daughter as if she was an adult. Dropping him off at "her house" really meant dropping him off with his ex-girlfriend who he was still with at the time he had entered prison. I wasn't comfortable with their relationship, but he assured me it was strictly about their daughter now. I made up my mind to trust him and keep my ill feelings to myself. I didn't want any drama. Besides, if he did have something still going with his ex, he was awfully bold to have me drop him off at her house.

I was glad to drop him off in the broad daylight because his daughter didn't live in the best neighborhood. Vailsburg had its good sections and its bad. This definitely wasn't one of the good. Her street was narrow and half the houses on the street were boarded up. I double-parked a little down from the house he had pointed out to me. He got out, walked around to my side of the car, and leaned in for a kiss. "Hit me later when you get done at the police station, alright?" he instructed.

"Okay, later" I replied as I pulled off. I drove slowly watching him through my rearview mirror to see if the house he pointed out was actually the house he was going in. It was.

I drove down and crossed through the intersection. I wanted to make sure I was out of sight before pulling over. I didn't want him to think I was stalking him or anything. I wanted to call Detective Ramsey to make sure he would be there before I drove all the way across town to the station. He informed me that he may or may not be at the station, but that I should ask for Carlos Santiago, the sketch artist. He would be there and would be expecting me.

The station was bigger than I expected. There were officers dressed in uniforms as well as plain dressed officers busy walking back and forth throughout the station. Each one looking completely caught up in their work, hustling and bustling past one another. Doing the sketch went a lot faster than I expected. Carlos sketched fairly fast. When he was done he turned his large notebook around to me "How's this? Is there anything that you think I need to change or enhance?"

I stared at the picture he drew. It didn't look exactly like Ninja Rainy, but it was close enough. "No, this looks fine."

"Okay, I'll make sure Detective Ramsey gets a look at this, and he'll contact you to let you know what's next." He let me know. As I rose to get up from my seat, Carlos's eyes looked past me. "Oh, there he is now!" he said. I turned to see who he was talking about. Detective Ramsey made his way over.

"How did everything go?" he asked with an excited smile.

"Fine, I guess" I replied, looking at Carlos to weigh in.

"Here's what we got!" He held up the sketch.

"Good ... good. We should be able to get this released by the ten o'clock news." He said, eyeing the sketch over in approval.

"Okay then," I said, not knowing what else to say.

"I'll walk you out!" Detective Ramsey said as he held his hand out in front of him. We walked and talked. Mostly he asked me if anything new had come to me, which it hadn't. Then he went on to explain that they would release the sketch and have a hotline where people could call in to identify the ninja. I don't know why, but I didn't tell him that I had an idea of her real name. I didn't want to tell him that I had suspicion that she was actually my birth mother. I thought it best to pretend to be surprised when and if it came to air.

As we rounded the corner with me closest to the wall and him on the outside, we ran smack dab into another officer. "Oh! Excuse me!" I said startled, quickly backing away from the man's chest.

"Hey, Johnson! Watch it man!" Detective Ramsey said to Rock in a joking way. My mouth dropped open in slow motion as I caught his gaze. There were those eyes! My own eyes almost popped out of my head as I was caught in a trance connecting the dots as to where I had seen those same eyes.

"Heyyy Angie, what are you doing here?" He asked, looking at me. He looked a little different, but I couldn't figure out what exactly was different. He was wearing his police cap. I wasn't use to seeing him with anything on his head. I blinked slowly, my mouth still open, but no words formed. "Are you here about Mr. Burkwell?" he asked, avoiding my stare. Still, no words came out.

"No, she was here to help out with a sketch." Detective Ramsey answered for me.

Before I knew it, I snapped. "You sonofabitch! I know it was you!" I screamed as I lunged at him giving everything I had. I threw my fists. I clawed trying to scratch his eyes out. Everyone around stopped and stared as Detective Ramsey pulled me off of him, restraining me. "LET ME GO! HE DID IT! IT WAS HIM! HE'S THE ONE THAT RAPED ME!" I screamed for my entire audience to hear.

"Rape? Angie, what's going on? Are you okay?" Rock said, remaining calm, but looking nervous.

"Just calm down, Miss Delimar. Calm down!" Detective Ramsey said, still holding me.

"Let go of me! Arrest him!" I insisted.

"Miss Delimar, just calm down. Nobody's going to arrest anybody. Officer Johnson is one of our finest officers. I assure you; you're mistaken." He said trying to calm me.

"I'm sorry, man. I don't know what's going on, but I gotta go clock in." Rock said with his hands up in the air in the surrender position.

"It's okay. Don't worry about it, Johnson. I'll take care of Miss Delimar," Detective Ramsey responded. Now I turned to Detective Ramsey, grasping his shirt and pleading with tears forming in my eyes.

"Please! Please! I'm telling you, I know it was him! I'm positive. Please don't just let him get away like that! DO SOMETHING! PLEASE!" I pleaded.

"Alright now, Miss Delimar. Just calm down. Come with me." He was still holding me as he guided me down a hall. Rock went the other way, and the crowd of onlookers dissipated, going back to their own hustle and bustle. I was taken into a small interrogation room. It had one of those two-way glass mirrors just like on the movies. I started feeling nervous like I was a suspect.

Detective Ramsey pulled out a chair for me to sit on. Then he pulled a chair up for himself on the opposite side. "So you know Officer Johnson from another case?" he asked.

"No, I know him from the gym. It just so happens that he was on the scene of another case where the crime took place right next door to me. We work out together sometimes at the gym, and he's always flirting with me and asking me out all the time even though I told him I have a boyfriend." I started rambling.

"Okay … okay, slow down. Just take a deep breath and relax." Detective Ramsey said, trying to calm me down again.

I wouldn't and couldn't calm down though. "Look! I don't care how much of a good cop he is. I'm telling you, Rock raped me!" I was looking dead into his eyes.

"Rock? So you guys do know each other on somewhat of a personal basis?" he asked with raised eyebrows.

"No! I know what you're trying to say. I don't know him like that. Like I said, I just know him from the gym. He knows where I live, and I know it was him that night." I said in a calm but stern voice.

"I see … and how are you so sure it was him? When we spoke at the hospital you said you didn't know who raped you. You said it was dark out, and the parking lot light was out. Correct?" He questioned me like he didn't believe a word I was saying.

"Yes, it was dark, and yes, the light was out, but he was on top of me looking right in my face. I know it's him by those eyes … those hazel eyes." I said, saddening as I replayed the attack in my head.

"Do you understand this is a serious accusation you're making against a police officer, Miss Delimar?" He asked me that as if I were three years old.

I leaned into the table and stared Detective Ramsey down. "I don't give a shit who he is. I'm telling you he raped me, and you have to take that seriously. Otherwise, I'll have this entire department under investigation." I said through clenched teeth.

"Now you just hold on a minute. You better be careful making threats here." All kindness was gone from his voice. He was no longer interested in calming me down or treating me like the victim that I was. "A lot of women are confused in the days following their attack. They think every man they see did it." He said, trying to convince me of my own confusion.

"Well, I'm not saying every man did it. I'm saying Officer Johnson did it." I wasn't backing down.

He sat back in his chair in silence thinking for a moment. "Okay, we're still investigating your attack. Just let us do our jobs, and we'll let you know when we have something. Besides, you mentioned a man by the name of Ozzy from your job. We're still checking him out."

"That's it?" I said. "I'm just supposed to sit back and wait while my attacker, Officer Johnson, is free to go about his business?" I was in disbelief.

"Yes that's exactly what you will do. Do you want to know why?" he said with a straight face. I didn't respond. I just waited for his answer. "We confiscated your clothes, you know, and guess what we found?" He taunted me. I sat back, rolled my eyes, and exhaled loudly because I knew exactly what he was talking about. I had totally forgotten that I had those two bags of weed in my jeans pocket. He read my expression and continued, "Yup, that's what I thought. So if you think about going publicly with any of these crazy accusations you're making, you'd better think twice. I'll personally haul your ass back in here so fast and charge you with possession. You don't want that, do you?" He said, flatly.

I clenched my jaws together hard. I didn't respond. I just got up, took one last glaring look at Detective Ramsey, and opened the door to leave. By the time I made it back in my car, my face was covered in tears. My chest heaved up and down as I let out sobs. I was glad no one could hear me with my windows rolled up, and I hoped no one saw me either.

I couldn't believe it was Rock who had raped me. That alone had me reeling. I tried to regain my composure as I thought hard. I pictured the man in the ski mask, then Rock, then back again. I wasn't mistaken. I was one hundred percent sure it was the same person. My skin crawled as I thought about him forcing himself on me. As I thought harder, it all made sense. In all the time that I had known Rock, I had never seen him wear any type of hats or caps. Today he had on his uniform hat, and at the gym he wore that ridiculous bandana that day. I know ninja Rainy hit him pretty hard. She had to have left some type of bruise on his head. I only wished there was some type of way for me to prove it.

I called Cal to let him know I was done at the station, hoping he would provide me with the comfort I was so use to him giving over the phone. The phone rang and rang then went to his voicemail. I left a message for him to call me back.

After hours passed and I hadn't heard back from Cal, I decided to text him. Eventually, he responded saying he was going to go out with his cousins and spend the night at his grandmother's house. Although I was a little disappointed and suspicious; I decided not to be clingy. I understood that he hadn't seen his family in quite a while and probably wanted to reconnect with them.

I didn't want to be alone, especially knowing Rock was out and free to roam. I didn't feel like having to pick up and drop off May. Nor did I want to ask her to take the bus to see me even though I knew she would do it, and I was done with Cherlise. Other than that, there really wasn't anyone else to call. I started missing my mother and decided to go to her apartment. I still had some packing and cleaning left to do anyway.

Once I got to her apartment, I lay in her bed and made myself comfortable. I wrapped myself in her sheets and hugged a pillow tightly, trying desperately to smell her scent. My cheeks got wet as I smothered my face deeper into the pillow trying to muffle the sounds of my sobbing. I cried from loneliness. I cried for the rape. I cried at my helplessness. I cried for Cal. I cried from confusion. I cried from revealed secrets. I cried from anger and frustration. Most of all, I cried for my mother. It hit me like a ton of bricks that I would never see her again. I would never be able to run to her for comfort or share my feelings, fears, secrets, or emotions with her again. I was never in denial about her death, but for some reason it was just hitting me just how real it was.

No one understood or cared for me like my mother. I had been angry with her when finding out about the adoption, but the love my mother gave me far outweighed her secret. I forgave her in my heart and mind that very instant and made peace with it just like that. Yet that still did not remove my emptiness at the moment.

I cried like a baby missing its mother. I cried until I began to cough and gag. My eyes bloodshot and swollen, I cried myself to sleep. It was just dusk, but I needed to sleep away the pain at that moment. I slept straight through the night, still clinging to the pillow.

CHAPTER 20

I slept straight through noon on Sunday. My eyes peeked open. The sun felt warm and cozy shining through the window even with the blinds closed. I snuggled deeper into the sheets and ran my hand up and down the soft blanket. I was in no rush to get up. I didn't feel like crying anymore. I didn't feel like doing much of anything. So I just lay there.

About a half hour went by as I lay there, gazing in the sun's direction. I was removed from my trance when the phone rang. I could tell by the ring that it was Cal. The butterflies fluttered in my stomach the way they always did when he called. I stared at the phone for a second while trying to decide if I should answer or not. I was still a little hurt from the day before when he decided to hang out with his cousins instead of me. I didn't want him to hear it in my voice.

I took a deep breath and answered the call. He wanted me to pick him up from his grandmother's house. I agreed with no hesitation and told him I would be there in about two hours. I wanted to shower and eat something first. I wasn't really hungry, but I knew I needed to eat.

I pulled up outside of Cal's grandmother's house and called him from my phone. He came out looking well rested and crisply dressed. I wondered where he was planning on going. The door slammed loudly when he got in the passenger seat. He leaned over and planted a kiss on my cheek. "What's up?" he asked, cool and calmly.

"Nothing, sup with you?" I answered his question with a question like we usually did.

"What's wrong?" he asked. I guess I wasn't doing a good job of hiding whatever was going on with me.

"Nothing" I said in a high-pitched tone, trying to deny it.

"Oh, you got my phone charger?"

"No, you took it with you." I said, feeling blood rush to my face. I was starting to get angry. I already assumed he probably left it at his daughter's house.

"No, I didn't!" he said arguing with me.

I tried to remain calm as I replied through a tight jaw "Yes … you did."

"Oh shit …" was all he could say in return.

I couldn't hold the jealousy in. "You left it at your baby mama's house, huh?"

That started an argument immediately. "What? What the fuck are you talkin' about? No I didn't! It's probably in the house."

"Mm hmm, well go check and get it." I said, calling his bluff.

He did as told, but not before rolling his eyes and letting out a loud sigh of annoyance. I didn't want to be one of those nagging girlfriends. I really didn't. Nor did I want to wrongly accuse him of anything, but I knew. Call it women's intuition or whatever. I just knew his visit to his daughter's house was about more than just seeing his daughter. The more I thought about it, the angrier I got. The angrier I got, the harder I began to breath. My nostrils flared, and I felt like a crazy person about to snap—or, at least how I imagined they felt before they snapped.

He returned with no charger in hand. Standing outside the passenger door looking lost and confused; he motioned for me to let down the window. When I did he said, "I don't know what the hell I did with it!"

"I know what you did with it. You left it at your baby momma's house! I already told you that!" I shot back.

"Mannn, Angie, don't start this bullshit. I don't know where my charger is." He said, trying to calm himself down. It was too late for me to calm myself down. I was steaming with anger at this point. Sure, I had no real proof, but I just knew. That was enough for me, and I pulled off from the curb leaving him standing there with the screw face on.

I drove like a mad woman down the street, cursing him out aloud to myself as I did: "Dumb ass muthafucka! Who the hell do he think I am? Got me fucked up! Stupid ass ... *And* I'm returning all that shit that still got the tags on it at home." By the time I made it home, my armpits were on fire. I raised my arms in the mirror and saw two wet stains.

After tossing the shirt in the laundry basket, I took a damp cloth to my pits. Then I put on some fresh deodorant. I did exactly what I said I would. I headed back out retracing our steps from the previous day. I returned everything I had a receipt and tags for. Feeling partially vindicated, I decided to go see a movie. I didn't care that I was alone. At the moment, I wanted to be alone.

I sat in the dark, sparsely crowded theatre eating my buttery popcorn with my legs kicked up on the seat in front of me. I decided to see *The Passion of the Christ* to see what all the hype was about. My phone started ringing, and it took me a minute to get to it. I didn't feel too bad since there weren't many people in the theatre, but I immediately silenced the call and switched it to vibrate. I didn't recognize the number, but whoever it was really wanted to get in contact with me. The phone kept buzzing as it vibrated against the contents in my purse. I had to send it to voicemail three times before the mystery number left a message.

The movie turned out to be pretty good, and I understood why it was the talk of the year. I was glad that I decided to go to the movies because it calmed me down and took my focus off of Cal. I wasn't so glad when it was over though. I had nothing to do and no one to talk to. I contemplated movie hopping, but I was too scared. There really wasn't anything else playing that I wanted to see anyway.

I checked my voicemail on the way to the car. "Hey Angie, this is Matt. Um, Cherlise got locked up. She asked me to call you to see if you can help bail her out. Please call me back ASAP at five five five thirteen twenty-one. Thanks."

I was surprised to get a message from Matt, but not really surprised that Cherlise was locked up again. *Her and those damn tickets!* I thought to myself.

During the drive home, I thought about how much she had changed over the last year. She had become a lying, self-centered, man-chasing criminal. I thought about how she didn't even come to the hospital after she knew I had been attacked and how she outright stood me up on my birthday. By the time I was back at my apartment, I had decided I wasn't helping to bail her out. Better yet, I wasn't even going to return Matt's phone call. Yeah, one might think I'm a terrible friend, but I was thinking about what kind of friend she had been to me lately. The more I thought about it, the more I was okay with my decision. She was always so far up the crack of Matt's ass, making her world revolve around him. I figured it was time for Matt to step up and take care of her for a change. I was leaving it to him to find a way to get the money. They were on their Bonnie and Clyde shit not giving a damn about anyone else, so the two of them could figure it out on their own. Besides, I had enough to deal with.

I wasn't ready to go back to work that first week, but I didn't know what else I would do. I would just be home, thinking way too much, and being miserable. Everyone welcomed me back with sad, frowning faces and the soft, "I'm so sorry about your loss. How you doing?" I know everyone meant well, but I was tired of hearing and answering the same thing over and over. I tried to stay at my desk as much as possible, but that didn't stop people from coming by.

The first two days were the hardest, but eventually the repetitive condolence line ceased. I stayed quiet, kept to myself, and tried to just focus on my work. On that Wednesday, on my way out for the day, I ran into the pantry guy. "Hey! I haven't seen you around in a while. Were you on vacation?" he asked as he stopped pushing his cart that held pantry supplies in tow.

"Hey, I know. No, I wasn't really on a vacation. My mother passed away." I said to him.

"Oh my God, I'm so sorry. I didn't know."

"Thanks ... well have a good night!" I said, trying to continue my move towards the exit.

"Hey! Um, do you have a boyfriend?" he asked hesitantly. I was caught off guard and didn't really know how to answer. I wanted to be able to say yes as I thought of Cal, but Cal hadn't even tried to call me or anything after our fight.

"Mmm, it's complicated," was my final decision.

"Complicated?"

"Yeeeeah, I guess you can say I'm kind of on a break, but why do you ask anyway?" I said, trying to steer the conversation away from my dating status.

"Oh, well I was trying to find somebody to hook my cousin up with, but I didn't know you had a boyfriend, so never mind." He said it as though I was some kind of item he decided not to take at the checkout counter.

I was even more caught off guard. Even though it was rumored that he had a girlfriend, I guess a little part of me hoped he'd say something like "Oh I've been wanting to ask you out for a while now" or "I wanted to see if you had plans this weekend" or anything other than what he had just said. What made him think I wanted to be hooked up with his cousin anyway? What were we? Fourteen?

"Why are you trying to hook him up? He can't get a girl on his own?" I asked.

"Nah, I mean he can, but I thought you might be his type and I thought you were single." He explained. Now I was even more offended. Why did he assume I was single? I was getting annoyed just talking to him at this point, and I started to realize this conversation wasn't worth me getting caught in the rush hour traffic because I didn't leave on time.

I simply said, "oh," and walked on.

I couldn't lie. I had thought about Cal every day since our fight. Apparently he wasn't thinking of me since he hadn't even attempted a call, visit, or anything. I contemplated on whether or not I should call him the entire ride home. I decided to give myself a time limit. If I didn't hear from him by the weekend, then maybe I'd call.

I couldn't even justify calling. *He* was the one that fucked up! *He* was the liar and cheater! I started making excuses for him in my head: *Maybe he really didn't leave the charger at his baby momma's house. Maybe I assumed too quickly and overreacted. Maybe I reacted from all the stress I was going through.*

I hadn't heard anything from Detective Ramsey since I left the station the week before. I forgot to watch the ten o'clock news that night too, so I didn't know if he released the sketch of Rainy or not. I wasn't going to let it go, though, not that easy. It was weird. Before I felt eerie every time I caught Rainy following me, but now I was looking around every corner, over both shoulders hoping to spot her following me. She had disappeared the same way she had appeared, into thin air.

CHAPTER 21

I was actually looking forward to work that weekend. I felt at ease, at home at the club. It wasn't too stressful working there, and for the most part, it was fun. I knew it would be too loud to have the "I'm so sorry about your mother" conversations. I was relieved about that. Although I had spoken to Ronnie to let him know I would be back that Friday, the rest of the girls seemed surprised to see me back so soon.

As soon as I got behind the bar, Britt, Keisha, and Tee Tee embraced me in a group hug. Even though the music was bumping as always, they managed to yell out comforting words to me to let me know they were happy to have me back. "Girrrl, you missed it all!" Tee Tee started telling me.

I was disappointed to find out that Princess had gotten fired. Up until that moment, I hadn't even realized that she wasn't there. She usually worked Fridays. According to Tee Tee, she got caught stealing from the register and had been doing so for a while. She was also stealing from some of the girls' tip jars when their backs were turned. Part of me felt bad for her because I thought had Ronnie given her more hours, she might not have stolen. She had her son to take care of too. The other part of me now wondered if she had ever stolen from my tip jar as well. There had been a few nights where I knew I did really well in tips just to get home and recount a lower amount than what I thought.

That wasn't all the juice either. Tee Tee went on to tell me the aftermath to the shooting at the IHOP. As I already knew, the guy that lay in his woman's arms bleeding had died. What I didn't know, however, was that the woman was Ronnie's sister and that man his brother-in-law. For Newark to be the size city it was, it was still such a small world. I was hoping Tee Tee and the other ladies didn't tell Ronnie we were there. Of course they did. Naturally, Ronnie and his people were looking for the shooters. Now I hoped he didn't ask me anything about it. I saw one of the shooter's faces, but I had no desire to be a snitch. I felt bad for the woman and her husband, but nothing would bring him back now. I didn't want any parts in this. I had more than enough going on in my own life.

Tee Tee finished off her run down by telling me somebody had been there looking for me. "Somebody was looking for *me*? You sure they asked for *me*?" I questioned, not knowing who it could be.

"Yeah! I told him you wouldn't be here for a while because of your mom, but I didn't know you were coming back tonight." She explained.

"Well, what did he look like?" I asked, suspecting it was Rock. Although, I didn't think he knew I worked there. Still, I didn't know who else it could be. The only other person that would ever come there looking for me was Wally, but we were done with our business since Cal had been released.

"Mmmm, he was like this tall," she said holding her hand just above her head. Well that ruled out any hope of it being Cal because her hand wasn't high enough.

"Kinda on the light side, nice smile. He had dimples." She continued as she smiled and batted her lashes. "He looked older though." That was the end of her description.

"Older?" I repeated baffled.

"Yeah, well, older than us anyway." I thought hard, but had no idea who it was. From her description, it didn't sound anything like Rock.

"Well, I'm glad you told whoever it was I wouldn't be back for a while. No telling what kind of weirdo he might've been." I said, shaking my head as I continued topping off all the liquor on our speed racks. She laughed as she walked off to help a customer. I turned my attention to see who was working that night. There was no sign of Jillian, which eased my mind. I was debating back and forth on whether I should tell the other girls how she had taken me to the lesbian club.

The rest of the night was smooth. I avoided Ronnie at all costs, afraid he would ask me about the shooting and what I saw. Thankfully, he didn't. As the night wound down, I thought of Cal more and more. I missed seeing him and hearing his hoarse voice, his comforting words.

The dishwasher was broke as it often was. As I washed out glasses by hand, my mind wandered about. I landed on the decision to call Cal when I got off, but my eyes were fixed on the flat screen that hung opposite the bar. Usually basketball or football games graced the screen, but at this time highlights of the news played. The flashed image of Mr. Burkwell's face jerked me from my trance. The music was loud, so the TVs always had the caption feature turned on. I read the captions as I waited to see if they would show Mr. Burkwell's face again.

The caption came up line by line out of synch with the reporter's mouth, "Brian Burkwell was wanted as a person of interest in the homicide of his grandson, fifteen year old Mikell Jackson. However, since his evasion of the police, he has been named a suspect in the murder. He was captured this morning around ten AM while attempting to shoplift from this small convenience store behind me." The store was somewhere in Central Jersey. I didn't recognize it, but I did recognize Mr. Burkwell's face definitely this time when they showed his mug shot.

The reporter went on to tell how Mikell's body was found in the apartment and how the police had been searching for Mr. Burkwell for weeks now. The storeowner called the police after catching Mr. Burkwell steal a sandwich and some razors. I couldn't help but feel a little bad for him when they showed him again being escorted from the back of the police car into the county jail. He looked so old and defenseless trying to put his head down to hide from the cameras. I still couldn't imagine him doing something so heinous to his own grandson like that. If he had, I was convinced it had to be an accident.

I must have been really focused on the news because I didn't even see Jillian walk towards me. She snapped her fingers in front of my face to get my attention. "What's up, girl! Welcome back!" she said in a cheerful voice.

"Hey, I didn't even know you were here tonight." I replied, trying to be cordial. I wasn't really mad anymore about the lesbian club, but at the same time I wanted her to be clear that I didn't swing that way.

"Yeah, I just came in now to pick up my check." When she said that, I realized she was fully clothed. She continued in a sympathetic voice accompanied by the head tilt, "So how you doing?"

"I'm good. What's up with you?" I asked, less because I really wanted to know, but more just to be courteous.

"That's good. I'm chillin' … shit it's Friday! I'm off, and it's payday! I can't complain." She replied.

I smiled, but not with as much enthusiasm as she was giving off. She motioned with her hand for me to come closer as she leaned over the counter to tell me something in my ear. Even though the intention was a whisper, she had to yell over the music.

"Look, I don't want you to feel awkward around me. I know you're straight, and I would never try to take you to a club like that again. We still gotta work together, and I don't want that to affect our work relationship. Feel me?" I did feel where she was coming from. One thing I was about was getting money. I already had no intentions of letting that one little event affect our work relationship.

"Nah, I know. I know." I said, reassuringly.

"Okay, 'cause you know we still gotta be ready to double team 'em when I pull in them big dollar clients, right?" She said with a big grin.

I sucked my teeth before answering while returning the smile, "you already know!"

"Alright! Well I'm bout to get outta here, but I'm sorry about your moms too … for real. If you need to talk, forget about all that other stuff. You know my number. I mean that."

I rolled my eyes, "Thanks, I appreciate that. I'm good though. See you later."

"Okay, don't just be saying okay! You working tomorrow?" She asked.

"I'm not sure yet. Ronnie said he might want me to work Sunday since we lost Princess."

"Ain't nobody *lose* Princess. That bitch got fired!" She hollered out as she held her head back in laughter. I laughed too and shook my head. "Alright then, later, Angie." She said as she waved, walking away.

When I got home, I felt antsy. I didn't know why I was so nervous about calling Cal, but I was. The fear of the unknown was overwhelming. I wasn't sure how he would respond to me calling. It was late, almost three thirty in the morning, but I didn't care. I needed to hear his voice. With everything I was going through, I needed him. I needed to know if he was needing me too. I wondered if he was even thinking of me, or if he had moved on already within that one week.

Men never seem to feel the hurt the way women do. A woman could fall to pieces, no sleeping, eating, plenty of crying after a breakup. With men, it was a different story. They were on to the next chick within forty-eight hours of a breakup, not a second thought. All these things ran through my mind as I searched for his name in my phone. *What if he's with a new girl right now?* I thought to myself.

I took a big gulp as my heart began to beat fast. To my surprise, he picked up right after the first ring, and he sounded wide awake, "Hello?" he said, calmly. I could hear music and other voices in the background. From what I could tell, it sounded like all men.

"Hey, what's up?" My voice shook as I tried not to sound as nervous as I was feeling.

"Chillin', what's up wit'chu?" He replied. I loved his raspy voice. He sounded like someone who had smoked ten packs of cigarettes every day since he was ten years old, but of course he hadn't.

"Nothing, I was just thinking about you. Do you know who this is?" I asked, hoping he did.

"Of course," he said after sucking his teeth as though he was insulted.

"Who is it then?" I asked playfully.

"It's my wife!" I could feel his smile through the phone, and the butterflies in my stomach fluttered.

It was my turn to suck my teeth, "So I'm still your wife, huh?"

"Hell yeah! Why wouldn't you be?" he said in that way only he could say it in.

"You know why! I haven't talked to you in a whole week. You haven't called or anything." I wanted to know if he was still really mine.

"Yeah I know. That's cause I was just waiting for you, waiting for you to cool your hot ass down. You already know I don't deal with drama." He said, sternly.

"Yeah, I might've spazzed a little, but—"

"*Spazzed a lil'*? How bout you spazzed A LOT! Damn near ran over my foot!" He said, cutting me off. I started to laugh when he said that. "It ain't funny! You gotta learn how to talk instead of blackin' all the time babe … for real." He sounded like a father scolding their child.

"Well, I'm sorry, but you know why I did it."

"Nah, babe that was some dumb shit! Why would I even have you drop me off at my daughter mother's house if I was creeping with her? That don't even make no sense!" He sounded annoyed at the idea. I guess he did have a point, but I still wasn't satisfied.

"Well, you the one that left your charger there. What you expect me to think?"

"Man, I didn't even leave my charger there. I told you that shit already!" He said, starting to get mad all over again.

"Well, where was it then?" I challenged him.

"I DON'T FUCKING KNOW! I never even found it! Had to go buy a new one, Ms. Know-it-all!" I paused for a minute trying to decide if I believed him or not.

"Mm hmm, well whatever. Just don't let it happen again. Where you at?" I asked, changing the subject.

"I'm in New York. Had to take care of some business out here. Why?" he asked sarcastically.

"Just asking …"

"I'll be back tomorrow though. I'ma have my man drop me off there, okay?" I was happy to hear him say that. I couldn't wait to see him.

"Alright … what time?" I asked, knowing he wouldn't have an answer.

"I don't know yet. Just stay by your phone."

"Well, I wanna know because I gotta go back down to the police station tomorrow." I let him know.

"Oh yeah, what's going on with that?" he asked as though he had totally forgotten that I was ever attacked.

"Things are not so good, but I'll fill you in tomorrow."

"Alright, well I'll hit you tomorrow and see where you at."

"Okay," I replied. We said bye and hung up. I wanted to tell him that I loved him, but I didn't want to sound like a sucker. Plus I knew he was around his boys and didn't want him to have to be mushy. Although, I knew he wouldn't have cared who was around. That's just the kind of man he was.

I went to bed feeling good that night. I felt relieved to know that Cal still wanted me. I had mixed feelings about the fact that I was so happy to have him back in my life when I was the one who felt like *he* fucked up in the first place. It didn't matter at that time. I decided that I would start on a clean slate. I would be more trusting and try to control my emotions. I really wanted us to work. However, I knew it had been a week, and he was fresh out of jail. I wondered how many women he had slept with within that week and who they were. I planned to ask him when I saw him the next day too. Even with those thoughts, I still went to bed floating on a cloud. I was so in love and I was loving it.

CHAPTER 22

The next morning I wondered if I should've called Detective Ramsey before going to the station. I decided against it. I had a feeling he would just give me the run around if I called on the phone. I would just show up bright and early. If he wasn't there, I would ask for the other detective, Officer Green, or I'd just wait. I just hoped that I wouldn't run into Rock. I couldn't go through that again. I didn't know how I would react this time.

Once again, the police station was busy with everyone hustling and bustling about. After doing a quick scan of the room sure that I didn't see Detective Ramsey or Rock, I approached what appeared to be the front desk. Sitting behind it was a Hispanic lady, Puerto Rican maybe, on the phone. Her desk was covered with stacks and stacks of papers and manila folders. She looked like she was in her fifties but stuck in the eighties wearing a shiny, red, satin blouse. She wore a big fake pearl necklace and matching stud earrings. She wore plenty of rose blush, blue eye shadow, and bright red lipstick with black lip liner. Her hair was clipped up in the back in sort of an up-doo, but it was still big like she might've had a perm put in. I tried not to focus on it, but I couldn't help but notice the huge black mole hanging from her chin. I wondered if she had ever gotten it caught on anything.

I blinked hard as my eyes began to water from the smell of her strong perfume. Holding the phone with her ear to her shoulder, she used one hand to sift through some papers. "Uh huh, uh huh. I have it right here. Let me take a look in the system, and I'll give you a call back … uh huh, uh huh I understand, but …" she spoke as she held one finger up to me. Then she mouthed the words to me, "one minute," as she rolled her eyes at whoever wouldn't let her off the phone. I nodded patiently and took a step back as I waited, looking around the precinct.

There were about four other people sitting on the benches in the waiting area. I watched as two officers brought in a man who could only be described as homeless. One officer held him by the middle of the cuffs that were around the man's hands in the back. The other officer held him by the side of the arm guiding him towards the back of the station where I assume the holding cells must've been. The man didn't seem to be resisting arrest at this time, but he was babbling out loud to everyone: "JESUS IS THE SAVIOR, BUT Y'ALL DON'T KNOW! Y'ALL DON'T KNOW SHIT! DEVILS! NO DEVILS ALLOWED, BUT Y'ALL DON'T KNOW!" He alternated back and forth, babbling to himself as he twitched his head then broadcasting aloud to everyone.

My phone started to ring just as the lady behind the desk was ready for me. I looked at the phone, surprised Cal was calling so early. I silenced the ringer and didn't answer it.

"What'chu need, honey?" she asked in a sincere voice.

"Hi, I'm looking for Detective Ramsey."

"Okay, what's your name and what is this in reference to?"

"My name is Angela Delimar, and he's working on my open rape case." I said as I hushed my voice. I didn't want everyone looking at me knowing that I had been raped.

She seemed unaffected by what I had just said, but I guess she was so use to dealing with these types of cases. It was probably just business as usual for her. "Okay," she replied as she picked up the phone and dialed. "Hi, Ramsey, there's an Angela Delimo here to see you about her case."

"Deli-*mar*" I corrected her, but she didn't care.

"Uh huh, okay … bye bye now," she said, hanging up. "You can have a seat. He said he'll be right out to see you."

"Okay, thanks." I replied.

I took a seat on one of the benches next to a boy wearing headphones. He looked like a skateboarder and was deep into his world of music as he tapped along with his hands on his thighs. After sitting there for ten minutes, I figured it was as good of time as any to call Cal back.

"Hey what's up?" he answered.

"Hey, where you at?" I asked, wasting no time.

"Shit, I'm just over here at my cousin's crib. You home?"

"No, I'm here at the police station waiting to see the detective working on my case."

"Oh, why you ain't answer the phone when I just called you a little while ago?" He asked suspiciously.

"Because I was in the middle of talking to this lady here. You still coming over later?"

He paused for a minute before answering. Once he started talking I could tell it was to take a pull, probably from a blunt, "Yeah, what time you gonna be home? Better yet, just come pick me up when you done!" He instructed slowly.

"You high, ain't you?" I whispered, giggling.

"Hellll yeah!" He said, laughing back.

"Alright, well I'll hit you when I get outta here." I replied, and then we hung up.

As I sat people watching, I wished I had brought headphones like the skateboard kid or a book or magazine or something. The more I waited, the more impatient I got. My leg bounced up and down in anticipation. After sitting for an hour and watching three of the four people waiting do what they came to do and leave, I decided it was time for me to see what the hold up was.

"Excuse me," I said softly to the lady behind the desk. She looked up as though surprised to see me still there.

"Who were you waiting to see? Ramsey?"

"Yes, I was just wondering if he was going to come out to see me any time soon?" I was trying not to sound like I had an attitude.

"Hold on, let me call him again and see what's going on. What's the name again, baby?"

"Angela Del-i-mar" I responded, putting emphasis on the last name so she'd get it right this time.

"Okay," she said as she dialed. "Hiiiii, Detective, it's Maria again. Miss Delimar is still waiting—" It sounded as though she had been cut off. "Okay … oooh … well, what should I tell her?" she asked as she waited for a response before hanging up.

"Detective Ramsey said he had an unexpected meeting, and it's

still going to be a while. He suggested you come back another day."
She said. I knew in my heart there probably was no meeting, and he
probably had no intention of seeing me in the first place.

"Well, did he say when is a good time for me to come back?" I
asked.

"No, I'm sorry. You might want to just give him a call before you
come down, so you can be sure he'll be here." She suggested. I knew
that wouldn't make a difference if he was avoiding me.

"Well, is Detective Green available?" I asked.

"Detective Green?" she responded quizzically.

"Yes, from my understanding they are both assigned to the case. I
was originally told I could talk to either one of them."

"Okay, hold on let me check." She picked up the phone another
time. We waited in silence until she shook her head before hanging
up. "I got his voicemail. He's going to be on vacation for two
weeks." She explained.

"Well, who is *their* boss?" I asked, growing impatient.

"Well, that would be Captain Arnoldi, but he's not going to see
you." She said matter-of-factly.

"Well, I need to talk to someone about my case today. Detective
Ramsey told me a week ago that he would be in touch, and I haven't
heard anything since."

"I understand. He's probably just got a lot of cases pending right
now that he's working on. Captain Arnoldi is only going to tell you to
talk to Detective Ramsey first. Your best bet is to just come back
another day and call before you come." She said.

Feeling discouraged, I grunted out a "thanks" and walked out of
the precinct.

This time there were no tears, only anger. My breathing was hard,
loud, and forcefully blasting through my nostrils. My jaw was locked
and teeth clenched in frustration. I didn't know what I was going to
do. I thought about hiring a lawyer, but who had money for that? I
knew what would relax me. I wanted to smoke some trees. I needed
to zone out for a while.

I called Cal and let him know I was done, and to have some trees
ready for me. He kept asking me what was wrong over the phone,
but I wouldn't tell him. I assured him I'd tell him in person. I threw
in an old Sade CD to try to relax my mind and mood on the drive to
pick up Cal. I wondered when he would be able to get a car. I wasn't

really feeling the fact that I had to drive all the time, but at this time it didn't matter. I just wanted to see him.

As cold as it was, I pulled up to see Cal, his cousin, and two other guys sitting on the front steps. He nodded towards the car to let me know he saw me, said a few more things to his cousin and friends, and then rose up to leave. Once he was in the car, I couldn't contain my smile. I grinned up at him, but didn't say anything. "What's up?" he said smiling back. "Come here." He leaned in for a kiss. He reeked of weed, but I could smell a butterscotch candy in his mouth through the stench.

During the drive back to my apartment, I filled Cal in on all the details. He seemed to be getting more and more furious the more I told him. By the time we had made it into my apartment, he looked like how I had felt moments ago when I left the police station. After I was finished telling him everything, he took two long pulls from the blunt he had rolled and breathed smoke out through his nose before he said anything.

"So you know the dude that did it?" he asked calmly. His voice was calm and steady, but his squinted, red eyes and flared nostrils said otherwise.

"Yeah ... matter of fact, you remember that night you called me and they were investigating next door? I told you I knew one of the officers from the gym?" I asked, jogging his memory.

"Yeah ..." he answered.

"It was him." I said, quietly looking down. I pinched the blunt from his hands between my fingers and took one pull, breathing in deep. I exhaled and continued, "I didn't know at first it was him, but when I saw him in the police station, I was sure! I know it was him, babe." I took another pull and held my breath as I passed it back to him.

"The dude that's been trying to holler at you?"

"Yeah, he was always trying to talk to me, but I kept telling him I had a boyfriend." I explained like a child in trouble. Cal's calmness and silence was starting to scare me. I hadn't seen this side of him before.

I felt myself getting wavy as I watched the smoke twist and turn about the room. I felt glued to the couch. It took everything in me to turn my head to face Cal, and when I did, I felt like I was turning in slow motion. "I just don't understand why the detective doesn't believe me or if he does, he's not doing anything about it." I complained.

"Man, fuck them cracker ass pigs! I already told you, you can't trust no crackers! So this dude's name is Rock?" He asked.

"Yeah, I'm not sure what his real name is. I only know his last name is Johnson." He sucked his teeth as he shot his eyes at me out the corner of his sockets like I was making up the name. "That's his name!" I said convincingly with my eyebrows raised.

"Which station did you have to go to? The one on Main?"

"No, it was the one on Central and First." I told him.

He leaned back staring ahead deep in thought. "Alright …" was all he said and that was the end of that conversation. "Come here," he said softly as he squeezed my thigh. I hesitated for a moment, then snuggled up to him on the couch. He put his arm around me and looked me deep in my eyes. He waited a few seconds before saying "You know I love you, right?" This time his serious face matched his serious tone.

I tried to answer, but my voice got caught in my throat. I coughed to clear it gazing back into his brown eyes, "I do."

With his fingers pressed behind my neck and thumb placed gently against my jaw, he pulled my face close to his still holding my gaze. Finally he closed his eyes and pressed his lips against mine. I closed my eyes too and gave a gentle peck. We both opened our eyes, and as though we had spoken to each other through telepathy, we both closed them again and our lips met with much more force this time. Unleashing our tongues at the same instant, we explored each other's mouths passionately.

I grabbed his bicep and squeezed, feeling his muscle. He let go of my neck and ran his hand down the front of my shirt lightly stopping at my readily perky nipple, rubbing back and forth against it with his thumb with such ease, before he grabbed the whole breast and squeezed. Then he made his way to the other one and followed the same pattern. Both nipples were at attention, ready to come straight through my bra and shirt. I guess they were talking to him too. He let go and grabbed me around the waist with both arms, guiding me to his lap where I now sat facing him. He pulled my shirt up over my head. My girls were already popping out the top of my bra, so he complied and pulled my bra down to release them right in his face.

He licked slowly and gently, back and forth as he looked up into my eyes. His hands were pushing my waist down, so I was sitting on top of something nice and hard. Now he moved my waist back and forth as I started to grind. I felt my juices start to flow like crazy inside my panties. I was glad I didn't wear jeans that day, but jogging pants. It made it easy for me to feel him and him to feel me. It also made it easy for access as he slipped both hands down the back of my pants, squeezing and rubbing my ass. Then he took one hand and stuck it inside my panties, searching for my pool of wetness from behind. He found it and let out, "damn you wet, baby," as he slid his fingers back and forth. He stuck one finger in, and he was ready.

All in one motion, he pulled his hands out of my pants, stood and lifted me. I wrapped my legs around his waist. He went back to kissing me deeply as I held on during this frontward piggyback ride to my bedroom. He placed me down gently on the bed then stepped back and stripped slowly down to nothing but his boxers. I could see he was hard as a rock as his dick protruded through them. It turned me on more, so much more that I couldn't help but touch myself as I eyed it. I stuck my hands in my own pants and rubbed, feeling my own wetness as he watched.

"Yeah, do that shit," he said. He pulled my pants off slowly and my panties followed soon after. All the lights were on just how I liked it, and he wasted no time. He went straight for the main course. Kissing the inside of my thighs first, he spread my lips apart and licked around in circles on the tip of my clit. I watched for a while then let my head fall back as I felt a puddle forming beneath me as my juices flowed. I let out a soft moan as he stuck his finger back inside me, in and out, as he continued to lick in circles. He knew how to do it just right too, none of that insane, over the top, face burrowing or rough jabbing with the fingers.

Right when I was about to explode, he got up and smiled mischievously to let me know he had stopped on purpose. After scooting out of his boxers, he laid next to me and said, "come here" as he guided me into the sixty-nine position. He went right back to his task, licking and fingering me as I started on the other end. I kissed his stomach as I rubbed on his penis softly, stopping to massage his perfectly proportioned nuts every now and then. Then I went to work myself, kissing the tip lightly then sucking on it gently, just enough to drive him crazy. I could taste the pre-cum. I spit it back out on his dick then went all the way down with one deep stroke to the mouth. He let out a groan and slapped my ass. Taking that as a job well done, I continued sucking and slurping up and down until we were both ready to get to the business.

Cal grabbed a condom out of the nightstand drawer and instructed me to put it on. I did as told and squeezed his penis as I rolled the condom on. Still in the sixty-nine position, he lifted one leg to let himself out and gave me a little nudge forward "move up, but stay just like that," he said as I was bent over doggy style. Now positioned behind me, he rubbed my clit some more from behind, smacked my ass a few more times watching it jiggle before he tried to penetrate.

He approached gently, but it didn't matter. The physical trauma was gone, but the mental images were still there. As soon as I felt the tip of his penis, Rock's face flashed in my head clear as day. "Stop! I can't!" I said as I scurried away to the corner of the bed.

He sucked his teeth in frustration "WHAT THE FUCK, ANGIE!" he said, clearly angered by this. His outburst startled me like a baby, and I began to cry grabbing all my clothes from the floor and getting dressed in a hurry.

He stood watching me for a moment in confusion and anger then sat down on the edge of the bed. He breathed in deeply with his face in his palms. "Angie … what are you doing? Come here." He said it more calmly but still in a disappointed voice this time. I continued getting dressed. I stopped stiffly when I was done.

"I'm sorry, Cal. You know I wouldn't do this on purpose." I said with a tear stained face.

"I know. I know, but what's wrong? It seemed like you were all good then all of a sudden …" his voice trailed as he got up to put his boxers back on.

I stood frozen in the corner of the room. "I wanted to. It's just every time I … I just …" I couldn't finish my sentence. I didn't know how to put what I felt into words. He walked over and hugged me then took me by the hand and led me back to the bed.

"Come here. We don't have to do anything. I just wanna feel you next to me. Talk to me." He said, trying to comfort me.

"I'm sorry for giving you blue balls." He laughed even though I was genuinely apologetic.

"You didn't give me blue balls, silly." He said as he cuddled up to me from behind and kissed me on my neck.

"It's just every time we try to have sex, my mind automatically goes to the rape. I just see Rock's face in that ski mask, and I feel like I'm about to get raped by him all over again." I explained.

"Well, I would never hurt you or try to make you do anything that you don't wanna do. You know that, right?"

"I know, and I want to make you happy, but—"

"Sex is not the only thing that makes a man happy, Angie," he said, cutting me off. I sighed, turned and smiled at him shyly. "I'm for real. You need to know that. I'm not with you for sex. I'm with you for *you* because I love the shit outta you." He said in a serious tone. I laughed every time he said that, but I knew what he meant. He continued, "Yeah, sex plays a part in a relationship, but we'll get there. You just need some more time, and I understand that." He assured me.

"Thanks for understanding, babe."

"Why wouldn't I? And you don't need to be worrying 'bout that Rock no more. That's gonna get taken care of ... you hear me?" He asked sternly.

"Yeah."

We spent the rest of the afternoon talking, lounging, eating, and watching TV. It was great, and just how I hoped we'd be. Even though I was use to working Friday and Saturdays, I was happy to have that Saturday off, so I could spend more time with Cal. I cooked us a big brunch, cheese omelets, turkey ham, beef bacon, home fries, and French toast. We napped as late as we wanted, straight into evening, but eventually got up.

I showered first and got dressed. Relaxing in the living room while I waited for him to shower, I watched TV. "BABY!" he yelled from the bedroom.

"WASSUP?" I yelled back.

"Where you put my clothes?" He was walking towards the living room with a green towel wrapped around his waist. I stared at the few curls of hair on his chest as he got closer. I had completely forgotten that I returned all the clothes.

"Ummm ... okay don't get mad." I said as he stood there patiently waiting for me to explain with an expression of confusion. I continued, "You know how mad I can get, and I thought we were done, sooooo what had happened was ... I kinda took all the stuff back to the stores." I was surprised that he didn't get mad. He simply dropped his head and shook it back and forth.

His famous words, "come here," left his lips with a smirk. Feeling like a midget standing up to him, he pulled my arms around his waist and kissed my forehead. "What am I gonna do with you?" he said.

He put on his outfit from the previous day, and I took him to his cousin's house to get fresh clothes. We chilled there for a few hours, trying to decide what to do next. Evening was setting in and the night was still young. His cousin, Max, suggested we tag along with him, his girlfriend, Tiana, and some other people to a bar down the street. It was their hangout spot, and they all spent most Saturday nights there.

Chinks was a hole in the wall bar smack dab in the middle of the hood. There were two small rooms, and they both smelled funky as soon as we hit the door. Cal seemed to know everyone there, stopping to give dap to everyone who spoke to him. I felt out of place being there, but the music was bumping and I didn't care as long as I was with him. There was a pool table cramped in the back of the first room behind the bar. After getting some drinks, we all headed back there. I had my usual Grey Goose and cranberry. It was super strong. I didn't want to look like a lightweight in front of everyone, though, so I drank it down fast.

I sipped on my second one while Tiana and I sat on some high stools watching the guys shoot pool. When the DJ started bumping some classic club music, she grabbed my hand, "Come on! Stop being shy. I see you over there bouncing, Angie!" I glanced over at Cal who smiled back at me, then followed Tiana to the next room. It was even more packed in the second room. It served as the dance area even though there was no actual dance floor. People were just dancing wherever they found room. We squeezed right on in the middle as the speakers blasted "DEEP DEEP INSIDE! DEEP DEEP DOWN INSIDE!" I loved club music. It didn't matter whether it was old or new.

I held my drink in the air as I did my smooth two-step. Bouncing up and down, the vibrations from the bass felt good. Good music has a way to make everything right. I danced until I sweat. I didn't think about Rock, the rape, my mother's death, Rainy, or anything. It was just the music and me. By the time I finished my second drink, I was feeling it. My eyes were closed, but shot open when I heard Tiana in my face screaming my name. Once she had my attention, she motioned for me to follow her back to the other room.

We stopped at the bar on the way. "Girl, you was feelin' it, huh?" she said, grinning while she bounced and snapped her fingers.

"That was my shit!" I said, feeling more relaxed than when we first got there.

"Have a shot with me!" she yelled over the music.

I waved my hand shaking my head, "I don't know. I'm already feeling tipsy. I'm a lightweight, girl!"

"Girl, you good! Your man is here. We got you! Come on!" She leaned over the bar to get the bartender's attention. "Let me get a shot of Henny and ... what you want a shot of Angie?"

"Okay, Grey Goose." I said, giving in. We tapped cheers and Tiana threw hers back while I struggled, trying to drink mine down quickly. My throat burned and my eyes watered. It went straight to my stomach. By the time we made it back to the pool table, Cal was sitting on a stool waiting for another game, but he wasn't alone.

There was a woman standing in his face talking in his ear. She was tall, brown skin, sported a short texturized hair cut, and her frame was filled out. She wore tight, bright pink and green spandex leggings with stilettoes and a low cut tank top. You could see right through her leggings too. I wondered who she was and why she was talking to Cal. As Cal spotted Tiana and me making our way back over, he said something to the woman who looked in our direction and walked off.

Cal smiled at me as I approached, but all smiles were gone on my part. I didn't want to make a scene or ruin our evening, but I definitely wanted to know who that chick was. Cracking his legs open he pulled me into a spot to stand between them. I was swaying left to right, but I wasn't exactly sure if it was from the music or the drinks. I felt like the room was wavering a bit, but I held it together.

"Who was that?" I yelled in his ear.

"Huh?" I don't know if he really didn't hear me or was pretending not to hear to buy time.

I repeated the question, "Who was that chick you was talking to?"

"Oh, that was Rhonda, just some chick I used to mess with way back in the day in high school." He replied, waving it off like it was nothing.

"Oh, well y'all certainly looked pretty friendly and cozy."

"Angie, don't start. I haven't seen none of these people in a minute. You forget I was locked up. She was just saying what's up. That's all!" He said, trying to remain calm.

I decided to drop it for the moment and let it go. "Mmmm hmmm. Okay, if you say so." I said it with a raised eyebrow and a smirk to lighten the tension, but I was serious at the same time.

I was relieved to sit down when Cal's turn was up again. All of a sudden, I had an urge to pee really bad. Liquor has a way of doing that. Once I was in the tiny stall of the already tiny bathroom, I squatted and released for what seemed like an eternity. I don't know why, but long pees always seem like the best pees. I felt at ease again, but by the time I made it back to the stool, I had to go again. This went on for the next hour, taking trips back and forth to the bathroom. Each time, I had to regain my courage to get up and walk knowing I was probably staggering.

I knew I should've stopped drinking by that point. I don't know why I had the fourth Grey Goose and cranberry, probably because Cal insisted. I guess I was trying to prove that I could hang or something. I was done after that. We walked outside to leave and everything was spinning. I could barely walk straight holding on to Cal's arm for support. I held it together long enough to make it back to Max's house. Once we were there, I whispered to Cal "You gon' have to drive us home. I'm sooo fucked up right now." He looked down at me and shook his head with a smirk.

I was nervous with him driving home because his license was suspended, but I was definitely in no position to drive. He did the speed limits the entire way. If we got pulled over, he would've went back to jail so fast. I felt bad putting him in that position, but all I could think about at the moment was how drunk I was and how bad I had to pee again. I squirmed around in the passenger seat bouncing my legs. I think my squirming made him even more nervous driving.

Nevertheless, we made it to my place safely. I couldn't wait to get up to the steps. I ran to the bathroom and plopped down on the toilet seat, happy I didn't have to squat this time. I exhaled loudly and sat there for a few minutes when I was done. Finally, I stood up and washed my hands. The small room started to spin again. I felt myself sway back and forth with no control. Out of nowhere, PLANK! I fell flat on my ass on the floor with my back against the bathroom door. I laughed to myself out loud as Cal yelled through the door, "You alright?"

I responded through my laughter "Help! I've fallen, and I can't get up!"

He sucked his teeth first then said, "Move!" I inched up so he could get the door open enough to squeeze through.

He reached down grabbing me by both arms to lift me to my feet. I was drunk as a skunk, but I wasn't embarrassed yet. I didn't get embarrassed until the next phase. After walking me to the bedroom, Cal undressed me and put my pajamas on me. He instructed me to go to bed, but the rumbling in my stomach wouldn't allow me. I sat on the edge of the bed, leaned over. Shutting my eyelids made it all worse. Now, not only was the blackness spinning, but I felt like I was on a rollercoaster, and the drop was coming fast. Jumping to my feet, I bolted back to the bathroom slamming the door behind me. Clear liquid along with all the food I had eaten that day spewed out of my mouth into the toilet, splashing up on the toilet seat. I heaved until there was no more. I brushed my teeth and rinsed out my mouth the best I could, thinking it was over.

Little did I know, I made it back to the bed to lie down, and that just made it worse. Before Cal could even hit the lights, I was sitting back up on the edge of the bed with my elbows leaning on the dresser that sat alongside of it. No words necessary, he already knew what was coming and grabbed the little trashcan I kept in my room, placing it in front of me between my feet. My head rose and slammed back down on the edge of the dresser as dry heaves of green spit exited my mouth and entered the trash. My head rose again and slammed down on the edge of the dresser. One time, two times, three times, four until I lost count.

I felt a little better after the second round, but something in me knew it wasn't over still. So I stayed sitting frozen in the same spot, leaned over, head down. I felt Cal's warm touch rub my back. "You good now?" he asked, sounding sleepy. I could tell he was ready to snooze, but he took care of me instead. I shook my head and stayed put. He left and returned with a glass of water. "Here sip on this, little sips," he instructed. I did as told as he got on the bed and straddled behind me with each of his legs on the outside of mine. He continued rubbing my back as I sipped.

Round three was approaching, but this time I expected it, so I was ready. Nothing really came up this time, yet my body still went through the same motions jerking forward and heaving up air. My head continued to slam into the dresser, but I felt nothing but my stomach being squeezed like a lemon until every drop was out. In between one of the heaves, a fart slipped out loudly right on poor Cal. That's when the embarrassment really rushed in. "I'm so sorry!" I said with my head down, but too sick to move.

He didn't move either. Instead, he just rolled his eyes, continued to rub my back and said, "It's okay." At some point I finally made it in the bed and was able to stay asleep. Cal stayed up a little longer than me; I guess to make sure that I was really done this time. I only remember him whispering in my ear "Babe, I'm putting the trashcan right here next to you in case you gotta throw up again, okay?" I don't even remember if I answered back or nodded or what.

The next morning I awoke to a massive headache and the grumbling of my stomach. I was super hunger, but as soon as I tried to lift my head from the pillow it throbbed instantly. I let out a groan and Cal appeared from the living room. "You finally up?" he asked, looking at me like he had been waiting on me to do something.

I sat up slowly, "yeah, my head is killing me."

"You got some Tylenol or something to take?"

"Yeah, but I don't wanna take it on an empty stomach."

"Well, I need you to take me back over to my cousin's anyway, so let's grab something to eat on the way." He said.

"What time is it?" I asked, not wanting to move.

"Two fifteen."

"Damn, I don't feel like going to work tonight! I gotta be there earlier tonight too!" I said, wiping cold out my eyes.

"What time you gotta be there?"

"Six, but I guess I got a little time ... You know I gotta take a shower first, right?" I said in question form but it was more of a notification.

It was his turn to let out a groan of impatience this time, "hurry up," he said.

"Alright."

I took a fast shower as I tried to ignore the grumbling in my stomach that was growing stronger and stronger by the minute. Fully dressed, I met Cal in the living room. I rubbed my forehead "I'm ready ... damn why is my forehead hurting so much? Like right in the middle?" I asked out loud, but was more wondering to myself.

Cal snickered before answering, "You don't remember?"

"Remember what?"

"You kept banging your big ass head on the dresser last night when you was throwing up!" I paused for a moment slowly recalling the events

"Oh shoot, that's right! Yo, my bad last night. I did not mean to get pissy like that. For real, I usually don't drink like that but those drinks were strong."

"Yeah, you really shouldn't. You were a mess! Farted on me n' shit." He replied looking at me with a scowl. As soon as those words rushed out of his mouth, blood rushed to my face. Embarrassed wouldn't even describe how ashamed I felt.

I laughed nervously, "Oh my God. I'm soooo sorry ... damn I'm embarrassed. You took good care of me too."

"Don't be embarrassed, baby. Now let's go." He said as he rose from his seat on the couch and kissed my forehead.

CHAPTER 23

After stopping at a chicken shack to get something to eat, I dropped Cal at his cousin's house. I only had enough time to run back home, change, and go to work. I was in a rush to get to work so I didn't even notice the small note attached to my windshield until I started driving. It was too far for me to reach from inside the car, but it was securely positioned under the wiper. Once I found a parking space, I couldn't wait to pull the yellow post-it note from my windshield. There was only one line written in blue ink on it: *"If you know what's good for you, you'll stay away from the police station."*

I called Cal in a panic as soon as I read it. It took a few minutes for him to calm me down. He told me to go to work and not to worry about it. He kept saying he was going to take care of it. I didn't know what he could do, but I followed his instructions and went on in to work. I was going through the motions of working, but my mind stayed on the note all night long. I couldn't believe Rock had been bold enough to return to the scene of his own crime. I wondered what he meant by, "If you know what's good for you ..." Was it a threat of another attack? My eyes darted about the dimly lit club all night in fear.

Apparently, the crowd was thinner on Sundays. My tip jar wasn't even halfway full by the time the night was more than halfway over. It was a different crowd than Friday and Saturday too, calmer. There were more couples. That probably had a lot to do with my low tips as well. Men were less inclined to chat with me when they were with their women. The crowd was thin enough for me to spot a familiar face huddled in the far corner nearest to the door. Finally, she had resurfaced. It was Rainy.

She looked directly at me and watched me work. I wondered how long she had been watching me. I stared back at her, but she didn't seem scared off this time. She remained seated calmly in her corner all alone sipping on her drink. The club was dim, but the booth where she sat had a red light right above it, almost like a spotlight was shining directly on her. She was dressed differently this time, no ninja suit. It was the first time she didn't have that hoodie tied around her face. Her hair was just past her earlobes, cut in sort of a bob. It framed her round face nicely. I hadn't noticed how beautiful her eyes were before, big and bright. She was studying me, and I was studying her.

There was only one other bartender working with me, Keisha. "Hey Keisha, I'll be right back, okay?" I called over to her.

"Alright," she replied over her shoulder while she washed glasses out in the sink. I walked slowly towards the direction of Rainy's table. To my surprise, this time she didn't run off. She stayed put as though she was waiting for me.

Before I could make it there, Ronnie appeared out of nowhere, right in my face. He was so old school: tall, dark, heavy with a potbelly, and dressed in a burgundy Adidas tracksuit. He had on matching white and burgundy Adidas sneakers. He wore a burgundy Kangol hat that sat on a head full of cornrows. A small gold cross hung from his ear. He wore a thick gold chain around his neck, a gold watch, and had a matching gold tooth in the front of his mouth.

He wasn't alone either. "Angela, the girls told me you were at IHOP the other week when my brother-in-law got shot. This here is my sister, Carla." He said loudly over the music. Spit flew out of his mouth when he spoke. I looked in the face of the same woman who had begged for my help at the IHOP.

I gave a sheepish half smile, "Hi, I'm so sorry for your loss."

Her response was a cold stare followed by a slow, "thanks."

"If there's anything that you saw or heard, it would really help us out. Did you see anything?" Ronnie asked.

I looked at Ronnie, then to Carla, then back to Ronnie as I shifted in my stance. I hesitated before answering, "Uh ... no I didn't really see anything. It happened so fast." I said, trying to glance over their shoulders at Rainy's table. Carla's eyes were cold as ice as they seemed to penetrate right through me.

"Even if you only got a glance at whoever did this or anything, it would really help us out a lot, Angela. You sure you didn't see *nothing?*" he asked again.

"Sorry, Ronnie. You know if I did, I would tell you. I just dropped to the floor when I heard the shots." I said, telling the partial truth.

"Alright, baby girl," his voice boomed as he guided his sister to the back of the club. She turned and gave me one last glare on her way.

I turned my attention back to Rainy's table, but she was gone once again. I spun around in all directions looking for her. I ran to the door and swung it open, looking up and down the street. There was no sign of her. I hurried back inside and went to check the bathroom. She wasn't there either. I didn't understand it. I thought for sure I would be able to confront her this time. My heart sank at my missed opportunity.

The rest of the night dragged along as I kept hoping Rainy would return to her table, but she never did. I didn't want to go home alone that night, but Cal said he had some business to take care of. Part of me wondered if he was really with his daughter's mother or another woman. When I got home, I counted my tips: a measly eighty-two bucks. I hoped Ronnie wasn't planning on having me work Sundays regularly now that Princess was gone.

After changing my clothes and having some Ramen noodles for dinner, I turned on the TV in my room and lay in bed. I set my alarm for the next morning. I didn't want to go to work, but I knew I had to. I only had a few hours to get some rest, but I couldn't fall asleep. Feelings of guilt, fright, loneliness, and wonder crept through me one by one. I tried to justify my guilt about lying to Ronnie and his sister by telling myself that I really didn't know who had done the shooting. Sure, I saw one of the guys' faces, but it wasn't like I actually knew who he was. I had to protect myself too. I didn't want to talk and have them coming after me next. I wouldn't be of much help anyway. I only got a glance of the guy's face.

I kept hearing noises outside all night and kept waking up to look out the window. I was convinced Rock was watching me some how some way. I thought about calling in to work and telling my boss I would be in late, so I could go back to the police station. I knew I wouldn't be at ease until Rock was locked away. But what would going back to the station do? It was clear Detective Ramsey had no intentions of pursuing Rock as the rapist he was.

I tried to push the thoughts of Rock out of my mind only to have thoughts of my mother replace them. I thought about how much I missed my mom, and I thought about Rainy. I tried to rationalize her behavior. Why was she following me around but never trying to talk to me? Yet, she spent years writing letters to my mom trying to get in contact with me. How could she just drop me off at the hospital after saving my life and just split like that? None of it made sense to me. I had a feeling she disconnected her number on purpose too, and I didn't understand that either. It would seem like after all those years of trying to talk to me, she'd be happy to hear from me.

I lay staring up at the ceiling as I waited to fall asleep. Just after I drifted off, I heard a chirp. My eyes popped open as I waited for the sound again. *Chirp*. There it was again. I sat up trying to figure out what it was. My eyes fell on my smoke detector. I groaned, knowing that the chirping wouldn't stop until I changed the battery. I didn't even have the right size battery for it. I decided I would just take it out until I could buy one.

I turned on the light and returned from the kitchen with a chair to stand on. I twisted and jiggled the smoke detector until the case popped off. My nail broke trying to pop the battery out, but eventually I got it. The chirping stopped, but now my eyes fell on a tiny red light that was still lit. I looked closer and realized it was coming through an extremely small lens. I pulled on the lens with my fingertips until I yanked it out of the wall. I studied the lens closely until I figured out what it was, a tiny hidden camera.

I gasped and yanked hard on the wire trying to break the lens free. It was attached to a wire that ran into the wall. I couldn't get it, so I sprung to the kitchen to get scissors. I snipped the lens from the wire and the steady red light ceased. I couldn't tell where the wire ran to because it disappeared into the wall.

My mind went back to the day I found my lingerie out of place, hanging out of the drawer. I knew I wasn't crazy! I knew someone had been in my apartment, and whoever it was planted a camera in my smoke detector! I wondered how long the camera had been in the smoke detector and who put it there. I also wondered where they were watching it from. I thought about those nights I heard someone trying to come in through the front door. I wondered if it was Rock all along. None of this had started happening until he found out where I lived, but how could he get into my apartment unnoticed?

Management still hadn't sent anyone to change my locks after promising to do it immediately. I would make it a priority to call them first thing in the morning. I got no sleep that night as I stared up at the smoke detector feeling like someone was staring back at me. I knew the wire was cut, but I was still uneasy. I had no idea how many cameras were in the apartment or where else they might be planted.

CHAPTER 24

I was so happy for that Wednesday to come. I was finally going to have my awful bandage and stitches removed. I couldn't wait to get that thing off of my head. I was surprised that only a few people at work had asked me about it, at both B.I.G. Insurance and Ronnie's. I told everyone I was involved in a motorcycle accident. The story was I was riding on the back when someone cut my boyfriend off, and we flipped off. That was the best I could come up with. I didn't want anyone to know I had been raped.

I left work a little early to make the doctor's appointment. It worked out in my favor because after blasting out the apartment management, they sent someone out that day to change the locks and do a thorough inspection for other hidden cameras. I wanted to be home for both things. I trusted no one at this point.

I was going to my regular doctor for the follow-up. After removing the bandage and examining my head, he removed the stiches one by one. It hurt a little, and the doctor informed me it would leave a scar in my head. It didn't really matter since my hair would cover it anyway.

"So how has recovery been, Angela?" he asked.

"It's been okay. I'm just glad to finally get that thing off my head."

"Well, how have you been feeling emotionally?"

After taking a deep breath I answered with, "Well, it hasn't been easy to be honest."

"Did the doctors at the hospital refer you to a psychologist or therapist?" he asked.

"Yes ... but I haven't called." I confessed.

"Why not, Angela?" He asked, showing genuine concern.

I shrugged my shoulders and dropped my mouth open trying to think of a reason "... I don't know."

"I know it's hard making the first step to set an appointment, but I think it would really help for you to talk to someone, Angela." He scribbled something on a form and tore it off. "Here, this is a referral to a psychologist. She's really good. I'm going to tell the ladies at reception to give you her business card. I want you to make an appointment. You'd be surprised how much it helps to talk to someone about what you've gone through."

"Okay," I said to appease him, not knowing if I would actually make the appointment.

I really had no good reason why I hadn't seen someone yet. I don't know what was holding me back. I knew the doctor was probably right. I probably would feel better if I talked to someone, but for some reason I couldn't bring myself to make the appointment. Maybe I wasn't ready to talk about the rape yet.

I used the doctor's restroom before leaving. As I looked in the mirror running my fingers through my locks, I realized I hadn't had my hair done in weeks. I hadn't even realized or thought about it until now. It was time. I hadn't even thought about the fact that I would now need to find a new hairdresser. I decided then and there it would be a must do for that weekend. Maybe I would be able to find a shop that took walk-ins somewhere. I got the psychologist's card from the receptionist as instructed and tucked it in my wallet before leaving the doctor.

I went home and watched over the shoulders of the locksmith and the apartment inspectors. I watched their every move. The lock change was a quick job, and I was glad to have my new keys in hand. The inspector didn't find anymore cameras, but I wouldn't let him stop combing the apartment until I was satisfied that every nook and cranny had been covered. "Check that hole there!" "What about the shower head?" "The TV's?" I gave instructions to the inspector, and he patiently followed my orders. The wire that I cut the night before was traced to a laptop that sat in the attic of the apartment building. The inspector explained that whoever planted the camera probably was using remote access from another computer to watch me.

My stomach sank as I thought about all the things I did in the privacy of my own bedroom. I replayed the times Cal and I had attempted to have sex. I thought about all the conversations I had that I thought were in private. I felt ashamed and angry at the same time with no idea what to do next. I knew I could report it to the police, especially since I had the feeling it was probably Rock's doing. I knew no one would believe me, though. Even if they did, they probably wouldn't investigate it any further anyway.

That evening I picked Cal up and we headed to Red Lobster for dinner. At first, he complained about going there because he felt he wasn't dressed up enough. It was times like these that showed just how long he had been locked away. Even though I explained to him over and over on the way that nobody dressed up to go eat at Red Lobster anymore, he seemed more relaxed after we got there. I guess he saw he blended in just fine in his jeans, boots, and polo shirt.

Crab meat and juice splattered every which way as we went to work on our crab legs. We were both so hungry that the first fifteen minutes between us were silent as we devoured our delicious meals. Finally coming up for air, I took a sip of my pina colada. "So I think I'm gonna go back to the station on Saturday and demand to talk to that detective's boss." I said.

Cal dropped his fork in his plate as though my comment annoyed him. "Don't do that." He said, sternly looking into my eyes.

"Why?"

"Because I said so. That's why. Didn't I tell you that I'll take care of it?" he replied, inhaling deeply through flared nostrils.

"Yeah, but what do you mean you gonna take care of it? Take care of it how? Do you think you should really be going down to a police station? I would think you'd wanna stay as far away from there as possible." I replied with a little bit of attitude.

"See ain't nobody even say nothing about going to the damn police station! I said I'll take care of it and that should be enough." He was staring into my eyes.

I leaned back in my seat and crossed my arms. I had no idea how he intended to take care of it, but I hoped he wasn't going to do anything stupid that would send him back to jail. After a long silence, I replied "fine." I hesitated because I could tell he was agitated, "Do you know that I found a hidden camera in my damn bedroom?" He paused again with his fork midway to his mouth. "Yeah ... a camera,

Cal! I don't know how, but I have a feeling Rock got it in there some way."

"How you know it was a camera, and where you find it at?" he asked.

"I went to change the battery in my smoke alarm last night, and I found it inside of there. I'm sure it was a camera because there was a wire running into the wall. I cut it, but management had an inspector come and search the whole apartment today for any other cameras. He traced it to a laptop in the attic of the building. *That's how I know!*" I said defensively.

He chewed slowly in deep thought. "Look, just don't go back down to that station. I'm gonna take care of it, okay?"

I sighed as I wondered what was going through his head, "fine."

The rest of our meal was quiet. I felt like a child on punishment waiting for Cal to say something else. He didn't, and since I had to be up and out early for work the next morning, he had me drop him back off at his cousin's as usual.

The next morning at work, I ran into the pantry guy. "Good morning, lady," he smiled.

"Morning," was all I replied. I don't know why I was so offended by our previous conversation. Maybe the truth was that I was secretly disappointed he hadn't asked me out. He must've read my mind.

The next words out of his mouth were, "Listen, I'm sorry if I offended you the other day."

I pretended not to know what he was talking about. I brought my eyebrows down with a question mark expression, "What do you mean?"

"You know, when I was asking if you were single because I wanted to hook you up with my cousin?"

"Oh! Oh, please! I wasn't offended. I was trying to get out to beat the traffic. You know how Fridays are." I said, waving off the idea with my hand.

"Oh okay, good because I thought about it later like *I wonder if she was offended.*" He said through a chuckle. He continued, "I just asked because like I said I wanted to fix my cousin up with someone, and you're a successful, professional, cool, attractive woman, so I thought it would be a good match."

I smiled as I thought on the inside, "*yes!*" I said out loud to him,

"Well, thank you. It's all good though. I'm not offended ... and best of luck to your cousin."

"Yeah thanks ... So any updates on your complicated situation with your man?" he asked.

I thought it was a little nosey of him to ask, but I really didn't mind. "Well, it seems like it's always complicated, but at the moment we're back together and doing well."

"That's what's up."

There was an awkward pause until I thought of something to say, "Hey, where do you get your hair braided? I have to find someone new to do my hair."

"Oh, my sister's friend does it. She works out of her basement, but she does a real good job."

"Yeah, your hair always looks nice, and I'm far overdue to get mine done." I said, touching my hair.

"It looks fine to me, but I'll give you her number. What happened to your hairdresser?" He asked as he pulled his phone from his back pocket.

"Well, my mom used to do it so ..." I trailed off.

"Oh, I'm sorry," he said quickly as if he should've known.

"That's okay. I don't have my phone on me. Do you have a pen?" I asked, looking around for a napkin to write on.

"Nope, but I'll just stop by your desk later and give it to you."

"Okay, thanks a lot." I was truly grateful. Then someone came in asking where they could find extra cups for a conference. I took that as my cue to leave, and I waved a silent goodbye then walked back to my desk.

There was a smile painted on my face now. I felt satisfied to know pantry boy thought all those things about me. I don't know why I even cared when I already had a boyfriend. Aside from that, I would never date anyone from work. It was one of my rules. Still, I couldn't help but wonder what could be. He kept his word and stopped by my desk before leaving to give me the information. If I didn't know any better, I would've thought I was developing a small crush on him.

CHAPTER 25

I was happy to have my regular schedule at Ronnie's that weekend. Friday night was jumping as usual and tips were good. Cal even stopped by to see me for a little while. He sat at the bar, but that didn't stop the dancers from coming up to try to make their money. I wasn't mad because I knew they were just doing their job, but Cal swatted them all off like flies. Once everyone realized he was there to see me, they fell back. The other girls stared while I talked and laughed with him in between serving the other customers.

"So that's your mystery boyfriend?" Tee Tee asked as she nudged me by the sink.

I couldn't hold back my grin, "yep."

"I was starting to think you was making him up, girl! Cute ..." she teased.

I kept my grin in tack and boasted, "I know." We both laughed, and she went back to working the bar.

After promising he'd meet me back at my apartment later when I got off work, Cal waited for Wally to meet him there. Wally came in for a quick beer and they left. I never asked Cal about his business. I figured the less I knew, the better. I think he felt the same way. It was sort of an unspoken understanding we had. I had held him down and brought work in for him while he was locked up. My work was done now.

Shortly after he left, Jillian made her way over. "So that was your boyfriend?" she asked sounding a little jealous.

"Yeah, Tee Tee thought I was making him up." I chuckled.

"He's tall as hell! That's sexy though."

"Yeah," was all I replied.

"Why was you cock blocking? You could've let us make some money. You scared he might like what he sees here?" she asked.

"Please, wasn't nobody cock blockin' shit! He doesn't like strippers." I said proudly.

She held her head back and cackled like a wild hyena. "Girl if I had a dime for every time I heard that one…"

"Whatever, Jilli. Why do you care anyway? It's busy as hell in here tonight. I'm sure he wouldn't make you or break you." I said, getting tired of the conversation quickly.

"Yeah, you damn sure right about that!" she replied.

"Speaking of getting money, you just come over here to grill me 'bout my man or you gonna bring me some customers?" I asked.

"I know that's right!" she exclaimed. "Yeah I got a couple spenders over there. I'll bring 'em over in a minute, but first, I just wanted to let you know I'm having a little get together tomorrow night at my place after we get off. You should come." I looked at her with a blank expression. "I know. I know. It won't be like last time I promise. Everybody else is coming." She assured me.

"Everybody like who?" I asked, glancing over at the dancers. She already knew I didn't fuck with most of them like that.

"Only the cool people," she said trying to be funny. I rolled my eyes without laughing. "Tee Tee, Britt n 'em coming!"

"Really?" I asked as I turned and looked over my shoulder at them. I found it hard to believe that they were going after they had already warned me about her themselves.

"Yeah, for real. Ask them." She said, trying to convince me.

"Well I'll ask them before I leave, but for now, I'll just say I'll think about it." I felt uncomfortable about the idea.

"Alright, good enough. I'll be back." She said, sliding off to go bring some spenders over.

The guys Jillian brought over were indeed big spenders. It made the rest of the night easy because I didn't have to work hard for tips thanks to their generosity. I went home with three hundred twenty-eight dollars. That was a good night, and it made it even better to come home with Cal waiting in the front of my building for me. Every time I saw him was like my first time seeing him.

He hadn't made any more attempts to have sex with me. Part of me wondered if he was just giving me the time I needed. The other part wondered if he was getting it from someone else. That night he seemed really preoccupied. He picked at the late night dinner I cooked for us, and he didn't have much to say. It was a switch from when I had just seen him hours before at the club.

As we lay next to each other in bed, I couldn't help but ask, "Babe, what's good? You seem real distant."

"Nothing ... I'm good. You good?" he asked.

"Yeah ..." I responded. There was a long pause of silence that I couldn't let be. "You sure? You seem real quiet. You haven't even tried to push up on me or anything tonight." I persisted.

"You already know why, Angie. I'm not about to try to force you to do something you're not ready for." He said calmly.

"You sure that's why? You know sometimes I don't see you for days at a time. You sure you not just fucking somebody else? Like Rhonda or your baby mama?" I regretted the words almost as soon as they escaped my lips.

He grew agitated right away. "Don't start with that shit, Angie! Not tonight!"

"I'm not starting anything. I'm just asking." I said defensively.

"You always think I'm fucking somebody else. Didn't we just go through this? What the fuck, Angie?" He said sitting up in the bed.

"Well, you haven't tried anything with me. You acting all silent and distant all of a sudden. You're a man, so I know you have to be getting it from somewhere! And you still didn't answer the question." I said accusingly.

"Oh my God, what the fuck is wrong wit'chu? It's not all about you, Angie! You ever stop to think how much shit I got on my mind dealing with the business I deal with? I don't even have time to be fuckin' no bitches!" He insisted. I wasn't satisfied, but I didn't know what else to say. "I'm not gon' get into this with you tonight, Angela, not tonight ..." he said before grabbing a pillow and heading to the living room to sleep on the couch.

I felt dumb laying there in the dark alone. I wondered if I was being insecure. I hated to be the insecure chick, but what I said was true. He *was* a man and men have needs. I wondered what was bothering him so much this particular night though. My imagination started to run away with me as I thought of the possibility that maybe he was just with another woman. Maybe that's why he was so distant. Perhaps he had just come from doing the deed right before he came to see me.

The next day he had me drop him off downtown on the corner of Market and Broad. I didn't know why, and I didn't feel like I should ask given our conversation the night before. I asked if I would see him later that night, and he just said he didn't know and got out of the car when I stopped at the traffic light. I could tell he was still mad from the night before because he didn't even give me a kiss.

After I dropped him off, I went to the gym. I hadn't been in a while and really needed to. I spent an hour there and saw no signs of Rock or Rainy. Of course I was relieved not to see Rock, but was still secretly hoping to run into Rainy again. I took a quick trip home to shower and called the hairdresser to see if they took walk-ins. They didn't, but I was in luck as Monique, the stylist that pantry boy referred, said she could squeeze me in.

Her house was in the quiet suburban section of Hillside. I knocked on the side entrance as I was told to. As soon as the door swung open, the smell of relaxer rushed up my nostrils.

"Angela?" Monique greeted me with a big smile.

"Yes, hi."

She was short and petite with the exception of a massive behind that I couldn't help but notice as I followed her down the steps to her basement. It looked like she could topple over at any minute from that thing. Once we got in the light I could see Monique's brown skin was flawless, as was her hair. She wore a short cut kind of like Halle Berry.

As I suspected, someone was getting a fresh relaxer. I could see a woman rinsing the white stuff out of a little girl's hair. After saying hello to everyone down there, which was just Monique, one other stylist, and another woman who I guessed was the little girl's mother, I thanked her for taking me on such short notice.

"Oh, no problem at all. So how do you know Donny?" she asked.

"We work together. My mom usually does my hair, but she passed away, and I know his hair always looks nice. So I just asked him who does it." I explained.

"Aww, sorry about your mom. I know how you feel. I lost my mom six years ago." She continued, "But don't worry, we gon' get you back looking good which is the first step to feeling good!" I smiled out of appreciation.

Her hands felt good in my scalp. Lying back with my head in the sink was the first time I had felt completely relaxed in a while. I thought my scalp would be tender from the stitches, but it actually felt soothing. I closed my eyes as her fingers went to work, making gentle circles against my scalp as she shampooed me. The hot water she used to rinse my hair warmed my whole body.

I let myself slip away, only for a moment, in the perfect daydream. I saw Rainy's face sitting at the club as I made my way to her. She smiled as I got close, and then stood up to embrace me. No words were spoken. No words were necessary. I wore the necklace with my birthstone. She touched it with her fingers gently then took me by the hand leading me out of the club. My imaginary encounter only lasted for a brief moment before I was snapped out of it.

Monique tapped me when she was finished washing my hair to lead me back over to her station. I grabbed a *Hype Hair* magazine from a small stand that stood nearby. Right next to us, the other stylist blow-dried the little girl's hair. I glanced up periodically in the mirror to see the progress as Monique and the other stylist chatted with each other. I could hear the girl's mother fussing on her cell phone to someone.

After flipping through a few more magazines, I started getting antsy. I decided to strike up a conversation with Monique. "So how long have you been doing Donny's hair?" I asked.

"Oh let's see ... I guess it's been about two years now ... yup"

"Oh, okay ... yeah you do a really neat job on his hair." I couldn't think of anything else to say next.

I was glad she did, "Yeah, I love when Donny comes in. He's a trip! He keeps us rollin' with his stories."

"Really?" I asked curiously. Sure pantry guy was nice and could talk, but I had never saw him as being funny.

"Oh yeah! Leah, tell her 'bout Donny! Ain't he crazy?" she said, chuckling to the other stylist.

"Donny? She know Donny?" was her response as she giggled back.

"Yeah, that's how she found us. She works with Donny." Monique explained.

"Mmm mmm, I bet he keeps everybody rollin' at work!" she said, shaking her head.

"Well, I only see him sometimes because we don't work in the same department, but I guess I don't get to see that side of him" I said, joining in on the chuckle.

"Oh my God, he be having us dying in here! Don't he, Leah?" Monique said, continuing her laughter.

"You ain't never lied, girl! 'Specially when he start with his Toni stories." She said, shaking her head some more.

"Ugh, don't get him started," Monique replied.

"Who's Toni? His girlfriend?" I asked, being nosey.

Simultaneously, both ladies looked at each other and said "*GIRLFRIEND?*" then busted out in laughter. It seemed like what I had just said was the funniest thing they had ever heard. Still, I didn't get the joke.

"Uh uh, girl, Donny don't have no girlfriend," Monique said as she regained her composure. She continued, "Toni is his crazy cat."

I was immediately turned off. I don't know why, but I just didn't like the idea of a man having a cat. Plus I didn't really care for cats, period.

I just replied "oh okay." I felt a little embarrassed for so openly inquiring about his girlfriend. I didn't mean to come off desperate or even interested in his life at all. I didn't want to seem too nosey, so I didn't ask anymore about Donny, but Monique still had more she wanted to share.

"You don't know?" she asked, looking at me in the mirror.

"Know what?" I answered, clearly showing my ignorance. She gave Leah a glance as they shared an internal secret I was on the outside of.

"Donny plays for the other team, girl."

"Plays for the other team?" I repeated as if I didn't understand, but as soon as the words left my own mouth I caught on. "OH! Oooooh no ... I did not know that. *For real?*" I said in disbelief.

"Yup!" was Monique's confirmation.

"Wow, I had no clue."

"What a waste is what I say. That boy is fine!" Leah chimed in.

Although I agreed on the inside, I didn't want to show any enthusiasm about my agreement. "Yeah, I never would've guessed that—I mean not that gay men are supposed to look a certain way or anything ... I just didn't know, I guess." That was all I could say. That hadn't even entered my mind. I had nothing against gay men, but now I would have to see him differently. I had started developing a crush on him. I never noticed any flamboyance when I was around him, so I assumed he played the man in his relationships. I scolded myself for thinking this way. It wasn't my place to be thinking about who played what in someone else's relationship.

I picked up another magazine and decided not to strike up any more conversations while I was there. I was surprised to see Cherlise's number pop up on my phone, but I didn't answer when she called. I knew I didn't have good service on my phone in that basement, plus I didn't know if I was ready to talk to her yet. I wondered if she would ask me why I didn't call Matt back to help bail her out. I didn't really care at this point. In addition, seeing how the stylists had just told me Donny's business, I didn't think it was smart to have any personal conversations in front of these women. She didn't leave a message, so I decided not to call her back.

My hair came out on point, and I felt like a new person back at work that night. It wasn't until halfway through the night that I was reminded of Jillian's get together. I forgot to ask the other girls about it the night before, but Britt approached me about it. She asked if I was going and told me that they would all be there, her, Keisha, and Tee Tee.

"Weren't y'all the same ones warning me about her? I thought y'all didn't really get down with her like that?" I said, reminding her.

"We don't get down with her! Not like *that!*" This time I didn't have to wonder what she meant by that. "But shit, free drinks, and Nick is bringing some trees, so I'm going!" Nick was one of the bus boys at Ronnie's.

"Well, I don't know if I'm gonna go yet." I responded, still feeling unsure.

"Oh, come on! We obviously ain't going back to IHOP no time soon! We need a new after work chill spot, plus you haven't chilled with us in a minute." She begged.

"True … true. I might come. I'll let you know in a little bit. Let me hit up Cal and see if he's coming over tonight." I said with a wink.

"Ugh, look at you all sprung and shit!" She rolled her eyes sarcastically before walking away.

It was true. I was, and we hadn't even had sex yet. I texted Cal asking if he was coming over that night then waited for his response. It took him a while to respond, *"Nah I'ma just chill at Max's for the night."* He didn't have to say it, but I could tell he was still a little mad through his text.

"Are you still mad at me?" I had to know.

His response was *"No, babe I just think we need to chill for a couple days. I still love you, Angie."* I was relieved and a little offended at the same time. It was hard for me to see that my constant accusations about him being with other women were putting a strain on us.

I decided to give him the space he desired and replied, *"Okay I love you too babe."*

I had to admit I was looking forward to Jillian's get together, not so much because of Jillian, but because it had been a while since I chilled with the girls. So much had been going on that I couldn't talk to them about. I was looking forward to just kicking back and tearing it up, getting back to my normal life.

Jillian's house was just as nice on the inside as it was on the outside. Stripping had definitely paid off handsomely for her. She lived in luxury, and it was evident in every room of her home. I admired the black artwork that hung from her walls in the living room and hallways. A bearskin rug was sprawled out on the living room floor in front of a massive stone fireplace. The bamboo hardwood that ran throughout the main floor was immaculate. We passed the kitchen on the way to the steps leading downstairs, and it was huge with state of the art stainless steal appliances and granite countertops. I was convinced she had to have had a professional decorator put everything together.

The gathering took place in her spacious basement where there was a pool table and bar. A huge flat screen hung on the wall opposite the tan leather couch. I decided to take a seat at the bar where she was the server for the night.

"This is different having you serve me drinks for a change!" I said with a smile.

"I know, right. Don't worry, I started out as a bartender, so I know what to do. What'chu drinking?" she asked.

"What'chu got?" I said playfully.

"Girl, I got a fully stocked bar, everything you can think of and probably more. You like vodka? Rum? Yac?" I glanced over the bottles, and it did seem like she had everything.

"Hmmm, usually I drink Goose, but I think I want something different tonight. How about a Grand Mariner and pineapple please?" I asked politely.

"That's it? I was all ready to make you something fancy. I made them appletinis, mojitos *with* real mint leaves, and Britt got a long island! You sure that's all you want?" she asked excitedly.

"Yeah, I'll just have that to start with, I guess."

I looked around. There were about twelve people there in total. I knew most of them from the club, but maybe one or two I didn't. I saw Britt shooting pool with one of the bouncers from Ronnie's. Tee Tee and Kiesha were sitting in front of the flat screen playing some PlayStation game. The music played lightly in the background while everyone else chatted.

After I had my drink, I decided to go take a seat near the wall where I spotted Chucky and Freddie, the front door bouncers from Ronnie's. "OH MY GOD! MY WIFE IS FINALLY HERE!" Chucky teased as I slid a chair up to their table.

I smiled back shushing him. "What y'all playing?"

Freddie answered, "Spades what you know about that, lil' lady?"

"Please! I know how to play spades. You ain't said nothing but a word, son!" I said playfully. The truth was I only knew how to play the game. I was far from good at it.

"Alright get another person, and we'll deal you in." Freddie instructed.

Before I could turn around to see who was game, Jillian was standing over us. "Slide the table out some, I'm gonna play." She instructed.

After playing four games, we were tied. She decided to make it interesting suggesting we play for money. When she suggested one hundred a hand my eyes popped out of my head. I did well in tips that night, but I didn't want to just give it all away gambling. She must've sensed my hesitation as she winked at me and said, "don't worry we got this."

After a second drink, I didn't mind playing for the money. I just made up in my mind that I wouldn't go over what I knew I had on me. By this time, a few people started to gather around us. Some rooted for the bouncers and some rooted for us. Playing for money turned out to be to my benefit. In the end, we won three out of the five hands and I walked away with fifty extra dollars.

Once we were done with cards, I decided to join the viewers of Tee Tee and Kiesha's game on the couch. Someone passed me the blunt, and I took a couple pulls. Now I was nice and relaxed. It felt good to let my guard down and not worry about anything. The rest of the night at Jillian's went that way. It was a good call going to her get together, and I slept well when I finally made it home that night.

I don't know if it was because everyone else was around or because she knew I was definitely straight now or what, but Jillian was on her best behavior. She was a gracious hostess, and I decided it might be okay to chill with her again. To my surprise, I hadn't even thought about Cal, or what he might be doing. I felt carefree, and I had Jillian's get together to thank for that.

CHAPTER 26

The peace of mind didn't last for long. After a few days of sleeping alone, my nightmares of being shot in the head had returned. I had nightmares about Rock too. Sometimes it was a combination of both. I would see his face through the ski mask while he raped me over and over again. This time there was no Ninja Rainy to save me. He finished, and shot me in the head execution style.

Other times I dreamt about the IHOP shootout. Only in my dreams, it was Cal who was shot and killed instead of Ronnie's brother-in-law. I called out to Ronnie's sister, Carla, for help in the dream. She just stared back at me with that same blank expression she had at the club. My guilt was getting to me. I had no idea it would only get worse.

By Wednesday, I decided I needed to do something about Rock. I hadn't gotten anymore threatening notes. Still, I knew I wouldn't be able to move on until he was off the streets. I called to the station from work before I left. I didn't ask to speak directly to Detective Ramsey. Instead, I just asked the front desk if he was there and if they could find out if he'd be there for a while. When asked for my information, I gave a fake name and made up a pending case. After I had confirmation that he would be there, I headed to the station.

The same woman as before sat at the main desk, but she didn't remember me. I decided to stick with my fake name when she called Detective Ramsey for me this time. He was shocked to see me standing there when he came out to greet the fictitious Ms. Connor.

"Oh, it's *you* ... Miss Delimar," was all he said.

"Yes, it's me." I responded. The receptionist looked confused at our exchange.

Catching her expression, Detective Ramsey put on a fake smile and said, "right this way," as he extended his hand out toward the hallway.

He didn't bother taking me in an interrogation room this time. Once he had me alone in a tucked away section of a deserted hallway, he looked down at me through glaring eyes. "What are you doing here? I'm not going to allow you to come here and smear a dead man's name!" he hissed.

"*What?* You know why I'm here! I'm not here about a dead man! I'm here to press charges against my rapist, Officer Johnson! Now if you're not gonna do it, I demand to see your boss!" I said in a heated tone.

"You keep your voice down! Are you trying to pretend like you don't know?" he said, taking a step back and squinting at me as though he was trying to feel me out.

"Know *what?*"

"Officer Johnson is deceased. He was murdered last weekend some time. His body was found in Weekend Park on Sunday. Now you wouldn't happen to know anything about *that* would you?" he asked accusingly.

My mouth dropped open in disbelief. I would have thought I'd be relieved, but I was in more of a shock. I hadn't expected this news. I came there expecting to cause an uproar, demand justice for myself, make threats about suing the police station and such. I was totally unprepared for this, and I was caught off guard by Detective Ramsey's innuendo that I knew anything about it.

"Dead?" was all I could get out of my mouth.

"Oh, don't act like you didn't know. I know this is all an act. You come down here all of a sudden acting like you want to press charges, knowing damn well he was murdered." As he got in my face with awful accusations, spit flew from his mouth and landed on my cheek in his fit of rage. I stepped back thinking that he might become physical at any moment.

"I don't know what you're talking about! I didn't even know he was dead! I came here trying to get justice. I don't know nothing about killing nobody." My voice got louder as I defended myself.

He crossed his arms over his chest and stood up straight as he took a pause to stare me down. "Humph! Maybe you really don't know. It's not like you people read the news anyway." He said with a look in his eyes like he wanted to spit on me, this time on purpose. I stepped around him and hurried down the hall and right out of the police station. As I made my way down the hall he called out to me, "DON'T THINK THIS IS IT! WE'RE WATCHING YOU, AND DON'T FORGET ABOUT THAT POSSESSION CHARGE!"

I didn't know how to digest or process the information I had just gotten. I knew I hadn't seen Rock at the gym in a while, but I figured he was just keeping a low profile because of what he had done. Murdered? I wondered how he was murdered and who else would have it out for him. Rainy had immediately come to mind. She was always following me, so it would have been easy for me to lead her right to Rock. She did, after all, come to my rescue out of nowhere. The fact was I didn't know this woman at all. I had no idea what she was capable of. That thought scared me. I wondered if she had mental problems or if she had ever done anything like this before.

Up until then, I had only talked to Cal through phone calls and text messages since our heated argument. I hadn't seen him since the morning I dropped him off. I called him to update him on the news I had just received and for comfort.

"What's up," is how he answered.

"Oh my God, baby I'm down here outside the police station and they just told me Rock was murdered!"

I started to ramble, but Cal cut me off, "Uuuuggh, oh my God, Angie! See you don't fucking listen! I told you not to take yo ass down to the station! Didn't I tell you—just stop talking and come pick me up right now at my cousin's crib!" He demanded and then hung up on me just like that.

I looked at the phone, puzzled. I tried to call him back twice, but he didn't answer, so I did as told and headed straight to Max's house. I didn't understand his anger with me. I was a little disappointed that he hadn't stayed on the phone with me to say calming things like he had so many times in the past. I felt like he was really starting to get annoyed with me. I wondered if he was going to break up with me when I got there. My heart began to speed up with nervousness at the thought of that.

When I pulled up, he wasn't outside. I blew the horn and he came out from the back of the house. Anger and annoyance was written all over his face. He didn't even say hi or anything when he got in the car. My greeting was met with, "drive," as he rolled his eyes and shook his head. I did as told even though I didn't know where I was supposed to drive. I think that was the most heated I had ever seen him.

After just driving straight for a while, I mustered up enough courage to ask where I should be going. "I don't know just drive to a park or something." He said as he let out a sigh. I decided to drive to a little park that was part of the Clinton Ave. Elementary School. I pulled in the parking lot and turned the car off. I turned towards Cal, but he still hadn't said anything.

After sitting for a few moments I felt I had to say something, "Soooo?"

He shot darts at me through the corner of his eye, "Shh!" He shushed me as though he was trying to hear something as he looked around nervously. Finally, "Come on."

It was cold and I didn't want to, but I followed his lead and got out of the car. We walked down a short path towards the playground area, finally taking a seat on a metal bench. It was hard and cold on my butt, but I knew better than to complain at the present moment. Cal saw me start to shiver with my teeth chattering and put his arm around me pulling me closer next to him. I felt at ease. That was the Cal I knew and loved.

"Aaaahhh, Angie Angie Angie ... I don't know what I'm gonna do with you ... you know I love the shit outta you, right?" he asked with softer eyes.

"I know, and I love you too," I said as I looked down at the ground.

"But sometimes that's a bad thing," he continued.

"It's not a bad thing." I said, grabbing his hand to hold it. He shook his head.

"Angie, you gotta start listening to your man. Don't you trust me by now?" he asked.

"Yeah, I do but—"

"Well, but nothing then! Fuck, Angie. I tell you I'll take care of ol' boy and instead of leaving it alone you go down to the police station. Didn't I already tell you them pigs don't give a shit about you or your rape?" He cut me off getting agitated again. I didn't respond. "Angie,

I love and care about you, not them pigs! So why would you put your trust in them over me?" He asked.

"I wasn't putting my trust in them over you. I know you said you would take care of it, but I didn't know what you meant by that. I just wanted to see him pay, and make all this go away. That's why I went down there."

"That's what I'm talking about right there! It shouldn't matter that you don't know *how* I'ma take care of something. You should just trust me if I say I'ma do it!" he scolded.

"Well, I'm sorry. You're right. I should've trusted you. But finding that hidden camera in the apartment and that threatening note ... I haven't been able to sleep, and you been giving me the silent treatment. Shit, I'm scared, Cal!"

There was a brief pause then he sighed, "Angie, I had that camera put in." I opened my mouth to respond, but he cut me off, "Don't get mad. I had Wally put it in a while ago before I even came home. I just wanted to keep an eye on you, especially after hearing you talking to that Rock dude that day I called you. I needed to make sure you weren't lying."

I couldn't believe what I was hearing. I was just as confused as mad. "WHAT ... THE ... FUCK, CAL! ARE YOU *CRAZY?* WHO THE FUCK DO YOU THINK YOU ARE SPYING ON ME? AND HAVING SOMEBODY ELSE BREAK INTO MY APARTMENT?" I stopped there at a loss for words.

"I know. I know. You have every right to be mad, but just know I only did it because I love you. I wanted to make sure you weren't cheating on me, and I wanted to keep an eye on you."

"Keep an eye on me? You really are crazy. You had some random nigga in my apartment? Do you know he went through my drawers? How did he even get in there without anyone seeing him or breaking my locks?" I fired off questions.

"The first night he tried he said you were home, and he almost got caught when he heard you come to the door. So I had him do it when I knew you'd be working at the bar, and it was late so no one would be out. I'm sorry, Angela."

"*Sorry?* You have a stranger break in my apartment and plant a camera to spy on me and all you can say is *sorry?*" I could feel my eyes popping out of my head in disbelief. So that was the rattling I had heard at my door. The thought sent chills up my spine.

"Wally's not a stranger. He's like a brother to me. I don't know what else to say. I just love you so much and you're beautiful, Angela. I found it hard to believe that you wasn't fucking somebody else."

"So who the hell has been watching the footage?" I asked, thinking Wally must've been watching it and reporting back to Cal.

"*Me!* He linked it so that I could watch you from a program I had put on that cell phone I had when I was locked up. I had it removed before I gave up the phone though. So don't worry." He explained like it was no big deal. I didn't know how to deal with it. I sat quietly in shock. "C'mon, Angie don't be mad at me over this. Nobody else ever watched it except for me. I swear." He said, raising one hand in the air with the other on his chest. My face was frozen in anger. I wanted to forgive him, but this was too much. It wasn't normal.

"Well, I guess someone else got to Rock before you did because apparently he's been taken care of." I said, changing the subject out of fear. This man before me was apparently crazy, and I wasn't about to upset him outside in this deserted park alone. He looked me dead in the eyes with a serious look. All this time he kept saying he would take care of it. The meaning didn't dawn on me until now.

My eyes grew big at the realization. I jerked my neck back and squinted my eyes at him waiting for him to say something or change his expression to change my mind about my most recent epiphany. He didn't flinch.

"Cal, what did you do?" I asked, afraid of the answer. He just hissed and rolled his eyes. I grabbed his face pinching his cheeks between my thumb and forefingers as I turned it directly to mine. "Cal ... did you already know Rock was murdered?"

"Look, I told you I would take care of it, and I did. That's all you need to know." He said coldly.

"No, that's not all I need to know! What the hell, Cal? You *killed* him?" I asked, now dropping his hand and backing away from him.

"Shhh!" he shot back.

I lowered my voice, but still had the same question, "Cal, please tell me you didn't kill that man."

After a brief pause he responded, "Okay, fine, I didn't kill him."

By this time I was pacing back and forth, chanting to myself, "oh my God oh my God oh my God."

"Angie, sit down please ... look, he wasn't no man no way! He was a rapist, a pig, an animal!" he barked the words at me.

"Still, Cal, still …" I trailed off.

"Still *what?*"

"Still, you weren't supposed to kill him!" I almost shouted.

That's when he grabbed my arm and sat me down. "Keep your voice down! Look this muthafucka knocked you out and forced himself on you, or did you forget that?"

"Of course I didn't forget! Did you forget it's *me* it happened to? I think about that shit every night. I can't sleep for fear of seeing him in my dreams. So don't say that shit to me!" I hissed in the lowest tone I could control.

"I know babe, and that's why I had to take care of him. You're my heart. Someone hurts you, and it's like they're hurting me. I told you I got you through any storm, and I meant that!" He said with a pleading look in his eyes.

"I didn't ask you to do that, Cal." I said, scolding him.

"You didn't have to ask me. It needed to be done. Now you can sleep, baby. Nobody's gonna hurt you now." He replied as he tried to hold my hand. I snatched it away.

"How the hell am I supposed to sleep with the cops watching my every move now?" I said, clenching my jaws.

"What'chu talking 'bout, Angie? Ain't nobody watching you. Don't be paranoid."

"Well that's what the detective said today. Apparently, he thinks I know something about the murder … and now I do!"

"What did he say?" I could hear a hint of worry creeping into his voice.

"He just asked me if I knew anything about it and said it's not over. They'll be watching me."

"Oh, they ain't got nothing. They just trying to scare you, Angie." He said, dismissing me again.

"They do have something! He threatened me with a possession charge for the weed they found in my jeans the night I was raped."

"You had weed on you? They not gon' bother you for that, Angie. You don't even have a record or anything. It would be a waste of their time." I wasn't sure if he was trying to convince himself or me. "Look, I'm not gonna let anything happen to you. Just don't say anything. I mean you don't know anything anyway. Just keep your ass away from that police station!" He demanded. I didn't respond. I was lost in my own thoughts and panic. "You hear me?" he asked sternly.

"Yeah yeah" I replied.

"Don't *yeah yeah* me, Angie. You know you're hardheaded. Keep your ass away from that station, Angie!" He said with a serious look on his face.

"OKAY!" I said, getting annoyed.

I didn't know the person I was sitting next to as well as I thought. I reflected back on all the conversations we had at our visitations. I asked him once before if he had ever killed anyone. He never gave me a straight answer, but I knew that he carried a gun. I just didn't know just how much he was capable of. For the first time ever, I was sickened by Cal. Don't get me wrong, I was definitely disgusted by Rock and what he did was unforgiveable. I wanted him to pay for sure, just not this way. I thought about how Cal might've killed him and settled on the assumption that he probably shot him to death.

My thoughts ran on and on as we sat there in silence for those brief moments. I thought about his demeanor when he demanded I not say anything or go to the police station. Sure, he loved me, but now I was wondering if he'd ever hurt me. If he could kill a man without a second thought, who's to say he wouldn't kill me if I upset him too much? Fear of the man I loved so deeply began to creep in and take over.

I jumped the next time he reached to grab my hand. He looked at me strangely before saying, "come on, it's getting cold." I didn't want him anywhere near me. He was ready to come home with me, but I was too afraid. I made up an excuse telling him how early I had to be at work the next morning, and I didn't want to have to get up extra early to drop him off. He seemed to buy it, and I was relieved to get him out of my car when I dropped him back off at his cousin Max's house.

I got no sleep that night. My nightmares grew worse. First I dreamt of a decayed Rock lying in a shallow grave at Weekend Park. He held his arms out begging to me, "I'm sorry, Angie. Save me, Angie," but I just stood there as Cal shot him repeatedly. No matter how many times he shot him over and over, Rock just wouldn't die. He just stayed sitting up in the grave with his arms extended like a zombie. Then the dream changed, and Cal turned the gun on me. He made me get on my knees execution style and uttered one word only, "sorry." Then he shot me right between the eyes.

CHAPTER 27

It was no surprise that I was exhausted the whole next day at work. I didn't even hear Renee as she stood at my desk. "I'm sorry, were you talking to me?" I said, trying to focus.

"Yeah, I just wanted to tell you we're getting ready to go into the conference room to have cake for Vanessa's birthday in ten minutes." She whispered.

I felt so awkward being in a room where the person of the hour knew I hadn't contributed to her celebration. It was embarrassing, but what else could I do? If I didn't go at all, it would just draw more attention to the situation, and she might take it even more personal. It definitely wasn't. I found a corner in the back of the room to sit quietly. I only stayed long enough to sing happy birthday and watch her cut the cake. I waited for the first person to walk out. As soon as they did, I slid out right behind them.

During my walk back to my desk I spotted the pantry guy huddled in a far corner near the water fountain with another guy. I had seen this guy plenty of times in passing, but I didn't know him. They were talking, but it seemed like a private conversation. I thought back on what Monique had told me, and I wondered if this other guy was gay too. I began to make up a whole story in my head about how the other guy was probably married, and they were having a secret love affair on the down low. I must have been staring too long because the pantry guy looked up right at me. He gave a big smile and waved. I waved back and refocused my eyes in front of me.

It was too late. I had drawn attention to myself by staring. When he finished his conversation, he made his way over meeting me at my desk. "Hey! Monique told me you went and got your hair done. It looks nice." He said, still smiling. He was always smiling.

"Yeeeeah, thank you! She did a really good job. I'm glad I went to her."

"Told you she'd hook you up! What she say about me?" he asked, batting his eyelashes. I wasn't sure what to say. My mouth had already gotten me in trouble once at work. I didn't want to make that same mistake again.

"Oh, they was just saying how funny you are and you be having them cracking up." I answered.

"Who is *they*?" he asked.

"Oh, the other stylist that works there, Leah?"

"Oh yeah! I forgot all about my boo-kee, Lee Lee!"

"Yeah, I would definitely go get my hair done there again," I said.

"Good, I'm glad you liked her." He said, before walking off.

I was glad I didn't slip and say anything about him being gay. I didn't know if he was out of the closet or not or if other people at work knew. I decided it was none of my business either way. It did make me feel better about the rejection I had originally felt when he wanted to hook me up with his cousin though.

Over the next few days, I avoided Cal at all costs. I was uneasy, and I didn't know what to do or how to feel about what he had done. He called and texted me several times. I ignored the calls but answered his texts with the brush off. He wanted to see me, but I continued to find excuses not to see him. I knew I couldn't keep on doing this because I was scared of what he might do to me. What if he got worried that I was going to snitch on him? What if I tried to break up with him? He might get mad and kill me too.

I finally decided I would see him, but not alone. I told him through text to come by the club on Friday night when I had to work. That way we would be around a crowd full of people. I felt more comfortable there in general, anyway.

It was the usual scene on Friday. Britt, Keisha, and Tee Tee were behind the bar with me. It was busy, so we hustled back and forth making drinks, flirting with customers, washing glasses, etcetera. Jillian was there too, and things were back to normal between us. She brought over some big spenders as usual, and we had a good time taking their money.

Cal entered the bar about midway through my shift. Although his presence was still the same, I didn't get the same feeling I usually did when I saw him. The fluttery butterfly feeling I usually felt in my stomach was replaced by flip-flops. My heart fluttered, but not in the same way either. It was more of a frightened speed up. My armpits began to perspire a little as well. When he made his way over towards the end of the bar where I was, I raised my arms a little higher than usual as I dried a glass in hopes to catch a breeze underneath them.

He grabbed a stool and slid right up in front of me. "What's up?" he said as he leaned over for a kiss.

"Hey," I leaned over and gave him a quick peck on the lips.

"What's good?" he asked.

"Shit, same ol' same ol', it's busy as always in here."

"I see that," he replied. He tilted his head to one side and looked at me through loving but worried eyes. "So why you been avoiding me, Angie?" he asked. I opened my mouth prepared to answer with denial, but he cut me off "—and don't try to act like you don't know what I'm talking about either, Angela."

I decided to go with denial anyway. "I haven't been avoiding you, Cal. I just been real busy. That's all."

"Oh, all of a sudden you been busy. Miss me with the bullshit, Angie. You know damn well what I'm talking 'bout! You don't answer my calls. Every time I try to see you, you give me an excuse. Your ass hasn't been busy in all the time that I've known you. Now all of a sudden you busy? *For real?* That's the best you could come up with?" I expected him to be angry, but he had a look of hurt on his face, not anger. I had never seen this look on him before, and it reached out to my core.

I paused for a few moments just looking at him, unsure of how to respond. I didn't want to upset him or hurt him more, but I didn't know what else to say to keep the peace. "Come on, you know why I been avoiding you, Cal. That was some crazy shit you dropped on me! How did you expect me to react? I don't know what to do with that!" I exclaimed with wide eyes.

He leaned in, "Lower your fucking voice, Angie!" He was right. I had started getting a little loud. I could see Britt looking at me from the corner of my eye.

I sighed heavily, "What do you want me to say?"

"What'chu you mean what I want you to say? I want you to say you still love me, and you still with me. I still got you. You still mine. That shit ain't 'bout nothing. You need to just forget about that. That nigga deserved everything he got, and you know that. Maybe you don't wanna admit it, but you know I'm right." He said.

I couldn't believe what I was hearing. He had absolutely no remorse for killing a man. In all the months I was getting to know him, I failed to realize just how cold he could be. What did he mean by *"he got everything he deserved?"* Now I wondered exactly what did he do to Rock. Did he torture him before offing him? All kinds of heinous thoughts started to cross my mind.

"I still love you, babe. You know that, but I just feel like I don't even know you right now." I said as calmly as possible.

"What? What the fuck kinda shit is that to say? Angie, you trippin!" He shook his head in a slow disapproval. He shifted in his seat nervously as he tried to think of what to say next. I couldn't believe what I was seeing. Tears started to form in his eyes. I prayed for both of our sakes that he wouldn't start crying right there in front of everyone. We already had some attention on us. I didn't need any additional attention like that.

I took his hand in mine and stroked it lightly in hopes to calm him some. "I still love you, baby. I just need some time, okay?" He closed his eyes and breathed in deeply, held it, then released slowly. When he reopened them, the tears were gone.

"Alright, I understand. Just know I love the shit outta you. I would do anything for you, Angie. I don't want to ever see you hurt … and you know I would never hurt you, right?" He said with puppy dog eyes. The fact was I didn't know. I didn't know who this person was. I hesitated then nodded. "For real, I need you to know that, baby." He said before kissing my hand.

It was perfect timing for Jillian to bring over some customers. She escorted two men by their hands up to the bar where we were having our private conversation in front of everyone. They sat down next to us, and she gave me the eye. "Look babe, I gotta get back to work before Ronnie sees me talking to you and starts trippin'."

Cal glanced over at the guys and sucked his teeth, "Alright, well just call me when you get off please."

"Alright," I said.

"For real, Angie! Don't just be saying alright. I wanna talk to you okay?"

"*Okaaay.*" I assured him.

He walked off, and I scooted over to Jillian and the two men she brought over. "How you gentlemen doing? What can I get you to drink?" I spent the next hour with them, taking breaks only to help other customers. Talking and laughing with them helped put me back at ease some, and it made the time go quicker.

I hadn't seen Rainy since the last time she came to the club. Since this whole new development with Cal, I hadn't even been looking for her. I wasn't even surprised when I spotted her spying on me this time. She sat alone at the same table she sat at before. We made eye contact just as we had before, but I was so use to the failed attempts at actually talking to her. I didn't even try to rush right over this time. I kept my eye on her and she kept hers on me, but I continued working. We would be closing soon anyway.

Once we shut down the bar, I saw her slowly rise from her seat and leave out the door. I didn't rush, but I had every intention of confronting her again if she was still around when I left the bar. She must have been tired of running away as well because she was standing right outside of the club when we all finally came out. I said goodnight to the girls and walked over to her. She didn't budge this time. She stood there with her feet firmly planted as if she was waiting for me to approach.

Here she was right in front of my face, just standing. I had the courage to walk up to her face, but nothing happened after that. I just stood there looking at her. This was the first time I got a really good up close look into her face. It truly was like looking in a mirror; only she was darker. I studied her every feature, but still said nothing. Her eyes were sad and hopeful at the same time as she stared back at me, studying me in the same way.

Finally, she broke the silence with a kind smile, "Angela ... you're so beautiful." She said it as if she couldn't believe it herself. I still didn't know what to say, so I said nothing. "I know you probably know who I am by now. I've thought about this day for years, and now I don't even know what to say." I stood there silently and let her have the entire conversation with herself. "I'm really sorry about your mom," she said. I don't know why that struck a cord with me, but it did.

"You don't know anything about my mother!" I snapped. As soon as the words left my mouth, I regretted saying them.

She didn't seem phased by my comment though. Instead she continued, "I know you probably have a lot of mixed feelings and emotions right now, and I know you're probably wondering why I've been following you around like this …" Her voice trailed as I could see her struggling to find the next words to say.

Before she had the chance to continue, I heard my name being called from a few feet away. "*Angie!*" Cal called anxiously.

I spun around to see him walking towards us. "How come you didn't call me yet? I told you to call me when you got off. I knew you wasn't gonna listen!" He said angrily.

"I *just* got off just now! Damn, you didn't even give me a chance to get home good." I shot back.

"Well, I told you to call me when you got off, not when you got home. I wanted us to chill tonight." He said with an aching in his voice.

"Well hold on, I'm talking …" I turned to motion towards Rainy, but she was nowhere to be found. She wasn't there anymore. I looked back and forth. "Dammit!" I said out loud even though I was cursing myself.

"What? Talking to who?" Cal asked, looking at me confused.

"Never mind" I said sadly. "Come on."

I was glad that I hadn't parked too far. I wanted people to see Cal and me together just in case of anything. Everyone would be able to say he was the last person I was seen with. I was terrified to go anywhere with him alone. I couldn't think of a way to get out of it quick enough though. I wasn't expecting him to be waiting for me when I got off of work.

That night, I lay stiffly in bed as he tried to cuddle with me. Each kiss he placed on my neck felt like a kiss of death. I tried to get my breathing under control. Like the animal I now thought he was, he must have sensed my fear, "What's wrong?" he asked as he continued planting kisses on my neck and back. We lay on our sides as he spooned me from behind. Usually this was my favorite cuddling position, but not tonight. Tonight I just felt rigid and scared.

"Nothing," I lied in response.

"You still scared from the rape, huh? I know, but you don't have to worry about that anymore. I took care of it, and I took care of it because I love you. You don't have to live in fear anymore." He spoke to me like a child. He seemed to have no clue that he was the one I was afraid of. He kissed me a few more times before squeezing me tight and whispering in my ear, "It's okay. You know we don't have to do anything. I just wanna be close to you and keep you protected."

It seemed like forever waiting for him to drift off to sleep. I wanted to slide from his grip and sneak out, but I had nowhere to go. Plus I didn't want to take the chance of waking him. I spent the entire night lying stiffly beneath his grip. I was too afraid to fall asleep, so I never did.

CHAPTER 28

I was relieved that he wanted me to drop him back off at his cousin's house the next day. I spent that whole first half of the day pretending everything was okay. I kept glancing at the clock nervously, counting down the time I had to drop him off. I had already decided that I would find a good reason not to see him after I got off work this night. I hoped Jillian or someone else would have the after work plan already set. That way I wouldn't even have to lie. It didn't even matter to me where we were going to go. I would say yes to anywhere just to escape Cal.

I spent that whole day thinking about how to make that escape. Sure, Saturday was covered, but that was just one night. I contemplated going to the police, but if they weren't prepared to help me before they probably wouldn't help me now either. Detective Ramsey had already accused me of having something to do with Rock's murder. If I came forward now, they would definitely think I played a part in it.

I breathed a sigh of relief when we finally pulled up to Max's house. "Okay babe, I'll see you later, right?" Cal asked.

"Well probably not. I'm supposed to go out with the girls after work. You know we usually get together on Saturdays after we close the bar."

He looked at me as though reluctant to believe me. "Well where y'all going?"

"I'm not even sure yet. We'll probably just go to Jilli's house again.

That seems to be the new after party spot since IHOP."

"Oh alright, well just hit me up and let me know. Maybe you can scoop me after you leave there." He said.

"Okay," I said as I leaned in to meet his already waiting lips for a kiss.

During the entire ride back home to change, I thought of Rainy, her face, her voice, her smile. Every woman at the bus stop along the way looked like her. Every pedestrian crossing in the cross walk looked like her. I had missed my chance to have a conversation with her. Hindsight is always twenty-twenty. Now I thought of all the things I could have and should have said. Instead, all I did was hiss one line of anger to her. I pictured in my head how the rest of our conversation would have went had Cal's ass not shown up and ruined it.

I also wondered why she disappeared again. I was starting to get real tired of that. It seemed like she was ready and willing to finally have a real conversation with me, but she ran off as soon as I turned my back for one second. Once again, I was left not understanding her or her actions. There was no telling when I would see her again. All I could do was wait now, and the next time I would have something better to say to her.

I was so preoccupied at work that Saturday night. My mind bounced back and forth from Rainy to what I would do about Cal, so it was no surprise that I didn't even notice Cutie, Gordon Hopkins, come into the club. I didn't even look up when he ordered his whiskey sour with Johnnie Green. I just proceeded to make it. When I spun around to serve it to him, he caught my attention.

"It's about time I picked the right night to come in here. I've been looking for you." He said. I looked up and for some reason his smile made me nervous. I miscalculated where I was setting his drink down and tipped it right over the edge. It spilled right in his lap.

"Oh my God, I'm so sorry!" I said as the blood rushed to my face. I grabbed some paper towels from under the bar and rushed around to the other side. "I am so so so sorry. Here." I patted his pant leg where the splatter took place. Surprisingly his demeanor didn't change one bit.

He grabbed my wrist softly, "It's okay. Here let me do that. Really, it's okay, love."

Thoroughly embarrassed, I handed him the paper towels in my

hand and returned back to the other side of the bar to grab some more. He continued patting his pants dry as I wiped the little bit that spilled on the counter. "I'm so embarrassed. I don't know where my mind is. I'm so sorry, Gordon." I said, trying to regain my composure before I found another way to embarrass myself.

"I said it's okay. It's nothing a little detergent won't get out. Now stop apologizing, beautiful." He was smooth and his words were comforting.

I smiled, "Here let me make you another one."

I took great care to gently place his drink down in front of him this time, and I made sure to put extra Johnnie in it. He pulled out his wallet, but I stopped him, "This one's on me, okay?" He shrugged and thanked me, putting his wallet away. "So how you been?" I asked.

"I been fine, but I'm better now that I get to see your beautiful face again." I smiled and I kept myself from saying something sarcastic in response.

"How have *you* been, Miss?" he asked.

"I been okay."

"Just okay?" He said, leaning down to meet my eyes with his.

"Well, a lot has been going on, but I'm good." I replied.

"I see ... care to share?"

I smiled politely before answering, "no, not really, but thanks."

"You sure? I'm a really good listener."

"I appreciate that, and I'm sure you are, but I don't really know you like that." I was just being honest. He was cute as hell, but he was still a stranger to me.

"You don't know me like that?" he chuckled before continuing, "Well you should really let me get to know you then."

"We've been over this before. I'm sorry, but I have a boyfriend." I answered, tilting my head to the side with a look of "sorry" on my face.

"I know. I know. I just thought I'd give it another shot. Do you know how many times I've been in here looking for you? I even asked that girl over there where you were one day." He motioned towards Tee Tee.

"Ooooooohhh, *you're* the mystery stranger! Yeah she told me someone was in here looking for me, but I didn't know she was talking 'bout you!" I said, laughing. "Well, I really should get back to work, sir" I said with a smile.

He gulped down the rest of his drink and replied, "Okay, I understand." He got up and turned to leave, but turned around quickly as though he had changed his mind "If you change your mind, you know how to get in contact with me."

"Okay, night!"

I knew nothing about this man, but he had me feeling all tingly inside. If only for a brief moment, he had taken my mind off of Cal and Rainy. His engaging smile floated in my mind for the rest of the night. He seemed nice, but then again, all men seemed nice in the beginning. It was nice to have options, but I was in no rush to date anyone new, especially not until I decided how to shake off Cal and I was over my rape.

I joined the rest of the ladies who were standing around at the other end of the bar. "Hey where's it at tonight?" I asked. I needed to make sure I had every reason not to go home after work.

"I don't know. That's what we were just trying to decide." Keisha answered.

"Jilli said she not trying to host tonight," Britt offered.

I started to get worried that I would have to go home. "Well who else stays open late besides IHOP?" I asked.

"I don't even know," Keisha said as though thinking out loud. We all saw Ronnie coming over at the same time and broke up our huddle. We already knew what he would say and none of us wanted to hear his mouth.

I went back to serving customers, but as the time ticked by, I became more and more worried. I did not want to go home by any means. I needed to devise a plan and fast. By the time the night was winding down, no one had come up with a plan. I got desperate. I did a quick mental check of my apartment trying to remember how clean and tidy it was. I decided it was in passable condition for company and told the girls they could come to my place to chill. The girls were on board, but I told them my place was pretty small so to keep it on the hush. I didn't have enough room or drinks for all the security and anyone else to come.

Jilli made it her business to find her way to me before we closed for the night. "So Angie, how you gon' have the after party and not invite me? That's fucked up!" she said with her arms crossed.

"Shhhh! Damn how the hell do you know? Besides, I thought you wasn't up to hanging out tonight?" I said, looking around to make sure no one else had heard her spill the beans.

"I hear everything. I got ears everywhere you know, and I said I didn't feel like *hosting*. I said nothing about chilling at someone else's expense." She said, smiling.

"Oh, well I didn't know. Come then, but please don't tell anyone else because this is a last minute decision, and I don't even have a big place like that to have everybody over." I explained.

"Okay, cool."

I was happy that I made the decision to have the girls over. Cal wasted no time blowing up my phone as soon as I got off work. I ignored the first two calls, but was more than happy to have the girls as background noise when he called the third time. I was relieved to be able to tell him the girls were over, and I didn't know how long they'd be there. I knew he wouldn't crash the get together, and I could tell he was discouraged when I told him I didn't know when they were leaving.

Britt brought the weed this time, and I already had some Grey Goose and Hennessey for everyone. We had our usual good time smoking, drinking, playing cards, and gossiping. "You know Ronnie said that his sister swears up and down that one of us saw more than we said we did at the IHOP that night." Tee Tee said. My heart sped up, but I tried to remain cool. I couldn't tell if she knew specifically it was me holding out or if she was just speaking in general. If she didn't know, I sure didn't want to give myself away.

"What? He told you that?" Jilli asked.

"Yup."

"What did he say?" I asked.

"He just said that Carla said she thinks that at least one of us had to see something."

"Well, why would she think that?" Britt asked.

"I have no idea. I told him I don't know what she's talking about, that we ain't see nothing, and if we did, we would want to help." I was at ease again once she said that knowing Carla hadn't pointed out anyone in particular, but the guilt lingered in me.

It was closing in on four in the morning, and everyone started coming down from their clouds. Yawning faces with watery eyes surrounded me. Keisha was the first to leave, and Tee Tee followed. Jilli and me continued playing cards as Britt fell asleep on the couch.

After a couple more rounds of cards, I became tired as well. We looked at Britt at the same time who was now snoring with her mouth wide open.

"Let's mess with her," Jilli whispered. I snickered nodding along. First I took a straw and tickled her ear with it. She swatted the side of her head but didn't wake up. I did this about three times as we cupped our hands over our mouths to silence our laughter. Then Jillian took her finger and wiggled her bottom lip. Britt tossed a little on the couch. She closed her mouth, swallowed and smacked her lips a couple times before letting her jaw slowly drop back open. By now we were doubled over in our silent laughter. Next Jillian grabbed a can of mixed nuts I had sitting on the coffee table. She took a peanut out and tried to throw it in Britt's mouth. She missed and hit her chin.

I motioned and mouthed the word "stop" to her because I didn't want Britt to choke in her sleep, but it was too funny. It took Jillian three tries before she got it in her mouth. Britt jumped up in confusion and spit the peanut in her hand.

"What the hell?" she said sleepily. We burst out in laughter. "Y'all play too fuckin' much!" she said through an embarrassed chuckle.

"Girl, you better be careful sleeping with your mouth open like that. No telling what somebody might wanna stick in there," Jillian said as she winked at me. I continued with my laughter.

"Shut up, Jilli! Nasty ass …" Britt said as she got up and stretched. "Damn, I'm tired as hell. I'm bout to leave y'all." She said as she grabbed her coat.

"Alright, Britt Britt. See you next weekend girl," I replied as I opened the door for her departure.

"So what about you? You not tired yet?" I asked Jillian.

"Nah, I'm a night owl. I don't even wake up til' three in the afternoon sometimes."

"Wow, must be nice." I replied.

"Yeah it is … you know you can do it too."

"You forget I have a regular nine to five during the week." I said.

"You can always quit that wack job and dance."

I laughed at that, "I don't think so."

"*Why not?*" she asked indignantly.

"It's just not for me."

"What do you mean it's not for you? What you saying you too

good for that?"

"Well ... shit, yeah! I'm not knocking you or any of the other girls for what y'all do, but it's just not something I'm interested in doing." I explained. I could tell she was still offended, but I was just being honest.

"Humph! Bet you wouldn't be saying that if you just got a lil' taste of that money, but anyway ... how you doing, Angie? I mean how are you dealing with your mom passing and whatnot?" she asked, switching her tone.

"Wow, well, I mean it's not easy, but I'm doing okay."

"You always sum everything up by saying you're okay. I can see you're okay, but are you *really* okay?" she pressed.

"Yeah! Why you ask like that?"

"Well, I saw you and your dude having your lil' argument last night. Everything okay with that?" she asked. It was hard to tell if she was being mischievous, nosey, or genuinely concerned.

"Yeah, we good," was all I said.

"Angie, I know we got off to a weird start, but I only ask because I'm genuinely concerned. At work and the last time we kicked it, it's been cool, right?" she asked.

"Yeah," that was true, but I didn't see her point.

"Well, like I said before, you can talk to me. Don't let that one lil' incident ruin everything." It was silent for a moment as I thought about whether I should confide in Jillian or not. The truth was I did need someone to talk to. I just wasn't sure she was the right someone. I didn't want her going back telling all my business.

I decided I would only tell a little bit. "Well a lot of shit has been going on, too much to run down the list, really."

"Well, we can just talk about whatever you're comfortable talking about."

"Well don't tell anybody but—"

"Angela, I'm not gonna tell anyone anything. I'm not like that. For real." She cut me off.

"Well, you better not ... I was raped like a month ago."

"Damn, for real?" was all she said.

"No, for fake! Of course for real!" I said, mocking her.

"Damn, by who? What happened?"

"It was this guy that I know from the gym. We work out together sometimes, and he's always asking me out, but you know I got a boyfriend or whatever, so I always brushed him off." I wringed my hands together as I continued, "Well, there was a murder next door and he was one of the officers that came here to help with the investigation."

"Wait—there was a murder here? Like the apartment next door or the building next door?" she asked with wide eyes.

"Yeah, next door, as in the apartment next to mine."

"Aw, shit. Why didn't you tell me I was coming to the hood? People gettin' bodied n' shit!" she said half joking, but half scared at the same time. I sucked my teeth and looked at her with an annoyed look. "Okay, go ahead. I'm sorry."

"Anyway, I ran into him while he was here, so he found out where I lived. I guess he waited for me to get home that night or something. I don't know. All I know is he attacked me outside in my parking lot, hit me over the head with something—that's why I was wearing that bandage before." I explained.

"Oh, I just thought you were trying something new, bad fashion move or something."

I gave her the same annoyed look again before continuing, "Yeah, so after he knocked me out, he raped me." I decided to leave out the part about Rainy coming to my rescue.

"Wow! You really have been going through it. So what happened? Did they catch the guy or what?" she asked.

"No, I had been going back and forth to the police station trying to press charges, but the thing is that he was a cop. So of course they weren't trying to arrest one of their own."

"He *was* a cop? What'chu mean *was*?" she was confused.

"Well, he was just murdered last weekend. They found his body in Weekend Park." Tears began to fall as I thought about Cal being the one that put him there.

Jillian grabbed my hand and squeezed it. "It's okay. I understand … I haven't told many people about this, but I was raped too. I never even reported it."

"What? You were?" I asked in disbelief.

"Yup, three years ago. One of my regulars from the club … never looked at men the same." Now her eyes began to tear up. "Ugh, see, now I'm 'bout to start crying." She said as she wiped her eyes and waved her hands back and forth to dry them.

"I'm sorry, Jilli," was all I could manage to croak out.

"It's okay. It's done now."

"Why didn't you call the cops or report him or something?" I asked.

"I don't know. I felt embarrassed. Plus you know they probably wouldn't even take me serious with me being a dancer and all." She was probably right.

"Well, does the guy still come to Ronnie's? Is it someone I know?" I asked.

"Nah, I haven't seen him since."

There was more silence for a while as we both reflected back on our misery. "You know what else?" It felt good having an outlet, and I thought I could trust her.

"What?" she asked.

I paused before making the final decision to confide in her some more. "You know Carla? Ronnie's sister? She's right." I said solemnly.

"Right about what?"

"I did see one of the guys that shot her husband at IHOP that night." I confessed.

"What? Really? Why didn't you tell them, Angie?"

"I'm scared to death, Jilli! I mean it's not like I know who they are or anything. I just happened to see one of the guys' faces. I only got a glimpse anyway." I said, trying to downplay it.

"That ain't right, Angie. You know that, don't you?"

"I knooooowww! Don't you think I feel horrible about it? I looked that woman right in her face and lied. And I know she knows it was me because she even called out to me for help that night. I didn't even help her, Jilli," I said as I dropped my head shaking it back and forth in guilt.

"Damn …" Jillian shook her head too, but in disapproval by what I had just shared with her.

"If you saw what they did to that dude, you would've been scared too, Jilli," I began to weep.

She just looked at me for a moment, deciding what to say next. "I know…" She said as she rubbed my back. "Don't worry, I won't say anything, but you should think about telling Ronnie the truth. They deserve that, Angie." I sniffled and nodded. Jillian got up and walked to the bathroom returning with some toilet tissue for me to blow my nose. I tried to clean my face up, but the tears kept coming. The guilt was overwhelming, and it showed.

"Don't worry. I probably would've done the same thing, Ang." She said as she resumed rubbing my back. "Stop. You're too pretty to be crying," Jillian whispered as she gently pushed my hair away from my face.

"Thanks, Jilli."

"Don't worry about it. That's what I'm here for girl." She ran her fingers along my cheek stroking it softly. Then her hand reached my chin where she brought my face halfway to meet hers, and before I knew it, her lips were pressed up against mine.

I drew back and jumped up immediately, "Whoa! What the fuck, Jilli?"

"I'm sorry. I'm sorry. I thought—"

"I don't know what the hell you thought, but I already told you I don't go that way!" I cut her off in a rage. I was standing in a stance ready to fight.

"Damn, my bad. My bad. You gotta understand that I find you very attractive. Do you know how hard it is to be around you and have to pretend like I'm not feeling you?" Her confession sounded and looked almost pathetic.

"Yeah, I'm not really try'na hear all that. I'm sitting here opening up to you like a dummy and all you wanna do is fuck me! Just like a nigga…" I was heated.

"No, no you really can trust me, Angie! I'm not gonna tell anybody anything, and I really do care about you. I just … I just got caught up in the moment, I guess."

"You guess? Well guess this—it's time for you to get the fuck out." I said in the calmest tone possible.

She huffed from frustration, dug both of her fists into the couch, and pushed herself up. She started to walk towards the door. I was two steps behind her, prepared to slam the door right on her heels. Suddenly, she turned and used one arm to grab me around the waist and the other around my neck in an attempt to pull me in close. In one swift motion, I swung my right fist and punched her in the face. I missed my target, which would have been the nose or lips. Instead, her eyebrow started to leak blood. What started out as a come-on, turned into a two-person brawl.

She grabbed my hair and yanked my whole body down causing me to lose my balance and trip over our feet onto the floor. Now she was on top of me choking me in a tight grip between her hands. She was a little stronger than I expected. "Bitch, you must've lost yo damn mind! You think you just gon' punch me in my face and I wouldn't hit you back!" Her face was twisted in a distorted ugly scowl as she hissed her words at me. I clawed at her hands trying to get free but she didn't let up. I squirmed and pushed her chest until I was able to squeeze one leg through her straddle with my knee bent to my chest. With all my might, I shot my leg out and kicked her between her legs, right in her pussy bone. "Aw FUCK!" she groaned, and I was released as she flopped over on her side wincing and grabbing at her crotch. "BITCH!" she hissed loudly in pain and agony.

I wasn't done. Now not only was I infuriated by her trying to force herself on me, but now she had just tried to choke me to death. I didn't want to waste too much time out of fear she would recover and retaliate quickly. All the memories and flashes of Rock's face flooded in. I wasn't about to let this happen again. A switch went off inside me, and I was in full defense mode. My eyes searched urgently for the nearest object I could find. I spotted my five-pound dumbbells in a corner behind my small table. It wasn't in my reach, but I made a fast break for one of them scrambling to my feet quickly. Five pounds doesn't sound heavy, but it's heavy enough to knock someone out I soon realized. I grabbed it and as soon as I turned around, I could see Jillian turned on her stomach slowly trying to get to her feet. I came down with all my might hitting her in the back of the head with the weight. Once! Twice! Before I knew it, I lost count of how many times I had hit her, maybe five. Maybe seven. It wasn't until she stopped moving that I even noticed the blood on my hands, the dumbbell, the carpet, and even some splattered on the leg of the table.

My eyes were wide in surprise at what just took place. I jumped back and gasped as I waited for her to call me more bitches or jump to her feet. Instead, there was just silence. I was out of breath, panting, "Jilli?" I called to her softly. Nothing. "Jilli!" This time I called a little louder and nudged her body with the tip of my foot. Still nothing. I crouched down slowly balancing on the balls of my feet. My hands were shaking something terrible as I reached out to touch her. I shook her lightly and her head fell to the side. I started to cry frantically as I turned her over and shook her hard, "JILLI! JILLI! GET UP!" I demanded. Her body was lifeless.

I stood up and cupped my hand over my mouth to muffle my sobs. I did a short pace back and forth as I looked at the apartment. I ran to my room to get my phone and began to dial 9-1-1. I froze before pressing "send" on the phone. A sudden panic rushed over me. I was already suspected of having some type of involvement in Rock's murder. I became afraid quickly that I would spend the rest of my life in jail. I reasoned that no one would understand that it was just an accident. Plus, if Detective Ramsey got any kind of wind of this I was sure he would make sure I rotted in jail. He was already holding that possession charge over my head.

I snorted heavily and breathed deeply trying to calm myself down to think. *Think think think, Angela!* I looked down at the blood on my hands as they continued to shake. I thought about calling Cal but the thought left my mind as quickly as it came. I put my phone down on the table and rushed to the bathroom. I washed my hands feverishly. I scrubbed them so hard in scorching hot water, taking care to wash under my nails as well. I glanced up at the mirror and noticed some blood on my face. I wasn't sure if it was from the spatter or if I put it there when I had my hands muzzled over my mouth. The sight disgusted me and I felt my stomach toss and turn in agreement.

The next thing I knew, Grey Goose and mixed nuts were coming up. I didn't even bother to try to make it into the toilet. I just let the contents land right in the sink. When I was finished, I washed out the basin quickly with cleanser. Then I brushed my teeth and scrubbed my face hard with a washcloth and hand soap. The blood was gone but my skin was still crawling where it had been, so I continued scrubbing until my cheeks burned with rawness.

Next, I flicked the light on in the bedroom and took my clothes off. I grabbed a plastic bag that was hanging on the door handle and turned it upside down emptying out all of its contents onto the floor. I stuffed the clothes in and tied the handles into a knot. I threw on some sweats then grabbed a scrunchie and tied my hair back quickly, stopping every so often to glance to the living room to see if Jillian had moved. She hadn't budged an inch. I grabbed random clothes and random toiletries stuffing them into an overnight bag. I grabbed my pocketbook and my phone before putting on a coat. I turned off all the lights and took one last look at Jillian before I rushed out.

My heart thumped hard and heavy as I galloped down the stairs, taking three steps at a time. There was no warming up the car this time. I pulled out of the space quickly and sped right onto the street without stopping to look first. Luckily, no one was out driving this early in the morning. I wasn't sure where I was going. I just needed to get out of Newark as fast as possible. It wasn't until I passed a cop car that I realized I was speeding. I checked my rearview mirror to see if he was going to pursue me, but he didn't. I couldn't think until I made it to the highway. Even then I still didn't know where to go.

CHAPTER 29

I spent the next two hours driving south on the New Jersey Turnpike with no clue where I was going. There weren't many cars out, so it made my getaway easy. I was wide awake on adrenaline, but my eyes grew weary. The sun was coming up, and I knew I had to pull over somewhere. I checked the signs to see where I was. I saw signs for Philadelphia, and I decided I would keep driving until I made it across the bridge.

It was another forty-five minutes before I made it. I drove around until I found the first motel that looked open. It was a small, dank inn. On any other day, I never would have dreamed of staying somewhere like this, but I knew I didn't have a lot of options at the moment. The place looked deserted except for two cars in the parking lot. I pulled in close to the office and looked around nervously before getting out.

A bell rang above the door when I entered. It smelled like cigars and the one small window that displayed the lit "Open" sign was clouded with dirt. I could barely see my car through it. I waited a minute or so before ringing the small bell that sat on the desk. I wondered what the purpose of the bell hanging over the door was if I still had to ring this other bell to get someone's attention. Still no one came, so I tapped it again, this time twice. "ALRIGHT! I'LL BE RIGHT THERE!" an agitated, dry voice said from the back of the office.

An old white man with a bald spot and white hair on the sides of his head came limping to the front. He wore a green sweater vest over a dingy white work shirt. His hunched back was hard to ignore as he shuffled to the desk. It looked like it took all of his energy to stand up.

"Yeah?" he croaked out hoarsely.

"Hi, I'd like a room please."

"Uh huh, just you?" he asked. I didn't want to tell the truth and say yes. I didn't think it was safe for a woman traveling alone to let people know she was alone, especially in unfamiliar surroundings.

"No, my boyfriend's waiting in the car." I lied. He looked out the window, but I knew he couldn't see much through the cloudy glass.

"It's sixty for the night or four-ten for seven days. How many days you staying?" he asked. I had no intention of staying there for a whole week. I didn't even want to stay there one night. I just needed a place to collect my thoughts before I made my next move.

"Just one night."

He licked his finger before opening a receipt book and flipping through it. He wrote some things in then asked "cash or credit?"

"Uhhh, let me see ..." I sifted through my purse until I found my wallet. I only had twenty-three dollars. That's when I realized I left all my tips in the canister I kept them in at home. I sucked my teeth and thought out loud "*damn!*" "You take Visa, right?"

"Yep! I'll just need to see some ID," he said. I didn't want to show him ID because I knew it would be a matter of time before the police were looking for me, but I knew I'd be gone by the time they traced my credit card there. I felt grossed out handing him my ID and credit card knowing he had just slobbered all over his finger.

There was no computer there. Instead, he had some old fashioned device where they take an imprint of the credit card and make a carbon copy. He did that and handed me my cards back along with two room keys. I was surprised that they were actual keys instead of the plastic key cards every other hotel and motel used. This place was old as dirt.

"Alright we run a nice, quiet place here. Please be mindful of your noise level and please leave our room the way you find it. You're in twelve. It's up on the second floor." He instructed. On any other day, his comment would have set me off. I possibly would've cursed him out and told him exactly what I thought of him and his dinky old ass motel.

Instead, I just said "yeah." I didn't know what he thought I was there to do. I wasn't going to be having band practice in the room or doing anything to trash it. I just wanted to sleep for a couple of hours before I made my next move.

I headed back to the car and drove to a parking space closer to the room, so I could see it from my window. I looked around suspiciously, but there didn't seem to be anyone there except me, at least that's how it looked and sounded. The room was small with the bare necessities. There was a phone, a TV, two twin beds, and a small table. I turned up the heat in the room before removing my coat and started my inspection. I began with the beds. I stripped the first bed down to check the cleanliness of the sheets. There was a short, curly hair on the sheet. I checked the other bed to see if it was any better. It wasn't. There was an unidentifiable stain on it of a brownish color. I decided the bed with the hair was the lesser of two evils and removed the hair from the sheet.

Next, I checked the bathroom. It wasn't much to write home about. I pulled back the shower curtain and two roaches scattered in opposite directions in the tub. One ran down into the drain and the other hauled ass up the wall. I wanted to leave, but my eyes were too tired to drive anywhere, and I knew switching rooms would probably be a waste of time. I stared at the mirror. I watched way too many investigation shows. Every time I visited a hotel or motel, I thought there were hidden cameras somewhere. Given my recent findings at home, I guess I wasn't totally paranoid for nothing. I wondered if the mirror was one of those two-way mirrors, so I did the nail test. I put my fingernail against the mirror and looked closely to see if there was a space in between my nail and the reflection. It passed.

I kicked off my sneakers and plopped on the bed. I knew I would have no problems falling right to sleep, but the room was too quiet. It gave me an eerie feeling like I was in that classic movie *Psycho*. I picked the remote up from the nightstand that stood between the two beds. I began flipping through the channels and discovered there was no cable there. Most of the channels already had the morning news starting, so I just left it on a random station and placed the remote back down.

I tossed and turned as the morning anchors reported. My eyes were closed, but I just couldn't fall asleep. All I kept thinking about was what I had just done to Jillian. Once again hindsight was twenty-

twenty. I scolded myself for allowing myself to even get in that position in the first place.

I turned from my back onto my side as the thoughts poured on endlessly. I wondered how long it would take for them to find her body. It was a whole week before anyone realized the stench from the apartment next door to me was a rotting body. The difference was that I was sure someone would be looking for Jillian before a week would pass. Panic set in next. *Oh shit! What if I left some evidence there? Duh, of course you left evidence. The evidence is the dead corpse in your apartment! What was I thinking? I shouldn't have run. I should've called the police. No, maybe I should've dismembered the body and hid it in different places or something. No, that's horrible and disgusting. At least someone would be bound to find her. They're gonna know right away it was me. The girls were the last ones to see Jilli alive, and they left her alone with me. Of course, I could always blame it on Britt. She was still with us. It would be her story against mine.*

I began to disgust myself with the thoughts that raced through my brain. How could I even think of doing things so malicious, conniving, and out right wrong? I was in a more than tight spot and had no clue how I would get out. I thought of the only person I knew that I could trust with my secrets and wouldn't turn me in— Cherlise.

My heart pounded as the phone rang. My first call went unanswered, but I continued calling until she finally picked up on the fourth call. "Hello?" she answered blandly.

"Hey Cherlise, thank God you finally answered!"

"What's up?" I could tell by her tone that she wasn't feeling me at the moment. I had to put my pride aside though.

"Listen, I really need your help." She was silent as she waited for me to continue. "I'm in a reeeeeal fucked up situation right now, and I don't know what to do. I didn't know who else to call …" I waited for her to say something. This time she did.

"It's funny how you all of a sudden have my number when you need something."

"I know you're probably still mad at me, but look we can hash that out later. You can curse me out all you want to then. Right now, this is something real serious!" I said with urgency. I felt a ball forming in my throat as I fought back tears. "Cherlise, I think I killed somebody." I said as the tears started streaming.

"*What?* Yeah right. What are you talking 'bout, Angie?" she said, half chuckling.

"Cherlise I'm serious. This is serious! This girl from the club was over and she tried to push up on me, and I fought her off then hit her in the head with a weight and she stopped moving. For real, Cherlise I don't know what to do." I was talking fast.

"Wait, wait. Is this supposed to be a joke or something?" she asked.

"Noooooo, I'm telling you it's not a joke!"

"So where is she? Did you check to see if she's breathing or has a pulse?" I scolded myself again in my head after realizing I had done neither one.

"No, but she wasn't moving at all Cherlise." I said.

"Yeah, but that doesn't mean she's dead! Go check her pulse. See if she's breathing." She urged.

I paused for a moment, "I'm not home anymore. I got scared, and I left. I didn't know what to do, so I drove out to Philly." As it came out of my mouth I realized how irrational I had been.

"WHAT? YOU JUST LEFT HER THERE?" she exclaimed in disbelief.

I started sobbing into the phone, "I-I just got scared. She wasn't moving, and I was scared to call the cops because I already got beef with them, and I just really didn't know what else to do. What should I do? Do you think I should just turn myself in?"

"I don't know what you should do, but I don't know how I'm supposed to help you. Matt don't even want me talking to you after you just igged his call when I needed your help so ..." I couldn't believe what I was hearing.

"So what? Just like that you gon' say fuck me? Damn Cherlise ..." I said disappointedly.

"Yup! Fuck you just like you said fuck me when I needed you. Good luck!" she said with hatred in her voice and hung up.

I stared at the phone through blurry eyes. I was hurt and mad with Cherlise, but I was more so desperate and worried about my current dilemma. The news was still on and as I wiped my eyes, I caught a glimpse of Mr. Burkwell's mugshot. I turned the TV up to see what they were saying about him this time.

A female, Asian reporter covered the story. She was standing in front of the prison where Mr. Burkwell had been awaiting his trial.

She was stiff and robotic as she spoke. "Right behind me at Southern Gate Prison is where prison guards found the lifeless body of seventy-three year old Brian Burkwell hanging in his prison cell early this morning. Brian Burkwell was a Newark man charged with the murder of his teen grandson. Sources say he was found at approximately five AM this morning hanging from a self-made noose fashioned from his own bed sheets. A thorough investigation is expected to begin immediately into how this could have happened. Burkwell shared his cell with another inmate who claims he heard and saw nothing. Prison officials on duty are being questioned about their whereabouts during this occurrence. An autopsy has been scheduled as well before the body will be released to Burkwell's family. Family and friends of Burkwell maintain his innocence and say this is a tragic loss all the way around."

It saddened me even more to watch this. I decided to call May, but after the second unanswered call, I gave up. I had no one. I began to think about what people would say about me if I were no longer here. I envisioned my funeral and who would be there. I felt hopeless.

My boyfriend was a murderer. I grieved the loss of my mother only to find out she wasn't even my biological mother. I began feeling sorry for myself knowing that my biological mother gave me up for adoption. *She could have at least tried to raise me. She didn't even give it a shot. She just gave me right up like it was nothing.* I thought to myself. I was a rape victim who had been treated as a criminal by the police. And now, I was a murderer too!

I buried my face into the pillow as my body jerked up and down from heavy sobs. These cries escaped from the pit of my stomach. I began to cry so much that I began coughing and gagging. I cried until the pillow was soaked with my salty tears. Snot ran down my nose, and I didn't even care. When the gagging got to be too much, I tried to take in deep, slow breaths. I walked to the bathroom mirror and looked at my bloodshot, swollen eyes. I was ugly, and I felt ugly inside and out.

I stood there thinking more and more about Mr. Burkwell. I bet the pressure got to be way too much for him or prison did. Either way, he must have felt hopeless just like me to kill himself like that. I returned to the bed and drifted off to sleep thinking about Mr. Burkwell and the position I was currently in. I tossed and turned as images of Mr. Burkwell's lifeless body swung back and forth through my dreams.

Sleep was restless, and suddenly, I found myself standing in front of the dresser that the TV sat on. I was rummaging through the bag I had thrown together and brought with me. After watching Mr. Burkwell's tragic story, suicide seemed like my only option left. I couldn't go to prison for killing Jillian. I wasn't built for prison. I didn't know anything about it and had no intention of finding out. Just the fact that I had left the scene of the crime didn't look good for me.

With no one to talk to, I felt entirely alone. I concluded that I wouldn't be missed anyway, especially once people found out what I had done. I started to think about the best way to do it. I didn't want to hang myself like Mr. Burkwell. I had always heard that people defecated on themselves when they were hung. That was a gross way to die, I thought. I suddenly wished I had a gun. That seemed the like the quickest way to do it. I tore open my bag to see what I had thrown inside that would help me with my new mission. I found a bottle of aspirin. I didn't think one bottle was enough for an overdose, so I kept searching. There were no additional bottles. The only thing I found to assist me was a small pair of scissors used for manicures. A knife or blade of some sort would have been better, but since that wasn't available, I had to use what I had on hand.

I decided the suicide was to take place right there on the bed. I fluffed up the pillows after filling a glass from the bathroom with tap water. I never drank tap water but it was good enough to do the job. I downed the entire bottle of aspirin in three gulps followed by the tap water. I waited a little while until I started to feel funny before I moved into the second phase of the plan. I rolled my sleeves up to the biceps. I held my left arm out on my leg then raised my right hand with the scissors hooked on my thumb and index finger. I came down hard, plunging them into my wrist and quickly spread the scissors open to make a deep gash.

The pain was way worse than I could've prepared myself for. I groaned loudly in agony as I stared at the scissors sticking out from my arm. Blood gushed out quickly. I took a deep breath and pulled them out fast. I growled, groaned, and rocked back and forth in pain. I didn't know if I could go through with the other arm, but I had to do it. My left arm was getting weak fast, so I had to act quickly. I switched the scissors over to my left hand. They slipped out from all the blood that was now oozing down. I picked them up from the bed sheet and came down quick and hard again on the other wrist. I gasped and heaved as I opened the scissors in my flesh. The wounds were definitely deep. I pulled the scissors out and let them fall to the floor. Now I just lay there waiting, sobbing, bleeding like a fountain, grunting and groaning, and squirming from the pain.

This was taking longer than I expected, but after about ten minutes I started to feel dizzy and lightheaded. My wrists and arms grew numb and the squirming died down until I squirmed no more. I drifted in and out of consciousness. One of the times I was out, my stomach woke me up as I threw up on myself without warning. I immediately blacked out again. Lights out. That was the last thing I remember.

CHAPTER 30

The phone rang, jolting me out of my latest nightmare. I jumped up with my heart racing as I checked my wrists for gashes. They were fine. *Just another dream,* I thought to myself as I closed my eyes in relief. I grabbed the phone and saw that it was Cal. I silenced the ringer and sunk back into the bed. I couldn't deal with him right now.

I glanced at the clock and saw it was just after ten in the morning. I felt like I had been asleep much longer, but I was glad to know I still had two hours until checkout time. I needed that time to think and decide what my next move would be. I lay still for a minute or two collecting my wits until I felt a tickle on my arm. I pulled the cover back and looked down to see a roach running off of my arm onto the bed. I jumped up out the bed swatting my arm like a mad woman. The hard slaps I gave my arm stung and I started to itch all over. It was clear I needed to get out of there, sooner rather than later.

After inspecting the tub for anymore roaches, I took a fast shower and gathered my things to head for check out. I returned the keys to the old man in the office and got my bill. After getting directions, I drove to a Dunkin Donuts to grab something to eat. I decided to sit inside to eat and drink my vanilla frosted jelly donut and orange juice. I was surprised it wasn't that busy, but happy I could keep a low profile and not be disturbed.

I went through the contact list on my phone trying to see who I could call. There was no one. My options were limited. Somehow cutie must have sensed this from a far because at that instant I got an email from him: *"Hey, beautiful. I know I know you said you got a man, but I was just thinking about you and wanted to say hi. I hope that's cool. How are you?"*

This time I didn't hesitate in responding, *"It's cool. I could be better actually."*

"Why is that?" he replied.

"I got a lot going on right now. Kinda in a tight spot, and I don't know what to do."

"Care to share, love?" he asked.

I really didn't want to share what was going on. I didn't know this man. I might tell him and he might turn me into the police without a second thought. *"Not really, what's up with you?"* I asked, trying to change the direction of the conversation.

"I was fine until this lovely lady told me she's not fine. Now I'm concerned." He was so nice.

"I'm sorry. I didn't mean to put my burdens on you." I responded.

"You didn't. I asked, and you told me. I'm tired of all this emailing. Can I please have your number, so I can call you?"

I hesitated. Before I had a reason not to give him my number; that reason was Cal. Now, I had no intentions of being with Cal ever again. He didn't know it yet, but I'd hoped he would get the picture eventually and go peacefully. I sent Gordon my number, and he called right away. On the phone, he sounded just as good as he looked.

"I'm glad you finally agreed to let me call you, Miss Angela. Now … tell me what's bothering you, angel." He started off.

"I don't really wanna go into it on the phone, but I'm knee deep in a really bad situation right now." That was more than I wanted to say but hopefully enough to satisfy his inquiries.

"Wow, I see. Well I'm sure it's probably not as bad as you think. I told you before I'm a good listener if you wanna talk. I'm not here to judge and who knows. Maybe I can even be of some help."

"Thanks, but I highly doubt it. Plus I really don't want to drag you into my mess." I said.

"Let me worry about that. I'm a grown ass man. Nobody drags me into anything I don't want to be in. Why don't you tell me where you are, and I can meet you there? We can try to work whatever it is out together."

I didn't understand why he was being so nice and caring. He was a good-looking guy. I'm sure he could get any chick he wanted. Why was he wasting his time trying to help me? I was a total stranger to him. Maybe he was just trying to get in good to get some ass. I guess my silence ran a little long as I weighed out my situation versus my options.

"Helllllloooo? You still there?" he asked.

"Yes, I'm still here. I'm all the way in Philly though."

"Damn! What are you doing way out there?" he exclaimed.

"I drove out here last night—well early this morning to get away from the situation I'm in."

He paused this time before responding, "I see. Well stay put. I'm coming to you. Where are you exactly?"

"You're gonna drive way out here? You know you really don't have to do that, Gordon."

"I know I don't. I'm coming because I want to. I want to talk to you, and find out what's going on. I like how you say my name by the way." He said. I could feel his charming smile through the phone, and it was infectious. As horrible as I was feeling, he managed to get a smile out of me.

"Okay. I'm at the Dunkin Donuts on …" I went on to give him my location and some general directions how to get to me. Now I would spend the next three and a half hours waiting.

The two employees behind the Dunkin Donuts counter kept shooting me looks as I stretched out eating my one donut for as long as I could. I still continued sitting there after it was long gone. I didn't care how much they looked at me so long as they didn't ask me to leave. Time dragged by as I waited for Gordon. Cal called three more times during the wait, but I didn't answer. After the third unanswered call, he left a message then started texting me. I didn't answer those either. I didn't see the point in checking the message since I had no intentions of calling him back or hearing what he had to say. It was hard to believe that just weeks before I would've died if I missed one of his calls. Now I hoped I would never have to see or speak to him again.

I had my head down on the table, bouncing my leg up and down as I waited in anticipation. I looked up every time I heard a car pull up. Finally, I lifted my head to see a black Infiniti G6 pull up with all black tinted windows and shiny rims. Gordon stepped out of the car looking even sexier than he had at the club. He was dressed down this time in some jeans, black Jordans, black army jacket, a gray skully hat, and a red, gray, and black Armani T-shirt with a black thermal underneath it. I swallowed hard as I watched him walk in. He didn't walk cool like Cal. Instead he walked like he had a purpose, more upbeat.

I waved from my table, and he walked right over. He sat down across from me, folded his hands, and looked at me with raised eyebrows, "So?"

I cracked a nervous smile before answering "So what?"

"You know what. I want to know what's going on, pretty lady." He said.

I sighed heavily and looked down at my hands, which I had started wringing in my lap. "Well, first, thank you for driving all the way out here. I can't believe you did that." I paused before continuing, "You want to talk here?"

"Well, I don't really know this area or know where else we would go to talk. You know somewhere better? We can talk wherever you feel comfortable."

I looked around as I thought about it. There weren't a lot of people, but I still wanted to talk somewhere more private. "Can we talk in my car?"

"It's kind of cold out there, baby." He replied.

"I'll turn on the heat."

"You're gonna waste your gas, but that's fine if that's what you wanna do." He said, sounding defeated.

We got in the car, and I cranked up the heat. I blew my breath into my cupped hands as I waited for the car to warm up and the heat to get hot. "Okay, you can stop procrastinating now and tell me what's up." He said, looking at me anxiously.

I took another deep breath. "Okay ... I killed someone last night." I looked over at Gordon's face, but I couldn't read his expression. He just sat with a straight face. "Did you hear me?" I asked.

Then he cracked a smile and started laughing, "You're funny. What's *really* going on?"

"Gordon, I'm serious." I said softly. He was studying my face now trying to decide if I was serious or not.

"You killed someone?" he asked in a sarcastic voice of disbelief.

"Yes! I'm dead serious. That's why I drove out here. I left the body in my apartment and came out here because I was scared to call the police or 9-1-1." Now I was biting my lip.

I needed him to take me seriously. His eyebrows raised, and he drew his head back with wide eyes "You're serious." I didn't respond this time. I just looked with a straight face. "Wow, I knew you said you were in some deep shit, but I didn't think it was anything like this!"

"I knew I shouldn't have told you." I said disappointedly. I didn't know what I had expected to happen. We were strangers to each other. I highly doubt the first thing a man wants to hear from a woman he's just started talking to is that she killed someone the night before. I was kicking myself for revealing my secret.

"No, no I'm glad you told me, and I'm glad I came. I told you I want to help and that's what I intend to do. Now just tell me what happened take by take, slowly. Okay?" He said.

Now I eyed him with suspicion as I let out a slow "Ooo-kaaayyy." I ran down the early morning events for him. He sat completely still and silent as he listened to each word intently. "And that's it," I said when I was done telling my story. He had an intense look on his face like he was deep in thought. "Are you going to turn me in?" I asked as I grew impatient waiting for a response.

He took a deep breath then answered, "No … you're going to turn yourself in."

"I can't do that."

"You can, and you will." He responded sternly. The dominance in his voice irked me and turned me on at the same time.

Who did he think he was telling me I would turn myself in? I had no intention of doing that. I couldn't have Detective Ramsey catching wind of this through the Newark Police grapevine. Whether he found out about it or not, I knew I would do time, and I certainly wasn't up for that. I hadn't told Gordon about my already existing problems with the Newark Police and I wasn't ready to tell him. I think killing a woman was more than enough for a stranger to handle for one day.

My phone rang, and I saw it was Cal again. Shaking him was going to be harder than I thought. I might just have to get a new phone number altogether and go underground for a while or something. I quickly hit the silencer and threw my phone back in my purse.

"Your man?" Gordon asked.

"Yeah—well he's not my man anymore." I said sadly.

"Oh no? I guess he's not catching on. I can't blame him." He said.

"Well, I haven't exactly told him that it's over yet."

"Oh, I see, and why not?" he asked.

"It's complicated."

"Why is it complicated? You just tell him it's over, and that should do the trick." He said.

"Well, it's not that easy. There's more to it than that that I can't go into right now."

"Can't or won't?" he asked.

"I don't really want to talk about that right now."

He shrugged, "Okay … I guess."

"I can't turn myself in Gordon." I returned to the subject at hand.

"Why not?"

"Because I just can't. I can't go to jail." I replied.

"You won't go to jail. I'll make sure of it. It was an accident."

"Yeah, but it doesn't look good that I just left her there like that." I explained.

"Yeah, you do have a point. Still, you just defended yourself. That's crazy. I thought dudes were bad. I guess she thought she was gonna get you regardless of what you said." He said, shaking his head.

"I don't know what she thought. I had already told her I wasn't gay."

"Well, I have some friends that will help us out." He said.

"What kind of friends?"

"Lawyers." He answered.

"So now what?"

"Now we go back to your house. I'll make a few calls, and see if one of my guys can meet us there to represent you. Once the three of us come up with a game plan, we'll call the police. It's better you surrender yourself than they catch you and charge you with eluding too."

I sighed before answering, "Okay."

I was terrified of what would happen once the police were there, but what else could I do? Turn into a lifelong fugitive and stay on the run? That was no way for me to live. I would just have to face the music and deal with the consequences.

We went to a diner to get something else to eat before heading back to Jersey. I was impressed to find out that Gordon was a lawyer himself. He had his own private practice and seemed to be doing well. Gordon followed me back up the parkway, but he used his navigation anyway just in case we lost each other on the way. The ride was a long one.

CHAPTER 31

Dusk was settling in as we arrived back at my apartment. I met Gordon in front of the building where he parked. I shifted back and forth nervously as I waited for him to get out of the car. I wasn't ready to see a dead corpse up close and personal. I wasn't ready to talk about the happenings with a lawyer. I wasn't ready to face the police. I wasn't ready for any of this.

Gordon read my expression as he got closer. "Relax. Don't worry. Everything is going to work out just fine. You ready?" I wanted to answer no, but I just took a deep breath and unlocked the outside door. We made our way upstairs, and I was glad we hadn't passed anyone along the way. My hands shook uncontrollably as I fiddled around with the keys. I finally dropped them, and Gordon picked them up for me. "Just tell me which key." He instructed. I was surprised how calm he was acting about this whole scenario. I wondered what his motives were.

He opened the door and stepped inside first as I followed behind. "Well where is she?" he asked. I gasped as I looked down at the floor where I had left Jillian's body. I lightly nudged Gordon out of the way to get a clearer view. There was a little blood on the carpet but no Jillian. "Is she in the bedroom?" he asked. I was too stunned for words. With my mouth gaped open I rushed past him to the bathroom. No Jillian. I burst into my bedroom. She wasn't there either.

I looked around the apartment for clues, but there weren't any.

Jillian's coat and purse were gone. There were no signs of her. Baffled, I stood in my bedroom doorway trying to fathom where she could be. Gordon appeared behind me startling me, "She's not here?"

My mouth was dry as I found my words, "No ... no she's gone. I don't get it."

"Gone?"

"Yeah, I left her right here!" I said as I made my way back to the living room and stood over the bloodstain on the carpet. Blood spatter was still evident on the legs of the table and a little on the wall, just no body. "She was right here!" I repeated.

"Does anyone else have access to your apartment?"

"No, just me. Matter of fact, I just had the locks changed." I explained.

"Locks changed? Why?"

"Long story for another time. Right now I just gotta find out where the hell this girl is!" I said as my head began to spin from the confusion.

"Try calling her." Gordon's suggestion was a good one. I whipped out my phone and called, but the call went straight to voicemail.

"No answer," I said sounding defeated.

"Okay, I guess you can try again later. It's probably not safe for you to stay here, you know."

"You're probably right. I can go stay at my mother's old apartment, but what should I do next? I mean it doesn't make sense for us to call that lawyer or the police, and we don't even know where she is." I said.

"Yeah, well we should hold off on that for now until we know exactly what's going on. We should check to see if her car is still on your street though."

"Okay, that's a good idea." I replied.

I went back to the bedroom to pack a new overnight bag. I wasn't sure about going to work the next day, but I grabbed some work clothes just in case. I locked my place back up, and we headed out the back door. Gordon walked with me to my car. "Are you going to be okay by yourself? I know you don't know me, but if you rather stay at my place, you can. I don't bite." He said with a seriously concerned face.

"That's okay. I'll be alright. I just need to be somewhere away from this place, so I can think and try to find out where Jillian is. I'll be fine once I get to my mom's."

"Okay, well please call me once you get there, so I know you're safe. Don't worry your pretty little head. We'll figure this out together." He said as he moved in for a hug.

I spoke in his ear as we embraced, "Thank you so much for all of this."

"YO! WHO THE FUCK IS THIS, ANGIE?" I heard a voice yell out to us. That's when Cal walked up to us and yanked me by the arm.

"Ouch! You're hurting me! Calm down, Cal!" I said, both frightened and worried about what would escalate next.

"Nah, don't tell me to calm down! I been calling you all night worried that something happened to you, and you over here fucking another nigga?" He was furious.

"It's not like that, Cal. We weren't doing anything."

"Look brother, you need to let go of the lady's arm." Gordon stepped into the argument. I wish he hadn't.

"What? You fuckin' *my* bitch, and you think you gon' tell me what to do too? You need to mind your business and roll up outta here!"

"I ain't *rollin'* nowhere! Now you need to let her go!" Gordon shot back.

Cal did exactly that this time. He let go of me and spun around and punched Gordon in the eye, dropping him to the ground instantly. A kick to the ribs came next. I grabbed at Cal's arm pulling him away from Gordon with all my might.

"Cal! What are you doing? What's wrong with you? STOP!" I screamed at him. He was out of breath, and his nostrils flared as he took sharp breaths in and out. He was in a blind rage and for a moment I thought I was about to be his next victim.

"Get the fuck off me!" he said, snatching his arm from my grasp. He just stood there glaring at me as his chest heaved in and out. "I can't believe you, Angie. After all I've done for you, this is what you do to us?" He spat on the ground and shook his head at me.

"Cal, it's over, and you need to leave before I call the cops on you."

"Call the cops on me? Word? That's how we doing now? Alright, I got'chu Angela." He said then gave Gordon one more kick in the stomach.

"STOP!" I pleaded.

"Fuck you, Angie!" He said before shoving past me to return in the direction from which he had come.

Once I was sure he wasn't coming back, I crouched down beside Gordon and put my arms on his shoulders as he tried to get up. He shrugged me off, "So I guess that's him, huh?" He sounded angry, but I couldn't blame him. I felt horrible about what had just taken place.

"Yeah, that was him."

"Well, you should've told me he was crazy, shit." Gordon said as he got to his feet and brushed off his coat.

"Gordon, I'm so sorry about all of this. I had no idea he'd be here. I don't even know how he got here. Are you okay?"

"Besides my swollen eye and my most likely broken rib, yeah I'm fine, Miss Angela." He responded sarcastically.

I didn't know what to say or do next. "I'm sorry." That was the best I could come up with.

I ended up walking him to his car instead. He was limping and holding his ribs on one side. "Are you going to go to the hospital?" I asked worried.

He sucked his teeth before answering, "No, girl! I'll probably just wait til' tomorrow and go see my regular doctor."

"Are you sure? If your ribs are broken—"

"Yes, I'm sure! I'll be fine. You just make sure you call me when you get to your mom's and make sure you lock yourself in good. That boyfriend of yours is a nutcase." He said, cutting me off.

"He's *not* my boyfriend anymore, but okay, I'll call you when I'm in."

After Gordon shut the door and started his engine, I rushed back to my own car. I was terrified. I had no idea where Cal went or if he might've been lurking around somewhere in the shadows waiting for me. Gordon was right. Cal was obviously crazy. Why didn't I see this early on? How did I miss this?

During the drive to my mother's, all I could think about was what I would do about Cal and where the hell Jillian was. It was such a mystery. With all the commotion from Cal, I had completely forgotten to check for Jillian's car before I left. I was glancing in my rearview mirror the entire ride. Once I finally made it there, I looked around nervously before getting out of the car and rushing into my mom's apartment. I locked myself in like Gordon suggested. Still, I felt paranoid. I found myself peeping out of the blinds every so often to make sure no one followed me, in particular Cal. Unsure of what my next move would be, after texting Gordon, I left all the lights on in every room and the TV too. Needless to say, I didn't get much sleep that night.

CHAPTER 32

The next sound I heard was my phone ringing back to back. I tried to ignore it, but whoever it was, was being persistent. I didn't recognize the number right away, but I did recognize the voice right away. "Hi Angela?" It was Danika. I had totally forgotten to set my alarm to get up for work at B.I.G. Insurance. Trying to collect my senses, I frantically jumped out of the bed.

"Oh my God, Danika I'm so sorry! I totally overslept. I'm at my mom's, and I forgot to set my alarm." I pulled the phone away from my ear to see what time it was. It was eleven o'six, and I was supposed to be in by eight thirty that morning.

"Is everything okay? We were worried about you." She said in her robotic voice. They weren't worried about me at all. They just wanted to know where I was because the work was probably piling up on my desk.

"I'm so sorry. Yes, I'm okay, but I just had a lot going on this weekend and got in super late." I explained.

"Okay. Yeah I was wondering because I know it's not like you to be *this* late." I rolled my eyes at her comment.

"I know. I know. By the time I get dressed and get there, it'll be one o'clock probably. I'm sorry to do this, but I'm just going to have to take a sick day." I was in no condition to go to work. My mind was all over the place, and I probably wouldn't get anything accomplished anyway.

"Well, you could come in for a half day and still get *some* work done. You know I'm really not supposed to let you use a sick day if you're not really sick." This lady knew exactly how to get on my last nerve.

"I'm sorry, Danika, I'm just really not feeling up to it. If I can't use the sick day, that's fine. I'll just use a vacation day. I'll be in tomorrow." I said, trying to compromise.

"Well vacation days are supposed to be planned and approved beforehand you know, but I guess we can do it this one time. I just don't want the rest of the team to think that it's okay to do this. If I allow it for you, then everyone else might think it's okay." I wanted to reach through the phone and yank her by her ponytail.

"Well, no one else on the team has to know. I don't see why you would have to tell them, and I know I certainly won't." I replied through my clenched teeth, trying not to let my annoyance show through the phone.

"Okay, just don't make a habit of it. I'm glad you're okay. See you tomorrow, Angela."

"Okay, thanks, bye." I was glad that conversation finally came to an end. Sometimes I would rather have my fingernails pulled out with pliers than to talk to that woman.

I sat back down on the edge of the bed, stretched, and then rubbed my eyes. I still felt sleepy and wanted to crawl back under the covers, but I knew I shouldn't. I stared down at the floor as I tried to think about what I should do first. The previous night's events replayed in my mind. I had no idea Cal had so much rage in him. I felt horrible about what he did to Gordon. *Oh! Gordon!* I thought to myself. I needed to call and see how he was doing, make sure he was okay.

The phone just rang and rang until his voicemail picked up: "You've reached the voicemail of Gordon Hopkins. I'm sorry I missed your call. Please leave a detailed message, and I will return your call as soon as possible. Thank you, and have a wonderful day!" He sounded so cheery on his greeting. Most of the men I knew didn't even bother to record a greeting for their phone. If they did it would be something like, "I'll hit you back" or "You know what to do. Get at me" or something to that effect. He was so ... so ... *mature.*

"Hey Gordon, it's Angie. I was just calling to check on you and see how you were feeling. I'm so sorry about what happened last night. I also just wanted to thank you again for everything. Please call me back when you get a chance. Thanks."

Next I tried Jillian again. That call went unanswered too, straight to her voicemail again. I thought about leaving a message, but was too afraid. As far as I knew, no one knew what happened between us over the weekend, and I wanted it to stay that way. I didn't want to take any chances leaving any messages for her. I needed to speak to her directly instead.

My stomach started to growl as I looked around my mother's room. I hadn't made much progress in packing her things up. I only had two more weeks to get all of her stuff out of there. I decided to get up and make something to eat. There wasn't much left in her refrigerator. I ended up scrambling the last of the eggs that were in there and some turkey bacon that I suspected wouldn't be any good much longer. Then I got to work. I turned on the radio and started with her bedroom, removing her clothes from the closets and stuffing them into garbage bags for the Goodwill.

I had all of her closets and dresser drawers done and was trying to decide what to do with all the nic nacs she had on top of the dresser when the phone rang. It was Cal. I didn't answer, so he sent a text message: *"Angie I'm sorry. I know I fucked up but it's only because I love you. Who was that guy though?"* I ignored the text message and started wrapping the items from the dresser in newspaper. I received several more calls and texts from Cal apologizing and begging to talk to me. I continued to ignore him. That's when the voicemails started. He left three and each message was more intense than the one before. The last message said "ANGIE, I SWEAR TO GOD IF YOU DON'T ANSWER THIS FUCKING PHONE, I'MA BREAK YA NECK!" I knew it would be just a matter of time before he realized I was at my mom's. I had to get out of there, but once again I found myself with nowhere to go.

After I finished packing up the entire bedroom, I stepped back to take a look around with approval. I was glad I had made some headway. Reluctantly, I decided to call Aunt Sandy and ask if I could crash with her for a few days. I really didn't want to, but I had no one else to ask and nowhere else to go. She agreed after giving me the third degree on why I needed to stay there and how long I'd be staying. I hated asking people for favors, but I was desperate. I needed a place to rest while I got my plan together. I didn't tell her about Cal, since I managed to keep him my little secret all the way up until this time. I just told her that they were doing some remodeling to my apartment and that it felt too eerie staying at my mom's place without her being there. I had already made up my mind that I wouldn't stay at Aunt Sandy's any longer than one week, and I would pay her for letting me stay. She said I didn't have to, but I knew she wouldn't turn the money down either.

I looked over my shoulder every step of the way from the time I stepped out of my mother's apartment, until I made it safely inside of Aunt Sandy's cozy home. She lived with her boyfriend, Bo, in a nice area of Springfield. It was quiet, and it felt nice to be away from all the city noise. She made up the guest room for me and was the perfect hostess. Bo was a nice man, but never really said too much. It wasn't surprising that dinner was fairly quiet.

Aunt Sandy cooked some baked chicken, pilaf rice with gravy, and sweet peas. It wasn't bad. It definitely wasn't good either. I tried to smile when she asked how I was enjoying the food. The rice could've cooked a little longer. It was hard in the middle but I forced it down to be polite. After dinner, Aunt Sandy knocked on the door as I was getting settled in for bed.

"Come in."

"Hey Angela, do you need anymore blankets or anything?" she asked.

"No, I have everything I need. Thanks again for letting me stay, Aunt Sandy."

"Oh, you're welcome." After a long pause she asked, "Is everything okay, Ang?"

"Yes, everything is fine. I just need to get some rest, so I can get up for work in the morning." I replied, trying to give her a hint that I was ready to be left alone.

"Oh okay, well you know you can talk to me if anything is going on. Towels and washcloths are in this linen closet right here in the hallway and just help yourself to anything you see in the fridge."

"Okay, thanks so much. Goodnight, Aunt Sandy." I replied.

"Night." She closed the door behind her, and I finished changing into my pajamas.

The bed sat high and it was firm, but the sheets were soft and inviting. So were the feather down pillows. I sunk right in and drifted off when my phone started ringing. I exhaled and rolled my eyes assuming it would be Cal again. It wasn't. It was Gordon, and my stomach fluttered a little at the realization.

"Hello?"

"Hey beautiful, did I catch you at a bad time?" he answered.

"Hi Gordon, no you didn't. How are you? Are you okay? I just feel so bad about yesterday. I'm so sorry about all this." I rambled.

"Baby, calm down. It's okay. I promise. I'm okay. Now stop apologizing. You can't control what that fool ex-boyfriend of yours does!"

"I know. I know, but I still just feel horrible. If it wasn't for me, none of this would've happened." I replied, still feeling guilty.

"Listen, stop apologizing. Just forget about what happened. I'm a big boy. I can handle myself, and I'm fine. Now more importantly, how are you?"

I smiled on the other end of the phone before answering. "I'm fine. I'm staying at my aunt's house for a few days until I can figure out what to do next. I know Cal won't find me here so …" I trailed off.

"Okay, that's smart. Yeah, you need to stay as far away as possible from that maniac. Where does your aunt live? I would love to see you."

I hesitated before answering. For some reason, I still had some apprehension about Gordon. I didn't know this man, and in one day, I had managed to get him involved in my problems and beaten up. "You still want to see me after all of this?" I asked.

"Yeah! Why wouldn't I?"

"I don't know. I just thought all my baggage and drama would've definitely changed your mind by now." I said with a light laugh.

"Girl, please! I don't scare that easily. I want another chance to take you out. You know like a real date? Get to know you without all this other unnecessary nonsense dangling over our heads."

"Well, okay if you insist—"

"I do!" he said, cutting me off.

"Well I'm staying in Springfield. I guess you can come by and pick me up tomorrow after work."

"Okay, sounds good. I look forward to it."

"Me too, I'll text you the address." I said.

"Cool, have a good night, baby."

"Thanks, you too." I responded before hanging up.

I reached over and turned off the lamp next to the bed. A million thoughts ran through my mind as I lay there in the dark waiting to fall asleep. I wondered if I was moving too fast. I had just barely gotten out of a relationship with Cal. Should I really be going on dates this soon? Plus Cal's recent behavior and revelations had me questioning everything and everyone. How much did I really know about Gordon? He could be some kind of psycho too just waiting for his moment to reveal his true colors. Not to mention, this man was still married. For all I knew, he could have a crazy wife waiting in the shadows somewhere for her chance to pounce on me.

CHAPTER 33

I was surprised when I returned to my desk the next day to see that my rush pile had gone down some. I guess some people got a clue and got someone else to take care of a few of the accounts that I was supposed to work on. My email was another story, so I got right to work typing away on the keyboard. The hours flew by as I made headway with my work. Then the desk phone rang.

"B.I.G. Insurance, this is Angela speaking," I answered. I could hear someone breathing on the other end of the phone, but they didn't say anything. "Hello?" I tried again. Still there was just breathing for a few moments. Then the person hung up. I looked at the caller I.D., but I didn't recognize the number. I shrugged it off as the person having the wrong number and went back to work. Just then, Donnie popped his head over the cubicle wall.

"Hey! Feeling better?" he asked.

"Huh?" I was caught off guard.

"How you feeling? You were out sick yesterday, right?"

"Oh ... oh yeah I'm fine. How you doing, Donnie?"

"I'm great! Did you have a cold or the flu or something?" he pressed. It annoyed me whenever I returned from a sick day and people wanted details. I never knew if they were asking to make conversation, out of concern for me, out of nosiness, or out of concern for themselves if I was contagious.

"No, no cold or flu. Don't worry, I'm not contagious." I said dryly. He stood there waiting for me to go on and tell him what sickness I had, but I just looked at him.

"Oh, well at least it's not the flu, so that's good!" he finally said.

"Yup!" I really wasn't in the mood to chat. I wanted to get back to work.

"Yeah, I came over here yesterday, and they said you were out sick."

"Oh, yeah ..." I was waiting for him to get to his point while still trying to be polite.

"I wanted to invite you to my party that I'm having in a few weeks. I'm only inviting a few people from work. You know, just the ones I'm cool with, so keep it on the low."

"Oh okay, thanks for the invite. Where you having it?" I asked.

"It's gonna be at The Volt in Jersey City. I'll email you all the info and bring whoever you want. The more the merrier, but there's a theme, and you must come dressed for the theme or you can't get in. No party poopers!" he instructed as he chuckled.

"Oh, that sounds fun! What's the theme?"

"It's gonna be like a masquerade ball. So bring the sexy, and you gotta at least where a mask. We're giving prizes for best costume too so ..." This was the first time Donnie ever actually *seemed* gay to me.

"Okay cool, cool. Just email me the info, and I will most likely be there, and thanks for inviting me!" I said with a smile.

"No problem. Alright, I'll talk to you later. Let me go finish making these deliveries upstairs." He said as he pushed his cart full of pantry supplies past my aisle.

The rest of the day at work was uneventful, and I was happy to get out of there. I was excited about my date with Gordon. I had already laid out my outfit that morning. So all I had to do was go back to Aunt Sandy's, shower, and get dressed. I wasted no time leaving the office once five o'clock came. I had just unlocked the driver door to my car when a black Dodge with black tinted windows pulled up behind, blocking me in. The shiny rims kept spinning as the car stopped. "ANGIE!" a voice yelled angrily.

I spun around to see Cal exiting the passenger side. I tried to hurry to get my car door open. I jumped in the seat, but I couldn't move fast enough. Cal slid in the doorway preventing me from closing it. With both hands on the steering wheel I sighed in exasperation as I turned and glared it him.

"What do you want, Cal?"

"What'chu mean what I want? You haven't been answering my calls or texts! What's really good, Angie?" he asked as if he really didn't know the answer.

I spoke calmly and steadily in a low voice. "Cal, I already told you it's over. We're not together anymore."

"Just like that?" he asked with his face distorted.

"Yes, Cal, just like that."

"For real, Angie? You just gon' kick me to the curb just like that for that pussy ass nigga?" He said, getting louder.

"Cal, you are not the person I thought you were. You're crazy. You're out of your fucking mind!" Now I was getting louder. I was getting tired of this and tired of him calling and texting me. I just wanted whatever we once had to be over.

"What'chu mean *I'm outta my mind*?" he asked again as though oblivious to everything that had been going on.

"Cal, you're a murderer, and you hurt people. I don't wanna be with you anymore. It's over. What part of that can't you understand?"

He swung the door all the way open and crouched down beside me to look into my eyes. Grabbing my hand off the steering wheel, he held it in between both of his. "Angela, don't do this. That fag can't love you the way I do—shit he can't even fight! How's he going to protect my lady?" His voice was starting to crack as he looked at me with pleading eyes. I looked back into those same eyes that once made me melt and felt nothing.

"I'm not your lady anymore, Cal, and it's not about him. I barely even know that guy. It's about *you* and the things you've done. Killing people, beating up people you don't even know, spying on me with cameras … you ain't right in the head."

"Stop saying that shit, Angela! I fucking love you! You damn straight I killed for you, and I would do it again in a heartbeat. Who you know gon' be down for you like that?" he asked. I rolled my eyes and didn't answer. It was clearly like talking to the wall. I wasn't getting through to him.

"Fine! Fuck it! You wanna keep fucking that fagot ass nigga? Go ahead—shit you probably been fucking him this whole time anyway!" He said angrily as he stood up and slammed the car door. "Bitch!" he growled at me as he walked back to the car. My heart was racing, and my pits had began to sweat profusely. I had no way of predicting what Cal was capable of these days. I let out a slow sigh of relief as I looked in the rearview mirror to see the car speed out of the parking lot. I was glad our conversation hadn't escalated, and I was glad it was over. Now hopefully the calls and texts would stop.

I was relieved once I had gotten back to Aunt Sandy's house. I needed a shower bad. I also needed some time to calm myself down and relax before my date with Gordon. I didn't want to bring anymore drama or baggage his way. When I got in, Aunt Sandy hadn't made it in yet, but Bo was home slouched on the living room couch watching TV. He still had on his work uniform. I wasn't exactly sure what he did, but he wore khakis and a tan work shirt with his name on it.

"Hi, Bo!"

"Hey Angela, how you doing?" he asked.

"I'm good. How are you?"

"Good, good just waiting for the numbers to come on. Who knows maybe today will be my lucky day!" he said, smiling.

"Well, the best of luck to you, Bo!" I said, returning the smile as I headed for the guestroom.

"Hey, Angela can you do me a favor right quick?" he asked. This was probably the most I had ever heard Bo say at one time.

"Sure, what's up?"

"Can you just grab me another beer from the fridge?"

"Sure." I returned with his Bud Light in hand quickly.

"Thanks, sweetie. If you want one, just help yourself." He said.

"Oh, no thanks, Bo. I'm actually about to hurry and jump in the shower. I got a date!"

"Aww, sookie sookie now! Okay then." He said with a smile and wink before he turned his attention back to the TV.

I was moving fast as I lathered up with my apple scented Bath & Body Works shower gel. I inhaled deeply as I watched the suds slide down my body. I loved the smell of that fragrance. I rinsed off and stepped out of the shower onto the rug. The room managed to get steamy in that short time, and I couldn't see the mirror. I dried off quickly and massaged the same apple scented lotion into my skin. Then I hung my shower cap and tied the towel around my body. I reached for the door to turn the handle to leave but it was already slightly open, just an inch or so. I stopped and stared at the open crack in the door as I second-guessed if I had closed it all the way when I came into the bathroom. I couldn't make up my mind and assumed I must have been rushing and just forgot to close it. I made a mental note that next time I would be sure to lock it.

I hadn't brought many clothes with me to stay at Aunt Sandy's. So my choices were limited. I was glad that I did think to bring at least one dress. It was still freezing out, but it was either the dress or some jeans and a shirt that didn't really go together. I was just sliding on my shoes when Aunt Sandy tapped on the door.

"Come in!" She peeked her head around the edge of the door.

"Hey, Angela. How's it going?" she asked.

"Hey, Aunt Sandy. Good, how was your day?"

"Oh, chile', same ol' thang just a different day, ya know?" she said through a sigh.

"Yeah, I know what you mean."

"You look nice. I see you like to get fancy for work, huh?" she said jokingly.

I laughed before answering, "No, I'm actually about to leave in a bit. I have a date."

"*Oh?*" she responded. I smiled shyly.

"Yeah, his name is Gordon. I met him a lil' while back at work."

"I see...where y'all going?" she asked.

"I'm not even sure yet. We didn't really talk about it, probably just out to eat or something. We both gotta work in the morning, so I'm not trying to stay out too late."

"What does he do?"

Aunt Sandy didn't have any kids of her own, so I guess she considered me to be like a daughter to her. I could tell she was enjoying the girl talk. I beamed with pride when I answered, "He's a lawyer, has his own practice and everything."

"Niiiice. Momma taught you right! Marry you a rich man, Angie!" Then she lowered her voice to a whisper, "*somebody who can take care of you, not like Bo in there.*" She rolled her eyes, and I just smiled politely. I didn't care about Gordon's money, but it did feel better telling someone I was seeing a lawyer rather than a crazy ex con.

"Well, have fun girl. I'll leave the door open for you." She said.

"Thanks, Aunt Sandy. I don't plan on coming in too late though." I looked at my watch and just as I did, my phone rang. It was Gordon telling me he was outside to pick me up. I ended the call and said, "Well that's him! I'll see you later."

"Okay, have a good time, Ang." She said as she followed me to the front door. I had no idea she was so nosey. I guess she wanted to get a glimpse of what he looked like.

I could hear her mumble to herself as I walked out the front door, "Hmmm, an Infiniti ... not bad."

When Gordon got out the car to open the passenger door for me, I could see he was back in his work attire. He looked just as sharp in a suit as he did in jeans. "Hello, Beautiful," he said as he planted a kiss on my cheek and held out a small white box with a red ribbon around it.

I smiled, "Hi, Gordon. What's this?"

"Just a little something, nothing major. You like chocolate?" he asked.

"Yes, I do. Thank you." Once I was seated, I opened the box of assorted chocolates and ate one of the darker ones. It was filled with coconut. I was glad I picked a good one. It felt warm and toasty inside the car, and I was glad he had my seat warmer on already.

"How was your day?" he asked.

"It was okay." I thought about telling him about Cal's appearance then quickly dismissed the idea.

"Just okay?" he asked.

"Yeah, well, I don't exactly have the most thrilling job. I sit at a desk, type stuff on the computer, and push paper all day. How was your day?"

"I see ... well, my day was challenging, but I enjoy a challenge. I guess you know that by now though." He said as he glanced over at me with a smirk.

"Keep your eyes on the road. I want to make it home tonight. Why was your day challenging?"

"Relax, girl, you in good hands. We're having a hard time getting this doctor to release some medical records that can be pivotal to this client's case I'm working on." He explained.

"Oh. Well hopefully you'll get a good break and get what you need."

"Yeah, I'm sure it'll all work out in the end. It's just another pain in the neck, but I don't want to talk about work anymore. Let's talk about something less stressful." He suggested.

The rest of the ride was smooth and we held good conversation. Gordon turned out to be funnier than I expected, and I definitely needed the laughter with everything that had been going on. He took me to a delightful crab house in the city that sat on the Hudson River. It was too cold to sit outside, but the view of the river was romantic. I was glad I decided on the dress because I would have been severely underdressed had I worn the jeans. I didn't feel nervous or anything around Gordon. He was so down to earth and laid back. There wasn't one lull in the conversation the entire evening. We talked about everything. Finding out about his wife was a priority for me, so we talked about that too.

"So tell me what the deal is with your wife."

"What do you mean the *deal*?" He asked.

"You know what I mean. What's the story? What's the situation? Are you just separated? Has the divorce process been started? Why aren't you guys together anymore? Was it her fault? Your fault?" I fired off the questions with no regard.

"Okay. Okay." He said with a nervous laugh as he pumped his hands out in front of him. "Slow down. My wife and I were married for three years, together for five. Yes, the divorce papers have been filed and signed by us both, and it's nobody's fault. I guess people just change over time, grow apart. I wanted children. She didn't. She's a great person, and I still love her, but I'm not *in* love with her anymore. We both just realized we're not meant to be together. It was a mutual decision, and I wish her the best." He explained.

"So nothing in particular happened to cause the divorce? Nobody cheated on anyone? Abused the other one or something like that?" I asked with wide eyes.

He tilted his head back and laughed, "God, no! Nothing like that. Neither of us has felt happy or fulfilled in the marriage for some time now. We've done the counseling thing, but I think we both just had to come to terms that it's just time to say goodbye. There's no hard feelings between us or anything bitter like that. It's just time to move on." He said.

"Hmm … I see." I wasn't sure what else to say or ask, at least not at that moment. I was sure I'd have more questions to come later, though.

The conversation for the rest of the night focused around lighter topics. I'm sure Gordon was probably relieved to be out of the hot seat. I enjoyed his company, and he was the perfect gentleman. When he dropped me back off for the night, he walked me to the door. I expected him to try to kiss me on the lips. Instead, he kissed my hand

and thanked me for the good night. I was happy that he wasn't overly anxious to get physical like most men I had dealt with. I definitely wasn't ready for anything like that. Though I hadn't had any recent nightmares about Rock, I still wasn't past the rape.

It was eleven forty-five, and Aunt Sandy and Bo were already in their room asleep. I tiptoed into the guestroom and turned on the light. I changed into my nightclothes, set my alarm for the next morning, and lay down in the comfortable bed. Before I could drift off, I got a text from Gordon: *"I had a really good time tonight, Angela. Thanks again for letting me take you out. I look forward to seeing you again."* I went to sleep with a smile on my face that night and experienced a peaceful rest that I hadn't felt in a while.

CHAPTER 34

I was antsy all day that Friday. I kept glancing at the phone clock on my desk as the time ticked by. I was scheduled to work at the club, and I was anxious about Jillian. I still hadn't heard anything from her, and I'd given up on calling her. I bounced my knee up and down under my desk as I stared at my computer screen. I thought about calling out, but I knew I couldn't do that forever. I would just have to face my fears and handle the outcome however it came. I was mentally preparing myself for anything.

I went through my usual routine for Friday, stopping after work to pick up something to eat. Aunt Sandy's was too far, so I just went back to my mom's apartment to eat and rest up before heading to Ronnie's. My stomach did flip-flops the entire way there. I felt the nervous diarrhea coming on and hoped I'd be able to avoid letting it loose in Ronnie's nasty bathroom. That night, I didn't even bother having my usual Grey Goose and cranberry because I knew that might just make the diarrhea worse.

It was the usual scene when I got there. One of the dancers was bent over on the main stage making her butt cheeks clap as three men laughed and slapped her ass. Two other strippers slid up, down and around the poles on both sides of the platform. One guy threw a wad of singles up in the air to make it rain on one of the pole dancers. I caught the back of Ronnie walking towards the office in the back of the club. I was happy about that. Hopefully he'd stay back there for a while.

I headed to the bathroom quickly like I always did to make sure I looked okay. I held the diarrhea in and prayed the night would move fast. "HEY, ANNNNNG!!!" Britt yelled as I arrived behind the bar.

"What's up, Britt! Hey, Tee Tee! Hey, Keisha!" I said hello to the girls as I started checking bottle levels.

"They having a bachelor party tonight, so it's just you and me behind the bar." Britt explained as Tee Tee and Keisha headed back out on the floor with trays in hand. Whenever it was crowded or there was some type of party, they would double as cocktail waitresses and/or shot girls. Better them than me, I preferred to stay behind the bar where there was a barrier between the customer and me. Whenever you worked the floor, it was likely you would be groped or harassed at some point.

My hands were shaking so much from nervousness that I spilled a little of the Hennessy my first customer ordered. I took a deep breath and placed both of my hands down on the counter. That's when a hand reached over and tapped mine. Startled, I jumped. "Ay, girl!" It was Ozzy.

I rolled my eyes before answering, "Don't touch me! Didn't they throw you out of here?"

"Now you know they can't keep me out forever, doll. Ain't nobody gonna keep me away from all this ass n' titties!" he cackled as he tilted his head back. All I saw was a mouth full of rotten and missing teeth.

"What do you want Ozzy?" I asked through my disgust.

"I want *you*, girl! But I'll settle for the usual for now." None of his jokes were funny. I served him his shot of E&J and moved on to help the other customers before he could say anything else.

I kept glancing from left to right, looking for Jillian, but there was no sign of her. I was going to drive myself crazy before long, so finally I just asked Britt. "Hey, Jillian's not working tonight?"

"Oh, nah, Ronnie said he hasn't heard from her all week. She was supposed to work Monday and Wednesday, but didn't show up." She said.

"Oh, damn ... really?"

"Yup, *you* haven't talked to her? I know that's your girl." She said sarcastically.

"Oh, shut up, Britt! That is *not* my girl, and no, I haven't talked to her since last weekend."

"Yeah, I noticed she stuck around after I left ... care to share the details?" she asked with a smirk and one raised eyebrow.

"There ain't nothing to share! I told you I don't get down like that, and I told her too! All we did was kick it, and that was it."

"Mmmm hmmm, well, Ronnie said he hasn't heard from her all week, and if he don't hear nothing by tomorrow, he's gonna fire her." She said.

All I said was, "damn," and went back to work.

I was somewhat relieved that I wouldn't have to see her that night, but I was still baffled. Where could she be? None of it made sense. I would have to go back to my apartment at some point. I had to make it my business to check for her car.

A familiar face and a friendly smile interrupted my thoughts. It was Gordon. "What are you doing here?" I asked as he leaned in and kissed me on the cheek. I was getting used to that.

"I can't come see my favorite lady doing her thing at work? You know you're sexy when you're behind that bar." He answered. I smiled from ear to ear.

"What are you drinking?"

"How about you surprise me?" he smiled back.

"You sure you want that?" I asked, laughing.

"Yes, I'm sure. Just make sure I can actually taste the alcohol this time please." We both laughed at that.

Having Gordon there made me feel a little more comfortable. Talking and flirting with him made the night go faster as well. I spent the night going back and forth from chatting with him to serving the other customers. The tips were average. Not having Jillian there to bring over the big spenders did make a difference, but what could I do? Had I known that night would be my last one working at Ronnie's, I would've turned up my flirting and worked my charisma a lot more to get those tips.

At some point during the evening, I was leaned over the bar talking to Gordon when I glanced up. Sitting in a dark shadow in the far back corner of the club, was Cal. No drink, no lap dance, no nothing, he just sat there with his eyes fixated on me. He was frozen still. His eyes ice as he glared in my direction. It was creepy, and I didn't feel safe. Once he realized I made him, he calmly rose and exited the building.

I didn't realize that I had stopped talking mid-sentence to hold my breath in fear. "Hellllooooo! Earth to Angela!" Gordon chuckled as he looked back in the direction I was staring and waved his hand back and forth in front of my face.

"I'm sorry, my bad. I thought I saw someone I knew." I didn't want to tell Gordon it was Cal. I didn't want them to start fighting again; plus I hated putting my baggage on him.

"Oh, so anyway, what do you think?"

"Think about what?" I asked.

"Clearly, you are distracted. Everything okay?"

"Yeah, I'm sorry. Tell me again what you said." I said.

"Sunday. What do you think about us going to the Jacob Javid Center? They're having the Black Arts exhibit there, and we can go out to eat afterwards."

A smile returned to my face as I answered, "Yes, that sounds really nice."

Things picked up and got a little busy at some point during the night, so Gordon decided to leave. I felt bad that I couldn't give him my undivided attention, but I knew he understood I was working. I promised to call him to let him know I made it in safely that night. He kissed my hand then cheek and said goodnight.

Sometimes, when things got real busy like that at the bar, I didn't really pay attention to faces until I was actually serving the person. I didn't even see Rainy when she came in or when she walked up to the bar. In a rush, I placed a napkin down in front of her and asked, "What can I get you?" without even looking up. It wasn't until she gently placed her hand over mine that I raised my eyes to meet hers. It was as if time had stopped, and we were the only two in the club. I gulped and my throat was dry. Once again, I was at a loss for words.

Again, she took the lead, "Angela." Her voice was still soft even though she had to yell over the music a little. "Angela, I think it's time. We really need to talk." She said with begging eyes.

"Talk? Talk about what?"

"Us, your mother … everything," she responded.

"Us? Look, Rainy—"

"I'm not Rainy!" she cut me off.

I was puzzled, "Wait—you're *not?*"

"No, I'm not. That's why we really need to sit down and talk. I just want the chance to explain everything to you. After that, you can do what you want." She said. I opened my mouth to respond, but before I could get any words out, Ronnie's strong arm spun me around. Standing next to him was his sister, Carla.

My heart dropped and began thumping hard through my chest. My armpits began to perspire as I looked back and forth between the two of them. "Angie, my sister says you're lying about that night at IHOP. She said you saw everything!" He was visibly upset.

I scrunched up my face to make my answer more convincing, "Ronnie, you know if I had any information, I would tell you. I didn't see anything. I had my head down!" I turned towards Carla and continued, "I'm really really sorry about your loss, but I promise you I don't know anything. I really didn't see anything."

"Yes you did! Them niggas ran right past you!" She spat.

"Yeah, a lot of people were running by me trying to get to the door, but I didn't see any faces. I had my head down!"

"You's a fuckin' lie!" she said, pointing her finger in my face.

"Look, I'm sorry, but I don't know anything!"

"Yeah, you sorry. You a sorry ass liar!"

She was getting more and more upset as she confronted me. Ronnie stepped between us, "Angela, I can't believe you would do me/us like that! I gave you this job, and I been a good boss to you. You're fucked up!" I felt like shit inside because I could tell I had let Ronnie down.

"Ronnie—"

"You gotta go, Ang. I'm letting you go. Count out your tips, and I'll go write out your last check, but you don't work here anymore, Ma." He cut me off.

"You're *firing* me? You can't do that!"

"Look, my sister is 'bout three seconds away from busting your ass. I could just step aside and let her do it, but you're not worth it. Now get your shit!" He said sternly.

I did as instructed, not because I was afraid of Carla, but because Britt and a whole lot of other people had stopped and tuned into the show we were putting on. I was embarrassed beyond belief, and I really just wanted to find the nearest rock to crawl beneath. When I turned to collect my keys and phone from behind the bar, I noticed a folded napkin set in place of where Rainy, or the Rainy look alike, had just been. I opened it to reveal a short note: *Meet me in front of your gym tomorrow evening, 5pm. I folded it back and stuffed it down in my front pocket.*

Ronnie returned with my check in hand as Carla stayed glued in the spot she'd been standing, watching my every move with disgust in her eyes. I swallowed hard, put on my jacket, and glanced up at Britt. "Bye, girl," she said. A dry knot was lodged in my throat preventing me from speaking. I took my check from Ronnie's giant hand and waved as I walked out of the club for the last time.

I thought Cal left the club, but I should've known better. As soon as I made it to my car door, he crept up from behind and grabbed my arm tight. Flashes of the rape came flooding back, and I immediately started screaming and whaling with my other arm not even realizing it was him. He spun me around, pressed me up against the car window and cupped his hand over my mouth.

"Girl what's wrong with you?" he exclaimed. I think I startled him as well. I rolled my eyes and breathed heavily into his cupped hand once I knew it was him. My heart still raced, and I still felt a sense of fear because no one was in sight. Cal was still so unpredictable.

Slowly he removed his hand. "Cal! Why in the hell would you creep up on me like that! You know what I've just been through!" I said angrily as I clutched my chest.

"I know. You're right. I'm sorry."

"What do you want? I told you it's over, Cal!" I said.

"Yeah, I seen you with ol' boy in there. I just want to talk, Angie."

"We don't have anything to talk about. Now please move." I said, trying to nudge him out of the way knowing it wouldn't work.

"Please, Angie. Just give me five minutes. Please? I know you're still mad at me, but please just let me talk to you. Just five minutes okay?" It almost made me sad to see a grown, hard man begging so desperately.

"Well, I guess I don't have a choice the way you got me pinned up like this. Fine, five minutes, Cal. *Five minutes*!" I emphasized. He released me, and I crossed my arms.

"Angie, I'm sorry. I'm sorry for what I did to that pig. I'm sorry for spying on you. I'm sorry for beating up your new boyfriend." He said with a slight chuckle that let me know he wasn't really sorry for the fight with Gordon. "I'm sorry for everything. I just love you so much. I would do anything for you and to keep you. I can't stop thinking about you, and I want you back, Angie. I want you back. What I gotta do to get you back? I can't undo what I did to that pig, but if you want me to apologize to ol' boy, then I'll do that. I can do

271

that. I'll do whatever you want me to do. I just gotta have you back. You're the best thing that has ever happened to me. You know my moms was out there on them drugs and my pops never claimed me. The streets raised me. These niggas out here was the only family I had til' I met you, Ang. I never met anyone like you that loves me the way you do. I know I fucked it all up, but please just give me a chance to fix it, Angie. Please!" His begging almost made me feel sorry for him, but I knew he was sick in the head. I knew that I'd be a fool to go back to him and worse; I'd be putting myself in danger.

I had to think wisely before I answered. I knew anything could set him off at any moment. "Cal, I did love you at one point, but now … now you scare me, baby. Really, you scare me." He was silent as he shut his eyes. "I still care about your well being, Cal, but you need to get some professional help. You need to talk to someone—someone besides me … and … I think you should really turn yourself in—"

"What! You crazy! Ain't no way I'm ever going back to jail! EVER! I'll die before I let them lock me back up like some animal in a cage!" He cut me off before I could finish. "Come on, Ang. Don't be like this. Look, let me come to your crib, so we can talk some more. I know we can work this out if we just sit down and talk, right?"

"No, Cal. Not right. You cannot come over. I'm sorry baby, but it's over. I listened to what you had to say. Now just let me go, and accept it." I said sternly.

I could see the anger start to filter back into his eyes. He backed up slowly, nodding his head up and down. "Alright, Angela, go. I hear you … but just know you still mine. You still mine, and I'm coming for what's mine one way or another, so don't forget that!" There was a cold vindication in his voice like he had something planned. He walked off slowly down the street and I got into my car as quickly as possible. I didn't even let the car warm up as I sped away.

It was too dark on my street to look for Jillian's car that night. I would have to do it in the morning. As I pulled into my parking space, a fear enveloped me. My eyes darted all around looking for Cal, looking for Jillian, looking for Rainy—or her look alike, and even looking for Rock, even though I knew he was dead. I hated feeling so paranoid in a place I called my own. I actually ran from the car to the door as if someone was following me. I felt like someone was.

I did my paranoia check of the apartment, and it was all clear. Jillian's blood was still splashed about in different places. I felt my stomach whirl as I recounted that night. It was one-thirty in the morning, but I didn't care. I had to get the blood out of the carpet, off the wall, and off the table. I scrubbed like a mad woman. I scrubbed until it made my hands raw and sore. I showered and lay in my bed, staring up into the darkness. I couldn't fall asleep, and I thought maybe the living room couch might be better. I turned left and right on the couch trying to get comfortable, but it was weird hearing the silence of the empty apartment next door. My mind wandered to Mr. Burkwell and Mikell.

I tossed and turned some more before deciding to move back into my bed. I flicked on the TV and that made things a little better. At least it wasn't so eerily quiet. I still hadn't drifted off when Gordon called me.

"Hello?"

"Hey, Miss, what you up to?" he asked cheerily on the other end.

"Just watching TV, trying to fall asleep."

"Well I was just calling to make sure you made it home okay. Someone was *supposed* to call and let me know they made it in safely, remember?" He asked teasingly.

"Oh yeah, I'm sorry I totally forgot, but I made it in."

"You okay?"

"Yeah, I'm okay. A lot happened tonight at the club after you left."

"Oh, really? Like what? Do you want to talk about it?" he asked.

"Nah, not really. For starters, I got fired. But I don't really want to talk about it right now."

"Oh, wow, okay. Well if and when you're ready to talk about it, you know I'm here. It doesn't matter, day or night." He assured me.

"I know, thanks Gordon. I appreciate that."

"Alright, well go ahead and get your beauty rest. I'll call you tomorrow, love."

"Okay, goodnight."

CHAPTER 35

The next day I took my time getting out of bed. It was close to noon before I decided to get up, and that was just because someone's car alarm was blaring, preventing me from going back to sleep. I went into the bathroom and gagged immediately. The overwhelming stench of my own throw up still lingered in the sink where I'd regurgitated before fleeing the scene. Once again, I got right to cleaning and scrubbing. I poured bleach and Pine Sol down the drain to get rid of the smell. I cleaned the entire bathroom before peeing, brushing my teeth, and washing my face.

Once done in there, I started brunch. While I waited for my sausage to cook in the oven, I went to the bedroom to pick out an outfit for the day. I grabbed my jeans, which I had just thrown over a chair the night before, and stuck my hands in the pockets before tossing them in the hamper. I pulled out the balled up napkin that Rainy's look-alike had left for me the night before.

I sat down on the edge of the bed and stared at the writing. *Why didn't she leave a phone number or something?* I wondered. Today would be the day. I would finally find out exactly who this woman was who had been following me for months now. I promised myself I wouldn't freeze up this time. I would demand answers to all of my questions. I stared at the writing. I had seen this handwriting before. It was identical to the purple handwriting from the note left in my locker at the gym! I grabbed the metal box from on top of the dresser and took out the picture.

This looks exactly like the lady that's been following me, I thought to myself. I was one hundred percent sure this was the person who saved me from my attack that night. Now, I was sure of nothing.

"Ugh! I wish they'd turn off that damn alarm already!" I said out loud to myself. It had been going all morning. It would stop for a moment, and then just start right back up. I finished picking out something to wear. It was one of the outfits I usually wore to Ronnie's. I saddened as I recalled the events of the night before. I was honestly going to miss working there. I was going to miss the girls too. I'd probably never see them since we didn't really talk or hang out outside of work nights. I sighed as I dragged my slippers across the floor going back into the kitchen.

I was good and hungry and good and ready to eat. I pulled my chair up to my plate. Just as I opened wide to bite into my English muffin, someone knocked on the door. I rolled my eyes and sighed as I wondered who it could possibly be interrupting my brunch. I looked through the peephole. It was the lady from across the hall. *What does she want?* I thought as I swung the door open and pasted a phony half smile on my face, "Hi."

"Hey girl, I feel like I haven't seen you around in a while." She said.

"Oh, I know right? How's it going?"

"Fine, um I just wanted to tell you that I don't know if you can hear it or not, but your alarm has been going off all day." She said.

"Oh my God, that's *my* alarm? Yeah, I heard it, but I didn't even know that was my car!"

"Yeah, I went to get something out my car earlier and saw it was your car, but didn't want to knock on your door so early in the morning. Plus I thought it would've stopped by now, and it looks like one of your windows might be broken! I don't know if you already knew that either." She informed me.

My eyes widened as I gasped, "Oh my God, no. No, I didn't know any of that. I don't believe this!"

"Yup! Girl, whose man you been messing with?" she said trying to be funny. It wasn't funny, and I just stared back at her. "Girl when I saw that glass, I was like, ooh somebody is mad at her! 'Cause you know ain't no crackhead gon' break your window in the daytime." I guess she was able to see the humor in this that I couldn't.

I just rolled my eyes, "I don't believe this shit." I said out loud, but more to myself.

"Aw, I'm so sorry. I guess nobody else thought to come and tell you. I just didn't want your battery to die on you or something. Plus, it's supposed to snow tomorrow night so maybe you can hurry and get a new window today or at least tape it up real good." I guess the sense had suddenly returned to her brain.

"Yeah … well thanks so much for coming and telling me."

"Oh, you're welcome. Like I said, I would've come earlier, but I ain't wanna be knocking on your door all early like that."

"No, I'm glad you came and told me either way. Thanks." I said as I took a step back to start closing the door.

"You're welcome. Take care, hun."

After closing the door, I leaned up against it, shut my eyes tight, and growled through clenched teeth loudly. I didn't care if she or anyone else in the hall heard me. Upset couldn't begin to describe how I was feeling. I grabbed my keys from the table and a coat from the closet before changing into my Timbs. Then I headed out to see the damage.

The sun shined brightly, helping to melt a lot of the snow that was left. I pressed the button on my key to deactivate the alarm as I circled the car. There was a brick lying on the trunk. Whoever tried to break the rear window didn't throw the brick hard enough. There was a small hole and cracks, but it wasn't completely shattered. I pressed on it to see how sturdy it was or wasn't. I was thankful it didn't appear as if it was in danger of caving in completely. This would buy me some time in getting it replaced. I could just duck tape the hole for now, but I was still pissed.

Who would do this, and why? I asked myself. Only one name came to mind … Cal. He was certainly crazy enough to do this in broad daylight and not think twice about it. He definitely had the motives and the anger. He was becoming a bigger problem than I could have ever anticipated. Less than a month ago, he was my everything. Now he was a psycho maniac that I couldn't rid myself of. I needed to move from there and sooner than later. I needed a fresh start somewhere where he couldn't find me.

I found some duct tape in my tool bag and did the best I could with patching up the hole. I swept up the glass from the ground outside. I didn't need a flat tire on top of the broken window. The car still started, so that was good.

After working on the car, I returned to my apartment to eat my cold brunch. I had a missed call from a number I didn't recognize and a text from Gordon. He wanted to know what I was doing later and if I wanted to get together. I had told him nothing about my recent findings about my mother or Rainy, and I didn't want to tell him about my meeting with the look-alike. I just told him I'd be free after seven. We didn't make any set plans, but we agreed to meet up with each other then.

I cleaned up quickly and took a shower. I knew I needed to leave on time if I was going to make time to take a scan of the street to see if Jillian's car was there. Everything about that apartment felt weird to me now. I don't know if it was the rape, the surveillance from Cal, the recent vandalizing, or the bludgeoning of Jillian. Whatever it was, the place gave me the creeps. I decided instantly that I'd start looking for a new apartment immediately. I also decided I could no longer just sit by and let Cal run rampant through my life like this. I was going to take out a restraining order against him.

I left the apartment with three hours left until I was to meet the ninja lady. I drove up and down my block slowly until I came to Jillian's car. I could see two tickets had been left on the windshield, probably for Monday and Wednesday alternate street parking. She hadn't driven herself anywhere, so where the hell was she, and how did she get there? I hated having to wonder if she was somewhere dead or alive or somewhere plotting revenge on me. I just wanted to know and have it all be over.

Next, I headed to the only do-it-yourself car wash I knew of on Central Ave. I vacuumed out the back seat of the car where a little glass had come through the hole. As I was bent over, I heard a voice from behind me. "Wow, looks like you really pissed someone off!" Detective Ramsey chuckled as I stood up straight and turned around.

"What are you doing here?" I asked irritated. I really didn't need this, not today.

"Oh, I'm everywhere, honeybun!" he said grinning.

"Well, what do you want?"

"You know what I want. I want you to turn yourself in." he replied.

"*Turn myself in?* For what? I didn't do anything."

"Now, don't play stupid. You know *for what*, for Officer Johnson's murder. I know you had something to do with it. Don't tell me you didn't." He said more seriously.

"I already told you before, I didn't even know he was dead until you told me yourself. I ain't have NOTHING to do with it!"

"Don't get loud with me, girl! I'll haul your ass in right now and write you up for that possession charge. That's what you want, huh?" He threatened.

"How come you didn't apply this kind of effort to my rape case? Maybe Rock would be locked up now if you had—and still alive!" I snarled.

"Ha! Right there, see that? Now that almost sounded like a confession to me! What do you mean by that *maybe he'd still be alive?*" he pressed.

"Nothing," I hissed as I yanked the vacuum hose out of the car, tossing it on the ground while the machine was still going. I opened the car door and he slammed his hand against it forcing it back shut.

He got real close to my face, but I stared at the ground trying to shut him out. "Now you listen to me, bitch. You better think about confessing or getting a good lawyer 'cause I know you did it, and I'm coming for you. I'm all over you, watching your every move. One failure to stop at a stop sign, one lane switch without a signal, one fuck up, and your ass is grass! You hear me?" he said as his chest heaved up and down.

Though it was sunny, it was still cold outside, and I could see the sweat seeping through the pores on his nose. Now I looked up and glared into his eyes as I swung the door open hard, "I *said* I didn't do anything. Now I gotta go!" He took one step back, allowing me to get in the driver seat.

Before the door closed I could hear him getting the last word, "Yeah you go. Go now, because once I lock your ass up, the only place you'll be going is to the hole." He stared at the car until I was out of his sight. I could feel his hatred for me burning into the back bumper.

After I was out of sight, I pulled over on a side street to cry. My original plan was to head to the police station after vacuuming the car, but now I wanted to stay as far away from a police station as possible. I sat there for quite a while. Times like these I really wanted to smoke a blunt, but I was afraid to do that now too. Detective Ramsey had obviously been following me for who knows how long. He was watching my every move, and he wanted me to know it. I could easily blow the whistle on Cal. That would solve my problems with him, but how could I do that without being charged too? Detective Ramsey was clearly convinced that I had something to do with Rock's murder. He'd make sure I would go down with Cal.

I wiped my face with a Kleenex from the glove box then blew my nose. I took a deep breath and glanced at the clock. I had thirty minutes before I was to meet the ninja. I had to pull myself together. I had so many questions I was prepared to ask her. I wanted my mind clear for this conversation. I took another deep breath and shifted into drive. Just as I did, my phone began to ring. To my surprise it was Cherlise. I put the car back in park and answered.

"Hello?"

"Angie, it's Cherlise!" her voice whispered into the phone.

"Hey, Cherlise, what's up?"

"Angie, I need your help—Please don't say no. Please, this is serious." She said.

"Cherlise, why are you whispering? I can barely hear what you're saying. Are you crying?"

There was a silent pause before she continued, "Ang, listen. I need you to come get me. Please, this is serious." She repeated.

"What's going on, and why the hell are you whispering?" I was getting annoyed that I had to strain to hear what she was saying.

"Angie, please please just come get me. I know I fucked up last time when you needed me, but I really need you right now. This is life or death. I'm whispering because Matt's sleep, and I don't want him to hear me and wake up. Please, Ang, I'm beat up really badly." She said as she whimpered into the phone.

"*Beat up?* Wait—Matt beat you up?"

"YES!" she answered in a louder whisper.

"Oh my God, I knew that muthafucka wasn't shit! Where are you?" I was getting angry and fast. I felt my blood begin to boil.

"I'm home, please hurry. He's been beating me all day long, and if he wakes up ..." her voice trailed and there was another silent pause.

"Okay, Cherlise, okay. I'll be there in like an hour and a half." I had every intention on being there for my girl even though we'd been beefing a lot lately, but I wasn't trying to miss my opportunity to talk to the ninja and get answers for nothing. There may never be another chance.

"*Hour and a half?* No, Angie you don't understand! I need you to

279

come right now! If he wakes up, that's it! He's gonna kill me. I know it! Please, Angie, you gotta come right now. Please, I'll do anything." She begged. Now it was my turn to take a silent pause. "Angie? Are you still there?" she whispered.

"Yeah, I'm here. Okay I'm on my way, but you keep a kitchen knife or something close by in case he wakes up before I get there. I'm for real, Cherlise. You hear me?"

"Yeah, okay, I'll go grab one right now. Just hurry!" she pleaded.

"Alright."

I hung up and sighed as I shifted back into drive. I was torn. I was getting tired of this mystery lady following me and showing up everywhere. I was also getting tired of all the missed opportunities to talk to her. On the other hand, Cherlise did sound really scared on the phone. I wondered how long Matt had been beating her or if this was the first time and why. She did everything he ever wanted her to and more. What reason could he possibly have to put his hands on her? There was no reason.

I decided I would do both. I would swing by the gym quickly to tell the ninja lady that I couldn't stay and talk and hopefully get her phone number this time. Then I'd go straight to Cherlise from there. There was no street parking when I first got to the gym, so I had to keep circling the block. I wasn't paying ten dollars to park in the lot when I knew I wasn't staying anyway. I didn't see Rainy's look-alike the first three times I circled the block. On the fourth time I saw her dressed in her all black sweat suit with a black coat and hat. She was just rushing up the front steps to the gym when I blew my horn. She turned. I waved. She looked left and right like someone might be following her before she headed towards the car. I was double-parked and cars started blowing their horns at me as I waved my hand out the window for them to go around.

"Hey why didn't you park in the garage so you can come in?" she asked.

"I can't stay. My friend is in trouble, and I have to get to her right away. I just wanted to come by here real quick, so I could get your number so I can call you instead."

"I can't give you my number. Let's meet on Monday." She replied.

"Okay where? What time?"

"You know the Starbucks inside the train station?" she asked.

"Yeah."

"Meet me there on Monday at seven p.m." She instructed.

"Okay—can I at least know your name?"

She hesitated and looked over her shoulder before answering, "You can just call me Rowi for now."

"Okay, Monday." I said as she backed away from the window.

When I pulled up to Cherlise's block there were two cop cars and an ambulance in front of her building. I pulled into one of the driveways next door to her building, not caring that I shouldn't be parked there. My heart thumped as I thought of all the worse things that might've happened to Cherlise. As I rushed up to the front steps, an officer held his arm out and pushed me back.

"Just a minute, ma'am, do you live here?" he asked.

"No, but my friend Cherlise is in there. Please, I have to see her! Is she okay?"

"ANGIE!" I heard Cherlise's voice from behind me. She was waving me over from the back of the ambulance. I rushed over and climbed in to sit next to her.

A paramedic was working on her face. She was unrecognizable. Both of her eyes were black and blue. The left one was swollen completely shut. She was slurring as she answered the paramedic's questions because her jaw was swollen and broken, along with a fat top lip. Her nose was wider than I remembered, and I was sure it was broken as the dry blood sat beneath her nostrils. She was holding her right side beneath the jacket draped around her shoulders.

"Oh ... my ... God, Cherlise," was all I could squeak out as a tear fell from my eye. "Look at your face! What the hell happened in there? Where is that muthafucka?" Before she could answer, two policemen escorted Matt out of the apartment in handcuffs. There was blood smeared across his white T-shirt. No doubt it was Cherlise's blood because he looked perfectly intact. They secured him in the back seat of a squad car then proceeded over to us to talk to Cherlise.

"Ma'am, we took statements from your neighbors who called 9-1-1, but we're going to need your statement as well. We're going to have an officer meet you at the hospital okay?" he said. She just nodded her head.

Once he was out of earshot, I asked again, "Cherlise, what happened?"

She started to whimper, "He just lost it ... I mean we've gotten in fights before, but today … he just lost it."

"What do you mean you been in fights before? *He's hit you before?*" I demanded to know. She just nodded with her head down in shame. "Well, what happened? What set him off like this?"

"Remember the last time I got locked up? The time he called you to help get me out?" she asked.

"Yeah …"

"Well I—"

"Miss, we're going to need to take Miss Hickins to the hospital now. Are you going to ride in the ambulance with her?" the paramedic cut in.

"No, I'm going to follow in my car. Cherlise, I'm parked in somebody's driveway, so I can't stay there, but I'm right behind you okay? I'm coming straight to the hospital right behind the ambulance, alright?" I said reassuringly.

She nodded again and answered, "okay."

I felt like I was in an action movie weaving in and out of traffic trying to stay on the ambulance's bumper. We were at University Hospital for hours. Cherlise had one fractured rib, a broken nose, broken jaw, and one of her arms had been dislocated from the socket. The police took forever questioning her too. Couldn't they see her jaw had just been broken? She could barely talk. I couldn't deny it though. I was interested to hear the whole story as well.

Cherlise went on to explain everything to the police. She gave up everything on Matt, his boys, and the robberies she was involved with. Apparently, the only reason she had gotten out the last time she was locked up was because the cops had already been watching them. Once they got her on traffic violations again they were able to make her talk. The only reason she was able to be released and not be charged herself in the robberies was to snitch on Matt and the whole operation. That's exactly what she did. I guess she didn't think it through or know that Matt would find out sooner or later. Once he did, he went ballistic.

She was supposed to secretly have her conversations with Matt recorded in order to get a confession for the police. They had her believing that they would go easy on Matt and give him a light sentence of maybe a year or so if she did this. Somehow the word got to Matt first and of course he knew better. That's how the fight began.

I couldn't believe what I was hearing. I never would've thought Cherlise would agree to give up Matt. I know that had to be a last resort for her. "I never thought he would do this to me like this." She managed to eek out through her closed jaw. I rubbed her back as we sat in the hospital room waiting for her to be discharged.

"I know."

"I didn't even think he'd find out. They swore he wouldn't know!" she continued.

"You know you can't trust the police, Cherlise."

"I know. I know. I don't know what the hell I was thinking, but they kept saying they had me and my car on video and started saying I'd have to do like five or more years and stuff. Angie, you know I can't go to prison!" she said.

"I know … you did what you thought was best. I'm just glad somebody called the cops. He was about to kill your ass!"

"I just can't believe he did this to me. I feel so stupid. I should've left the first time he ever hit me." She shook her head in slow motion.

"Well, I'm just glad you still here, girl."

"I know, me too. I don't even know where I'm gonna go. I can't go back there. I know Matt's not getting out any time soon, but he might send his boys or somebody to do something stupid." She sounded worried.

"Don't worry, Cherlise. You know you can stay with me."

"Thanks, but then what? I can't afford to get a place on my own right now, Ang! What am I gonna do?" she said as she placed her face in her palms.

"Don't worry about that right now. We'll cross that bridge when we come to it. I gotta look for a new place myself. Cal's crazy ass keeps coming around. He done broke my damn window." I rolled my eyes getting upset all over again at the thought of it.

"Really? Your car window?" she asked.

"Mmm hmm. I got it patched up with tape right now. I'll have to go get it fixed Monday maybe—but yeah he's crazier than a little bit. I had no idea what I was getting myself into. I'm 'bout to turn his ass into the cops too!"

"Damn, really? For what?" she asked as she winced from the pain in her jaw.

"There's a whole lot to tell with that one. I'll have to tell you later."

Another hour later, the hospital finally discharged Cherlise, and a nurse wheeled her to the entrance while I pulled the car around. I must not have had any service inside the hospital because as soon as we started driving, my phone began to blow up with missed calls, voicemails, and text messages from Gordon.

"Oh shoot!" I said as I started going through all the messages once we were back inside my apartment.

"What?" Cherlise asked.

"Nothing. I just forgot I was supposed to be going out tonight."

"Going out where?" she asked.

"Just out with this guy I've been talking to."

"Oh really? Dag girl, you don't waste no time!" She teased. I smiled and excused myself as I disappeared to my room to return Gordon's call.

"There she is! I was starting to think you had enough of me already!" Gordon was always in a cheerful mood.

"Heyyyyy no, no of course not. I am sooooo sorry about tonight. Today has been a crazy day. Cal broke my window. Then I had to go get my friend and go to the hospital with her because her boyfriend beat her up really bad. I had a run-in with this detective ..." I stopped to sigh.

"Just breathe, baby. Breathe. Are you okay?" he asked.

"Yeah, I'm fine, but I definitely gotta move out of here. Anyway, I'm so sorry in the midst of all this drama I totally forgot about us tonight, and I didn't have service in the hospital. I didn't get any of your messages until just now."

"It's okay. I understand. Sounds like you had a very eventful day. Is your friend okay?" he asked.

"She's beat up pretty badly. I'm letting her crash with me for a while because she can't go back to her place right now."

"That's good. You're a good friend, Angela." He replied.

"I guess. Wish I was a better date." I chuckled into the phone.

"Don't worry about it. I'm not going anywhere. So Cal broke your window? You saw him do it?" he asked.

"No, I didn't see him, but he was at the club last night. He saw us talking, and he came up to me afterwards. He was real mad, so I'm assuming it was probably him." I explained.

"I see .... We're gonna have to do something about that dude. I don't like him terrorizing you like this. Why didn't you call the cops?" he demanded.

"I don't know. I knew he was long gone by the time I even realized what had happened. Plus I don't have any proof that it was him."

"Yeah, we gotta find you a new place ASAP, somewhere safe." He replied. "Well, go take care of your friend. Do you ladies need anything?"

"No, we're good. I think we're both just exhausted. They got her on all these pain killers, so we'll probably just watch TV and go to sleep."

"Okay, well you call me if you need anything—or if that Cal bastard comes back. I mean it, Angie!" He instructed.

"Okay, Gordon, but I promise we're fine."

"Alright, I guess we shouldn't go to the exhibit tomorrow considering everything, so I'll probably just come by to check on you if that's okay." He said.

"Yeah, that sounds like a good idea. I don't really want to leave Cherlise alone right now. I'm sorry. Just call when you're on your way over."

"Alright, night, sexy." He said.

"Night."

CHAPTER 36

Cherlise and I spent the rest of the night talking—well me talking and her listening mostly since part of her jaw had been wired. I filled her in on everything from the drama with Cal harassing me, to the mystery woman Rowi, to Rock's murder and Detective Ramsey's accusations, and Jillian's disappearance. She told me about Matt's abuse and how controlling he had become. It felt good to let it all out. I felt like I had my old friend back. It was a shame it took something like this for it to happen.

The next day we just lounged around the apartment with the exception of me running to the store. Since Cherlise couldn't eat anything solid for a while, I went to get her some Ensure protein shakes. Gordon stopped by like he said he would. I was always pleasantly surprised at how good he always managed to look no matter how he was dressed. That day he wore a graphic T-shirt with a thermal underneath, some jeans, a fitted Yankee cap, and some fresh white air forces.

"You must be the lawyer." Cherlise eased out from her clenched jaw.

"I'm Gordon, you must be Cherlise. Nice to meet you." Gordon answered as he stuck his hand out to shake hers.

"*Fine and he got manners too!* Do you have a brother?" Cherlise chuckled.

Gordon smiled shyly before answering, "No, only sisters. Sorry."

"Don't pay her any attention. I told you she on all that

medication!" I said sarcastically before we all laughed. "Gordon you want something to eat? I got some left over bacon from this morning. I can make you a BLT or something." I offered.

"No, that's okay. Can I just have a glass of water please?" As I pulled out the jug of water and poured, Gordon's eyes were glued to my every move.

"*What?*"

"Nothing, I'm just in awe of your beauty. I can look, can't I?" He asked, taking me in slowly from head to toe. I felt my temperature rise. Of course men called me beautiful before, but it was something about the way he said it and how he looked at me when he said it. I could tell that he wasn't just running game. He really meant it.

"I guess," I responded as a smile spread across my face.

"Awwww, that's so sweeeeet!" Cherlise chimed in. I rolled my eyes in her direction, but Gordon's eyes never left me.

"So when are you going to start looking for a new place?" he asked.

"I don't know. I need to start this week. It's just so much to do. I still have to finish packing up my mom's place for good. I only have one more week to do it. Then I'll have to start packing up this place."

"Well, you know I'll help however I can. I can meet you at your mom's one day after work this week and help you finish up. Then we can start here. I just really want you out of here, Angela. It's not safe." He expressed his concern sternly.

"I know. I know. Trust me; I want to get out of here just as bad as you want me to!"

"I gotta move too. Can you help me move too?" Cherlise asked jokingly.

"Oh, you're moving too?"

"Yep. I can't go back to my place. I gotta start looking for a place this week too. I can't stay here forever." She said in a more serious tone.

"Well shoot why don't y'all just find a place together? Save you some money ..."

Cherlise and I looked at each other. Neither of us was opposed to the idea, and Gordon was right; it would save us both some money. I really liked living alone, but with all that had been going on, maybe it wasn't a good idea for either of us to be alone for a while.

"I don't know. What do you think Cherlise?"

"I'm down with it! He's right. It will save us some money, plus we almost like family so ... might be fun," she replied.

"We'd have to get a two bedroom, though, of course—and somewhere spacious so we're not tripping over each other."

"Of course." She agreed.

"Well, we can start looking this week then."

"Yeah, I can start looking at some places while you're at work, and if I see something I think we'd like, we can go back together." She suggested.

"Yeah ... sounds like a plan." It was settled.

Eventually, Cherlise's medications kicked in, and she nodded off on the couch while Gordon and I sat at the kitchen table talking. "Gordon, I don't know where Jillian could be. Her car is still parked outside. I'm really nervous about it."

"Damn ... her car is still outside?" I nodded as his forehead wrinkled in deep thought. "That's so strange. So we know she didn't drive from here, and as far as you know, no one has heard anything from her?" he asked.

"Nope. Nothing. Britt said that Ronnie was planning to fire her if she didn't show up for work this weekend. I don't know what to do."

"Don't worry. Everything will be fine. Maybe you should just go to the police and tell them everything that happened." He said.

"What if they lock me up?"

"They won't lock you up. I promise. Besides, I already told you I got one of the best lawyers for you. You didn't do anything except defend yourself ... *right*?" He questioned.

"Yeah! Damn I shouldn't have left that night. I should've stayed here and called the police. I was just so scared. I panicked. I didn't know what else to do!"

Gordon stood up from his chair and walked over to my back and began to massage my shoulders. "Just calm down and try to relax. Trust me, everything is going to work out. You didn't do anything wrong. Tomorrow when we get off, we'll go to the police station and file a report, and I'll have the lawyer meet us there. Okay?"

"Okay ... Wait! No, tomorrow, I can't!"

"Why not?"

"Tomorrow I gotta do something after work. It's important." I said as I remembered my appointment with Rowi.

"More important than *this*?" he asked quizzically.

"Yes, more important than this. I don't really want to go into it right now, but I have something very important to do that I just cannot put off."

"Okay, well, we can go early in the morning or on Tuesday." He suggested. I did want to get it over with, but one more day wouldn't hurt.

"Okay Tuesday then." There was nothing in the world that would make me miss my meeting with Rowi again.

I shifted my head back and forth as Gordon continued massaging my shoulders. "Ahh that feels so good. I see you're a pro at this." I smiled up at him.

"I just want you to relax, babe. Just relax." I did as told, closed my eyes, took a deep breath and exhaled. I didn't even feel or hear Gordon bend down. I just felt the softest lips against my neck as he planted butterfly kisses in a row starting at my shoulder and traveling upwards toward my earlobe. Good cannot begin to describe how wonderful it felt. Inhaling his light cologne only made matters worse. Once at my earlobe, he stopped, placed his index finger against my chin and turned my face to meet his lips. Those nice juicy lips I hadn't been able to keep my eyes off of the first night I saw them, were pressed against mine.

He gave a firm, yet gentle peck then whispered into my lips "Just relax. I got you, Angie." Then another luscious peck followed. We both turned and looked at the couch when Cherlise began to shift around in her sleep, trying to get comfortable.

Suddenly, I became aware of what was happening, and I wasn't ready for it. I slid my chair back forcing Gordon to step back. "You alright?" he asked.

"Yeah," I answered looking down at the kitchen floor. I felt flushed and warm all over. He studied my body language before lifting my chin, so that I'd have to look him in the face.

"You sure?"

"Yes," I responded.

He paused for a moment as if taking in every detail of my face. "Alright, I guess I should get ready to go. Tuesday then, right?" he asked.

"Yeah, yeah Tuesday. And thanks for all your help, Gordon."

"Don't worry bout it, my pleasure, beautiful." He pinched my cheek before swinging his coat around his back to put it on. I opened the door, and he walked out into the hallway then turned around. "I hope I didn't move too fast or make you uncomfortable."

"No, it's not that. It's just … there's just some things we need to talk about. I just really need to take things slow." I answered bashfully.

"Okay, well, I don't have a problem with that. Whenever you're ready to talk, you already know I'm more than ready to listen. Okay?" he tilted his head to the side and looked into my eyes.

I smiled before answering, "Okay." That's when he grabbed both of my hands and kissed the back of each one, one at a time, before leaning in to leave a kiss on my cheek.

"Alright, I'll call you later."

"Alright," I said and closed the door behind him.

Cherlise spent Monday recuperating. I was jittery all day about my meeting with Rowi. I kept glancing at the clock and time was dragging by. I was so tired of going round and round and being followed. I would finally get some answers. Today would be the day. Around three o'clock, the desk phone rang and I answered, "B.I.G. Insurance, this is Angela." There was silence. "Hello? B.I.G. Insurance?" There was clearly someone on the other line, but they weren't speaking. I could hear a faint beeping sound in the background, but couldn't really make out what it was. I hung the phone up and stared at it, expecting the person to call right back. They didn't.

I knew it had to be Cal. I hoped and prayed he wouldn't show up in the parking lot today, not today. I didn't have time to deal with his craziness. I would have to figure out a way to shake him once and for all. I was glad about the move, but as long as he still knew where I worked, he'd have access to me any time he wanted. I couldn't afford to quit B.I.G. Insurance, especially after being fired from Ronnie's.

Ronnie's. My mind switched gears as I started replaying Friday's events. It was so embarrassing to get fired in front of the girls and everybody like that. As I sat staring at the phone and wondering if I'd look for another bartending job, Renee peeked over the top of my cube.

"Hey, Angela." She spoke in a low voice.

"Hey, Renee." Things still felt so awkward to me around Renee. Sure, I'd apologized, and she'd forgiven me, but I still felt bad for some reason.

"Hey, I'm passing around this card for everyone to sign for Gabby's baby shower." She explained as she handed the card to me. Gabby was another woman on the team who was due to have her baby soon. "You can sign it if you'd like, and everyone is donating some money to buy her a gift card. There's no set amount, just whatever you want to donate—only if you want to though! You don't have to, and there's no pressure. You can just sign the card if you want, or don't. I just didn't want to exclude you so …"

I hated things being so apparently awkward. I had become the office cheapskate. "Oh no, it's fine. Let me see what I have in my wallet." I said as I signed the card. Then I dug around and pulled out five singles as I wondered what everyone else had given. They probably gave more than five dollars, but all I had was twenties, and she wasn't getting a twenty.

"You sure? You don't have to." She repeated.

"No, it's fine. Please take it. Sorry I can't give more." I wasn't really sorry. I don't know why I said that.

"Okay no problem. Thanks." She took the card and money then moved to the next person's cubicle.

I rolled my eyes at myself. Now I would feel embarrassed every time anyone in the office asked me for money for anything, and they would all feel awkward asking me to contribute. I spun right to left on my chair trying to regain focus on my work after checking the time once more. This was the longest afternoon ever. I tried to keep myself busy for the rest of the day, but it was hard with all the questions flying through my head that I wanted to remember to ask Rowi.

I hopped out of my seat at 4:59 on the dot, hoping to beat some traffic. I don't know what kind of difference I expected one minute to make. Regardless, I just wanted to make sure I was at the Starbucks on time. I was flying so fast on the highway that I made it downtown to the train station way earlier than I needed to be there. I found a good parking space and decided to do a little window-shopping before it was time to meet Rowi. I had over an hour to kill, so I took my time strolling down the street going into different stores. I stopped at a stand to check out some bootleg CDs. I sifted through the stacks that were lined up on the table, but there was nothing that I really wanted, so I turned to continue strolling.

As I did, I heard someone call my name, "ANGIE!" I looked to my right and left then I saw Princess walking straight towards me, "What's up Angie?"

"Hey Princess! Long time no see!"

"I know right," she said as she opened her arms for a hug. It's a shame, but I checked my purse after she let go to make sure everything was still there. She might've been cool, but apparently she was a thief, and I wasn't taking any chances. "What's been going on girl? How's everything at the club? I know you heard Ronnie's punk ass fired me," she said, rolling her eyes.

"Yeah, I heard. What happened?"

"Girl, please. He said some bullshit about me stealing or something. I'm like, nigga, don't nobody need to steal shit from this lil' hole in the wall!" she said with an attitude.

I laughed, "Damn … so where you working now?"

"I been looking, but I haven't found anything yet. I'm still on unemployment, though, so …" she trailed off.

"Oh, well, I'm sure you'll find something soon. How's your baby?"

"He's fine, getting into everything, but he good." She replied.

"That's good."

"Yo, what happened to Jillian?" she asked. I felt my heart rate speed up a little. I wondered how much she knew and *how* she knew.

"What do you mean?"

"You know, how she wind up in the hospital like that?" she asked as if I knew.

"*The hospital?*"

"Yeah! You know she over at University right? Britt n 'em ain't tell you?" she asked, surprised.

"No. Well I actually just got fired from Ronnie's Friday, so …"

"*WHAT?* Get the fuck outta here! *You?* You were one of the good ones, Miss Goodie Two-Shoes. How *you* get fired?"

"Girl, it's a long story. Basically Ronnie's sister got me fired 'cause she claim I saw something that I didn't with her husband getting killed."

"*Her husband getting killed?* Damn when all this happen? I been missing out on everything!" she exclaimed.

"This shooting happened like a month ago, and we was all there, at IHOP after work. You know how we do … Well we was there, and her husband got killed, and she try'na say I saw the shooters."

"Daaaaaamn, that's crazy! So he fired you just like that?" she asked.

"Yup!"

"Damn, that's messed up. So what you gon' do?" she asked.

"I don't know. I might look for another job, but I still got my full-time job, so I'm good for now."

"Oh, you got another job? They hiring?" she asked.

I didn't even have to think about it. As far as Princess was concerned, the answer to that would always be, "No, not right now."

"Oh ... well good for you, girl. At least you got that."

"Yeah ... so what happened to Jillian?" I needed to get as much information as possible.

"Well, I saw Chucky the other night at Mink's, and he said she at University Hospital. She's been there for a minute. They're not really sure what happened. She was missing for like a week, and her grandmother started checking all the hospitals and finally found her. They said she was found laid out on Broadway with blood all over her, and her head was all bashed in. They think she walked there and collapsed, but nobody knows where she was coming from—don't you live over that way?" she asked.

"Yeah, not too far from there ... So she didn't tell anybody how she got there or anything?"

"Nah, she was in a coma for the first couple of days. Now she out, but she can't talk or anything and she got ... shoot what's that thing called when you can't remember shit?" she asked.

"Amnesia?"

"Yeah, she got am-i-nee-shia!" she tried to pronounce it.

"Wow ..." I was lost in my own thoughts now.

"That's crazy, right? I wonder what she was even doing over there."

"I know. That's scary. Do you know when they found her?" I asked.

"I don't know. I just know Chucky said she hadn't been to work for like a week, and Ronnie was ready to fire her ass too!"

"Yeah, I know. That's what Britt told me Friday when I was there." I said calmly as I looked down at the ground, wondering what my next move would be.

"Well, I gotta go catch this bus so I can go pick up my baby. Here take my number. We gotta hang out some time!"

I took out my phone and handed it to her to put her number in as I responded, "Yeah, most definitely."

"Well, it was good seeing you. Make sure you hit me up!" she said as she handed the phone back.

"Alright," I said as we parted ways. I knew I had no intention of ever calling her, but I wasn't about to tell her that right then.

Now I felt nervous as I checked my watch and continued to stroll down the street. I was fine as long as Jillian couldn't talk or remember anything, but what if that changed? Knowing the state she was in, I was rethinking my plan of going to the police station with Gordon. I went into a small, tight clothing store and sifted through some of the clothes on the racks but I wasn't really even looking at the clothes.

My mind was completely somewhere else until a saleslady asked me, "Hi, can I help you with anything?"

"Uh – no. I'm just looking, thanks."

"Okay," she said with a smile and disappeared behind some other racks. I had to get out of there. I felt uneasy all of a sudden. I spun around, left the store abruptly, and headed back up the street to the train station. I decided I'd just sit in the Starbucks and wait for Rowi.

To my surprise, she was already there thirty-five minutes early. She sat in a corner sipping on what I assumed was some kind of coffee. She saw me, but didn't budge or blink as I made my way over to the table. "Hi," I said as I slid the chair out to sit.

"Hi, Angela," she responded as she broke out into a nervous smile. We were both so anxious. I guess neither knew where to start as we both started talking at the same time.

"So who are you?" I asked at the same time she asked, "How are you?"

We both smiled, and she tried again, "You go ahead."

I didn't feel angry this time the way I'd felt that night outside of the club. "Well, who are you—and why have you been following me around like this?"

She looked down at her coffee as she fiddled with her hands around it. "Well, let me ask you this. How much do you know about your mother?" she asked.

"When you say my mother, are you talking about my mom, Candice, or my biological mother?"

"So you know about the adoption?" she asked.

"Somewhat, I just found out when my mom—Candice passed away. I didn't get a lot of information though."

"So if your mom didn't tell you, who did?" she asked.

"My Aunt Sandy. Well she's not really my aunt, but my mom's best friend."

"Yes, I remember her ... well, you know you do have a real aunt?" she asked.

"Really?" I perked up at the thought of it even though I was more interested in finding my real mom.

"Yes ..." she hesitated.

"Well? Who is she? Where is she?" I asked, barely able to contain myself.

"She's sitting right in front of you," she said with a shy smile.

"You? You're my aunt, for real? So you're the lady in the picture."

"What picture?" she asked with a puzzled look. I dug down in my purse and pulled out the picture, the necklace, and a few of the letters from the metal box then handed the photo to her.

She smiled sadly before answering, "No, that's Rainy!" Now I was confused as she handed the picture back. I glanced at her, then back at the picture, then back at her once more.

"Twins ..." I thought out loud.

"Yes, I'm your Aunt Rowina, Rainy's twin sister." She answered. My eyes widened as I stared into her smiling face.

"Really? You're really my aunt, for real?"

"Yes, Angela, I am." She answered.

I looked her up and down suspiciously then asked, "How do I know that you're not lying? You could just be some crazy psycho stalker!"

"Well, lucky for you, I came prepared. You're not the only one with photos!" She winked before looking in her large shoulder bag. Her hand came up with a small stack of Polaroids just like the one I had.

I was amazed as I looked through the photos. I could tell some of the photos had been taken the same day as the one photo I had. There were pictures of Rainy, Rowi, and me. There were pictures of them with my mom and dad. There were pictures of me from a newborn up until about two years old. I couldn't tell who was Rainy and who was Rowi, but I asked about each one. I realized there were more pictures of Rowi and me than of Rainy and me.

"There's not a lot of pictures of me and Rainy." I said.

"Yeah, I know, but you're welcome to keep those few if you'd like." She answered.

"Thank you ... so why did Rainy stop coming around? How come I don't know you or her? From what my Aunt Sandy told me, it was an open adoption where I should've been able to still see Rainy."

Rowi grew quiet and looked down in her lap as if the answer was there. "Well, it was supposed to be an open adoption. You see, my sister, your mother, was only fifteen when she had you. We were both into a lot of things back then—gangs, drugs, drinking, you name it. So it made sense for Rainy to give you up for adoption to a family that would be able to give you a good life. Your mom met a few different couples, but she handpicked Candice and Ricky because she really liked them out of everybody. For a while, everything was going smoothly with the situation. The more she got to see you and be around you, the more she loved you. That's when she decided it was time to get her life together. She did the rehab thing and stopped running with all the folks we was running with. She even got a nice little office job, and we got an apartment together. Then she started having ideas of getting you back, full custody. That's when everything went downhill ..." she trailed off as she shook her head.

"Downhill how? What happened?"

"Once she petitioned the courts to try to get you back, your mom wasn't trying to hear that. You were hers now in her eyes. She wasn't about to let Rainy take you away. So she stopped allowing Rainy visitations with you. She fought tooth and nail to keep you, and she won. She still saw Rainy as a threat, so she wouldn't let you have anything to do with her." She explained.

"But she still let you see me?"

"Yeah ... for a while anyway; until she found out that I was taking you around Rainy. That's when she stopped visitation altogether." She answered.

"So why have you been following me around like some kind of spy, and where is my real mother?"

"I had to follow you like that until I knew it was safe. I've been following you, well, really just checking on you for a long time now. I don't know what took you so long to notice." She admitted.

"Really? Oh my God. Well what do you mean you had to know it was safe? Safe from what?"

"Well after your mom stopped all visitation, Rainy didn't stop. She still kept showing up to your house, calling, and sending those letters there." She said as she motioned towards the small stack I had brought with me. "Eventually, Candice got a restraining order against Rainy, and that's what did it. That's what really made her start using again. It's like she lost her whole world after that. Nothing else mattered. So I started keeping tabs on you, but I had to be careful. If your mom would've found out, she'd put a restraining order on me too." She explained.

"Wow, I can't believe my mom would do that."

"I know that Candice really loved you. She just wanted to protect you. Once I found out that she had passed, I knew it was time we meet." She said.

"Well, are you going to tell me where my mother is? Will I get to meet her?" I asked with the anticipation burning inside.

"Yes, if you want to. I know she wants to see you." She answered.

"Well, where is she? When can I see her?"

"Angela, your mom is really sick. I can arrange for you to see her, but you need to know that she's not herself anymore." She said.

"Not herself? What's wrong with her?"

"Angela, Rainy has been diagnosed with schizophrenia. I'm telling you this not to scare you, but to prepare you for when you meet her—if you decide you still want to." She explained.

"Wow ... so she's crazy."

"She's *schizophrenic*. She hallucinates a lot, and she may or may not even recognize you. I just want you to be prepared for that. She can't help it." She responded.

I took a deep breath as I looked at one of the photos of Rainy, wondering how she looked now. Did she look like those crazy bums who hung out at the train station? Now I wasn't sure if I wanted to meet her after all, especially if she wouldn't even know who I was. "I can't believe this. My mother dies only for me to find out she wasn't my real mother. I find out I have a biological mom somewhere out there. Only now I find out she's crazy! This just can't be right."

"Angela, I know this is probably a lot for you to digest right now. Here, I can give you my number now that you know the situation. Give it some thought. If you decide you want to see her, we can arrange that. Either way, whatever you decide, I want you to know that we both love you, and I would love a chance to get to know my niece—outside of following you around." She wrote her number down on a gum wrapper and handed it to me.

I fondled the wrapper in my hands nervously, trying to decide what to say next. Rowi reached out and placed her hand on top of mine, "Angela I'm sorry you had to find out this way, and I'm sorry Rainy couldn't be there for you all these years, but know she wanted to so badly. We *all* wanted to be a part of your life!" I glanced up with interest wanting to know what she meant by *'we all.' Who else was there?* I guess she read my mind through my expression, "Angela … you have a whole family of aunts, uncles, cousins, and even a brother who would love to get to know you." I perked up at the idea of having a brother.

"Really? I have a brother?"

"Yeah! His name is Samuel. Everybody call 'em Stitch though," she said with a chuckle.

"Stitch," I repeated the name out loud. I couldn't keep my grin to myself as I thought about my little brother. "How old is he?"

"He's fourteen. He'll be fifteen in July. He stays with your Uncle Melvin and me, and we have a daughter, Kareemah." She said.

"Oh, is that the girl that was with you that night at IHOP?"

"Yup, that's my baby girl—your cousin! And that was your Uncle Mel there." She said proudly. "That was a crazy night with that shooting and everything. I was so worried 'bout you. You know some man was killed in all that mess?" she asked.

I looked down sheepishly, remembering the whole scene that night and the whole scene at Ronnie's, "Yeah, I know."

"Well, I should go. I need to go get dinner started. You think about what I said. You have my number now, so you be sure to use it for anything. Okay?"

"Okay, I'll give it some thought," I responded.

As she stood up, she grabbed my hand again and looked me deep in the eyes, "I mean it, Angela. If you need *anything*."

"Okay, I will." She squeezed my hand tight and smiled big before letting go and walking out of the Starbucks. I just sat there staring at the gum wrapper in my hand with her number sprawled across it, tapping my foot on the floor.

CHAPTER 37

"**I** think that's all the more reason you need to go to the police and tell them the truth!" Gordon was trying to convince me to go forward with our plan of confession after I told him the news of Jillian being in the hospital with amnesia.

"But I mean, it's not like she remembers anything, so what good is it going to do? The damage is already done."

"Yeah, but her memory could come back at anytime. Then if she tells what happened, you're definitely going to have to do some time for sure. Plus, you told me her car is still parked on your street! They're going to trace her last whereabouts back to your place eventually when they go to look for her car! It's the right thing to do Angela." He argued. Why did he have to be so good and noble?

"But if I tell them now after all this time, I might go to jail anyway!"

"It's better for you to go to them first and tell, than for them to find out you did it and come find you. Trust me! Now I already got the lawyer on his way there, so let's just go." he said.

I huffed and puffed before agreeing to meet him there as planned, "Okay, fine. I hope you're right."

I was glad we didn't go to the station that Detective Ramsey worked out of. We met Gordon's lawyer friend out front. He was a middle-aged white man, tall and lean with a bushy mustache. "Angela this is Tom Cardi; Tom, this is Miss Angela Delimar."

We shook hands, "Nice to meet you, Miss Delimar. Don't worry, we're going to take care of all of this and have you back to your normal life in no time! Just leave all the talking to me." He smiled a warm smile then held the door for me to enter into the station.

This station didn't have a receptionist type of desk like the other one. Instead, there was a big glass window when we first walked in. I did as told and let Tom do all the talking to the officer behind the glass. After their exchange, the officer motioned for us to sit in the waiting area. Ten minutes later, another officer appeared from the back and took us in through the main area of the precinct to a private room with a long table. The three of us sat on one side of the table and the officer on the other.

"So I understand you have some information you'd like to tell us." The officer said.

"Yes …"

"Okay, well?" he replied. I glanced at Tom before answering. Once he nodded his head with approval, I began my confession. I spent an hour explaining to the officer everything that happened with Jillian and me. He asked a lot of questions. Some Tom gave me the approval to answer, and others he told me not to. Gordon kept his hand placed on top of mine firmly the entire time. It felt good to have him there, but I was still nervous as I watched both the officer and Tom scribbling notes on their pads.

Once I was done, the officer left for a while and then returned with a detective. "This is Detective Graden. He's going to be handling this case." The officer informed us.

"*Case?*" I didn't like how that sounded.

"Miss Delimar, from what Officer Kemp has reported to me, there may be charges filed against you—assault and battery, leaving the scene of a crime, and possibly attempted murder with a deadly weapon. This is serious." His facial expression matched the seriousness in his voice. I turned to Tom with panic in my eyes.

"Let's not jump the gun, detective. We both know you have to talk to the D.A. and the victim's family before we know exactly what we're dealing with." Tom said.

"That may be true, but your client just confessed to bashing in the victim's head and leaving her there to die!"

"In self defense!" Tom argued.

"You can argue self defense all you want, but you know the victim's family is going to want to see justice served either way. Miss

Delimar you need to understand that it's highly likely you may have to do some time."

I glanced at Gordon quickly, released my hand from his grip, and slammed my palm on the table, "I told you this would happen!"

"Angela, it's okay. Calm down. We don't even know for sure that the family will press charges, and if the D.A. takes this to trial, it will be evident that it was all in self defense." Tom tried to assure me.

"*Trial?* Nah, forget all that! I'm not trying to go to trial, so they can lock me up! I have information that can help on another case!" I blurted out. I didn't even think before I said it, but at this point my only concern was saving my ass.

"What kind of information? What case?" Detective Graden asked. I shifted nervously in my seat and wringed my hands together trying to think. It was too late to take back what I had said.

"I have information about ... a murder." I said quietly.

"A *murder?*" Detective Graden said as if taken off guard.

"Yes ... a cop's murder." Gordon's head jerked around in my direction. He was apparently shocked as well. I looked at him with the words "sorry, I didn't tell you" in my eyes.

"Wait a minute, wait a minute. I need a moment alone with my client." Tom told the officer and detective.

"Sure," Detective Graden said before he and the officer rose and left the room.

"Angela, this was not part of the plan! I told you not to say anything unless I gave you the green light that it was okay. What is this about a murder?" Tom was clearly annoyed that I went against his instructions.

"If I give them information on an unsolved murder, won't they give me some kind of deal where I won't have to go to jail for this? Isn't that how it works?" I asked ignorantly.

"It's not quite that cut and dry, but please just tell me what you're talking about."

"Well ... about a month or so ago, a man's body was found in Weekend Park, Officer Rock Johnson. They still haven't solved his murder. I know who did it." I saw Gordon's eyes widen out the corner of my eye.

"*Well?*" Tom urged me to continue.

"His name is Calvin Shay."

"And how do you know all this?" he asked.

"Because ... he's my boyfriend—I mean *ex* boyfriend, and he told me." My knee began to bounce up and down as I wondered what Gordon was thinking.

Tom leaned back in his chair in disbelief, "He confessed this to you? Did he say why he did it?"

"Yes, I know why he did it ..."

"Take your time Angela," Tom coaxed. I looked down into my lap as I fought hard to fight back the tears that were welling up. One single tear dropped quickly and Gordon grabbed my hand again, attentively rubbing it.

I turned my attention to him now, "I'm sorry I didn't tell you all this, Gordon. It's just one big ol' mess I didn't want to drag you in."

"It's okay, just tell us everything now." He replied.

"Angela, tell us why he did it please." Tom asked again.

"He did it because of me. He found out ... that ... Rock raped me." The tears streamed faster now, and Gordon's eyes looked like they were ready to pop out of his head as his jaw clenched.

"Wait, so you knew the victim too?" Tom asked.

I nodded, "Yeah, we used to work out sometimes together at my gym, and I guess he followed me home one night or waited for me or something, and he raped me outside my apartment."

"Did you report the rape?" Tom asked.

"Yes! I even told them that I thought it was Rock, but they didn't believe me. Then when I told Cal he just got so mad ... so mad. I didn't know what he was going to do though. I knew nothing about it until after it had already been done." Tom sighed and dropped his pencil on top of the pad. He leaned back into the chair further and rubbed his head in confusion and disbelief.

"What's going to happen now? Will I be in even more trouble because I didn't come forward and say something sooner?"

"No, no I think this information will help a great deal. I know the D.A. will be anxious to close a cop killing case." Tom explained. We sat there in silence waiting for Detective Graden to return while Gordon tried to console me. Once the detective entered the room, followed by the same officer, I let Tom do all the talking.

I had to tell both stories all over again and sign a confession for each one. Detective Graden finished off the interview by saying he would have to talk to Jillian's family and the D.A. to see what kind of deal they could work out for me, but he and Tom seemed pretty confident that I wouldn't have to spend any time behind bars. Now the only thing I was worried about was Cal. He was still out there on the loose. If he found out that I turned him in, he would do way worse damage to me than Matt did to Cherlise. Detective Graden said not to worry because they would be picking him up first thing the next morning. So hopefully I only had to survive until then.

I don't think Gordon knew what to say. He was silent walking me back to my car. "Gordon, listen—"

"Shhhh, *you* listen. Don't worry your pretty lil' head about anything. We'll talk about all this later on. Right now, both of us have to get to work." He cut me off.

"Okay."

"And when are you gonna get your window fixed?" he asked as he twisted up his face, showing his disapproval.

"I don't know. I have to figure out where I'm going to take it first."

"We'll go tomorrow after work. I'll take you to my guy." I liked when he was firm with me this way for some reason.

"Okay, thanks as always, Gordon."

He kissed my forehead before opening my driver door for me, "I'll call you after work, babe. Be careful."

Even though I called Danika to let her know I would be late, she still wanted to see me when I finally made it in. I wasn't in the mood for this today. "Angela, I'm sure you know why I've asked to speak with you ..." she said, waiting for a response.

"I know, Danika. I'm really sorry that I was late this morning. I had to take care of something and it ended up taking a lot longer than I expected. I can stay late to make up the time tonight."

"Well making up the time really isn't the issue, Angela. You know your schedule is to work eight thirty to five and we made that your schedule because that's when we need you here. That's primetime for doing business. If that's going to be a problem for you, you need to let me know, so we can make other arrangements. When you're not here, we have to find someone else to do your work. That's not really fair to the rest of the team." She was laying it on, and I was trying hard not to go off.

I knew I was in the wrong for being late, but I just didn't feel like hearing about it right now, not today. I took a deep breath before answering, "I know. I understand, and again, I'm really sorry. It won't be a problem going forward."

"I most certainly hope not. Now, you can make up the time between today and tomorrow." She said sternly.

"Okay, thanks Danika." I rose from my seat thinking the conversation was over.

"Uh, Angela, that's not the only reason I called you in here." She said.

Oh boy, what else did I do now? I thought.

"It's been brought to my attention that you've been using the company's email for your own personal use. You know that's against our code of conduct here at B.I.G. Insurance." She cautioned. My heart sank, and my mouth became dry. Had she been monitoring my email now? I really couldn't stand this place anymore. I wasn't sure what to say next.

"Yes, I know, but I'm sure I've only used it a few times for personal use and nothing inappropriate."

"Uh huh, I see …" she said as she pulled out a sheet of paper from a manila folder. "This is an email sent from you to Renee on January seventeenth at twelve fifty-seven p.m.:

'Yeah I'm just gonna give the $5. It's only $5. There's like ten of us on this team. This chick is ghetto as hell. I know she's just going to go to the dollar store and get the card and balloons. So that's only like $5 at the most. What is she gonna do with the rest of the money? Plus she was just crying broke on the phone so how is she gonna ask everyone else for money when she don't even have none herself.'"

The blood rushed all over my body, and my armpits began to sweat as the embarrassment set in. "Danika, I didn't mean—"

"This is quite funny!" She said, trying to fight back her laughter. "I was thinking the same thing when she approached me for money for this—still! This is a place of business."

I smiled sheepishly, relieved and surprised she actually found it funny. "I'm sorry, and I actually didn't even mean to send that to her. That's what I get, I guess …"

"Oh! Bahahahahahahaha!" Danika couldn't control her laughter any longer once she realized that I didn't even mean to send Renee the email. I don't think I had ever seen her laugh before. I wasn't sure what to do. It was clear I was being reprimanded, but it was also clear that Danika had an interesting sense of humor. I sat there patiently with a painted smile on waiting for her to finish.

She regained her composure, sat up straight, and smoothed out the front of her blouse. "Please forgive me. That was very unprofessional of me." She cleared her throat before continuing, "No more personal emails, okay?"

"Okay."

" —and no more calling out or being this late!"

"Okay, Danika ... is there anything else?" I asked timidly.

"No, that's all for now, thanks." She said with her serious tone switched back on.

I returned to my desk with a slight smirk at the thought that I had actually made Danika laugh. I'm pretty sure no one else in the office had managed that yet. The rest of the day was smooth sailing, and I stayed an hour late to make up part of the time I missed.

Cherlise was excited to see me when I made it home. She'd highlighted a bunch of apartment listings that she wanted to go check out from the Star Ledger. Even through her wired jaw, she was talking much better than the day before.

"I'm thinking tomorrow I can go check out the first two places. They're walking distance from one another. The first one has central air and hardwood floors. Doesn't that sound nice? And it looks nice from that one picture there." She pointed to one of the listings.

"Oh yeah," was all I said.

"What's wrong? You don't like it? Maybe we should make a list of must haves," she suggested.

"No, it's fine. It does look nice from the pictures."

"Well what's wrong then? You seem down or something." She asked.

"Oh, Cherlise I don't even know where to start." I sighed.

"What? What happened? Did something happen between you and Gordon?" she asked, overly interested.

"No, everything is great with me and Gordon. He actually seems too good to be true, really."

"Oh ... well what is it?" she pried.

I told her about Rowi, Rainy, and the rest of the family that I had just learned about. I told her about Rainy's condition, about my brother, and about my hesitation to meet them all.

"Well that's a good thing, Ang! Shoot I wish somebody would come tell me that crazy ass woman that raised me wasn't really my momma! I'd jump on the chance to have a new family!" She said, rolling her eyes as I laughed.

"I know. Part of me does want to meet them but part of me is scared, I guess."

"Angie, that's your family! Your *real* family! I don't think you have anything to be scared of. Just go meet 'em!" she coaxed.

"Yeah, maybe you're right."

"Of course I'm right! There's no harm in meeting them one time. If you don't like them or whatever, then you don't ever have to see them again. You don't owe them anything." She said, jerking her neck and looking in my eyes.

"Okay okay okay already. I'll call Rowi and make some arrangements. I am nervous about meeting Rainy, though, since she's not in her right mind. She probably won't even know who I am."

"Well, you won't know that 'til you go, will you? This is the woman who gave you life! You owe it to yourself to at least see her once!" Cherlise did have a valid point.

"Okay, I know. You're right, Cherlise. Well that's not the worst of what's bothering me though." I confessed.

"What's up? What is it?"

"Well you know I told you Gordon got me this lawyer, and we were going to the police station today, so I could confess about Jillian ..."

"Yeah," she answered.

"Well, I got so scared Cherlise. The detective started talking 'bout I would have to do some time and I ... I snitched on Cal."

"WHAT!" she blurted out then winced from the pain.

"You okay?" I asked.

"Yeah, yeah. I probably shouldn't do that again." She said, rubbing her jaw.

"I just got so nervous and scared they were gonna lock me up right then and there, I just told them that Cal killed Rock!"

"Oh my God, Angie. What the hell were you thinking?" she looked worried.

"I know. I know. I'm just so scared that he's gonna come around here and do something, Cherlise. He's really crazy, like for real."

"Ummm, *ya think*? He killed a man, Angie! Of course he's crazy! Say what you want about Matt. He's done a lot of things, but I bet you he ain't never killed nobody!" she said, shaking her head.

"Well, he damn near killed *you*! Need I remind you?" I shot at her.

Her nostrils flared, and she glared at me through her embarrassment. "Look, I'm sorry, Cherlise. I didn't mean it like that."

"Well, how did you mean it?" she said with arms folded.

"I'm just scared, okay? Cal is out there somewhere right now, and I just moved to the top of his hit list!"

She shifted in her stance and softened her glare, "Well, we really gotta move fast now!"

I could hear my cell phone ringing from inside my purse, and I dug around to get it. "It's Gordon. I'll be back." I said as I headed to the bedroom to answer it privately. "Hello?"

"Hey baby, you busy?" he replied.

"No, I was just talking to Cherlise."

"Turn on channel seven!" he instructed. I could hear a mixture of nerves and excitement in his voice. I turned it on, and it was a breaking news story. Cal's mugshot was in the top right-hand corner of the screen and there appeared to be a car chase happening.

"Oh my God ..."

"That's him, right?" Gordon asked.

"Oh my God! Yeah, that's him! What the hell is going on?"

"They put the warrant out for his arrest this afternoon, and when the cops went to pick him up from his grandmother's house, he ran out the back window and forced a woman out of her SUV! Now they're chasing him down Route Twenty-Two!" He filled me in. I was frozen. It felt like I was in a dream. This was something out of a movie. "Angela, are you there?" Gordon asked.

"Yeah, I'm here. Hold on!" I ran back into the living room and turned the channel. "They're chasing Cal down Route Twenty-Two!"

"What! Are you serious?" Cherlise asked as her eyes glued to the TV.

"Look! That's his picture right there! He done high jacked some lady's car!" Both of our mouths hung open as we watched in anticipation.

"Baby, don't answer the door for nobody! You hear me? There's no telling where this fool is going or what he might do!" Gordon commanded.

"I just can't believe this."

"I know, but don't worry. They'll catch him." He assured me.

"I sure hope so ..."

They didn't. Cal ended up crashing into a guardrail somewhere in Annandale after a seventeen-minute chase. Then he got away on foot. The police lost him, just like that.

CHAPTER 38

The next three weeks moved fast, and there was so much going on. Cherlise and I did find a nice cozy two-bedroom in Bloomfield. I forfeited my rent for the remainder of the month, but it didn't matter. I just had to get out of there. Gordon was a godsend. He helped me finish packing up my mother's apartment, and I was glad to finally have that out of the way. Then he and two of his cousins moved Cherlise and me into our new place. Cal was still on the run from the police, but he hadn't made anymore contact with me. I kept in contact with Rowi over the phone. We talked every couple of days. She was a real easy person to talk to and funny. I was getting use to having a new aunt. I decided to take things slow with meeting the rest of the family though.

The best news of all was that the district attorney's office did uphold a deal for me. Due to the information I'd given them about Cal I was let off with a slap on the wrist in Jillian's case. I was charged with assault only and plead guilty. With that, I only had to do thirty days of community service and that would be the end of my probation. When they said that, I envisioned myself picking up trash on the side of the highway in an orange jumpsuit with one of those trash sticks. Lucky for me, it wasn't like that at all. Instead I just volunteered at Greater Zion Jesus the Christ Shekinah Mount Calvary Baptist Church twice a week, filing paperwork for the pastor.

Things would probably never be back to normal, but they were slowly falling into place. Gordon and I were dating regularly now, no interruptions—no crazy ex-boyfriends. I liked him more and more each day we spent time together, and he made it no secret he felt the same way. One night after dinner, we went back to his place to watch some movies. He had a nice open loft in Jersey City near the river. I was impressed. Though I tried to pretend like I wasn't. It definitely looked like a bachelor pad with the typical black leather sofas, but it was decorated very tastefully.

We were paying more attention to each other than we were the movie. This was a regular thing for us now. He started kissing my neck lightly before saying, "come here," as he turned my face to face his. He was a wet kisser, but a good kisser. He sucked on my tongue then flicked it back and forth with his. I pecked his top lip gently then sucked on the bottom one. He grabbed the back of my neck firmly for a second and pulled back to stop and look into my eyes. Then he went back to kissing me. I stroked the back of his neck with one hand and ran my fingers up and down along his rib with my other hand.

One of his hands found its way to my breast, cupped it, and then squeezed the nipple gently. I could feel myself pulsate between my legs beneath the skirt I was wearing. He rested his other hand on the side of my hip with fingertips rubbing against the side of my butt cheek. In an instant, we were all over each other. Then all of a sudden he stopped.

"What?" I asked, a little out of breath.

"Are you sure you want to keep doing what we're doing right now?"

"Ummmm, yeah! Why? You want to stop? Is something wrong?" I asked.

"No, not a damn thing wrong on my end!" He said with a smirk and chuckle before continuing, "It's just, I know you been through some traumatic events recently. I don't want to push you into anything you're not ready for."

I sat back and thought for a moment. I realized that all these weeks we'd been making out, I was always the one to stop us when it was getting heavy. I guess he was expecting me to do it again this time. Tonight was different though. Rock and the rape were the furthest things from my mind. I wanted Gordon, and I wanted him now.

"I know I've been hot and cold over the past few weeks with the rape and everything, but I'm okay tonight … *really.*"

"Are you sure? Just like that? I mean you still refuse to go see the psychologist. You haven't really talked to anyone about it. Angela, I just don't want you to do anything that makes you uncomfortable or that you'll regret." He said almost as if he was afraid.

"Gordon, I'm sure. I'm fine … are *you* okay? Do you think I'm going to change my mind and say you raped me or something? Rock really did rape me. I didn't make any of that up, you know." I was starting to feel defensive.

"Baby, I know. I never doubted that, and no, I don't think you'd do anything like that. I just want you to be sure. We have all the time in the world." He said, ducking his head down to my level to look me in the eye.

"I'm sure …" I said as I pulled his face back towards mine to meet my lips.

We picked up where we left off and began kissing slowly. Gordon got up and pulled his shirt off over his head. I kept my eyes on him, taking in every inch of his perfectly toned body. I knew he worked out, but *damn.* He put his hand out for mine, and I grabbed it as he helped me up off the couch. He then pulled my shirt off over my head as well. "Turn around," he commanded. I did as told, and he began kissing my back and shoulders as he unhooked my bra. Once that fell off, he massaged both breasts slowly and gently in each hand. I started to slide off my skirt, but he stopped me. "No, leave that on—the boots too." Then he gave a mischievous smile.

I turned back around to face him. He lifted my skirt, caressing my backside. SLAP! I jumped a little, then returned the smile as I unbuckled his belt, unfastened his jeans, and slid them down. Now standing in just his boxers at attention, I felt around down there as we continued kissing. I was happy with what I felt as I stroked it up and down a few times. That turned him on and he aggressively searched for my wetness. He found it and started rubbing lightly. "Mmmm," I moaned into his mouth and felt a little pre cum ooze onto my thumb. He bit gently on my bottom lip, and I almost lost it. I let go and felt a little lower. I felt around and cupped one but something wasn't right. Something was missing. I felt some more then jerked my head back in astonishment. I had never been in a situation like this, and it caught me by surprise.

"What? What's wrong? Why'd you stop, baby? That shit felt

good!" He asked, confused with one hand on my butt and the other on my clitoris.

I cleared my throat before answering because I didn't know how to say it. "Gordon ... um, you only have one testicle?"

He sighed and looked down, "Yeah, I only have one nut. I was born that way ... Is that gonna be a problem?" he asked. He wasn't even embarrassed a little bit.

"No, it's just—well ... I just wasn't expecting it. That's all. Kind of caught me by surprise, you know?"

"Well, everything works just fine. See?" he said swinging his thing back and forth and laughing. This removed the awkwardness and made me laugh as well. Then he pulled his boxers down so I could have a good look. "See? Nothing to be scared of!" He said as he grabbed my hand to put it back on his one testicle.

I was the one embarrassed, but he was right. If this was the one thing that I'd been waiting to find out was wrong with Gordon, then this was something I could deal with. I knew he couldn't be as perfect as he seemed all along, but if this was the one thing, if this was all, then *this* I could do. This was nothing compared to all the bullshit Cal and all the others before him had put me through. Shit, that just meant one less nut I had to worry about touching or licking.

CHAPTER 39

I guess I did something right during that night of passion with Gordon because I received a bouquet of pink roses the next day at work. A note was attached to them: *"Over the past month, I've gotten to know and experience pieces of you, and last night was a damn good piece. But I want all of you. Angela, tell me you'll be mine and mine only."* I smiled from ear to ear.

I grabbed the phone to call him, but Donnie popped up at my cubicle before I could start dialing. "You still coming to my party on Saturday, right?" he asked. I had forgotten all about it. He had told me so long ago.

"Oh, it's *this* Saturday?"

"Yes, ma'am! Don't tell me you forgot." He said, making an over exaggerated sad face.

"My bad, Donnie, I did forget but I'll still be there."

He perked back up and smiled as he handed me a small flyer, "Cool! Bring as many people as you want. Make sure you bring this flyer because it'll get you in on my guest list—and don't forget your masquerade attire!" he instructed.

I smiled, "Okay, I won't."

He walked away, towards Renee's desk. I reached for the phone again, but before I could pick it up, it started ringing. "Hello, B.I.G. Insurance?" Silence. "Hello? Hello?" I could tell someone was on the other end of the phone, but they didn't say anything, so I hung up. My heart began to speed up and I worried that Cal might be waiting for me outside of work again or something. As I stared at the phone an email from May popped up. She was asking what I had planned for the weekend, and if I wanted to hang out.

I had been so busy over the past few weeks that we barely talked. I responded and invited her to accompany me to Donny's party. My cell phone vibrated against my desk at the same time another email came in from May. It was a text from Rowi. Usually she called, but she probably guessed I was at work. *"Hi niece! I want to run something by you. Can you give me a call later when you get off work?"* Now I was curious to see what she wanted to tell me. Up until now our conversations consisted of the formalities, just getting to know each other—details about our lives.

I responded with *"okay,"* and turned my attention back to the email from May. She was on board for the party Saturday. We went back and forth a couple more times before I remembered Danika had been monitoring my emails. I cut the conversation short and told May I would call her later.

I didn't have a lot of work, surprisingly. So I spent the rest of the day trying to find things to keep me looking busy. I couldn't wait to get out of there to call Gordon. I had butterflies in my stomach as I hurried to my car. I hopped in, started the car, and proceeded to back out of the parking space. The road felt funny. The car was sort of wobbling up and down as I rolled back. I hit the breaks and then eased off of them slowly. It wasn't the road. It was my tire. "Dammit!" I said out loud to myself as I pulled back in the space and shut the car off. I walked around to the passenger side and there was the flat tire in the back. Even though it was a pain in the ass, I was just thankful I had roadside assistance.

I made the call and was told it would be approximately a forty-five minute wait before they could get to me. I sighed wishing I knew how to change the tire myself, but there was nothing I could do; so I just waited in the car. I decided to call Gordon while I did. "Hey, baby, how was your day?" he asked with anticipation in his voice.

"It was goooood."

"Oh yeah? Anything in particular make it so gooood?" he asked. I could hear his smile through the phone, and I was smiling back on the other end.

"Well a certain somebody sent me this lovely bouquet of roses. You know anything about that?"

"Hmmm roses, roses, I might have something to do with that." He replied.

"They're so beautiful, babe. That really made my day. Thank you."

"Oh, you're welcome. A beautiful bouquet of roses for a beautiful lady—Excuse me, *my* beautiful lady." He said confidently.

"Oh, *your* lady?"

"That's right! I know you read the card, and I know you not gonna break my heart like that, are you?" He asked as if he already knew my answer.

"Yes, I read the card, of course. You're too sweet. And yes, I will be your girlfriend. You sure you want me to be your girlfriend though? Are you ready for all this craziness?" I asked, chuckling.

"Girl, please! You ain't giving me nothing I can't handle over here!" We both laughed at that. "So what's going on? You home already?" he asked.

"No, I'm still at work sitting in the parking lot. I got a flat tire."

"For real? Damn, okay I'm on my way!" he said with no hesitation.

"No, it's okay. I already called roadside assistance."

"What'chu you call them for? You know I would've came and took care of that." He said, scolding me.

"I know, babe, but I didn't want you to have to go out of your way to come up here, and plus, I'm paying for it so…"

"I guess, but I'm your man now, and that's what I'm here for. So next time you call your man, you hear?" He said half sternly, half jokingly.

"Yes, sir!" I joked back.

"How long did they say it's gonna take?"

"They said like forty-five minutes." I answered.

"Okay, well, I'm still stuck at work myself finishing up a few things. Call me when you make it in. Better yet, call me if they're still not there when they're supposed to be. I'll stop by later to see you if it's cool."

"Okay, that's cool. See you later."

After we hung up, I called Rowi next. "Hey, Angie!" she said excitedly when she answered the phone.

"Hi, Rowi, are you busy?" I still hadn't gotten use to the idea of calling her aunt.

"No, chile' just got in from work a little while ago. 'Bout to see what I can whip up for dinner right quick." She replied.

"Oh okay, yeah I'm still stuck at work myself. I got a flat tire, so I'm just sitting in the parking lot waiting for roadside assistance to get here."

"What! Oh, Lord Jesus, are you okay? Is anyone waiting with you?" she asked worriedly.

"No, but I'm fine. There's still a lot of cars out here, and people still coming out of the building to leave."

"Oh, well you keep those doors locked while you wait, okay? And you ask to see the guy's ID when he gets there!" she instructed. It was cute how protective she was.

"Okay," I said, chuckling lightly.

"For real, girl. It's too many crazy ass people out here nowadays. And just cause we ain't talked about it, don't think I forgot about that night that man forced himself on you. Lord knows what would've happened next if I hadn't hit him. Yeah, we ain't talked about it, but I damn sure ain't forget!" I got quiet on my end as I replayed that night in my head. All I could see was Rock's eyes glaring into mine.

"Angie, you still there?" Rowi said into the phone.

"Yes, I'm still here. Sorry 'bout that."

"Well, I won't keep you on the phone too long. I wanted you to call me because I wanted to run something by you. Now you don't have to say yes if you don't want to. I'll completely understand. It's your decision okay?" she prefaced.

"Okay."

"I'm going to visit Rainy on Sunday up at the institution. I'm taking Stitch, and I wanted to see if you might want to go—Like I said, don't feel pressured. I know we've only been talking a few weeks now, but I thought it might be nice for her to see you. I know it would make her day, and I know Stitch is real anxious to meet his big sister." She explained delicately.

"Wow … I don't know what to say. Do you think she'll even know who I am?"

"Well, she definitely has her good days and her bad days. Some days she don't know any of us, and some days it's like she's her regular self. So we really have no way of knowing. I do know that when she's the Rainy we all know, she always asks about you. So I know she hasn't forgotten you, Angela. She ain't never forgotten you, baby." She said sadly.

"Well, can I let you know something by Friday? I'd like to think it over a bit." I had mixed emotions.

"Sure, sure of course. And if you decide to go, Stitch wanted me to ask if maybe you'd like to come over to our house for Sunday dinner afterwards with us—me, Stitch, your Uncle Mel, and Kareemah. He's so anxious to meet you, Angela. You're all he been talking 'bout ever since I told him about our first real sit down. He's such a good, sweet boy. He really is." I smiled silently on the other end. "But you go ahead and think about it. I don't want to rush you into anything. I know it's a lot, so you just take your time and think about it and let me know, okay?" she said.

"Okay, I'll definitely get back to you by Friday. What time are y'all going up there?"

"Visitations start at eleven, so we'll probably leave about ten-thirty. You can meet us there or you can park at my house, and we can ride up together. It's up to you." She said.

"Okay, well, I'll let you know. Thanks, Rowi!"

"Oh, no problem, honey. I look forward to talking to you soon. You be safe." She instructed.

"Okay, bye bye."

I hung up, and the butterflies had returned to my stomach. The thought of finally meeting my real mother in person had me reeling. I was curious, nervous, and scared all at once. I didn't know how I'd feel if she didn't know who I was. Even though I knew she was sick, I wasn't sure if I was ready to handle that just yet.

The tow truck pulled up behind me exactly forty-five minutes from the time I'd gotten off the phone with roadside assistance. I popped my trunk and handed my ID to the technician. He went straight to work and propped my car up with the jack. I stood by watching as more people left work and lent nosey stares as they made their way to their own vehicles. You would've thought they've never seen or gotten a flat tire before the way their necks bent.

The technician's nametag said "Jack" on it. Jack didn't say much except when he finally got the tire off and examined it as he put it in the trunk in the spot where the spare had been. "You see this here?" he called me over. I looked where his flashlight shined. It landed on a tear in the rubber. "Now there's no nail or glass or anything that I could see in or around your tire. You see how this is here? Somebody slashed your tire, ma'am." He informed me with a concerned look.

317

"WHAT! Slashed?" I exclaimed.

"Yup, maybe a knife or razor possibly, but this was definitely done intentionally I hate to tell you."

"Oh my gosh! I can't believe this. First the broken window, now this!" I said, more so to myself than Jack.

"Oh, so this isn't the first incident? Somebody got it out for you?" he asked.

"Yeah, I'm pretty sure it's my crazy ex." I said sadly.

"Wow! That's crazy! Usually you see this type of behavior from females, not from men!"

"Yeah, I know," I mumbled as he went back to work putting on the new tire.

I didn't notice until the technician handed me his clipboard to sign paperwork that I was trembling. My hand shook as I tried to steady the pen. "Thanks, ma'am. Here's your copy. I hope you're able to shake that crazy ex of yours. This ain't good at all." He said as he tore off a sheet of paper and handed it to me.

"Tell me about it. Thanks." I folded the paper and headed back to the driver door to get into the car.

I called Gordon again on my way home just to vent my concerns about the tire and what Jack, the technician, had just told me. He tried to calm me down as much as he could over the phone and assured me that he would meet me at the new apartment shortly.

Cherlise was sprawled on the couch watching TV when I entered. Her jaw had healed and so had her ribs, but she still hadn't been back to work yet. I was starting to question if she still even had a job. I didn't want to be insensitive to her recovery or make assumptions, so I kept telling myself I'd give her another week before I'd ask what the deal was.

"Hey, Cherlise," I said tiredly.

"Hey, Ang, what's wrong? You're home late tonight."

"I know. I had a flat tire and I had to wait for roadside assistance." I replied.

"Oh damn, I'm sorry. Everything's okay now though?"

"Yeah, I just have to go get a new tire tomorrow. I can't be late to work, though, so I don't know how I'm gonna do it. I might just have to ride on this donut 'til the weekend or something. I don't know." I sounded exasperated.

"Well, why do you have to get a new tire? Can't you just get that one patched?"

"Nope! Apparently somebody slashed my shit." I said, shaking my head as I took off my coat and hung it up on the coat rack we had in the corner.

Cherlise had done a lot of the decorating, and I had to admit it looked way better than my last place. It was more inviting. We kept the couch I already had, and bought most of the decorations from Target and the dollar store. She made everything come together very nicely.

"WHAT! Somebody slashed your tire?" she asked slowly.

"Yup, that's what the tech said and he showed it to me too."

"Daaaaaamn. What the fuck! Who would wanna slash your tire? I mean, *damn*! Who you piss off like that?" she asked as if really racking her brain for an answer.

"I don't know. I really think it's Cal. You know they still ain't catch his ass. I knew it wasn't safe. Now I'm like, what if he followed me here? What if he knows where I live now?"

"I don't know, Angie. You better get you a gun." She said with wide eyes.

I burst out laughing. "A gun? Girl, what am I gonna do with a gun? I don't know how to shoot no gun! Shit, I don't even know where to buy a gun!"

"I'm for real, Angie. This nigga is crazy. You gotta fight crazy with crazy! I can talk to my cousin about getting you one. We'll figure out how to shoot that shit later!" Now she was laughing.

"I don't know, Cherlise. What if I accidentally shoot myself in the foot or something?"

"Girl! You ain't gonna shoot yourself!" she said while rolling her eyes.

"What? That stuff really happens. People think they got the safety on or the gun ain't loaded or whatever, then BLAM!" We both laughed some more before the doorbell rang. "Oh, that's Gordon ... my boyfriend," I said while giving Cherlise a look.

"Ehm ehm, boyfriend? Did I just hear you correctly?" She cleared her throat with a grin.

"Yup, you heard me!" I said, grinning back.

"Oh, so y'all official now? Oh shit! Are you going to tell me when and how this went down?" she questioned.

"Yup, but I can't tell you right now. I'll have to tell you after he leaves." I winked as I pressed the intercom "Who is it?"

"It's me!" he replied.

"Me who?" I asked as Cherlise and I looked at each other and giggled.

"Me, Gordon, your man, your boyfriend!" We snickered harder before I finally buzzed him in.

We greeted with a nice tongue exchange once he made it upstairs. "Whooooooo!!" Cherlise hollered as she covered her eyes.

"Girl, hush!"

"Hi, Miss Cherlise, and how are you today?" Gordon asked.

"I'm doing just fine, but not as good as the new happy couple." She teased. Gordon smiled bashfully, and I cut my eyes at Cherlise.

"How are you, baby? You calm down some?" he asked.

"Yeah somewhat, I guess. I just don't understand what he's still doing around here. It's like he's not even afraid of being caught by the police!" We took a seat at the new kitchen table. We got it from a second-hand store, but it was way nicer and sturdier than my last one.

"Don't worry. I'll call the detective first thing in the morning and let him know what's going on. In the meantime, I bought you this." He reached in the pocket of his coat and took out a small keychain-size can of mace. "Put this on your keys and have it out anytime you're walking to or from your car, okay? You just unlock it like this." He instructed as he showed me the tiny switch on the mace can.

"Thanks, Gordon. I'll feel so much better once they catch his ass. I can't take this anymore. I don't even know how I'm gonna get my tire replaced. I absolutely cannot go in late anymore. Danika is not going for it."

"Baby, stop worrying! I'll take you to work early in your car, and then go get it done and pick you up after work. Okay?" He said.

"Really? You'll do that for me? You're the best!"

"What did I just tell you? I'm your man! That's what I'm here for. I hope I don't have to keep on reminding you of that over and over." He said before leaning in to kiss me on the cheek.

I smiled, "I know. I know. I'm just not use to this, but thanks."

"Stop thanking me! You not use to it because you use to messing with those lame dudes that do dumb stuff like slash your tires and whatnot, but I'm not trippin'. I know I can show you better than I can tell you." He said and winked before planting another kiss on my lips.

"Oh my gosh! GET A ROOM!" Cherlise yelled from the couch before making a barfing motion. We all laughed in unison at that.

CHAPTER 40

"**A**re you sure?" I asked in desperation.

"Yes. I'm really sorry to hear about your car and the problems you've been having, but Calvin Shay is definitely *not* in your city and hasn't been for some time now."

"I just don't understand. It doesn't make any sense." I said into the phone, but more to myself. It took Detective Graden a couple of days to return my and Gordon's calls. Now that I had him on the phone, I couldn't believe what I was hearing.

"My office received a tip that Mr. Shay was laying low with some relative in Baltimore. As soon as we heard, we got a team on surveillance right away. They've been monitoring his every move for at least two weeks now. We're just waiting for the right time to close in, but he definitely hasn't been anywhere near New Jersey. So I'm sure he couldn't have slashed your tire, Miss Delimar." Detective Graden explained. I was speechless.

"Wow, I don't know what to say. I thought for sure it was him. I just don't know who else would do this or why."

"I'm really sorry. Maybe it was just some neighborhood kids up to no good. You know they have their own little initiations and whatnot." He reasoned.

"Yeah, maybe." I didn't bother to explain that it happened at work in a corporate park. There really was no neighborhood to speak of.

"I'll give you a call after we have some new information. We

322

should have an update for you after we make the arrest." He offered.

"Okay, thanks Detective Graden."

I sat parked outside of May's building, breathing heavily. I hadn't called yet to tell her I was there since the detective called me first. We had plans to go shopping for some masquerade costumes for Donny's party the following night. Thoughts raced through my mind as I thought back to my slashed tire. The anxiety grew worse now, knowing Cal had nothing to do with it. I should have felt a sense of relief that he was nowhere near, but I just felt panic. Nothing added up.

Once I finally let May know I was waiting outside, she came right out. I hadn't seen her since my mother passed. There was something different about her. I just couldn't quite put my finger on it though. It wasn't until we were in the dressing room at one of the costume stores that I realized what it was.

"May, have you gained a little weight?"

She smiled beaming from ear to ear, "Mayyyyybe! Why? I look fat?"

"No, not fat, but your face just looks rounder or something, and your hips are a little wider."

"Well, I was going to tell you a while ago, but with everything that was going on with your attack and your mom passing and everything, I figured I'd wait." She said.

"Tell me what?" May didn't get out or do too much, so I wondered what she could've possibly been keeping from me.

"I'm pregnant!" she exclaimed excitedly. My mouth dropped open and my eyes grew wide.

"WHAT! Pregnant? Since when? By who? Are you serious?"

She laughed as she hung the costume she'd just tried on back on the hanger. "Yes, I'm serious. I'm going to have a baby, and I'm four months pregnant."

"*FOUR MONTHS!!* And you're just now telling me?"

"Shhh! You've had a lot going on, and we haven't had a chance to just hang. I wanted to tell you sooner, but I wanted to decide what I was going to do first. I didn't want anyone to know until I was sure I was keeping it." She explained in a whisper. It took me a moment to process the information.

"I can't believe it! You're gonna have a baby! Congratulations! When can we start planning the shower? Are you scared? Do you have any names picked out yet?" I had to calm myself down. "I'm sorry, I know I'm asking a lot of questions. It's just 'cause I didn't know! I had no idea. Wait, who is the father?" I asked.

"I know. It's okay. I haven't picked out a name yet, and I'm thinking about having the shower at Tony's probably when I'm at eight months or something. Are you gonna help me plan it?" she asked.

"Of course! I can't wait. This is so exciting! Now we can go shopping for baby clothes. Do you know the sex yet?"

"No, not yet. I haven't made up my mind if I want to know yet." She answered.

It was strange that she still had not answered my question about who the father was. As far as I knew, she didn't have a boyfriend, and she wasn't seeing anyone. Had she been anyone else, I wouldn't pry, but I felt close enough to ask her again.

"Okay, so how come you won't answer my question? Who's the baby daddy?"

She rolled her eyes at the term, "baby daddy," before answering. "It's ... it's complicated."

"Okaaaay? So?" I pressed.

"Look, I rather you just meet him in person. I've been seeing him for a while now, but I haven't told anyone because ..." she trailed off.

"Because what? Who is he? Is he married?"

"No! He's not married, and you wouldn't know him if I told you. I just haven't said anything because I'm kind of ... embarrassed." She said with a funny look on her face.

"Embarrassed why? Is he ugly or something?"

"No!" she answered defensively.

"Is he ... handicapped? He don't have no arms or legs or something?"

"Hahahahahaha! No, Angie! Of course he has his arms and legs!" She couldn't stop laughing.

"So what is so embarrassing then?"

"He's just from a different generation than us. That's all." She finally admitted.

"Oh that's it? So you got you a young whippersnapper? Girl I ain't mad!"

"Look, I rather you just meet him, so you can see what I see in him. He's so smart and he spoils me like crazy. You see this?" she held out her arm, so I could get a good look at her watch. I hadn't noticed it with her long sleeves, but now it was hard to miss. It was a Rolex with diamonds that dazzled even under the dull light in the dressing room.

"DAMN! Where youngin' get that kind of money from? Is he a drug dealer?"

"Girl, no! You're so crazy. He's in real estate. He does really well too, but that's not why I'm with him. I think I'm really in love with him, Ang." She said in a tone I'd never heard her use before.

"Awww, I'm so happy for you, May-May!"

May was on the quiet and reserved side. I don't think I'd ever seen her with a man or heard her speak of any male interests the whole time I'd known her. It was nice to see that she'd found someone too.

"Oh, so this means you can't drink when we go out tomorrow. Hell, you can't drink for the next five months or so!"

"Nope, that's the real reason I didn't go out with you on your birthday. I didn't feel like making up reasons why I couldn't pour it up with y'all, and I wasn't ready to tell you the news yet. But I wanna go out tomorrow and get my last little partying in before I start to really show, and I can't hang." She explained in a down voice.

"Ooohhh, yeah! I knew you ain't have no damn headache that night!" We both laughed. "So when do I get to meet your knight in shining armor? Oooh! We should do a double date, so you can meet Gordon too! Did I tell you we made it official? He's my ... *boyfriend*." I said with pride.

"No, you didn't tell me! I'm so happy for you two. Yeah, we definitely gotta plan something soon, so everybody can meet. Why don't we take them to the party tomorrow? Might be fun." She suggested.

"Hmmm, yeah that might be fun. We can just pick them up some simple masks to wear."

"Yeah, I know Sampson will be game. Do you think Gordon will want to go?" she asked.

"Oh, *Sampson*, so that's his name!" I teased. "Yeah, if he doesn't have any other plans I'm sure Gordon will go too."

We didn't see anything at the first two stores, but the third was much better. We bought both Sampson and Gordon Court Jester masks in two different colors. I bought a black and gold half facemask for myself along with a matching corset. May bought a red mask just for the eyes and an off white gown. I knew it was presumptuous of me to buy Gordon's mask, but I knew if he was available he'd want to spend time with me—even if it was at a gay masquerade party.

After I dropped May back off and we finalized our plans for the next night, I swung by home to get an overnight bag. Then I called Gordon to let him know I was on my way over, even though he already knew I was coming. We already planned to stay in at his place, and he was going to cook us a nice steak dinner. Not too soon after I walked in the door, and we exchanged kisses and hellos, I got a call from Rowi. Friday came so quickly I'd forgotten to call her with an answer about Sunday even though I had definitely given it a lot of thought.

"Hi, Rowi, I'm so sorry I totally forgot to call you today."

"That's okay, honey. I know you're a busy workingwoman. I don't want you to feel like I'm pressuring you or anything. I'm really calling because Stitch keeps bugging me to." She explained through a nervous chuckle.

I could tell she was sincere about not wanting to hound me. I felt flattered that Stitch was so interested to meet me. I was probably just as curious about him as well. "Aww, I can't wait to meet him. Honestly, I was still a little undecided up until you just said that. You can let him know that I will see you and the family on Sunday. I'll drive my own car and meet you at the institution."

"Oh, boy, you have no idea how excited he's gonna be to hear that! All week long all I've been hearing is: *Auntie, did you find out if my sister is coming Sunday? Are you gonna call my sister, Auntie?*" she said laughing.

"Well, you can tell him you finally talked to me, and I'll be there bright and early. Then I'll come to dinner to meet everyone else afterwards as planned."

"Okay, Angie. Thank you, this is going to mean so much to him—and Rainy too." She said.

"You don't have to thank me. It's time I meet everyone."

"Okay, well I'll text you the address and I'll see you Sunday!" she ended the call excitedly.

I decided I'd drive my own car instead of riding along with them just in case things got uncomfortable. I could just leave at any point if

I wanted to. It was only Friday, but the butterflies and anticipation started to kick in prematurely for Sunday. What if I wasn't the type of big sister Stitch was expecting or hoping for? Would I even know what to say to him—or Rainy? What about Melvin? I'd totally forgotten how I'd spoken to him at the IHOP. What would he think of me?

None of that mattered once I felt Gordon's hands against my temples massaging gently. He had a way about him that just put me at ease. All my anxiety seemed to just disappear when he was around. "Dinner will be ready in about fifteen minutes." He informed me before leaning over the back of the couch where I was seated to plant a kiss on my forehead. I smiled and closed my eyes for a moment before kicking my feet up.

CHAPTER 41

I was surprised to find Cherlise cleaning up around the apartment when I got in from Gordon's Saturday afternoon. "Hey."

"Hey, Ang! What'chu 'bout to get into?" she asked as she polished the coffee table with Pledge.

"I'm just about to relax for a bit before I head back out for the night."

"You going out tonight? Where you going?" she asked.

"We're going to this party my co-worker is having at Volt in Jersey City."

"*We?* Who's *we,* and how come I wasn't invited? See how you do me?" she said sarcastically.

"No, it's not like that. I thought about inviting you, but then I invited May—"

"Oh, *never mind!*" she cut me off and waved her hand.

"Dang why you say it like that? You ain't even let me finish!"

"Because you know that girl don't like me, and she ain't never even met me. Every time y'all go out it always just has to be y'all two, and whenever you invite her to come out with us, she always has something to do." She said.

She was partially right. "You didn't let me finish though. I would have invited you, but she kind of turned it into a double date. Gordon is going, and she's bringing her man, some mystery man she been seeing."

"*Mystery man?* Oh, so what makes you think I couldn't find a date?" she asked.

"Yeah, she just told me yesterday she been seeing some young dude, and she finally wants me to meet him or whatever. The double date was her idea …Well do you have somebody to bring?" I asked, already knowing the answer.

"That's not the point. You still could've asked me, but I don't really feel like going out anyway. I'm still recovering, you know." She was giving me a hard time, but I knew she wasn't seriously mad. I rolled my eyes and sucked my teeth before chuckling.

Still recovering, my ass, I thought to myself. "So guess what?" I decided to change the subject.

"What?"

"I'm going to meet my mother and my brother tomorrow."

"REALLY, ANG? That's what's up! I'm so excited for you!" she said, and I could tell she really meant it.

"Yeah, and I'm going to meet my uncle and cousin too. We're going to the institution first to see Rainy, and then I'm going over to Rowi's house after for dinner. She said my brother has been asking about me a lot."

"Aww, that's so sweet. How do you feel about it?" she asked.

"Honestly, I'm a little nervous. I'm not sure what to expect or what they might expect of me."

"Angie, how long we been friends now? Since I don't even know when. You ain't got nothing to be worried about. Just be yourself, and if they don't like you well, fuck 'em! You get up out of there and come home!" she said in a way only she could.

I smiled, "Yeah, you right. Fuck it! If they like me, they like me. If they don't, they don't!"

After Cherlise finished cleaning, she cooked and we just chilled for the rest of the afternoon into the evening. I'd hoped to fit a nap in, but it didn't happen. Instead we watched TV and shared a blunt until it was time for me to get dressed.

"What the hell!" she burst out laughing when I emerged from my room in my costume and mask.

"What? You don't like it?"

"It's different, but why are you wearing that?" she asked.

"Oh, it's a costume party, a masquerade party."

"Oooh, okay, now it makes sense. Oh, yeah, well that's cute then. I thought you was just wearing that as a regular outfit." We both started laughing.

Gordon was punctual as always. I answered his call and told him I'd be right down. "Okay, he's here. I'm out. See you tomorrow!"

"Tomorrow? You sleeping at his house *again*?" she asked as though it was an inconvenience to her.

"Yessss! I am! Is that a problem?"

"Whatever, girl! Just don't do anything I wouldn't do!" she cautioned.

"Girl, I'm grown! Bye!" I closed the door before she could come back with a smart remark.

We arrived at Volt first and waited outside near the line for May and Sampson. A masquerade party was actually a great idea. It was fun to see all the different costumes. Gordon said he felt silly wearing his mask, but I begged him to wear it at least until we made it inside. I could see his face tighten as we watched all the flamboyant men prance and flutter through the line and into the club.

"I promise we won't stay out too late. I just want to at least show my face, and May really wants me to meet Sampson. Maybe we can even leave early enough to hit a different club." I offered.

He sighed, and gave me a look. "You didn't tell me this was gonna be a gay club!" He said in a low voice from the side of his mouth.

"It's not! But I did tell you that Donnie is gay. What did you expect?" I said with a sympathetic smile.

"I know, but I mean … I didn't expect it to be like *this*."

I grabbed his hand and stroked it. "I promise we won't stay long—hour and a half tops!" Then I stood on my toes and poked out my lips for a kiss.

Gordon leaned down and stopped just at my lips, "Fine, but you better not leave my side!" Then he gave my lips a peck. I smiled and batted my lashes.

An all black Jaguar pulled in front of the club with dark black tinted windows and black rims. That's when I saw May step out. She shut the door and stood looking around before the car pulled off. "MAY!" I waved and called to get her attention. Once she spotted me, she smiled and made her way over.

"Hey, girl, all these masks out here. I was like, 'I'm never gonna find her in this crowd.' I was about to call you." She laughed nervously as she reached out for a hug.

"Yeah, I know. I like seeing all the costumes though. May, this is

Gordon; Gordon, May."

"How you doing, May? Nice to meet you." He said.

"I'm good, thanks. Nice to meet you as well. Sampson dropped me off, so I wouldn't have to walk. He went to park. You know I just get so tired these days." She said.

"I can only imagine. Mr. Sampson got a nice car! I like that Jag, girl." She smiled bashfully. We waited some more until I saw a man walking towards the line holding his mask in hand. He was young, very attractive, and smiling in our direction. "Is this him coming now?"

"No, that's not him … I wonder how far he parked gosh." She replied as the man walked up to his friend who was standing in line a few people behind us.

"Oh, I think I see him coming now." She said as she looked down the street. There were quite a few people out walking down the street that night. Some looked dressed ready for the party and others looked like passer byers. The partygoers trickled into the line. Some were in pairs or groups; others solo. I was waiting to see which one was Sampson, but everyone just kept getting in line behind us.

"Oh, babe you finally made it. I was getting worried that something happened to you." May said as she leaned down and kissed Sampson. He was so short I didn't even see him walk up amongst all the people that were walking on the street. He had to be five feet at the most, but that wasn't the most disturbing part. I know that probably wasn't the main reason May was embarrassed. Oh no, it could have been the fact that he walked with a cane or that he had the toilet seat head with nothing but gray patches of hair working the perimeter of his head. Perhaps it was just the obvious fact that this man was old enough to be her grandfather!

"No, nothing happened, princess. It just took me a while to find a parking space."

"Angela, Gordon, I'd like you to meet Sampson, my boyfriend." She beamed proudly.

Gordon shook his hand first, "Good to meet you, Sampson."

I was puzzled and my face probably showed it, "Hi, how are you?" That was all I could think to say because that's what I was actually thinking. I was thinking we probably needed to get him to a seat right away before he keeled over and died right there outside the club from exhaustion. I was also thinking shame on May for making that old ass

331

man walk so far by himself.

I couldn't wait until we got inside. I had to find a way to get out of earshot of Sampson, so I could find out what the hell May was thinking. Then again, who knew if he could even still hear anyway. I was glad Donnie was standing right by the entrance once we made it in. This way I wouldn't have to search for him through all these costumes and masks.

"AAAAAANNNNGIE! You made it!" he exclaimed over the house music that was playing. He was wired up on something, but I had no idea what.

"Hey, Donnie, nice costume! This is my boyfriend Gordon and this is my friend, May and Sampson." It was difficult for me to refer to this old goat as my friend's boyfriend. I just wouldn't.

I could see Donnie was confused through his haze as well as to what this old man was doing at his party. "*You bought your granddad to the club?* I ain't mad! Is it his birthday or something? My uncle wanted to go to the club for his eightieth birthday too." He said to May. He was serious too, which made it all the more awkward.

I started to say something, but before I could, Sampson just slapped Donnie on the back and laughed the whole thing off. I was glad he took it so lightly, but I could tell May was a little embarrassed.

"Well the bar is back over there. Two for ones on everything until eleven, so drink up! We'll announce the winner of the best masquerade costume at midnight, and here's your tickets for the raffle."

"THANKS, DONNIE!" I yelled over the music as we inched along.

The dance floor was packed and the music was too loud. I wondered if this was good for May's baby. "WHAT DO YOU SAY WE GET THESE LADIES SOME DRINKS?" Sampson yelled to Gordon. He nodded in agreement, and we followed behind them as they paved our way through the packed club. It took a while for them to squeeze in at the bar to order for us. This was my perfect chance to ask May about Sampson while their attention was at the bar, and we stood behind them where they couldn't hear us.

"Girl! I thought you said you had you a young whippersnapper!" I said as I yanked on the sleeve of her dress.

"No, *you* said I had a young whippersnapper. I never said one way or the other. I just said I wanted you to meet him."

"Yeah, but May, he has a freaking cane for goodness sakes!" I said to her.

"Yeah ... *And?* Gordon is older than you too!"

"Yeah, but he's not old enough to be my grandfather!" I burst into laughter.

"See, and this is exactly why I didn't tell you or anyone else about it. I love him, and he loves me. I don't understand why everyone has to be so ignorant and judgmental about it!" She shot back. She obviously didn't find anything funny, and I could see tears welling up in her eyes. Instantly, I felt bad.

"I'm sorry. I'm sorry, May. I was only joking."

"No you weren't!" She whimpered over the music, and the tears she tried to fight back began to fall one by one.

"Aww, May don't cry. I'm so sorry. You're right. I am being ignorant. I'm sorry, please stop crying." I begged, but it was too late. I tapped Gordon and yelled into his ear that we'd be back. Then I took May by the hand and headed off to look for the bathroom.

I got directions from one of the buff bouncers that stood guard nearby. On the way there, I felt a hard bump into my shoulder. "Excuse you!" I said to the person. The way the men were dressed in there it was hard to tell if it was a male or female, but whoever it was it seemed like they bumped me on purpose. They were wearing a full gold and black mask with a gold and black joker jumpsuit. They just stopped and stared me up and down before I proceeded to the bathroom.

"People are so fucking rude!" I said to May as we finally entered the bathroom.

"Yeah, I wonder what that was all about." She had calmed down some, and I blamed it on the hormones.

"May, look at me. *Look!* I really am sorry. That was insensitive of me to act like that. Will you please accept my apology? You know I say dumb stuff sometimes." She had her arms crossed, and a woman in the bathroom stared at us while she waited for an empty stall. I stopped my plea for a minute and stared back at her until she looked away uncomfortably. Then I looked back at May, and we both laughed. I wet a paper towel and handed it to her to wipe her face.

"Thank you, I accept your apology. I know most people won't understand it, but he really does make me happy, Angie. He's so excited about the baby. He doesn't have any kids, and he didn't think he could even make any anymore. You know you're like my closest friend. That's why I wanted you two to meet. I know if you just get to know him, you'll love him too."

"Aww you're right May. I'm sorry. You know if you're happy, then I'm happy for you." I said as I hugged her tight.

"Thank you."

"Now how did you meet him?" I asked.

We spent a few minutes in the bathroom while she fixed her makeup and filled me in on the details of how they'd met. I could tell through the excitement in her voice that she really did love him oddly enough. I didn't understand it, and as she talked my mind wandered to how she could bring herself to have sex with him. I wondered if he had gray hair on his balls and if he used Viagra every time they did it. I shuddered at the thought.

We met the guys back at the bar near where we'd left them waiting with May's club soda and my cranberry and vodka. There were no seats, so we just walked from here to there periodically. Once they switched from house music for a little bit to some Top 40's, and we all danced. Sampson moved pretty swiftly on that cane, and May seemed to be having a good time. Donnie even bumped into me at one point and asked Gordon if he could have a dance with me. He was just as wired as he was when we came in, and he had me sweating. I couldn't keep up with him on the dance floor, but we had a good time. We ended up staying two hours, but Gordon didn't seem to mind so long as I was close by.

"You ready to leave?" I asked in his ear. He raised his eyebrows giving me a look that said he was ready, but he didn't want to say he was if I wanted to stay longer.

"Are *you?*"

"Yeah, I'm ready. You wanna hit up another spot or just go back to your place?" I asked.

He shrugged, "I don't know. It's getting late. By the time we get somewhere else, we'll only have like a half an hour to party so ..." I looked at the time on my phone, and he was right.

"Okay, we can go then." I said then turned around to let May know we were leaving. They were ready too, so we huddled up to pave our way through the crowd again. I stopped and yelled to them, "YA'LL SEE DONNIE ANYWHERE? I WANNA SAY BYE TO HIM RIGHT QUICK!" Everybody shrugged and shook their heads as we stood grouped together looking in different directions for him.

All of a sudden there was screaming and people trampling in different directions out of nowhere. We all looked around confused, and all I heard was, "ANGIE GET DOWN!" as Gordon dove for me. Everything was going in slow motion. I heard May's shrill scream as she looked in the same direction Gordon had been looking. It was the gold and black joker again, just standing there, but this time her mask was pulled up resting atop her head and her hand was extended precisely in my direction as if she was pointing directly at me. It felt like slow motion, but at the same time it all happened so fast. It looked like … *Jillian*, a bald, stitched up, disfigured Jillian. The club was dark, but the disco lights flashed on her just enough for me to catch a glimpse of her face. By the time I realized it was a gun she was pointing, I only heard the POP! POP! POP!

ABOUT THE AUTHOR

Just Jewel is the author of Two Way Mirrors, The Mini Poetry Project, and A Drop of Jewel blog site. Visit the author's website at Adropofjewel.com.

www.ingramcontent.com/pod-product-compliance
Lightning Source LLC
Chambersburg PA
CBHW020331180626
46812CB00001B/150